BELLWEATHER RHAPSODY

ALSO BY KATE RACCULIA

This Must Be the Place

Kate Racculia

BELLWEATHER
Rhapsody

HOUGHTON MIFFLIN HARCOURT
BOSTON · NEW YORK
2014

For information about permission to reproduce selections from this book, write to Permissions, Houghton Mifflin Harcourt Publishing Company, 215 Park Avenue South, New York, New York 10003.

www.hmhco.com

Library of Congress Cataloging-in-Publication Data
Racculia, Kate.
Bellweather rhapsody / Kate Racculia.
pages cm
ISBN 978-0-544-12991-7
I. Title.
PS3618.A328B45 2014
813'.6—dc23   2013026339

Book design by Chrissy Kurpeski
Typeset in Filosofia OT

Printed in the United States of America
DOC 10 9 8 7 6 5 4 3 2 1

"Natalie Takes the Elevator" was previously published in *Printer's Devil Review* (Spring 2011).

For all the players, no matter their part
(Nigel too)

The Players

The Program

SATURDAY, NOVEMBER 15, 1997

Allegro Furioso

SUNDAY, NOVEMBER 16, 1997

Grave e Cantabile

Postlude: AND AFTER

There is nothing with which every man is so afraid as getting to know how enormously much he is capable of doing and becoming.

Søren Kierkegaard

Every love story is a ghost story.

David Foster Wallace

SATURDAY
NOVEMBER 13, 1982

The Hotel Bellweather
Clinton's Kill, New York

MINNIE GRAVES IS a bridesmaid.

She hates it.

Her bangs are crispy with Aqua Net. Her ponytail is so tight her forehead aches. Her feet throb in shoes that are a size too small, Mary Janes dyed special to match the totally rancid dress Minnie's big sister, Jennifer, picked out just for her. There's a thing called a crinoline and she has to remember to always cross her legs and it's a total pain in her twelve-year-old ass. And it's pink. "It's not pink, it's *cranberry wine*," Jennifer said, but Minnie, whose big brother, Mike, tells her about all the horror movies he watches, thinks she looks like someone dumped a bucket of pig's blood on her.

Minnie's mother told her that, when the wedding started, Minnie would forget the crinoline itched and just be happy to see her big sister get married to Theodore. But Minnie's mother lied: Minnie spends the entire ceremony glaring laser-beam eyes at Theodore's stupid stomach, thinking it's really appropriate that he's named after the fat chipmunk. The priest talks for*ever*, and then, because she is part of the poofy-dress brigade, Minnie can't go with the rest of her cousins for cheese and crackers and little hotdogs wrapped in bacon—she actually has to stay and take pictures with these mo-

3

rons, and act like she's happy and everything is totally awesome, and pretend she doesn't know what she knows about her big sister. What she saw in the mirror this morning. She smiles so hard her cheeks hurt as bad as her smashed toes.

The photographer wants to take pictures of the bride and groom by themselves. Minnie is free; she doesn't wait for her parents or her brother, she just walks away. She thinks that if she stays a second longer she is going to throw up or haul off and punch someone, because she feels hot and itchy and awful and she doesn't know how to talk about it. She stomps across the hotel lobby, away from the ballroom where she can hear the rest of her family gobbling those bacon hotdogs and blabbering—probably about how beautiful Jennifer looked, and wasn't Theo handsome.

They are all so *stupid*. Minnie feels like crying, they're so stupid.

At the elevators, she pushes the triangle pointing up. It turns yellow under her thumb. She doesn't really care where she goes, she just wants to get away, so she steps in and pushes the first button she sees. Seven. It's cracked. When it lights up the cracks glow like little bolts of lightning and Minnie wonders how many times you have to push a plastic elevator button to crack it. She steps on the heel of one shoe, then the other, and nudges them off her feet.

The car is small, with mirrors on all sides.

When Minnie blinks she sees Jennifer this morning. Standing with her back to the bathroom mirror, looking over her shoulder at a low bruise the size of a cantaloupe, the right spot for a kidney punch.

"Since when don't you knock?" Jennifer says. "Beat it, Bug."

"Did I do that?" Minnie asks, because they shared a bed last night, and Minnie has been known to run hurdles in her sleep.

Jennifer's reflection tilts its head and her eyes are sad when she says, "No, honey." And Minnie notices the bruise is yellowish on the edges. Bruises don't turn that color until a few days after you fall, or run into a table, or wipe out on your skates.

Minnie doesn't know why but her stomach aches. This feels— important. Important, and scary, and Jennifer—who has never told her little sister a single private grown-up thing—says she can't tell

4

anyone about it, okay? It doesn't matter. Theo loves her. She knows Theo loves her. He promised her he'll never do it again, and she believes him.

"Now beat it, Bug. For real."

In the elevator, Minnie blinks and blinks but she can't see anything except bruises reflected to infinity.

When the doors open, she bolts into the hallway and feels afraid. This is the biggest hotel she's ever been in. Not that the Holiday Inn where they stayed when they visited Hershey Park was much competition for anything, but the Bellweather is so big, so in the middle of nowhere, it's scary. She knows she's in the tallest part, the tower, but there are hundreds of rooms and empty ballrooms and swimming pools (more than one!) and long dark halls with dark doors.

Stepping into the Bellweather for the first time was like being swallowed. A nice old man with a bow tie gave her a piece of candy and leaned down to say "Welcome to the Bellweather!" while her parents checked in, but it didn't really help. He offered to take her and Mike on a tour, to the auditorium, the library, the shops, and the indoor squash courts, whatever those were; he was super-excited about showing off but Minnie didn't want to go. She still can't shake the awful feeling that the lobby, with its brick-red and gold and white curlicue carpet and red and gold fabric on the walls, is the stomach of some giant animal, that the old crooked chairs facing each other in half circles are rows and rows of teeth.

And it smells. It smells like Pledge and broccoli and Grandpa, and the first thing Mike said when they got off the elevator was "Come play with us, Danny!" And she really *did* haul off and punch him then, because he knows how scared she is of that movie. He went to see it last Halloween at the drive-in. It's her own fault, she realizes; she asked him to tell her about it. "It's the scariest thing you'll ever see," Mike said, wiggling his eyebrows. "There are these two little twin girls, about your age, and their dad chops them up with an ax and you see them, like, all bloody, with their parts strewn all over the hall. And they haunt the hotel and they're really lonely, so when this kid Danny shows up on his Big Wheel—well, they just want to play with him. But ghosts don't play very well with the living."

She didn't know which was scarier, getting chopped up with an ax or having no one to play with for eternity but your sister.

She shivers and looks down the hallway. It stretches on and on in either direction, the lights on the walls low and flickery. Minnie realizes she is holding her shoes, one in each hand, and thinks they're the only weapons she has.

Against what? A little boy on a Big Wheel? Two little girls, hacked to pieces with an ax?

No, she tells herself. Don't think about that. That's just a movie. It's not real. It didn't happen.

She calms down for a second, but only for a second, because now that she's not afraid of little girl ghosts she's remembering that her sister just married a jerk. "Theo is an asshole," she tells the hallway.

She smiles a real smile for the first time all day.

"Theo is a total asshole," she says, a little louder.

Something thumps nearby and she starts, giggles.

"Theo is an asshole!" she shouts.

A door in front of her explodes and a man, his chest a bursting red balloon, flies out and crumples against the opposite wall. He lands with his face turned toward her and his eyes are bright blue and open, bloodshot with shock. There is a smell of hot metal, and Minnie, stunned, squeaks. She takes a step backward.

Then she takes a step forward.

Minnie Graves, who has never in her life had cause to be frightened of anything not contained on a television or movie screen, who has a surfeit of imagination and twice as much curiosity, convinces herself none of this will hurt her. She only knows that she wants to see this man up close, to discover what has ejected him so violently from room 712. Her bare feet are silent and the carpet is soft, and she crouches by the man's body. He reminds her of her Uncle Bill: younger than her parents, older than her sister or Theodore. He is wearing a tuxedo with a sort of wide belt the color of Smurfs. His chest is a pile of red meat, bright against his white shirt. Minnie has to squint to look at it, like she's looking straight at the sun.

He's not dead the way Grandma Harris was dead last April. He's not dressed neatly or lying with his hands crossed over his chest, cheeks too pink and waxy.

He is still warm. He's leaking parts of himself. Minnie's head fills with cold white static.

She hears a creak and a groan and looks up into the broken doorway of 712. There is a woman in a beautiful wedding dress, floating in midair—but then Minnie realizes she must be standing on a chair and only looks like she's floating because her dress is so poofy and full. It makes her think of an upside-down cupcake. It's prettier than Jennifer's, Minnie thinks, and feels guilty.

"Little girl," the woman says to her. Her voice is low and thick. "Little girl."

Minnie stares at the woman, at her dark hair and pale skin. There is an orange electrical cord looped around her neck and Minnie feels the same sickness in her stomach as when she saw the bruise on Jennifer's back. She knows this moment is dangerous, and she knows she should tell people—she should run down the hall and start banging on doors and screaming, but she can't. For some reason, she can't.

And she doesn't.

"Little girl," the woman says again. She is wearing long white gloves. She pulls one off and drops it to the floor. "Could you pick that up for me please?"

"*Don't,*" says the dead man.

He gurgles red between his lips and grabs her arm and squeezes, hard, and Minnie finally screams, and pelts first one shoe and then the other at his bloody chest, and runs. And runs. She flings herself against the emergency exit at the end of the hall, pounds down the stairwell, hides her shaking self beneath the last set of stairs, beside an exit door that she is too frightened to walk through, and collapses.

The next thing she knows are warm hands on her face—*Bug, Bug, wake up!*—and Minnie rouses, hiccupping for breath, to the concerned dark eyes of her new brother-in-law. She screams blue murder. She kicks, she punches him. She drags her fingernails across his face. Photographs taken after the youngest bridesmaid was discovered playing hide-and-seek in an emergency stairwell all show Theo with four angry pink welts strafing his left cheek, a marked man.

Her parents pull her off their freshly minted son-in-law, apologetic and confused, not yet calmed from the rush of worry and adrenaline that their missing daughter inspired, not yet aware of the man and the woman outside and inside room 712. Her mother's first thought is of the missing shoes—*I swear, Minnie, they were the same dye lot as the dress, there's no way we can ever get a more perfect match*—shoes, at that very moment, that are confounding the hell out of the hotel manager and the local police. Not that anything about the mess in 712 makes any sense: not that a happy young bride, just married in the morning, should have any cause to commit an apparent murder-suicide during the first few hours of her honeymoon.

Minnie's parents will discover this later, long after the reception, after a clerk at the front desk remembers that the colors of the Graves-Huppert wedding match the bloody Mary Janes. By then, Minnie will be asleep. When her parents wake her to talk to the police, again she will scream and kick and fight like an animal, afraid to be awake in a world of so many monsters.

THURSDAY
NOVEMBER 13, 1997

Andante Misterioso

1

Heaven Help Me for the Way I Am

RABBIT EXHALES A puff of November breath and worries. Every minute they spend outside in the cold, his bassoon is getting more and more out of tune. He blows on his hands. Why didn't he remember to bring gloves? Or a hat? It's November in Ruby Falls, they're spending the weekend in the Catskills, he knows better. His butt is numb where it connects with the cold concrete. He hugs his bassoon case to his side, under his armpit, but it isn't helping. His Discman is heavy in the pouch of his sweatshirt, but he'd have to unbutton his coat to get it. Anyway, his sister would be seriously offended if he slipped headphones on in her presence. No matter how freezing his ears might be, he knows Alice can't stand not being listened to.

His sister dances back and forth, zigzagging from the bottom step to the top, rehearsing songs from *Mame,* which the drama club is putting on the first week of December. She's covered "We Need a Little Christmas," "My Best Girl," and "The Man in the Moon," which isn't even her song to sing. Alice, of course, is Mame. She pirouettes on a high note and slides sidesaddle down the metal railing in the middle of the steps.

"Hey," she says, nodding at the front lawn. "You see the billing?"

Rabbit squints at the official school sign, its movable letters currently admonishing the students and parents of the Ruby Falls Central School District to bring their donations of canned goods and other nonperishable items to the next football game. Beyond it is a plywood signboard, staked into the freshly frosted ground, white with large gold and black lettering and a stylish cartoon of a flapper holding a trumpet like an old-fashioned cigarette wand. It reads RUBY FALLS HIGH DRAMA CLUB PRESENTS *MAME* STARRING ALICE HATMAKER.

He smiles a frozen smile at her. Alice isn't wearing a hat or gloves either. Her cheeks are blotchy pink but she doesn't look as though she feels a thing.

"Next stop," she says, "Statewide. Then Broadway, of course." She claps. "Soooo excited! Are you? Excited about your very first time?" She yanks up the handle on her brand-new rolling suitcase — cherry red, the color of Luden's cough drops — and leans against it. "Aren't you excited?"

He nods. He *is* excited. This — pale, twitchy — *is* his excited face. Rabbit Hatmaker is excited, and also anxious and terribly worried that something happened to Mrs. Wilson, because she's almost ten minutes late picking them up, and if *she's* any later, *they* are going to be late getting to Statewide.

He hugs his bassoon case tighter. He imagines his instrument's gleaming black plastic constricting, sparkling silver keys fogging under the warmth of his fingertips. Five years together, and he's hardly ever left her out in the cold. Mr. McGurk, former head of the RFH music department, introduced Rabbit to his bassoon when he was in seventh grade. "Bert," he'd said (he never called Rabbit by his nickname), "I need a bassoonist in junior high band. It's a lot like that saxophone you're playing right now, only there are two reeds wired together instead of one, so you can't bite down on it. You have to curl your lips around your teeth and hold it between them, soft but firm, like this." McGurk's mouth disappeared beneath his mustache in a flat, lipless line. "Li' dis!" he repeated. "That's called your *embouchure*."

The district owned two bassoons for student use, and McGurk presented Rabbit with one in a long flat case that seemed too small to contain it. But she was all there, in five separate pieces. A heavy boot. A bubbled bell. A graceful swooping bocal. Two joints, a wing and a tenor. Like a puzzle he solved every time he played, lining up the keys and pads, the corked ends fitting snugly into the right holes. Before he'd ever wrapped his lips around a double reed, Rabbit loved that bassoon. It was strange and singular and it made sense, and when he was first learning, it was two inches taller than the top of his head. He loved that about it too, that he was master of this mammoth instrument. He named her Beatrice.

Rabbit and Beatrice have been waiting to go to Statewide for years. Every March, starting in seventh grade, Rabbit prepared a solo for ASM. He could never remember exactly what the acronym stood for, Association for School Music, or Student Musicians, something like that — regardless, every spring ASM held competitions across the state of New York. The kids playing the hardest-level solos and receiving the highest scores each year were eligible for the ASM conference festival held the following fall, known as Statewide: a long weekend retreat at a resort in the Catskills, concert band, orchestra, and chorus made up of the best student musicians and vocalists from Queens to Boonville, with a packed schedule of intense all-day rehearsals culminating in a Sunday of concerts. Statewide was a huge deal, one step away from the big show. Everyone knew that the top music schools in the country, the Juilliards, the New England Conservatories, the Westings, saw the festival as a sort of farm team and went scouting for scholarship recruits. Only a handful of kids *ever* made it from podunk Ruby Falls, and never more than one kid a year. They were immortalized in McGurk's office, in photographs and notecards and press clippings tacked alongside the yellowing programs and playbills that represented his twenty-five years of teaching at RFH. Rabbit, in McGurk's office for his weekly lessons, memorized them. 1984: Claire Walker, RFH valedictorian, now playing with the horns of the Chicago Symphony Orchestra. 1988: Billy Fasman, youngest of the Fasman family, sang tenor at Tanglewood.

1996: Alice Hatmaker, drama queen extraordinaire, high school headliner. His other half.

He'd been jealous that his sister went to Statewide when she was a junior, but just a little. They'd never been particularly competitive about their achievements, probably because Rabbit was universally good at almost everything he tried (basketball notwithstanding) and Alice was great but only at a few select things. He sat beside his parents at Alice's Statewide concert, anonymous as anyone else in the audience. Rabbit felt awkward. Not excluded, exactly, but a beat early. There was something there for him in that strange old hotel, he could feel *that* all right, but it wasn't ready for him, not yet.

Last March had been everyone's final chance. Rabbit was looking down the barrel of his senior year. McGurk was looking down the barrel of his retirement. McGurk coached Rabbit through a level-six solo, a lively syncopated sonata in four movements by Telemann, tapping out the time with his fingertip on the edge of Rabbit's music stand. ASM held the competitions at a different school every spring, so Rabbit was lost from the moment he and his father entered the west wing of Fayetteville-Manlius High School. He'd been slotted at 6:30 on a Friday night — the last solo of the day — and Rabbit could tell that his judge, a thin woman with streaky blond hair who was rubbing her temples even as she greeted him, had checked out hours ago. He sat down and dampened his reed. It was a science classroom; there were rows of long lab tables with gas jets and sinks, and a poster of the solar system over the chalkboard. He thought of McGurk tapping tapping tapping, keeping gentle time. He thought of his father sitting outside in the hall, leaning forward with his elbows on his knees, cupping an ear toward the closed door. The judge asked him to run through several scales and to begin whenever he was ready. And Rabbit, as always, found himself the moment he began to play.

She clapped. She actually *clapped,* his judge, and got up to shake his hand when he'd finished his piece. Maybe she'd heard too many flutes and violins and not enough bassoons that day; maybe she was just overjoyed the day was over. Or maybe he'd been really good, as good as he'd felt himself to be — his insides matching his outsides, everything attuned. She gave him a perfect score.

Rabbit was going to Statewide.

He didn't know that for sure, of course. Not until late September, when he received a congratulatory letter, a folio of music, and various forms requiring his parents' signatures, a full day before his sister. She said she was happy for him, she hugged him and assured him he was going to love every second of it, but there was a distinct difference between her happiness on Friday and on Saturday after she'd received her own conference acceptance.

"The Hatmaker twins broke the curse," he told McGurk. He hadn't been able to reach him the day before, when the good news was his alone; retirement, said McGurk, meant never having to answer your telephone. "Two Ruby Falls kids in one year."

"I knew you could do it, Bert," said McGurk. Rabbit could hear a dog barking in the background. "That's great news. That's great, *great* news."

Rabbit wanted to say more. A lot more. About McGurk's replacement, Mrs. Wilson, whom he wanted to like but couldn't, and not just because she wasn't McGurk; he had a sixth sense for liars and secret keepers, and she was at least one, if not both. About how much he *missed* McGurk, period. It was different at school without him. It was lonelier. And he wanted to ask McGurk a question that would have been impossible to ask while he was still Rabbit's teacher: whether the rumors were true, that McGurk had been living with the same guy for the past twenty years, and that the guy was in fact his boyfriend. He wanted to ask if he, McGurk, was like Rabbit — gay — and whether being and not telling anyone was eating him alive too.

But he didn't. Of course he didn't. The stories about McGurk, they were just rumors. He didn't want to insult McGurk if he was, you *know,* and he didn't want McGurk, if he wasn't, to *be* insulted and consequently weirded out by Rabbit. It was too complicated, too frightening and risky. Rabbit needed to talk to someone he trusted, someone *like* him, and while he felt, deep down, that he and McGurk were very much alike — he couldn't. He didn't have the words.

"Thanks for everything" was all he ended up saying.

It was the closest he'd ever come to telling someone the truth, and over the next seven days he slipped into a bleak, blank misery. Not because he'd almost told someone he was gay, but because he *hadn't.* Having skirted the opportunity, having come so close and swerved, Rabbit realized how mortally exhausted he was of not being himself—completely himself. In the fall of his senior year, he had reached the point of no return. He was more tired of lying than afraid of what might happen when he stopped.

Which was saying something. The only fistfight he'd ever gotten into was when Dave Hollister got hold of his sheet music and picked on him because the bassoon part was labeled *fagott.* "It means 'bundle of sticks' in German!" he'd shouted at Dave before kneeing him in the groin, after which Dave laid him out with a single punch. And Dave Hollister was his *friend*—or friendly, at least; they sat at the same long lunch table.

He had to believe if he chose his audience wisely, it wouldn't be like that. It wouldn't have to be.

Which is another reason, moments from Statewide, why he's nervous as hell.

He blows into his freezing hands. Mrs. Wilson is now twenty minutes late. Alice plunks herself down on the step beside him and stretches out her legs, swiveling her ankles to the right, then the left, humming more highlights from *Mame.*

He's going to tell his sister. Tonight. Or tomorrow. Statewide is the perfect opportunity to come out to her. They'll be together, away from home and their parents, with time and space to themselves. If he tells her in the next twenty-four hours, she'll have three days to acclimate to the idea, three days for her magpie mind to be distracted by something shinier, more scandalously shareable.

He already knows how he's going to do it. He's going to ask what happened between her and Jimmy Kopek, her first real boyfriend. Jimmy seemed a decent enough guy, way more vanilla than Rabbit liked and honestly kind of dumb; Alice was so clearly, ridiculously out of his league, as far as talent and personality were concerned, their relationship had never seemed very real to Rabbit. Alice was playing the part of Jimmy Kopek's Girlfriend, he assumed, until something juicier came along.

Then Jimmy called last Sunday. Rabbit had answered the phone and handed it to Alice without suspicion; Jimmy seemed just as

Jimmy-like as all the other times he'd called. Until Rabbit got up in the middle of the night to use the bathroom and heard his sister crying softly, he hadn't a clue anything was wrong. They were definitely done, though. On Monday she took the bus home with Rabbit instead of getting a ride in Jimmy's Geo. All of the signs were there: she had been dumped. Alice Hatmaker, star of the show, had been *dumped.*

He's insanely curious, of course, but he's also genuinely concerned. Alice has never had an emotion she didn't want to shout from the hilltops, so the fact that she's hiding the Kopek situation is worrisome. In spite of everything, she isn't a bad person. She doesn't deserve to be hurt. In some ways he knows his sister far too well, but in others, not at all. He wishes she would look to him as a confidant. And while confidences are flying around—

She's his sister. She's his *twin.* If he can't tell the person with whom he shared a womb, how can he ever tell anyone?

A yellow station wagon emblazoned with RUBY FALLS CENTRAL SCHOOLS, caution lights mounted on the roof, pulls up to the curb.

"We're going in *that?*" Alice says. "We're taking a *short bus?*"

Mrs. Wilson waves to them from the driver's seat.

Natalie Wilson has been the head of the music program at Ruby Falls High for just two months and two weeks, but already she knows that the Hatmaker twins are the kind of blessed creatures that occasionally bob to the surface of small-town high schools: strange and petite, matched like elfin salt and pepper shakers. Glossy black hair in a short bob and a short Caesar, dark brown eyes and round noses. Frightfully talented. Between Alice's voice—bright, bigger than the entire town—and Rabbit's bassoon, the Hatmaker name is synonymous with musical achievement. They aren't picked on, as far as Natalie can tell, but they aren't exactly the king and queen of the prom, and if they didn't have each other, she suspects they'd be horribly lonely. Natalie remembers too well how it feels to be talented and seventeen.

She watches as the twins slide their luggage into the back. Everything about Alice, from her talent to her own idea of herself, is obvious, and she is obviously not amused that she'll arrive at Statewide as a conquering senior in a canary-yellow station wagon with a retractable stop sign by the driver's window. Honestly, Natalie would have fought harder to rent a regular car if she hadn't suspected that a school vehicle would royally piss Alice Hatmaker off. Humbling teenagers has turned out to be one of the few consistent joys of her teaching career.

Alice slams the rear gate. She's frowning so dramatically Natalie can't stifle a laugh.

Rabbit, now, Rabbit Hatmaker is different. He pauses as his sister climbs into the back seat. It's clear to Natalie that he's wondering whether it would be ruder to sit in back with Alice or weirder to sit beside his teacher in the front, and whether it is better to be rude or weird.

Natalie lets him decide without any encouragement. He chooses to sit up front.

"Hi, Mrs. Wilson," he says. "Thanks for driving us."

"Thanks for making Statewide," Natalie says. "I haven't been to one of these festivals in years. Since I was a student."

"*You* went to Statewide?" Alice sneers.

"Something very much like it," Natalie says.

"What did you play?" Rabbit asks, more softly than his sister.

"Piano," she replies. Their faces are rosy and they both sniffle in the sudden warmth of the car. "Sorry you had to wait in the cold."

She was late, but she isn't terribly sorry. The fact is that when Natalie should have been putting on her coat, driving her car over to the bus garage and trading it for the district's vehicle, she was sitting at her desk in her office, staring out the double-paned window into the rehearsal room. The room was always set up for band, folding chairs down and music stands at the ready. The window was old, plastic and warped, and in the odd reflections she could imagine every child who'd passed through this school, who'd played music in this room—glints of light bending and flashing and vanishing as she turned her head. They were moths. Ghosts. They passed by and through. Some were talented, some were terrible. They all played their songs and the room didn't change, and that was the whole story. The whole message. She couldn't turn away. The transience of life was so clear and crystal-sharp she wanted to throw herself on it and die.

So she sat there and stared, breathing.

She eases the station wagon down Route 12 in silence. They are officially on their way. On their way to hours and hours of endless, soul-deadening rehearsals for the Hatmakers, and hours and hours of endless, inane workshops and receptions for Natalie, should she be so bored as to consider attending. She is honestly kind of angry they made Statewide, and that she, newly hired, toeing the line, volunteered to chaperone. She prefers to spend her weekends drinking and napping, though when she made that argument to Emmett, it only strengthened his insistence that she go.

Rabbit fidgets in the passenger seat. He's opened his coat, and she notices a Discman peeking from the pouch of his sweatshirt.

"What are you listening to?" she asks.

"Uh." She caught him off guard. "Oh, you mean—um, Weezer?"

"The newest album?"

Rabbit blinks at her. She's unsure whether he's confused that she knows Weezer is the name of a band, or that she referred to their CD as an album.

"It's their second CD, and, um." He tilts his head. "I'm not sure. It's really different? Like, it's really . . . a lot angrier."

"I think it's brilliant," Alice says from the back seat, and then belts, apropos of nothing, "*God damn you half-Japaneeeese girls!*"

Natalie catches Rabbit's wince. They smile at each other sideways in the silence that follows his sister's outburst.

"I think maybe I just need to listen to it for a while longer? You know, how, sometimes you don't know how you feel about something until you've had time to process it?"

She's suddenly irritated by the way he poses his statements as questions. It reminds her of her husband, Emmett, who seems to have abandoned declaratives completely since last spring. She sets her teeth.

"Like, at first I didn't think I liked *The X-Files*—"

God, he *is* Emmett.

"But then the more I watched it, the more I liked it, and now it's one of my favorite shows?"

Emmett had watched *X-Files* on the night of the break-in. It had been a Sunday. Who breaks into someone's house on a Sunday night? Only a real asshole, a real desperate asshole. Natalie remembers walking into the den and there was Emmett, hand sunk in a bowl of popcorn, staring glassy-eyed at Scully and Mulder investigating some dank basement.

"This show is one big commercial for flashlights," she said, and Emmett said, "Shhhhh, this is an important—"

Something jumped out of the dark of the television screen and Emmett flinched, launching popcorn everywhere. She laughed at him, and he said, "Aw, shit," but laughed too, and she said, "Clean up when you're done and come to bed."

This is what the newspaper said happened next:

MAN DIES IN BREAK-IN

Minneapolis—A man died Sunday night after allegedly breaking into a private residence on Stratford Street. Around 2 a.m., Edward Hollis, 20, of Minneapolis allegedly forced his way into the home. After rendering one occupant unconscious, Hollis reportedly attacked the second homeowner in the master bedroom. He sustained one bullet wound at close range and was pronounced dead at the scene.

The newspaper did not say that Natalie had brushed her teeth and hair and slipped into one of Emmett's old dress shirts, thought about reading but decided she was too tired, and turned out the light. The newspaper also neglected to mention that she lay awake for a long time worrying about the Monday to come, when the school board was to vote on whether to reallocate money away from the music program for the third year running; and that she cried a little to herself because she hated that this had become her life—this endless fight to justify her existence, losing ground one steady inch at a time—and she was too exhausted to do anything about it but cry.

That, hours later, she felt the mattress jostle.

"Have you, um . . . seen it?"

Natalie starts. Yes. Yes, she saw it. She was there and she knows what she did.

"It's a TV show."

"Rabbit's got a crush on Scully," says a girl's voice.

She shakes her head. The gray road stretches ahead of her.

"I do not," says Rabbit.

"Who wouldn't?" says Natalie. She smiles at him and then catches his needling sister's eye in the rearview mirror.

Unbelievable. Freaking unbelievable.

Alice knew, from the first time she saw her, that there was something deeply wrong with Mrs. Wilson. Weirdo Wilson. When you talk to her, she acts like she doesn't hear you the first time. She looks kind of *beyond* you, not at you. And that *face* she just shot Alice through the rearview—two parts bitch to one part psycho—that proves it. The rumors are true. Some of them, maybe all of them: that she's in the witness protection program, that she testified against a Mob boss out in the Midwest, that she strangled a man with her bare hands.

God, she's a Freak with a capital F. Maybe that's the attraction. Maybe Rabbit's still waters run freak-deep, and that's why he didn't sit in the back with his own sister.

"Are we there yet?" Alice asks.

She rests her chin on the back of Rabbit's seat and palms his skull. His hair is thick and bristly. She's told him she does this because she loves the way it feels, which is true, but mostly she does it because she believes rubbing her brother's head brings her luck. Before opening nights, before concerts, before the solo that qualified her to be in this car, she rubbed her brother's head. Her little brother (by three minutes and twelve seconds) is her good-luck charm, and she is beyond superstitious. The greatest performers— the singers, the dancers, the baseball players—all are. We came by it easy, and we know how easily it can be taken away.

"We have about two hours and forty-five minutes to go," Weirdo

Wilson reports, and it isn't Alice's imagination that her voice sounds gleeful. The woman totally has it out for her, which Alice can only attribute to a case of raging jealousy. *Get over it, lady. Not my fault you used to be pretty good and now you teach mouth breathers to play on the downbeat.*

When you're not chaperoning shooting stars. Oh, she thinks, *I should write that down.*

She gives her brother's head an extra rub. Then she reaches over the back seat and snags her JanSport.

Alice has been writing her autobiography, collecting anecdotes, accolades, playbills, and photographs, since middle school. She carries it with her everywhere and writes in it at least once a day. It's an old Trapper Keeper she begged her mother to buy her before the first day of third grade, so it's pretty ratty-looking at this point, but that's part of its charm. The Velcro flap makes a satisfying *fzzzip* as she opens it. She clicks and unclicks and clicks and unclicks the pen clipped to the divider and passes her hand over the cool smoothness of a college-ruled page.

Here I am, she writes. *Route 81. A little after noon on Thursday. My second year at Statewide. A shooting star being chaperoned and chauffeured in a freaking short bus.*

Have feeling of impending doom. Laid out a tarot hand for myself last night. First I played Temperance. The Star. Harmony and balance, good things coming in the future. Good news for Statewide, right? Then what card do I play next but DEATH.

They say it doesn't necessarily mean you're going to die, only that you're going to change. But then why don't they call the card CHANGE instead of DEATH?

She taps the pen on the paper and clicks and unclicks it again.

Her mother thinks it's just a journal, but it's much more than that. It's the definitive dossier for her posthumous biographer. Alice knows how these things work: she started young, which she knows means she has to end young too—talent like hers eats you up, flames you out brighter than the sun. You can't conquer fate. You can't change your destiny, no matter how tragically avoidable. Talent made you doomed.

And beautiful. Alice's voice, in fact, is the only part of her that doesn't feel ugly. She's petite, but like a gnome rather than an elf or a pixie. Her eyes are too large for her face and her nose too round, and her ears are too small considering the scale of the rest of her features. And her body—ugh. She can hardly bear thinking about it. Becoming aware of her body and realizing it was uniquely deficient occurred simultaneously and subtly, so that Alice herself couldn't have distinguished one intelligence from the other. Her ugliness was something deep and total and *felt,* constantly, a perpetual discomfort in her arms and her thighs and her stomach and butt and face and hair and hands and feet and nonexistent breasts.

When Alice spoke or sang, though, she became her true self. Technically, Rabbit had been the first to speak, but Alice compensated for the delay with sheer quantity. She made adults listen to her, made other kids listen to her, made her brother listen to her, and when she smiled back at them and continued to talk, she held them. She sang with the radio (more like *at* the radio), in the shower, with her mother at the piano—she sang anything at any time, anywhere, to make herself feel good.

It wasn't until she first sang on a stage that Alice began to understand her full potential. Ruby Falls held a school talent show every winter. It was a joke. The district (and the talent pool) was so small that the same kids were always performing the same acts: Holly Wilcox would do a gymnastics routine to that "sail away" Enya song; the McCallister brothers would lip-synch to a Beastie Boys song. Alice had never tried out, had never been even vaguely interested, until she overheard Molly Brotowski bragging in the cafeteria about the private voice lessons her parents got her expressly so she could make her debut at the talent show.

"I can sing Molly Brotowski into next week," she told Rabbit. Rabbit had a mouthful of pudding cup but nodded vigorously. "She's not so special," Alice muttered. In truth, Alice was incredibly jealous of Molly's private lessons, and when she complained over dinner that night that her parents didn't take her singing seriously enough, her father called her bluff. "Try out," he said. "If you get into the show and go through with it, we'll talk about lessons."

Auditions were held on a Tuesday afternoon in the junior-senior high auditorium, where the show itself would take place in a few short weeks. Alice had never set foot on a stage before—a real stage, with real curtains that could be drawn aside by ropes and pulleys, facing a real audience of empty seats in old blue upholstery tattooed here and there in Bic by bored study-hall students. The moment felt enormous. Her heart began to pump wildly and she paused at the top of the steps, her foot in midair, before stepping firmly on the blond wood.

She was home. The sensation was immediate and powerful, and Alice, eleven and glowing in the low lighting, her throat itching with song, didn't feel anything but gorgeous. She waved to the owlish accompanist, who began to play ABBA's "S.O.S." *Be unpredictable*—that was her mother's advice. *Don't blend and they'll remember you*. Unlike Molly and the two other girls who had butchered "On My Own," who were memorable, sure, but not the way they wanted to be.

Alice sang the paint off the walls. She had never sounded this good. Not in the shower, not in her bedroom, not in the backyard or the kitchen or when following Rabbit around to annoy him. Not when her mother played in the evenings and sang with her, not even when she'd been practicing for this audition. Singing on this stage, her voice freed to fill a whole auditorium, was what Alice Hatmaker was born to do, and now that she was doing it, she knew exactly who she was. Molly Brotowski, with her shitty Eponine and her private lessons, didn't matter; the ugliness that infected every last inch of her flesh didn't matter; her brilliantly good brother who pretended that he didn't look at her with pity sometimes didn't matter. Hell, the talent show barely mattered. She was beyond it.

Alice Hatmaker was a star.

The Trapper Keeper open on her lap, Alice pages back through her years, more than a little in love with her own recent past. A playbill from eighth grade, when she played Miss Adelaide in *Guys and Dolls*, the first time in RFH history an eighth grader brought down the house. A scrap of red fabric from the dress she wore as Nancy in *Oliver!*, taped next to a photo of her in costume. God, she loved that dress. It made her body feel like someone else's. She flips all the way to the beginning.

To whom it may concern, she reads. *I, Alice Hatmaker, do solemnly swear that what you are about to read is the absolute true and unadulterated story of my life. This is only the beginning, but I'm going to fly so high, so fast, I'm going to break the sound barrier.*

Her signature takes up the entire bottom half of the page.

Her name in these old programs, seeing herself in these old pictures, reading words she remembers writing, all make her feel as though she actually exists. The past is solid. She can stand on it. She can dance on it if she wants.

The future is different. Like the remaining sheets in her Trapper Keeper, blank and finite.

She looks at her watch and frowns. Rehearsal starts at three o'clock. It's now a quarter to three, and they haven't gotten off the highway yet.

"Hey," her brother says, his voice catching. "How much longer, do you think?"

He's stressed all to hell. Her nervous bunny of a brother, king of all worrywarts.

"We're going to be a little late to the first rehearsal," Wilson says. "I'm sorry about that. You can blame it on me."

"You said it," says Alice, glaring at her through the rearview.

They pass it at the exact moment she realizes its faint purring isn't the blood in her own ears. A motorcycle, a black and silver motorcycle, roars beside them. It's heading in the same direction.

"Take me with you," she whispers at the window.

2

Rabbit Makes an Entrance

RABBIT IS BREATHING hard as he assembles Beatrice. Usually he puts his bassoon together with the utmost care — she technically isn't his, plus she's old and her cork is prone to flake. But the last time he looked at his watch it was twenty minutes past three, twenty minutes late to his first rehearsal, for God's sake.

He almost trips over his suitcase, which he hasn't taken up to his room yet; there just wasn't time. The Statewide orchestra is rehearsing in the hotel's auditorium, which is beautiful and falling apart; it looks drastically older than it did just last year when he came to watch his sister perform. Three of the seats in the row where Rabbit has unpacked Beatrice have lost their spring and lay flat as tongues coated in threadbare red velvet. He sucks on a double reed and hoists his bassoon. He enters the orchestra from stage right, weaving between music stands and folding chairs and stepping over cello posts. There is one empty seat in the second row of woodwinds — his seat, since he is the last to arrive, of course. He takes it and looks around. He was so concerned with sneaking in as quickly and quietly as possible that only now does he notice how loud the auditorium is, full of the din of musicians warming up.

Piccolos spike, basses saw lazily. The trombones, who all seem to know one another, occasionally break into "Louie Louie." And in a flush of relief and confusion, Rabbit realizes he is not the last to arrive after all.

The bassoonist on his right, a chubby girl with fat yellow curls, smiles at him. "No one knows where he is," she whispers. "They're all running around like crazy trying to find him. Like, how hard is it to show up on time?" She bobs her head. "Sorry. Didn't mean you. But you're not the conductor."

Rabbit smiles weakly. Talkative seatmates make him uneasy.

"I'm Kimmy," she continues. "You must be Bertram Hatmaker. That's an incredible name. Like something out of *Masterpiece Theatre*." She points at the top of his music stand, where he notices two parallel pieces of tape wrapped over the edge. "We all have our names taped to the top of the stands, facing out. I hear it's because Brodie likes to get personal when he yells at people."

"Brodie?"

"Yeah, the conductor? Fisher Brodie? He's totally crazy. I've never been in a group he's conducted before, but my friend Joe goes to Westing and has him for a few ensembles and says he's *majorly* disturbed."

Small-town Ruby Falls naturally insulates Rabbit from the gossip of the larger student musician community, and he is fine with that. Alice, however, has made it her business to know everything about everyone, and now Rabbit remembers his sister gasping when she learned who would be conducting the orchestra. He should have paid attention, but Alice gasps so often, it's impossible to tell when it might be for a good reason.

A bang comes from out in the auditorium, barely audible over the cacophony. Rabbit cranes his neck, but his view is blocked by the oboist in front of him, or rather, by the oboist's hair, which is twice as wide as it ought to be. There is another bang, louder than the first, and then someone barks, clear over the noise, "OI!"

And Fisher Brodie is suddenly *there*, like he's bounded the length of the auditorium and up the conductor's podium in one enormous stride. Rabbit's first impression of Brodie is of a human spider, a wide-eyed daddy longlegs, and when Brodie props his spindly arms on the stand at his podium and barks "OI!" again, just as loud but so much closer, Rabbit wishes he were anywhere in the universe but here.

Everyone stops playing, transfixed by the strange new creature in their midst, this wiry man who has yet to blink in their presence. He stands up straight and says, "Now tha yuhv had yer coodly warm-oop, whyn' we spill sum blud?"

Rabbit has never heard a Scottish accent in person before, and it enters his brain on a two-second delay. *Blood?* he thinks, but Brodie has already moved on. "Haggerty!" Brodie shouts at a lanky girl hunched over the timpani. "Set some eighths on a C!" Haggerty flinches but complies. "Schwenk! Sixteenths on B-flat!" is hurled at a boy cradling his tuba like a life preserver. Brodie flings instructions like knives, and the musicians, trained to respond without a thought, spew forth a horrifying sound, a deep and dreadful noise. It goes on for too long, it lurches and growls. It seems that Brodie calls upon everyone. Everyone except Rabbit. And just when Rabbit thinks he has escaped forced participation in this aural nightmare, Brodie looks straight at him and shouts, "Hatmaker! Give me—"

Brodie stops, then crosses and thrusts his arms to the side. The orchestral beast he has created slumps over in a jumble of honks and bleats.

"Bloody hell kind of name is *Bertram Hatmaker*?"

Rabbit dies.

"Never mind." Brodie tosses a hand, dismissing everything having to do with Rabbit Hatmaker in one casual gesture. "That was horror, children. Did you hear it? Horror." He turns to the side and his profile is that of a heron or a mantis, something alien and starved. "My name is Fisher Brodie," he says. "But you already knew that."

He lifts his arms and one hundred teenagers set their bows, raise their horns to their lips, and do not blink.

Brodie lowers his arms and the orchestra relaxes.

He raises them again and the orchestra tenses for action. Brodie smiles like this is the best game he's ever played. He lifts and lowers his arms several times in rapid succession and the musicians snap and relax, snap and relax, jerking like marionettes.

"Quite a hive mind you've got. 'Cept for Hatmaker here. Oi, Bert. B-flat."

Rabbit has been sitting dumbly, ignoring each of Brodie's commands, because he can't quite believe this is what Statewide is like. This isn't what *any* group he's ever played in has been like. It *does* have a hive mind, a weird humming mentality perched on the edge of action, desperate for instruction. He assumes it must be because he's never played with student musicians of this caliber before, but he can't tell if they're good or bad or merely perfectly trained.

"Oi. Bert." Brodie waves his hand at Rabbit. It looks odd, and Rabbit's first thought—that Brodie's hand is strangely insubstantial, transparent as it flutters in the air—is rapidly replaced by *Shit, he means me,* and he wraps his lips gently around his double reed. He hasn't played so much as a note all day, and Beatrice wobbles before producing a relatively in-tune tone. It is the only sound in the entire auditorium, and Rabbit, now wondering if this is how it feels to be on the verge of a panic attack, loses breath after a scant five seconds.

Brodie tilts his head. "Well, that was inspiring," he says. "Right, then. You should have received a packet of sheet music when you were asked to participate in this magnificent celebration of youthful artistry, and I trust you've all practiced until your fingers and lips bled. How wonderful for you. Wonderful but unfortunate, because we're not going to be playing any of it." He drops to a squat and reappears with a small stack of photocopies. "I realized that it was all shite, really. We'll be playing this instead."

Rabbit, who hasn't practiced as much as he probably should have, but who didn't think he could be more shocked by this circus, feels gut-punched. They were supposed to be playing Handel, a Mendelssohn suite. Selections from Holst's *The Planets*. All shite? And they were expected to learn something completely new in the space of—what? Three days, in time for the concert on Sunday?

"Och, maybe we'll still play 'Jupiter.' Your mums will love it," Brodie mutters. He hands a stack of parts to the first-chair violin on his left, another stack to the first cello on his right. Photocopies flutter their way back down the rows. A thin girl, her hair pulled high in a glossy jet-black ponytail, takes the stack of woodwind parts and stands up to distribute them. "Here," she says, her voice small and cold with rage as she hands Rabbit his music.

And now he understands why. The piece Brodie is springing on them is Claude Debussy's *Afternoon of a Faun,* and the thin black-haired girl, who retakes her seat as first-chair flute, is the key soloist. She flips her ponytail over her shoulder and inhales violently. Her back is stiff and straight and she holds her flute like a cudgel. If Rabbit didn't think Brodie would throw something at him—a music stand, his shoe, perhaps his entire body—he would turn to chatty Kimmy and ask who she is. She carries herself like someone whom other people are expected to know, perhaps for their own protection.

"Why do you play that?" Brodie says it conversationally, casually, to the dark ponytailed girl. "Why do you play that flute?"

She responds by glaring at him.

"Right, then. You." He points over Rabbit's head at someone in the back row, in brass. "Why do you play that French horn?"

A boy in a crisp white shirt and navy tie fiddles with the bridge of his glasses and clears his throat. "Because . . . I'm good at it?" he says.

"Wrong." Brodie points at the girl playing third-chair trumpet. "Goldstein. Why do you play that trumpet?"

"Because it's loud as hell," she says, inciting a wave of anxious laughter.

"Not wrong, but not quite right either. You, Libdeh. Why do you play that viola?" Brodie pauses for a second and continues before Libdeh has a chance to respond, "Which really is the question for all time, really. Why does *anyone* play the viola? Just a violin trapped in puberty. Moving on. Or rather, coming back. Miss—am I pronouncing it correctly—Fah-chelly?" She neither corrects nor confirms his attempt. "Tell me why you play that flute."

"My mother makes me," she replies with a sneer, and Rabbit wonders how old she is. Her voice is young, immature. Statewide musicians are typically seniors, with some juniors, but there isn't an age requirement. He supposes that a freshman or sophomore would be eligible, should she happen to be prodigiously talented.

Brodie crosses bony arms against his thin chest. "This piece of music," he says, "this *Prélude à l'après-midi d'un faune* — sounds classy, doesn't it? That's the French for you. But I love the French, they have their priorities right. They believe in eating fine food, drinking good wine, and fucking their brains out. That's what this piece of music, this beautiful, classy-sounding piece of music, is about — the pursuit of lust! The *dream* of sublime satisfaction. And that's the reason you play that instrument. You play because you get off on it."

Rabbit giggles out loud. It's half nervous release, half genuine amusement. He cannot picture himself, let alone any of these other band nerds — with their ties and their nervous tics and their ramrod-straight backs — playing orchestral music *because it turns them on.*

"*Yes. Finally!*" Brodie throws his hands up. "Thank you, Hatmaker. I knew you'd go first. You'd have to have a sense of humor with a name like that. But *Christ,* you're a humorless lot! Maybe you *aren't* getting off. Maybe you play these instruments too much. You know they're a means to an end, not the end itself?"

The orchestra is completely silent, completely still.

"If a tree falls on a trombone when no one is around, does anyone care?" Brodie asks.

No one responds. Brodie frowns and points at Rabbit.

"Do you care, Bertram?"

Rabbit's breath is coming in short little puffs now and he fears he really *is* having a panic attack, which makes his breath shorter and puffier. Because he *does* care. He cares so much about music that what Brodie is doing offends him personally, and maybe it's the panic, maybe it's the fear, maybe it's the adrenaline building in his bloodstream, but in a sudden flash Rabbit Hatmaker realizes he is this orchestra's only defense against a madman.

"*Yes.*" He stands up, planting Beatrice on the floor like a staff. "I care."

Brodie's head snaps back. He opens his mouth but Rabbit cuts him off.

"I don't ask for much, and neither does Handel, or Mendelssohn, or Holst, since they're . . . dead. But I'm not dead, I'm here, and I don't want to get yelled at." Rabbit feels like the top of his head will lift off. "A little respect—"

"Don't go quoting Erasure at me, Bert—"

"My name is Rabbit!"

"Good Lord," says Brodie. "*Rabbit* Hatmaker?"

"Bastard," hisses the young ponytailed flautist, and at first Rabbit thinks she is referring to *him*. But no: she is withering Brodie with a glare that wishes him dead. "You bastard," she says again, her voice hateful and precise. It makes Rabbit's arms prickle.

"Rabbit Hatmaker." Brodie laughs, hooting like an owl. "Parents have a bit of an Updike fetish, do they?" Rabbit, flushing, realizes he is still standing and plunks into his chair, shaking. For a boy who treasures his anonymity, he has failed spectacularly at maintaining it, and less than an hour into the festival. Bassoonist Kimmy, beside him, gives him an approving nod and a smile. Rabbit raises his head to see the entire woodwind section twisted in their chairs toward him, all with expressions of awed compassion and gratitude. Rabbit flushes brighter—flattered and, curiously for him, emboldened.

"D'you've a sister named Bunny?" Brodie asks.

"My sister's name is Alice," Rabbit says.

"Ah, Lewis Carroll fanatics. Naturally. Tell me, Rabbit, are your parents still dealing? Because I'm going to need some heavy-grade narcotics to put up with you lot for the next four days. Bloody hell." He raises his hands to conduct again but the hive mind has been shattered. Half the orchestra composes itself to play, while the other half glances around nervously, unsure whether this mad conductor is anyone worth following.

A smile passes over Brodie's face like a shadow. If Rabbit hadn't been staring at him in terrified defiance, he would not have seen it.

"Come on, children." Brodie snaps his wrists to attention again.

"I'm not rabid. And I thank Master Bertram Rabbit Hatmaker for being a sport. Perhaps he's the only *real* musician among you."

"You bastard."

She says it much louder this time, and, like Rabbit before her, stands up to say it. "You megalomaniacal bastard," she says, shaking her glossy ponytail back. "Tell me, why do you conduct?"

Brodie is taken aback. His body tenses and he doesn't blink as he stares at the young girl in silence. This outburst is not orchestrated — not like Rabbit's was, which Rabbit now understands. He feels duped. Used, an unsuspecting soloist.

"Is it because you're good at it?" The girl takes apart the first joint of her flute. "Because your mommy and daddy forced you to?" Without breaking his gaze, she reaches down for her case and repacks her instrument. "Do you conduct because *you* get off on it?" She snaps the latches shut.

Brodie doesn't speak, doesn't move.

"I think," she says, "it's not the music but the *power*. Master of your miniature universe." She stalks through the orchestra, out of woodwinds and through second and first violins, to the front of the stage, until she and Brodie are less than four feet apart, Brodie immobile and elevated on the conductor's podium, the ponytailed girl below.

"Jerk off on your own time," she says. "Not on mine."

Rabbit thinks she must be older than she looks.

3

Roommates and Mothers

ALICE IS MAD as hell at Weirdo Wilson for making her late. But somewhere between watching Rabbit pelt off to his own rehearsal and pulling her new rolly suitcase up the threadbare hall carpet toward room 712, she decides to embrace it. Now it will be impossible for her *not* to make an entrance. She will open the big double doors of the grand ballroom, naturally drawing all attention from the in-progress chorus rehearsal. The whooshing air will tousle her hair and she'll smile with her lips and her eyes and even her nose. She learned how to smile with her nose when she was maybe eight or nine, making faces in front of the bathroom mirror; it was a subtle but definite lift of the tip that, on the face of an actress less skilled, read as a mere flared nostril. Alice suspects this is a gift of genetics, the way a person can be double-jointed or have different-colored eyes.

She slides her key into the lock of room 712 and parks her suitcase at the foot of the far bed. She frowns at the limp brown bedspread, the defeated pillows. "This one's mine," she tells her invisible roommate, who no doubt arrived on time and has yet to realize her insane luck at being paired with Alice Hatmaker, returning Statewide superstar. Alice plans to take the girl under her wing, introduce her to everyone she knows—though most of the people she met last year were graduating seniors, there are sure to be *some* familiar faces—and everyone she only just met. There's bound to be a party in someone's room both Friday and Saturday nights; Alice will get this girl in. Last year, Alice's roommate had been a mousy little nerd who played clarinet in the concert band—who was, like Alice, the only student attending from her district and therefore randomly assigned a roommate—but she hadn't shown any interest in the underside of Alice's wing. Or anything, in fact, other than practicing her clarinet, doing homework, and going to bed by ten o'clock.

She hangs up her dress clothes for the concert on Sunday, a neat black pencil skirt and romantically flouncy white blouse, and tucks her new shoes beneath them. Jeans and shirts and the satiny purple top she bought to wear to the various parties get folded and tucked into the giant shared dresser. And then she sees it. It stings her from the bottom of her suitcase, one unmistakable edge peeking from beneath a pair of pink pajama pants.

It is a picture of her and Jimmy Kopek. From the prom last year, the junior prom, which was a lot more fun than Alice ever expected. When you go to a school as small as Ruby Falls, the last thing you want to do on a Saturday night in late May is put on a long dress and dance awkwardly with the same fifty or so people you see five days a week, your classmates more like coworkers than friends. But Jimmy Kopek asked her. Jimmy Kopek, who was quiet and cute and nice. She and Jimmy were chemistry lab partners. He let her copy his homework when drama rehearsal ran too late for her to finish the night before. She introduced all the combustible experiments as though Jimmy were a magician preparing to amaze a rapt crowd and she was his charming assistant.

"And now," she had said that day, the day he asked her, "Kopek the Magnificent will turn on the Bunsen burner and heat the mysterious liquid. Sir, your pipette."

"If I promise not to saw you in half, will you go to the prom with me?" He was looking down at the gas jet, adjusting the height of the flame, his eyes hidden behind thick plastic safety goggles. Gossipy Lilah Horowitz, eavesdropping from the lab table behind them, tilted her head like an overeager Jack Russell. The tilt convinced Alice that Kopek wasn't kidding. He had asked and meant it. It was the first time she'd ever been asked to a dance, which was something you wouldn't expect; Kopek, when she told him this later, admitted he'd been sure someone else had beaten him to it. He had asked casually so he could laugh it off as a joke if necessary. That's the irony of fame, she'd told him. Everyone assumes a star has already been sought by another, but nine times out of ten, she takes herself to the ball.

In the prom photo, Kopek is smiling a shy, close-lipped smile, but his eyes are crinkling, a sign he's two seconds away from one of his snorting laughs. One arm is dangling awkwardly at his side and the other, at Alice's direction, is thrust out proudly like a circus barker. Alice, presented by Kopek the Magnificent, is wearing a short black dress with a chevron pattern of white sequins and a bright pink top hat. She has one arm behind Kopek's back and the other rests dramatically on the crook of a black cane. Later, after going to the Perkins on the boulevard for eggs and bottomless hot chocolate at one in the morning, when Kopek dropped her back at her house, she hooked the cane around his neck and pulled him close for their first kiss. Then she gave him the pink top hat as a souvenir. Alice was always great with props.

Why is this picture here? she asks herself. *Who put this here? Why would they do that?*

She blinks and her throat feels thick and achy, and then she remembers that she started packing for Statewide two weeks ago (she needed adequate time to determine how many and which costume changes would be required), and Jimmy Kopek broke up with her only last week. So *she* did this. She did this to herself. She cannot think about this for one second longer, so she dumps her socks and underwear and pajamas on her bed and shuts the suitcase, zips it closed, and drops it on the floor.

The door opens.

Alice doesn't have time to compose herself before a striking girl with a high black ponytail enters. "Hey," the girl says in instinctive

36

greeting, and then, to herself, "Shit!" as she throws what looks like a flute case on the closer bed. It bounces and flies off the mattress to the floor.

Alice has never met this girl, but she recognizes her immediately.

It's Jill Faccelli. She's fourteen years old. She's been studying the flute since she was four and has been playing as a soloist with professional symphonies since the age of eight. She has been profiled in magazines, in the *New York Times,* and all the Greater Syracuse newspapers when she and her mother first moved to the area. Alice had followed her for a while, had been fascinated by this dark-haired girl who now called the same part of the world home, who was sustained, presumably, by the same general environmental conditions as herself: the amount of fluoride in the water, nutrients in the soil, pollen and mold concentrations in the air. Her mother is Viola Fabian, whom Alice also knows by reputation as a brilliant musician and a horrendous bitch. Alice feels they ought to know each other, she and Jill, and now, standing less than five feet apart in the same hotel room, Alice thinks they *do* know each other.

Jill shakes her head and her ponytail bobs cheerfully despite her grave expression. Her hair is so black it almost looks blue, and her face is red and patchy with white. "Sorry," she says, her eyes tracing the thrown flute case's trajectory, and Alice understands she is apologizing not to her but to the instrument. Alice shoves her underwear in the dresser and approaches, one palm out to—what? Wave hello? Shake her hand? Proximity to fame has stunned her silly.

"Hi!" she says, too loud even by her own theatrical standards. Her pulse threads and she feels herself blushing. "My name is Alice Hatmaker. I'm your roommate."

"Jill."

"Welcome to Statewide!"

Jill's eyes shift from right to left and her brow creases. She is preternatural. Alice has never stood this close to someone like Jill Faccelli, someone touched by a talent so great it creates its own atmosphere. Her ability is a tangible thing, a crackling magnetic field searching for a route through which to pass electrons to the ground. Alice has a fleeting absurd thought that this strange magic will leach like radiation into her own greedy tissue and bone. She breathes in deeply.

"You're creeping me out," Jill says. "Why aren't you at rehearsal?"

"I'm not stalking you, if that's what you mean." Alice is horrified these words are coming out of her mouth. She laughs nervously.

"The thought hadn't entered my mind until now."

"I'm sorry. We got off on a strange — I'm — I was running late. My chaperone got us here late, and I wanted to unpack before going to rehearsal."

"Us?" Jill brushes past Alice and picks up the flute.

"My brother and I. He plays — he's in the orchestra. Are you in the orchestra?" Alice shakes her head. Of course Jill's in the orchestra; they say there isn't a pecking order, but there is, and the best woodwinds and brass are in the orchestra, where there are fewer of them.

Jill doesn't answer. She hugs the flute case against her chest, propping her chin on one end. She looks younger than she is, as young as twelve, and Alice realizes that at the same age she was making faces in her mirror, learning how to smile with her nose, Jill was crossing in front of the Boston Symphony Orchestra to play to a packed house.

Alice droops a little. She feels tragically normal.

"Hatmaker?" Jill says, and Alice nods, excited to hear her name spoken by this magical creature. "That figures. Hey, listen —"

The door opens again, and Alice frowns, wondering how many keys the Bellweather cut for this particular room. Then she stops, because the woman with the white ponytail who enters is none other than Viola Fabian.

The temperature drops at least ten degrees.

"There you are," says Fabian. "What did I tell you? You've been here all of fifteen minutes and already you're pissing and moaning." She sighs and puts her hands on her hips. "I swear to Christ, Jelly, there are faster, surer methods of matricide."

"You weren't there, Mom. You don't know what he did."

"It doesn't matter what he did," Fabian says. "It only matters what *you* do."

Alice's brain says *Don't stare don't stare* but she can't help it, she stares, because mother and daughter are so similar and so different. They are severely beautiful, otherworldly, and intense. But while standing beside Jill was thrilling, standing beside her mother is—Alice catches herself, because even though she is prone to melodrama, she seldom feels this strongly—standing beside Viola Fabian is frightening. Where Jill presents possibility, Viola is all coiled threat. Alice thinks of her own mother, of curly-haired Harriet Hatmaker, handing her an oversize red mug of chicken-and-stars soup when Alice had chickenpox, telling her they would fight chicken with chicken. Viola has never made her daughter a bowl of soup in her life, Alice thinks; she has never tended her when she was ill or tucked her in or held her when there was no comfort but to be held. Alice wonders if anyone has ever tended Jill, in any way, and if her intelligent ferocity is what happens when a girl has had to teach herself how to be human.

"What do you want?" Jill asks. She has dropped the flute to her side casually, but Alice notices there is nothing casual about the way her fingers grip the case. "This isn't what we agreed."

"And you agreed not to have a tantrum. But you did, and that means it's your own fault that you're here now." Viola opens the top dresser drawer, which is half full of Alice's things. "If you'd behaved properly, you wouldn't have to suffer the indignation of watching me search your room."

"Actually, those are mine—" Alice bites her tongue, because neither Jill nor her mother seems to remember she's there.

"I knew you would do this. I knew you wouldn't be able to leave me alone for ten seconds. I haven't even unpacked yet, *Mother*."

"Then how do you explain this?" Viola holds up a red lace bra that Alice wears because it forces her chest up, making it easier to hit the high notes.

"That's *mine*," Alice says, ripping it out of Viola's hand. She swallows, and feels perfectly high. "And I'd like to ask you to leave, please, Dr. Fabian. This is not your room, I am not your daughter, and my things are none of your business."

Viola's head and shoulders pivot. For the first time, she trains all her attention on Alice.

It's like being caught in a tractor beam.

"I'm sorry, you are—?" Viola says. "And why aren't you at rehearsal?"

"I'm Alice," she says. "My chaperone got me here late."

Viola approaches and stares at Alice. Her eyes are hard and flat, and Alice, whose talent for charming adults is almost greater than for belting a song to the rafters, feels utterly outmatched.

"What makes you think you're special?" Viola asks.

"I don't—"

"Oh, you do. You think you're very special indeed. So special that you can take your time getting to rehearsal. So special that you tell me your first name only, and order me out of my own daughter's room at the festival I am in charge of. I'll tell you what else I can see, very plain: you're not special at all. But I would like to know, out of simple curiosity, what *you* think makes you special. You teenagers." She smiles, a broad, true smile. "You make me laugh."

Alice's knees buckle. She has no defense against a grown woman, an adult, dressing her down for no reason other than to hurt her. And she is hurt, terribly, because Viola Fabian has seen into her private and terrified heart. For what Alice fears most of all is that there is absolutely nothing special about her, that there are hundreds of thousands of other Alices, that everything she ever dreamed of becoming was only pretend.

"I'll see you at dinner." Viola leaves and doesn't bother to shut the door.

After a long, still silence, Jill walks up to Alice and puts a cold hand on her arm. "I know you thought you were being brave," Jill says. "But that was stupid."

Alice looks up at Jill—at *the* Jill Faccelli, who is now looking at Alice as if *she* knows *her,* and can't help but be a little happy.

"Is she always—?" Alice half asks, before feeling rude.

Jill shuts the door and crosses to the closet, from which she removes a scuffed black suitcase. Baggage routing tags sprout from the side handle, a bouquet of ciphers: LAX, LHR, CDG. That suitcase, Alice knows, has been all over the world, has followed Jill to London and Paris and Berlin and San Francisco and New York and God knows where else. She looks at her own bag, brand-new, naked, and untraveled.

"Oh, yes," Jill says. "She is always like herself." She flings her suitcase on the second bed and unzips it in one fluid motion. "She is never not Viola Fabian. She is never not correct, she is never not to be obeyed, she is never not the first, the middle, and the last word on everything. She is the reason I exist and the reason I need to do whatever she tells me. She is why I have a roof over my head, why I do not starve, why I live the life that I live. And it is because of Viola Fabian that I play the flute, that I am a musician at all, that I am a genius." She pauses and gives Alice a small but honest smile. "I meant it when I said it was brave of you to stand up to her like that. To stand up to her at all."

Alice shrugs and tries to pretend this compliment hasn't made her entire year.

"And I meant it when I said it was stupid," Jill says, and begins to unpack. "Now she knows who you are."

4

Natalie Takes the Elevator

ALL THESE YEARS, Viola has been waiting in the elevator. Natalie knows this is impossible—or at least highly improbable—and yet there she is. When the doors part, Viola Fabian, the woman herself, is standing inside as if she's been shut up there for the past two decades, biding her time until Natalie pressed the call button. Every detail is just as she remembers. The ponytail, which was mostly white even in Viola's mid-twenties, is now the color of paper. The exquisite gray wool suit could be the exact same one if the lapels were a bit wider. The frozen blue eyes and the sloping reddish brows—proof that Viola has, at some point, been something other than a white witch—and the mouth, painted the color of dried blood, are still poised for a glare, a doubting arch, a cutting remark that once had the power to stake Natalie through the heart.

Natalie's body moves itself forward, crossing the threshold from the dim sixth-floor hallway of the Bellweather into the ancient elevator car. Viola even smells the same. Natalie has compartmentalized so many things about her—that's Natalie's former therapist talking, Dr. Call-Me-Danny; he dropped fruity jargon like "compartmentalize" and "avoidance behavior" every third word—that she's begun to forget some of the details. But the memories are all there and floating up from the cold storage of her subconscious. Viola smells of lavender and something burnt. A hot wire. Singed toast. Natalie is suddenly afraid she's going to cry.

She didn't even cry after the break-in.

"Which floor?" Viola asks.

Her voice—Natalie blinks, and just as suddenly knows the tears aren't going to come—her *voice* sounds different. Smaller, more human. How is that possible when everything else is precisely the same? Unless it's Natalie's ears that hear differently.

"Lobby," she replies with a small croak. The elevator doors slide together, sealing them inside. "Thank you."

Viola has already pressed L and settles back to the middle of the car. She sniffs. She looks at her watch. She does normal things for a stranger sharing an elevator to do. But they aren't strangers; they are far, far from strangers.

Natalie clears her throat. "Here for the festival?"

Viola stares straight ahead. "Yes" is all she says.

"I have two students attending, chorus and orchestra. Both seniors." Natalie swallows, feels she is talking too much. "Did you travel very far?"

"Everywhere is far from this godforsaken armpit."

Natalie bites back a smile. Classic Viola. Then she frowns, bruised. This, she imagines Dr. Call-Me-Danny would say, is a "complex emotion."

Why doesn't Viola recognize her? How can she not remember Natalie Wink?

The first time Natalie Wink met Viola Fabian, one was ten and the other twenty-six; one was a student, one a teacher; one was awestruck and one was abusive. That, said Dr. Danny, was the simple truth. Natalie, who was there, knows it's sort of half the truth, that it contains pieces of the truth—gnawed on, mangled, and spit back out—and, in any case, that it was never simple.

It began with a piano. Her parents had a piano, an upright they'd inherited from her mother's mother, and Uncle Kevin, her mother's youngest brother, would sometimes play it when he came up from San Francisco for Sunday dinners. But this piano—Natalie had never heard a piano sound so pretty or so sad. It danced. It dipped. The vinyl popped.

Laurie and Nancy, her older, painfully normal sisters, were out with friends. Natalie had been sent to bed early so that her parents could talk to her uncle about life in the city—Had he found a job yet? Those types in the Haight weren't the most reliable employers. And he'd been kidding, right, about this being the first square meal he'd had all week?—but she'd crept back to the landing at the top of the stairs. Uncle Kevin always brought records with him, trying to *expand their consciousness,* which her parents never played while Natalie was (officially) awake.

She lay on her back and tipped her head over the top stair. The sad piano and a man with a warbly voice walked her through a sunken dream, until a single step appeared, a strong step made of sound followed by another, slightly higher, and another, higher yet. The piano got mad, and faster, she'd reached the top of the steps and with a rush of violins the entire world fell away. She leaped out into nothing and floated, held up by music. She had no idea what the man was singing about—sailors, cavemen, and lawmen were all involved—but it didn't matter. It was beautiful. Her fingertips tingled. She wanted to run downstairs and flip open the lid of her grandmother's piano and play it right then and there, but she didn't. She listened to the next song instead. And the next. Her mother's voice grew louder, she was getting upset; Natalie could picture Uncle Kevin running his hands through his bushy red hair until it stood three inches off his head. Natalie wished they'd shush. She pushed their voices aside and listened to the record and fell deeper and deeper in love.

When her uncle came upstairs to use the bathroom, Natalie was still curled on her back, head hanging over the top stair, giddy and giggly.

He crouched beside her. "Didn't you go to bed an hour ago?" he asked. "Sit up, Natty, all your blood's going to pool in your brains."

"Who was that?"

"You mean on the record?"

She raised her head, dizzy, and nodded.

"You liked that?"

"It's the best music I've ever heard."

"Then I'll tell you what. Tomorrow morning, look in the record cabinet. Filed under B for Bowie."

She listened to all of *Hunky Dory,* but especially "Life on Mars?," again and again. Uncle Kevin walked her through the basics, about sharps and flats, scales and counting beats. She listened more. She listened harder. The music echoed inside her mind and came out through her hands, one note, one chord, one measure at a time. She went straight to the piano when she got home from school. She spent every Saturday and Sunday dancing her fingertips down and over and across the keys.

She begged and pleaded with her parents for lessons, real private lessons. Uncle Kevin mentioned he'd seen a conservatory student play a piano concerto to a standing ovation, and Natalie knew, as soon as she heard her name—*Viola Fabian*—that this woman would be her teacher. *Had* to be. Her mother caved first. It was her mother's mother's piano, after all, and Natalie had only been two when her grandmother passed away. The drive from Millbrae to San Francisco to meet Viola Fabian was etched permanently in Natalie's brain: how the rolling brown hills gave way to long blocks of pastel row houses, to city stoplights and street corners and crowds of people, and how Viola could be in any one of them.

Viola met with Natalie and her parents in one of the practice studios at the conservatory. They compared calendars, discussed fees. Natalie eyed the twin baby grands with greedy joy. She ached to show this strange and beautiful young woman—younger than her parents, maybe even younger than Uncle Kevin—how talented she was. How alike they were.

Viola asked Natalie's parents to step out of the practice room while their daughter played for her. "Having you around makes us that much more nervous," she told them, and winked at Natalie. The room, soundproof and close, felt like a secret clubhouse as soon as they were alone. Viola asked her to run through her scales, major, minor, and chromatic. She asked her to play a prepared solo, and

Natalie played, of course, "Life on Mars?" Viola gave her a hand-written sheet of music to sight-read. Natalie knew she hadn't performed perfectly—sight-reading wasn't her strength, to say the least—but she knew she'd played well. She'd felt that sweet rush of weightlessness she always felt when she played, when the music lifted her high on its back. Through it all, Viola had said nothing beyond an instruction. She paced the small room (which felt smaller as time went on), winding the end of her white-streaked ponytail around her index finger, her brow furrowed, her lips pursed.

Natalie laid her hands in her lap and waited, hopeful.

Viola smiled at her with all her teeth and said, "You were sloppy on all your scales, but especially the full chromatic, which was pretty goddamn awful. That was the worst pedal work I've ever seen in my life, frankly, but it was still better than your sight-reading, which was a goddamn disaster. It's laughable that you thought to audition with *that* piece of pop trash, but it's not your fault; no one ever told you what to play. You taught yourself, and it shows. You aren't ever going to be great, but if you want to try to be good, I can help you. Learn this," she said, offering a sheaf of music. "All of it. By next Tuesday."

Natalie didn't know what else to do, so she smiled. Decades later, she would tell Dr. Danny that at that moment she knew, she *knew*—instinctively, deep in her gut—that Viola Fabian was dangerous.

But she didn't listen to her gut. She hadn't yet learned how.

Natalie is sick with the coincidence of it all. For them to have last seen each other on the other side of the country—seventeen years have passed since that sweltering day. Seventeen years: the midpoint of her life to date, almost exactly.

"Yes," she says, "everywhere *is* far from this godforsaken armpit." Natalie coughs. Her throat is itchy. "I'm from Ruby Falls. Way upstate. High school music program director." Why is she still talking? Why can't she stop? "Moved from Minneapolis this summer."

"So you know."

"Know?"

"Snow."

Ah, the weather. Of course they would get around to talking about the weather. That's what you do in an elevator, after all.

Natalie nods. "I know snow."

She and Emmett had talked about what they were going to do next, after the body was buried and the lawyers introduced her to the phrase "justifiable taking of life" and it was clear nothing would happen beyond Natalie's being written up in the *Minneapolis Star Tribune* as a heroic homeowner. Well, Emmett had talked; Natalie had shouted. *"We are leaving!"* she had yelled at him when he calmly, all things considered, pointed out that running away would solve nothing. She had shouted, *"We are going somewhere else!"*

Upstate New York, then, was somewhere else. More like nowhere, except for the hometown of Emmett's friend from college who was willing to put in a good word with the schools in his district hiring chemistry and music teachers. And in this elevator with Viola Fabian is somewhere else entirely—another world in another time, from another era of her life. Anger comes over her like a wave of nausea, because Natalie cannot imagine that Viola Fabian's path to this elevator has been anywhere near as disappointing as her own. And where is the justice in that?

"Have you heard the latest?" says Viola. "About this storm bearing down on us?"

"I thought it was only supposed to be four to six inches—"

"Four to six *feet*." Viola stretches a smile tight over her teeth. "Enough to bury us alive."

Without thinking, Natalie's hand slips inside her blazer—to touch, reassuringly, the butt of her gun.

Viola had, among other things, taught her how to recognize a threat.

Viola Fabian taught Natalie that good wasn't good enough. Neither was great. The only acceptable level of achievement was *brilliant*, which is exactly what Viola made Natalie become. Natalie was the one everyone talked about after recitals, playing solos much harder, with more fire, than her fourteen years would suggest she was capable of. She entered solo competitions and won. She auditioned for adult-level concerto competitions and placed. Every single thing Natalie attempted musically, she excelled at, and every single time someone praised her, she was sure to mention that it was nothing, that it was all thanks to her mentor, to Viola Fabian. Natalie was too young and awed by her developing abilities to question Viola's motives or methods. Viola had made her successful; success had made her pliant.

Mostly Viola used words—*Stupid. Moron. You're nothing special, you know. You're lucky to have me*—but not always. The first time it happened was almost funny. Natalie and Viola were sitting side by side at the piano in Viola's practice room at the conservatory while Natalie murdered a sonata. She was tired and hungry; she'd taken the bus straight from school without grabbing so much as an apple. Her hands were sore, tingly. She was desperate not to show Viola how exhausted she was, but Viola could always tell.

"What's your problem today? You think Schumann likes it when stupid teenagers shit all over his music?"

"Of course not," said Natalie. "Sorry."

"Again. From letter F." Viola stretched her arms behind her head and crossed one leg over the other. One pump, red and spike-heeled—she always wore pumps, even with jeans—dangled from her toe and she caught it in her hand. "One two three, two two three—"

Natalie limped along until she came to a particularly complicated passage of thirty-second notes, and her body, that betrayer, gave up. Her fingertips slipped and landed on the keys in a jumble.

"Oh, come *on!*" said Viola, and smacked Natalie in the side with her shoe.

Natalie flinched. Then she half smiled, puzzled. "Ow," she said absently.

"Again," said Viola.

Natalie rubbed her ribs. "That hurt."

"It was supposed to. Again."

Natalie took a deep breath and began at letter F. She walked this time instead of limped, her fingers tensed.

She got halfway through before her hand cramped.

Viola jabbed her with her heel.

"Ouch!" Natalie said. "What the hell?"

"It's working, isn't it? That was better. Again."

Natalie was angry now. The still childishly chubby flesh below her ribs burned, stung by a size six and a half stiletto wasp. She attacked letter F. And when she ran into that field of thirty-seconds, she hit every single note as hard as she could. She punched them. She knocked them out.

"Told you," said Viola, and smacked her one last time. Natalie took it without a word of protest. She had a bruise beneath her ribcage, never bigger than an egg, never smaller than a grape, for the rest of the time she was Viola's student.

By the time Natalie realized what Viola was doing, it was too late. She was a senior in high school, and nothing whatsoever about music made her happy. Music was something to win, to be first and best at. She snapped at her parents and was too proud to apologize. She shrank from Uncle Kevin because it was easier than admitting the truth. She listened to all of *Hunky Dory,* to *Ziggy Stardust* and *Heroes,* and tried to feel lovely and strange and weightless, but she couldn't; she played the piano, she listened to music, and nothing stirred, nothing sang inside. Natalie was earthbound and ordinary, marooned, alone.

Her parents threw a graduation party for her on a too-hot June night. Natalie, who didn't particularly want a party in the first place, gamely put on a sundress and stole a beer from the refrigerator in the garage. She was two bottles in when Viola arrived, looking, in her gray suit and power pumps, like a court clerk dispatched to serve the party a summons. Natalie had been going to her weekly lessons as if everything were normal, had betrayed no hatred toward her mentor for tainting the first pure love of her life, so there was no reason for Viola to suspect she was unwelcome. But unwelcome she was; here, in the backyard strung with pink and purple paper lanterns, in the house that had once echoed with David Bowie, Natalie watched this wicked big sister from across the lawn and wanted her to die. She was mortified to have borne Viola's cruelty and considered it kindness, humiliated by the understanding that all the awards and accolades were a celebration of something sick and wrong, something ugly between them.

She hid in the house, in her room. She watched the sun set on her last few friends and relatives in the backyard while she drank more beer. The party sounded like a success — she heard laughter, loud voices. She closed her eyes and tried to imagine how she could tell her parents the truth about Viola. She could hear them already: *Listen to yourself, Natalie. You're being melodramatic. Histrionic.* Viola was mean, Viola was a bitch, but Natalie had *allowed* her to be. And she, Natalie, was going to college in the fall. That was a natural cut-off, wasn't it? Couldn't this all just go away by itself?

There was a light thump on her door and Natalie turned and there was Viola, letting herself in. She looked like she didn't want anything in the world but to eat Natalie's heart out of her body.

"*There* you are. Everybody's missing you down there." She leaned against the dresser, her eyes skimming the beads and knickknacks and Bonne Bell lip-glosses of Natalie's girlhood. "But *of course* you're up here, hiding in your room like a spoiled brat."

Natalie didn't say anything.

"Your father tells me you're going to Indiana." Viola sniffed. "I was surprised you didn't tell me yourself. What gives? You've been so *quiet* lately. We haven't talked in months. Really, Natalie — is everything okay? Are you afraid about graduating, going off to college?" Viola sat on the bed next to her, pretending to be concerned. Next she was going to ask to brush her hair. "Maybe you're feeling a little anxious that there's an awful lot of competition out there. That maybe your best years are behind you?"

Natalie closed her eyes. The beer bottle in her hand was empty and her stomach too full. She sloshed.

Viola's arm circled around her back, giving her a squeeze. "Your best years *are* behind you, kiddo," she said in a voice slicked with cheer. "That's the way it is. Sure, you'll go on, you'll go to school. You'll learn how to write and how to teach music, and you'll probably teach but you won't write, and you certainly won't compose anything worth remembering. Then you'll marry someone and have children and you'll say you played piano once but you won't have sat down at yours in years. You'll get rid of it. You'll sell it, and you won't be happy, but you won't quite be able to put your finger on why. I'll tell you why. Because that's the way it is, Natalie. That's life when you're nothing special. And I'll tell you something else. This is a *much* easier lesson to learn when you're eighteen instead of forty." Viola grinned.

"You're welcome," she said.

The bottle was a baton in Natalie's fist. Viola raised her hands to protect herself and Natalie slammed the bottle into the meat of Viola's forearm and she knew she hadn't broken the skin but it was going to leave a bruise, a beautiful bruise, giant and swollen and black. She swore she heard the bone ring, low like a brass bell. Natalie, elated, feeling as if she had planted a flag on the moon, lifted the bottle again, and this time Viola was too stunned, too slow—this time, Natalie swung down and smashed her on her temple, right near the hairline.

Viola cried out. Closed her eyes, brought her hands up to cover her face, tilted and swayed on the edge of the bed. Natalie saw a tear of blood well, bright as a jewel, on Viola's forehead.

Natalie dropped the bottle on her pink braided rug.

She didn't think she would learn anything worse from Viola than that she was nothing more than an instrument, a toy to be tuned up and broken, but in her room on the night of her graduation party, Natalie learned that she was not the hero. Viola was not the villain. They were somewhere in between and nowhere at all, both of them alike.

Natalie brought the gun with her to Statewide on impulse, tucking it in her luggage between her sweaters and skirts and travel-size shampoo and conditioner. It had drifted into her mind while packing, as it often did, accompanied by a simple thought: *I might need that.* If she had asked herself why, for what possible reason could a chaperone at a weekend festival for teenage musicians need the protection of a .38—*other than the obvious ones, right?*—she wouldn't have had a real answer. Not then and not now, other than as a kind of insurance against everything she couldn't anticipate. It was easy to bring, easy to carry. It's compact but pleasantly heavy in her jacket pocket, a gift passed to Emmett from his father. She'd made a point of not knowing much about it before the break-in, but now, now that she knows the pinch, the jerk, the flash of firing it, she can't keep it out of her mind.

Emmett will miss it if he happens to check the safe in the den, but Emmett is spending the weekend with Kevin and Lou, playing poker, watching football, maybe road-tripping up to Canada for the casinos. She doubts he will so much as look.

She doesn't have a permit to carry it. She carried it out of her home and out of her hotel room just the same.

But Natalie is not going to kill Viola Fabian. Natalie, old at thirty-five, "clinically depressed" and more than slightly bitter, is never going to kill anyone ever again, even if she feels like it and even if the person deserves it. However, and she thinks Dr. Danny would agree, it might be therapeutic to *frighten* Viola. To gently remove the gun from the inside pocket of her wrinkled-from-the-drive blazer and ask if Viola knows who she is. *Do I look familiar? And do you remember what happened the last time we met?* She would press the red emergency button on the elevator panel and the car would jolt to a stop and she would face Viola, her Viola, and she would corner her in this tiny elevator car, which smells like old shoes and dust and a hint of ammonia from the housekeeping carts that are pushed on and off every day.

The hairs on the back of Natalie's neck stand up like spikes because this is a very insane thought she is having. Danny would probably say that it is "willfully self-destructive" and "pointlessly violent," and while Danny is usually "full of shit," for once Natalie would agree. But it is a thought that feels good, and she is a fan of feeling anything good at all these days, even if it is also insane. She senses a big smile pushing up from deep inside, from the bottom of her stomach. It surfaces on her face with something like a tiny laugh.

The elevator has reached the lobby. The doors open.

Natalie's more disappointed that she would like to admit.

There is no pretense of politely summarizing their elevator conversation—no blathering on about enjoying the festival, that perhaps they'll see each other at dinner, which will begin in a few short hours. Viola Fabian moves quickly to be the first off. She glances over her shoulder and looks straight through her former pupil, pinning her to the back of the car.

"Get over yourself, Natalie," she says.

5

The Face of the Bellweather

AROLD HASTINGS NEVER forgets a face. He's seen them all: the faces of businessmen checking in, florid and bright, clearly meeting their mistresses. The faces of their mistresses checking out, hollow-eyed, leaving the businessmen to their wives. He's caught the frozen, silly-surprised eyes of housekeepers smoking dope in the penthouse suite on eleven and housekeepers and bartenders groping each other in the service passage in the sub-basement, pushing their friends in laundry-cart races from one end of the low concrete tunnel to the other. Children crying in the library, pale cheeks shiny with tears, unclaimed by blank-faced parents—paged immediately—until they'd finished their highballs in the bar. Local high school kids booking rooms on prom night, blinking virgins on the verge whom he'd later catch streaking through the halls in the middle of the night, wide-eyed with their first taste of sex.

Hastings has also seen twenty-nine Statewide music festivals (and this one, the thirtieth), every one since the Bellweather began hosting the event in the late sixties. As other conferences and festivals, intimidated by the Bellweather's palatial resort grounds, moved on to newer hotels, cheap but charmless chains in towns more accessible from major highways, Statewide continued to book at the Bellweather. Probably because it was easier than finding another facility large (and, to be truthful, empty) enough to host more than two hundred guests for an extended weekend; to feed them breakfast, lunch, dinner, and a banquet on Saturday, all with vegetarian options; to provide the auditorium, ballrooms, conference rooms, and lounges for rehearsal and performance spaces. In fact, Statewide is the only annual event of its size the Bellweather has on its booking schedule. Without it, Hastings doubts the hotel would be open at all.

He's been the Bellweather's concierge for forty-six years, since he was twenty and the previous concierge, his Uncle Chester, died of a massive stroke in the hotel lobby: on his feet behind the concierge desk one minute, jotting a note in his appointment book, and dead on the carpet the next. Hastings has stood behind that same desk and watched his hotel get older and shabbier, the guests following suit. Where once the businessmen wore three-piece suits and hats—always hats—now they showed up in rumpled shorts and polos dotted with coffee drips. Families that had looked crisp and excited about their vacation in the Catskills were now tired and distracted, making a quick stopover on their way to other, more thrilling destinations when they bothered to come at all. He can mark the decades through the kids' appearance alone. The Statewide students began as a sea of impossibly shiny, straight hair, puka shells clicking and bell bottoms flapping. Their hair got higher and puffier, their concert ties skinnier, and their shoulders broader, and now they look as though they barely bothered to bathe before swaddling themselves in plaid and flannel.

But this girl—this girl standing at the check-in desk. She doesn't belong to any of those memories and yet she's familiar. He's seen her before. Where? How? If she's here for Statewide, she's late, though he doubts she has any connection to the festival. She's young but not a teenager. Her blondish-brownish hair is pulled back in a sloppy bun and she's unzipping a dark blue field coat that makes her look like an enormous blueberry. She's large. A big girl, not just tall but round. She has the look of acquired fat, of sadness weighing on her in the form of flesh. A whisper of tenderness mixes with his déjà vu.

Sheila at the front desk is greeting her, welcoming her to the Bellweather, and asking politely for her name. Sheila Czeckley, his check-in girl extraordinaire, is the only other person at his hotel who has the slightest comprehension of what real customer service looks like.

Hastings points his good ear in their direction, but the girl's voice is too low, too quiet for him to make out. He hears a gentle jingling instead.

The girl has a dog. Hastings grins, confused. A small dog, half fox by the look of it, with big pointed ears that flop when he shakes his head. He, the dog, is wearing a red vest with a white cross on it. His tail wags at the sound of his mistress's voice.

Curiosity killed the concierge, he thinks, and leaves his post.

The check-in and concierge desks are on the same side of the lobby, separated by the entrance hall to the west wing and its assorted ballrooms and business suites. A ghostly harmonic murmur wafts by as he crosses the open carpet: the sound of the Statewide chorus warming up. It lifts his steps. Hastings waits all year for this weekend, for his hotel to be full of life and song again.

"Welcome, welcome!" He hails Sheila and the large girl. "Have you come for the festival?" The feeling of having seen her, of knowing her—when Hastings looks into the girl's face, the sense that he knows her is so powerful he rocks on his heels. The carpet bounces him back. "Hello," he says, much softer. "Hello and welcome to the Bellweather."

Her eyes are large, gray, and her face—it's odd that she has any effect on him at all, because her face is as forgettable as blank paper. She looks like any young woman running to fat. Her cheeks are full, her chin pointed.

"Are you here for the festival?" he repeats. She blinks. "Statewide. The Statewide school music festival. I hope you'll be with us through Sunday. That's when they'll hold the concerts, right through there." He points across the lobby to the auditorium's closed doors. "The orchestra's rehearsing in there now if you'd like to hear them."

Her dog shakes his head again, jangling his tags.

"What's his name?" asks Hastings.

The girl bites her lower lip. "August," she says. "He's a working dog. I'm training him to be a working dog. For the blind."

"That's wonderful."

She doesn't respond.

Sheila smiles and hands over the key to 407. It's one of the Bellweather's nicest rooms, in a corner of the tower overlooking the rear grounds, the old Olympic-size pool and nine-hole golf course sloping low in the distance. Not that the pool or the golf course has been tended very well; he can't remember when anyone last played a round. Nonetheless, he's glad Sheila has recognized the importance of making this singular guest feel comfortable, special, and looked-after.

"We're here for whatever you need," Hastings says brightly. "Stop by the desk, give us a call any time, day or night. Enjoy your stay, Ms. —?"

"Graves." The girl shoves the key in her coat pocket, looking down at the counter. "C'mon, Aug," she says to the dog. "C'mon, let's go."

Hastings watches them disappear into an elevator car. Then he turns to Sheila, who shrugs.

"Made the reservation two months ago," she says. "Credit card. E-something Graves."

Hastings fiddles with his bow tie.

"What?" Sheila says.

"What what?" says Hastings, smiling.

He shakes his head. Sheila grins and dips her hands into the pockets of the hotel's uniform maroon blazer. The elbows are shiny with age.

"It's the damnedest thing," he says. "The damnedest thing."

Hastings is back in 130. He's lived in this room of the hotel since — well, it's been years now since Jess left him. It was supposed to be a temporary living situation (can't beat the commute, he used to joke), but Hastings knows this single, smoking room is where he'll spend the rest of his life. He's put a few pictures on the walls, a few articles clipped from the newspaper. Detective novels, old library castoffs, fill the drawers of his nightstand. Hastings is a junkie for crime, for mysteries, particularly of the unsolved variety. The closet is full of his blue and brown and tan suits, the closet floor a jumble of his blue and brown and tan wingtips and loafers. The bathroom sink is speckled with reddish-blond hair from his beard, and his toothbrush is perched at an angle on the porcelain.

Every morning, Hastings inspects himself in the full mirror on the back of the room door, underneath the emergency-egress instruction placard. His face, the face of the Bellweather—unlike the Bellweather itself—has changed little in the past forty-six years. He is still vaguely boyish, blue-eyed, clean-shaven, and friendly, though his short hair is white at the temples. He hasn't lost much of his six feet two inches and his teeth are all his own, though he has to wear glasses to read anything, big black frames he chose because they reminded him of a young Michael Caine. For all forty-six of those years, Hastings has tied his own bow tie every day. They are dark red and match the carpet of the Bellweather lobby, or they did years ago, before the carpets had been trod to mauve by hundreds of thousands of feet.

He naps every afternoon from three to four, the slowest time at the front desk, not that the front desk of the Bellweather exactly has busy times anymore, not even during Statewide. Rehearsals last until four-thirty. There's an hour break before dinner, when Hastings will be back at his post before retiring for good at eight. But today he can't fall asleep. Today he closes his eyes and sees that girl, that blurry girl he knows he knows.

Hastings looks at his watch. Three in the afternoon is the perfect time to call Jess.

His wife, after she left, moved back to England to be with her family. "So who are Caroline and me, some people you used to work with?" Hastings had shouted, and Jessica—God, he could still picture the look on her face: hurt, tired, and a little righteous—had picked up her suitcase without another word. Her father, a widower, had been a doctor in London and retired to a small village somewhere in Wales.

After years and years of silence, on an otherwise unremarkable

Thursday, Hastings had picked up the phone and called his wife to say hello. There was never anything promissory about their conversations. Oh, maybe the first few times they spoke, Hastings thought they were taking tiny steps toward a new future. Over time it became clear that both Harold Hastings and his wife were settled and set, that neither of them had any desire to move or to change, but that both of them were lonely, and they knew each other well—too well to live together in the same place, but well enough to be able to pick up the phone any time of day and talk.

Hastings dials Jess's number. As it rings, he pictures her tromping in from the vegetable garden she keeps outside the kitchen door, wriggling her feet out of large green wellies and tucking unruly strands of frizzy white hair behind her ears as she lifts the receiver from the cradle.

"Jess," he says, and she laughs.

"Knew it was you."

"How'd you know?"

"Who else would it be?" He can hear her smile, shrug.

There's a long pause. Hastings unbuttons his collar and pulls his bow tie loose.

"So why are you calling?" Jess asks. "Something worrying you?"

How did she do this? She used to know everything without having to be told, but they'd been sharing the same bed at the time, which made it that much harder to keep secrets. How could she tell *now*, in another life and another country, all the way on the other side of the ocean?

"It's Statewide," he says. "Another Statewide."

"And how do you think it's going so far?"

"So far, so good. Except—well, one thing. No, two things. You remember Doug Kirk?"

"Isn't he in charge?"

It's been over two weeks and Hastings still can't believe the phone call he received from Helen Stoller, Doug's secretary, on behalf of the incapacitated president of the Association for School Music. Kirk has been the head of ASM for years. Hastings always held him in high regard, not least because he brought a bottle of excellent Scotch with him every November and wasn't stingy about sharing it. Every Statewide Saturday night, right after the banquet, Kirk—who bore an alarming resemblance to a mustachioed Kirk Douglas—would plunk two tumblers down on the concierge desk. They drank to Statewide. They drank to the Bellweather.

This year, that toast isn't going to happen. This year, instead of striding around the Bellweather like the captain of a galleon (the only captain Hastings would even consider being first mate to), Doug Kirk is in a coma.

"It was a coronary," Helen had told him, her voice quavering. "And now he's in a coma. They don't know what brought it on, he was always so careful about his heart. Went to the doctor regularly, I booked all his appointments . . ."

"Helen. Helen, slow down—"

"What am I going to *do,* Mr. Hastings?" He had never actually met Helen Stoller, but she'd been Kirk's secretary for as long as he could remember. In Hastings's mind, she looked a great deal like his own mother.

"I'm sure there are other—" But there were no others like Kirk. Hastings felt a sudden terror of everything ending. "Please, Helen. This isn't what Kirk would want. I'm certain he will be fine, and I'm certain you'll be able to find a substitute for this year."

Helen Stoller sighed. "Anyway," she said, "that's up to the advisory council. I was just calling to tell you—to tell you. I knew you'd want to know." She sighed again. "I'll be in touch once we know more."

Helen was in touch, two days later, with the news that Kirk's condition was unchanged but stable, and a Dr. Viola Fabian would be heading the festival this year. Something about the way Helen said her name—*Viola Fabian, Doctor* Fabian—made Hastings's skin crawl. Helen, who looked like Hastings's mother, wasn't at all happy that this Viola Fabian would be serving in Kirk's stead. And the fact that Fabian hasn't introduced herself to Hastings yet has done nothing to change his first, albeit secondhand, impression of her.

"Kirk's in a coma," he tells Jess. "Heart attack. He's been replaced with a sub this year."

"That's awful. Oh, Hastings, I'm sorry. I know you really liked him. I hope he pulls through."

"Me too." He can hear a voice in the background. Voices. Who else is there? Who is with his wife? "What's that sound?" he asks.

"I've got company, but first—you said there were two things on your mind. What's the second?"

"This girl." Her face has already vanished from his mind. Her face is gone. How can her face be gone when the gut-deep feeling he knows her, he knows her, how does he know her, is stronger than ever. "You ever get déjà vu?"

Jess laughs. "Only when I'm talking to you," she says.

6

Bad Rabbit

ABBIT'S PARENTS, LAPSED Protestants, had managed to pass along the big-ticket ideas of Christianity, but practically speaking, Rabbit had learned Judeo-Christian history from the school of Indiana Jones. Bambi's mother taught him about loss, and he was too in love with dinosaurs to entertain the idea of a literal seven-day Creation schedule. Charlie Brown (or rather, Linus) told him the Christmas story; *Jesus Christ Superstar* covered the crucifixion. He did not regret his secular education. He may have been baptized Presbyterian, but music was his true religion.

In his earliest memories he was sitting on the floor in the family room, in front of the giant stereo his parents had bought themselves as a wedding present, his face pressed into the padded fabric of one speaker. The fabric was prickly against his forehead but his nose fit perfectly into a little groove, and he could feel music spilling like molten gold through his entire body. He'd sit back on his heels when the song was over and his father, an accountant and amateur drummer whose (still-unrealized) dream was to open a jazz club and coffee house, would say "Order up!" and put another record on the turntable. Rabbit's favorite albums were by Earth, Wind &

Fire (syncopation made his brain feel like it was laughing) and *Also sprach Zarathustra,* its opening rumbling like an earthquake. And he loved *The White Album,* and when his mother played ABBA on the piano and they'd sing together (though Alice couldn't do it without being a total showoff), and the *Star Wars* soundtrack, and of *course* Zeppelin. For six months in 1984, he had asked his parents to play "Stairway to Heaven" instead of a bedtime story.

Rabbit and Disney's *Fantasia* turned ten and fifty, respectively, in the same year. Rabbit had only seen pieces of it on TV—the Disney Channel liked to play "The Sorcerer's Apprentice" and the dopey Beethoven scene as filler between shows—but it was his father's favorite movie of all time. His father had first seen it in a theater in college (high as a kite, he said, with a hushed *don't tell your mother*) and had been waiting twenty-one years for it to return to the big screen. It had changed him, he said. It had opened him to music in new ways. So when it was rereleased for its half-century anniversary, his father skipped work, pulled Rabbit and Alice out of school, and bought them all tickets on opening day.

Rabbit had never seen him in such a state of excitement. His father's eyes blinked furiously behind his glasses, and his smile was so broad and wide Rabbit wondered if his lips ached. Except for a few hassled-looking parents with very young children, they were the only people in the theater—it was a Friday matinee on a school day, after all—and Alice, typically, wouldn't shut up about how amazing this was going to be, how magical, because she knew what their father wanted to hear more than anything was how very much like *him* his children were. Alice was always good at knowing what people wanted to hear and giving it to them in symphonic stereo.

Rabbit was less enthused. It was exciting to be out of school, but he was suddenly worried about his dad. What if the movie wasn't as incredible as he remembered—and how could it be, after twenty years? Not in college, not on drugs? The parts Rabbit had already seen weren't exactly mind-blowing; those silly flying horses were for little kids, and he found the story of the sorcerer's apprentice acutely frustrating (if Mickey Mouse was stupid enough to mess with the magician's hat, he deserved all the trouble he got). Rabbit's stomach soured in anticipation of having to pretend, first to enjoy the movie, and then not to notice his father's disappointment.

The toddlers in the theater fussed and Alice knocked over her soda at the end of "The Nutcracker Suite," because, she whispered theatrically, she was so caught up she forgot where her foot was. During the Beethoven segment, with its dippy fauns and centaurs and baby unicorns, Rabbit dared to glance at his father. The wide smile was still there, the blinking eyes — and then they were gone, and so was all the light streaming back at them from the screen. A child shrieked in the sudden dark and people began to rustle, but Rabbit's father grabbed his hand quickly, gently, and whispered, "Don't worry, it must be the light in the projector, the music's still there" — and Rabbit really, truly heard Beethoven's Pastoral Symphony for the first time. His eyes stung from the blackness, so he shut them and felt the music sweep him up faster and higher than he'd ever flown with his head mashed into the stereo speaker. He soared on the breeze of a brilliant spring day. The sun poured warm honey on his shoulder blades and he ran ahead up a small hill, bare feet tickled by springy new grass, and rolled down the other side, laughing. When the rain came, he shivered and ducked for cover, but it was gone soon enough, and what it left behind was a sense of the perfect rightness of this time and this place. Of himself — perfectly right, perfectly at peace with his family in the dark. He laid his head back contentedly and let out a long breath.

His father squeezed his hand. Alice was muttering something but Rabbit couldn't make it out, and didn't care to. His father squeezed his hand again and Rabbit knew then that he needn't have worried, that his father couldn't possibly have been disappointed in the moment he'd dreamed of for decades. The wait, in fact, had been necessary, because what he'd been waiting so long to experience was the joy of sharing something so sublime with his children.

Rabbit had never understood music before as an agent of connection, as a way for people not only to feel within themselves but to feel *among* themselves, a language that brought common souls into conversation. Beethoven could talk to him and could talk to his father, and he and his father could talk Beethoven to each other. Rabbit was a very shy child, more often spoken to than with. A recurring theme of parent-teacher conferences, beyond his academic excellence, was concern over his apparently self-imposed isolation. But on the day that Rabbit felt the Pastoral Symphony vaporize his body and plug his soul directly into his father's, he realized he had found his native tongue.

He had just started fourth grade at Ruby Falls Elementary, old for his year despite how young he looked; he was eligible to sign up for lessons on an instrument of his choosing. Uncharacteristically for Rabbit, he didn't worry that no such instrument existed. He trusted that it was out there, and that he would find it when it was ready to be found, and that through it, Rabbit Hatmaker would be able to talk. To his family, to his teachers, to people he'd never met. To animals. To the universe. Maybe to God.

That was the second of two revelations in his tenth year on earth. The first had already occurred that summer, at the swimming lessons his mother had been forcing on him and Alice since they could walk, when he got his first crush on a boy. On Mattie DeLuca, who was bused to the community swimming pool from his house in the city of Syracuse, who was eleven but just as short as Rabbit, who had olive-colored skin that glowed like a perpetual tan and the tilted-head cool of Ralph Macchio.

Nothing happened, yet everything had: Rabbit discovered something fundamental about himself without understanding what it meant. And he felt instinctively that it was something he didn't want to talk about. It was secret and safe inside his mind, and he would keep it there, in a sacred part of himself, until he knew what to do with it.

As Rabbit grew older, he felt the world become unfriendly. He began to worry, more than he had ever worried before, about what he was and what he wanted, and what it meant his life would be. It didn't stop him from knowing, but he worried that it would be the only thing anyone would ever see about him—that if he told his father or his mother he was gay, they would never see anything else. "Here is our gay son," they would say. "Here is our gay son who plays music and is kind, but did we mention that he is gay? Because he is. Gay."

And if the only thing the world saw about him was his gayness, how could anyone ever fall in love with *him?* Would he *have* to go to parades and wear rainbow-striped buttons? Would he *have* to love Barbra Streisand? Would *all* his friends have to be gay, not that he had ever met another gay person (that he knew of)? Would he ever be able to *not* have this secret?

Rabbit worried about all of these things. He also worried about graduation and about college, and whether he would know his own mind if Alice went to a different school (or, maybe worse, he worried that he would love his independence so much, he'd never want her around again). He worried that his sister was setting herself up to be disappointed by real life, and, Pastoral Symphony notwithstanding, he worried that his father was already disappointed, would never open up that coffee house he dreamed of, would never be truly happy. Rabbit worried himself into a hole for the people he loved, for the world at large, and if he hadn't felt that organized religion had no love for men who loved other men, he probably would have become a priest. He worshiped and found peace, at the age of seventeen, the only way he knew how: in the temple of Beethoven and Debussy, of David Bowie and Led Zeppelin. They filled his secret heart and made it less afraid.

Alice will not shut up. This is not a new phenomenon. Rabbit thinks by now he should have developed a survival mutation, a sub-chamber of his brain like an overflow tank that siphons off and contains his sister's endless talking. Less than five minutes after Rabbit checked into his room after that first rehearsal, Alice was at his door. About half an hour has passed since then—Rabbit has unpacked all his clothing, set up his toiletries in the bathroom, taken a quick shower, and changed into a crisp new shirt; they have left his room, walked the long creepy hallway, and are waiting for an elevator to take them down to the grand ballroom, to dinner—and he is certain his sister has not stopped speaking for longer than three seconds, which is the amount of time necessary for her to take a breath. He has gleaned that her roommate is famous and crazy, and her roommate's mother is even crazier and a total bitch.

Rabbit knows when to nod and when to raise his eyebrows, when to say *Are you kidding?* and when to say *She did not.* He does it seamlessly, thoughtlessly, as though he were actually engaged in the conversation and not silently overwhelmed by the events of his own afternoon. As it went on, his first rehearsal did not exactly improve. The flautist's storming out was definitely the most dramatic moment. But then they had to sight-read *Afternoon of a Faun* without the key soloist, stumbling from measure to measure, losing count and coming in at the wrong places. He heard the trumpets and trombones muttering mutinously behind him. Even mild-mannered bassoonist Kimmy on his right couldn't wipe the scowl from her face. Through it all, Fisher Brodie yelled and pinwheeled his arms and lobbed Scottish insults like lawn darts. But he didn't pick on any one person again; that dubious honor would forever be Rabbit Hatmaker's.

The elevator opens at the fourth floor and more students get on. Alice doesn't stop talking. In fact, one of the new riders is in the chorus, so Alice, renewed, starts talking with her about *their* rehearsal, and how incredibly tacky their conductor is. "Did you see her pants? God, she dresses like my mom—it's like my mom is conducting the chorus. Can you imagine? The whole program would be Barbra Streisand and Celine Dion. The whole thing!"

Rabbit frowns at his sister. They both know their mother would make a great conductor. Does he really need dinner? Can't he grab a packet of peanut M&M's from the vending machine on his floor and call it a night? Because this, he now sees, is what he can expect for the next three days. This elevator is the weekend in miniature, with his sister talking to people she's only just met as though they're her dearest friends—this is what Statewide is. It isn't about music, it isn't about beauty and art and life and death, about connecting to others, soul to soul. It's about *nothing*. It's about air passing through lungs and metal and wood and plastic, making sounds, making noise. His heart deflates. There is no way he can tell Alice he's gay when he cannot even tell her to shut up.

The elevator doors open on the lobby. He hears singing in the distance. Kids practicing, he thinks. Dinner, according to the festival itinerary, is a buffet set up in the grand ballroom in the east wing of the hotel. He follows his sister and her new friend, who he's figured out is named Chrissy. Chrissy tosses flirty little eye flicks in his direction that Rabbit doesn't have the energy to feel guilty about. The east wing is in slightly better shape, newer and more anonymous-looking than the rest of the Bellweather. Rabbit is surprised he notices this much, because he feels he's being pulled along by a tremendous tide, a bit of flotsam who wouldn't be able to fight his own drowning.

The singing is louder now. The singing is not practicing, Rabbit slowly realizes. It's a performance, and it's coming from a handful of young men in matching black T-shirts and jeans standing to the right of the grand ballroom's open double doors.

Rabbit's feet stop working. His back straightens. His pupils dilate, his lungs expand, his cheeks flush. Every part of him pops, juiced. They are singing that song, he doesn't know what it's called, about wanting to use your love toniiiiiight, they are singing it *a cappella,* and the man in front, the man singing the solo, bears more than a passing resemblance to a college-age Ralph Macchio. They sort of dance, the singers, but it doesn't feel dorky; they have an innate cool, a casualness and a swagger, that makes them charming. Their throats and faces are wide open and they are smiling into a horseshoe of onlookers, which the soloist, a full, bright tenor, is working shamelessly. His eyes are brown. His hair is dark. When he sings that he doesn't want to lose your love tonight, his eyes crinkle and his lips curl up in a smile.

Rabbit Hatmaker is in love.

His sister and Chrissy and everything in his life that was slightly or more than slightly annoying fades away to nothingness. Rabbit has been punched in the heart. He knew, he *knew* it would happen like this someday, and he thinks he will liquefy with joy, with gratitude that he is here, in this one spot on earth at this one time in history, for *this* man to be singing *this* song and for Rabbit to hear it.

"Yeah, *that's* the gayest thing I've ever seen," Chrissy says.

Rabbit snaps back.

"They're not gay, they're college guys. *A cappella* clubs are how you get laid if you're not a jock," Alice says. "Do you have eyes? Look at the lead guy. God, he's cute. If he's gay, I don't want to be straight."

Rabbit inhales sharply.

Alice pushes herself up on her toes and tries to catch the tenor's eye.

Panic flares in his chest. Rabbit blushes and takes hold of his sister's arm. "Hey, I'm starving here," he says. "Let's go eat. C'mon. Chrissy? Food? Like, now?" He needs to get her away, they all need to leave, the song is over and he doesn't know which he is more afraid of, should the tenor acknowledge them—that Rabbit will make an ass of himself or his sister will make a move.

Rabbit enters the ballroom behind Alice and Chrissy, herding them like distracted cats toward the end of the buffet line. If he hadn't just fallen in love, Rabbit knows he would be disheartened by the pale, wet food stretching before them, borne above small blue Sterno flames, in dented silver warming pans. As it is, he looks on the grayish slices of roast beef and the weirdly off-white mashed potatoes and smiles, happy in the knowledge that the tenor is in the world. He disturbs a layer of skin across the vat of gravy and daydreams about a situation, a moment, when they might meet. In the elevator. At the ice machine. Maybe they're staying on the same floor. What's his name? What school does he go to? He's had crushes before, Mattie DeLuca was just the beginning, but this is in a whole other realm of feeling. Rabbit never believed gaydar was a real thing—but is this how it feels to fall for someone he might actually have a shot with, someone *like* him? Is it like reverse magnetism, that in order to be drawn violently there needs to be the same charge on the other end?

The ballroom is full. It takes a while for Alice to find a table with three empty seats for them to join. The scene reminds Rabbit of their cousin Patty's wedding a few years ago, with an ocean of round tables and one long, skinny table, perpendicular to the buffet, where all the key players—the head administrators, in this case—are meant to be seated. He doesn't see Mrs. Wilson yet. He thinks he should tell her about what happened at rehearsal, though he doesn't know what it could possibly accomplish. But he figures Mrs. Wilson, unlike his sister, will at least listen to him.

Alice is making introductions for everyone. "Hi!" she says to the assembled souls at a table in a far corner, beneath a tall window with pendulous maroon drapes. "My name is Alice Hatmaker. I'm in the chorus, and so is my friend Chrissy Spanowitz. And this is my brother, Rabbit." Rabbit manages a twitch of a smile as his sister swings into her seat. "So who are you?"

There are two boys from the same school near Buffalo, Nate and David, who clearly don't like each other but are bonded by a mutual desire for familiarity. Next to David is a tall girl with close-cropped blond hair and bright pink lipstick who introduces herself as Chastity. She shakes her head like she has a tic, her long silver earrings jingling every time. Chastity is from "the city," a fact she confirms repeatedly during dinner with comment after comment about all the crazy things she's done in the Village. Next to Chastity is another girl, with curly red hair and glasses, who looks as if she'd rather be back in her room reading Shakespeare, and who leaves without a word immediately after half-finishing her plate of limp vegetables. The three other kids also know each other, from local county and city music festivals if not the same school—a boy and two girls, who introduce themselves as Harrison Map, Violet Smalls, and Jennifer Czerny. Rabbit thinks they might also be from New York City. They possess a worldliness that Rabbit associates with kids who grow up taking the subway and seeing homeless people on a regular basis, unlike Chastity, who he suspects may have moved there in middle school, and may not even be named Chastity.

"So what are you in, Harrison?" Alice asks, cutting a slice from her meat. "No—wait, let me guess. You're not in the chorus, because I would remember you." Harrison cocks his head and grins.

He has brown hair that flops over his forehead, and he is wearing a light blue button-down, the top button open to reveal a white crew-neck undershirt. Catholic school dropout, Rabbit pegs him. Trumpet. Band. "First violin in the orchestra," Alice guesses.

"Nice try." His voice is surprisingly deep. "First trumpet, concert band."

Rabbit smiles at his pasty food. He is in love, and he cannot lose.

"Curses!" Alice shakes her fist in the air. "And *you've* all been here before, right? You look familiar." Not to you, they don't, Rabbit understands; his sister just wants them to know that she's been here before too, that she is One of the Twice Chosen. Two of them actually *do* look familiar to Rabbit. The girls may have been sitting behind him in orchestra, in brass or percussion. His heart ices with the possibility that they will out him.

"This is my *third* year at Statewide," Jennifer Czerny says. She's pocket-size and blonder than anyone Rabbit has ever met. He wonders if her doll-like feet are dangling inches off the floor. "I'm what you might call a French horn prodigy." Harrison and Violet laugh, though Rabbit has no idea why. "I'm in the orchestra," she continues, and grins at Rabbit. "With your infamous brother here."

Rabbit freezes. Then, flush with love, he makes a choice: to bask in this moment.

His sister skips like a scratched CD, a heartbeat of quiet absence. He feels her turn in her chair to face him with a stiff smile.

"Oh *really*," Alice says. "My infamous brother. In the orchestra. What are you holding back from your own sister, you little punk?"

Rabbit shrugs and shovels mashed potatoes into his mouth. They're instant and taste like salty baby food.

"You didn't tell her?" Jennifer hunches conspiratorially in Rabbit's direction, her tiny chest practically in her plate of food. "Bad Rabbit."

This is *killing* Alice, and Rabbit kind of loves it. She punches him in the arm, a little harder than she really should.

"You were there." He tips his chin at Jennifer. "Why don't you tell the story?"

Harrison is looking at Rabbit with narrow, amused eyes. He might be cute, if Rabbit didn't suspect him of being a humongous preppy dillweed.

"Okay—so." Jennifer takes a sip of something pink from the glass in front of her. "Fisher Brodie's conducting, right? And he's late, like, really super-late, and we're all sitting there onstage waiting for him to show up. And when he finally does, it's clear he's off his meds. The guy fucks with us for fifteen minutes, asking why we're here, why we're musicians, blah blah whatever. But then! *Then,* he says that we're not going to be playing any of the music we were sent, that we've been practicing for weeks. Says it's all terrible. And then your brother here, brave little Rabbit, stands up and is all like, *Fuck you, man. Fuck you, man, fuck your bullshit, you have no right to talk about Mendelssohn like that, I mean, who the fuck are you?*"

Rabbit's insides are howling with laughter. He could kiss this tiny toy girl right on her truck driver's mouth.

Jennifer waves her hands in the air, still pretending to be him. *"Fuck you and your bullshit conductor patriarchy! You don't own us! You don't own the fucking music, you fucking twat prick asshole! Rarrrrrrrr!"*

Alice's eyes are flicking from Jennifer to Rabbit, Jennifer to Rabbit, trying to figure out if *she's* being fucked with.

"It's all true," says Violet. "I was there, hanging out in the back with my trombone." Violet's hair is done up in tiny braids that run straight back across her scalp, collected by a fat ponytail that flops from shoulder to shoulder as she speaks. "You're one badass rabbit, Rabbit. I think you gave Faccelli the idea to get the hell out."

"Faccelli." The word falls from Alice's mouth and sits on the table. It is just a word, but Rabbit knows his sister well enough to understand she is saying she is not amused.

"Jill Faccelli? You know, the *actual* prodigy at this festival?" Violet gives Jennifer's ribs a playful dig with her elbow. "Your brother started the rebellion, and Jill finished it by walking out of rehearsal."

"I know who Jill Faccelli is." Alice clears her throat. "*Jelly* is a friend of mine. She's my *roommate.*"

"Well . . . *Jelly* is having a terrible day." Jennifer lets out a snort of laughter. Violet and Harrison join her. Rabbit can't quite, because he knows that Alice's pride has been wounded—and then he suddenly finds that he *can* laugh. The whole time Alice was babbling on about her roommate and her drama and her*self,* she was talking about the girl with the dark ponytail who ditched rehearsal—the very girl Rabbit had a story to tell her about, if she had shut up long enough for him to tell it. It's kind of funny. It's really kind of funny, and Rabbit laughs out loud too.

He feels his twin draw into herself, diminished. He swallows a few final laughs.

"Oh, come on, we're just taking the piss," Jennifer says, and takes another gulp of the pink stuff.

"What are you, a Spice Girl?" Alice says.

Violet rolls her eyes. "Anyway. Are we doing this thing tonight? This haunted party thing?" She's asking Harrison, but she's not being secretive, and Rabbit likes her for this. He likes her even better when she addresses the whole table and says, "If you're not busy later, we're getting together in Harrison's room. Five-thirty-three. You should stop by."

Chastity's earrings jingle uncontrollably as she nods in the affirmative, and Chrissy, sensing Alice's stock plummeting, chimes in that she'd love to go. Alice crosses her arms over her chest.

"Haunted?" she says. "Wasn't Halloween last month?"

"So you don't know about the *hotel* either?" Jennifer says snottily. Rabbit is beginning to rethink his urge to kiss her. "I thought you said you'd been here before."

"I *have*—"

"The hotel is haunted. *Actually* haunted." Violet—Nice Violet, Rabbit has decided to name her—props her elbows on the table, blocking Jennifer from another retort. "Back in the eighties, on her wedding day, a girl hanged herself after blasting her husband to hell with a shotgun. Happened right in the hotel. She's the most famous ghost here, but, like, have you seen *The Shining*? And have you walked around upstairs by yourself? This place is *creepy*. Ghosts up to here." She holds her palm flat above her eyes. "This weekend is their anniversary. Of their wedding *and* of their deaths."

"Harrison has a Ouija board," Jennifer says.

"How do *you* know about this?" Alice asks. She's uncrossed her arms but Rabbit can tell she is still deeply annoyed—at Jennifer, and at him. The latter is a new feeling, and not entirely unpleasant. "Sounds like the kind of bullshit kids tell each other on the playground. You know, Pop Rocks and Coke killed Paul from *The Wonder Years*. My mom bought a cactus from Pier One and it exploded into a thousand baby spiders."

"It probably *is* total bullshit. But where's the fun in that?" Nice Violet says. She pushes back from the table. "I'm gonna get dessert to go. Everyone—around nine, nine-thirty, room five-thirty-three. BYO." She scrunches her nose at him. "See you later, Bad Rabbit."

Alice has pushed her own chair back and stood before Rabbit notices she's moved. "I'm not feeling so great," she says, addressing no one in particular. "This food is terrible. I'll see you later."

Rabbit is not the same person who woke up in Ruby Falls this morning, in his childhood bed with its blue-and-green-striped sheets. *That* Rabbit would have leapt to his sister's side without thought. *This* Rabbit is sitting down and his twin sister is leaving and *he is not following*. He feels her hesitate, knows she is tugging on that strange flap of soul, the overlap they've always shared; but the part of him that laughed, the part of him that is still buzzing with love, knows he is not ready to leave just yet. Knows he doesn't have to.

"See you later," he says. He doesn't look at her when he says it, but he knows she hears him—because she does leave, her offense receding like a car with a stereo thumping bass, losing volume as the distance between them increases.

Jennifer is leaning so far forward she *is* pressing her chest into her food. Rabbit wonders what's in that pink stuff she's been drinking.

"Jeeeeeesus. You had to grow up with that?" she says.

"We shared a womb," he replies, still stunned by his daring.

Jennifer pulls a face and sits back, a lump of mashed potato clinging to her shirt. "She must've come from the bitchy side."

"She got all the crazy-whore genes," Chastity says, giddy to play this game.

"She's not even that good," Chrissy, the turncoat from chorus, says. "She's okay, I guess. If you enjoy the sound of cats being thrown into blenders."

There is something intoxicating about this. Rabbit, who has never gotten drunk, imagines this must be what it feels like, his face warm and his mind dulled, his spine and tongue loosened, his gut tingly with the thrill of doing something he has never done before.

"Or chipmunks being fed firecrackers," he says.

Jennifer laughs riotously, as if it's the single funniest thing any human has ever said. Harrison claps him on the back, and Rabbit wonders for a moment whether Harrison is gay too. He really is sort of cute. He isn't the tenor, though. The tenor is out there, and Rabbit is going to meet him this weekend. He smiles.

Bad Rabbit is out.

7

Who You Are

NATALIE IS SKEWERED. Pierced, shish-kebabed. Viola Fabian instructed her to *Get over yourself, Natalie,* and for hours she's been walking around with a spear through her guts. She's surprised she didn't clothesline anyone while she was filling her dinner plate with sad brown food (and come to think of it, the sad brown food is likely making her feel worse). Now she's lying on her bed, staring at the flaking ceiling and prodding the sore point of entry with her fingertips, wondering if she's inadvertently toothpicked herself to this mattress, like a slice of tomato in a club sandwich.

Get over yourself, *Natalie.* Get *over* yourself, Natalie. The whole time they were standing in the elevator, Viola knew who she was. But of course she knew: Viola Fabian was omniscient. Is omniscient. Is here in this hotel.

Dr. Danny would think this is fate. He would call this an "opportunity for healing." Natalie is starting to think it is fucking *hilarious,* that maybe she ought to give more serious thought to the handgun on her nightstand in conjunction with Viola Fabian's sudden reappearance in her life. Surely this can't all be a coincidence; it could, in fact, be the universe's way of suggesting a course of action. She's already got blood on her hands. What's a little more?

Is this the first weekend she's had by herself, alone without Emmett, since the break-in? Natalie cocks her head back into the pillows and jiggles her legs. It *is*. It *is* the first weekend on her own; the first hours, the first day that is totally and completely her own. Since.

She sits up on the edge of the bed, belly and back aching, and surveys her room, anxious, desperate for a detail that might derail her brain. The room is not without its charms. All the furniture is old and heavy, made from dark, knotty wood, and the bedding and curtains are warm and thick, the color of overripe apples. It smells odd, shut-up and unaired. Is she the first person to stay in this room since last year's Statewide? There's no way a hotel this enormous, a *resort*, essentially, in a town this remote and depressed, could be fully occupied year-round, at least not since the middle of the century, when she can imagine families coming up from New York to spend their vacations in the country. Her skin prickles and she stands. A tomb. That's what it reminds her of—a mausoleum. Nicely appointed, but not meant to be lived in so much as lain in, forever.

She's cold suddenly, cold and shivering, and she has to get up. She has to get out. She pulls on a pair of jeans and a plain black shirt and leaves her crypt, shoving the key in her back pocket and the *Do Not Disturb* hanger on the doorknob. When she was a kid—the kind of kid who went to recitals not unlike this—she and her friends would giggle whenever they passed a *Do Not Disturb*–tagged room, knowing, in their infinite teenage wisdom, that it was code for *Do Not Disturb the Sex We Are Having*. Today her tag is code for *Do Not Disturb My Firearm*. If nothing else, being a grownup meant having the freedom to speak euphemistically.

She walks down the hall. The farther she gets from her room, the more the sharp pain in her middle subsides. As a child she loved to explore, to peer into the deep cupboards and closets at her grandfather's farmhouse in the Central Valley. There were very few old places—by East Coast standards—in the Bay Area; California looked like it had been built in the twenties and repainted once in the sixties. When she came east as a teenager with her parents to visit her father's sister in Boston, she had been shocked by how old everything felt, how lived in and wise, marked by the people who came before. The past was layered under the present like sheets of tissue paper, still visible if you focused your attention long enough to see below the surface.

The elevator panel tells her she's in the main tower of the hotel, that the tower has eleven guest floors, one basement, one lobby, and one rooftop lounge. She presses the top button. The car, after a gut-dipping moment of weightlessness, ascends.

For the second time that day, she's unprepared for what the parting doors reveal. She'd assumed the lounge would be an abandoned general-use area—an ancient, chugging sauna reeking of chlorine, an assortment of treadmills and stair steppers all turned toward one television, closed captioning scrolling—but it is a jungle. A forest. She allows herself a short befuddled laugh and walks into a giant greenhouse. The ceiling is made of glass panels held in place by a web of cast iron. Around the perimeter are ferns in enormous clay pots and shrubs and bushes, heavy with flowers, planted in low beds sunk into the tile floor. The moon is full (she frowns, knowing the seething mass of hormones on the floors beneath her will be powerless to resist its tidal pull) and illuminates the lounge with cold light. Stars wink across the surface of an enormous round swimming pool in the center of the room, blue-tinted bulbs wobbling just below the surface.

Natalie might as well be standing on that moon. She feels light. She feels—she swallows—she feels almost good. It's a physical memory, this feeling: a phantom stirred up. Standing in this bizarre and beautiful moonlight, high above the hotel, alone and unknown, she almost remembers how it feels to—

How it feels to be—

She raises her arms and dives headfirst into the pool. The water is icy, sharp, and every part of her shrieks happily. Her clothes are made of lead. She didn't even take off her shoes. They tug her down but all the rest of her resists. It's incredible to feel so lifted, so buoyant. She opens first her mouth, strange chemical water rushing over her tongue, and then her eyes. She twists onto her back and looks up at the night sky through the water and the high glass roof. The sensation of coldness is starting to subside. Natalie spreads her arms and legs wide and imagines the calm of flying underwater. Then she kicks her legs together and propels herself along the bottom of the pool, the moon, high above, never leaving her sight.

Viola may have hollowed her out once upon a time, but Natalie didn't stay that way. Over the years, she's filled herself with everything she could think of. In college, at a sprawling state university in Indiana, she filled herself with music theory and student teaching, with beer and pizza. Out of school, she filled herself with hard liquor and more pizza. She tried filling herself with work, conducting jazz and blues ensembles in addition to the required concert bands and orchestras, taking on private student lessons as Viola once had, spending almost every waking hour tapping out tempos with the flat of her hand against her knee. She met Emmett at her first real job (he was called in to sub after the regular chemistry teacher set his beard on fire during a classroom demonstration), and she filled herself with marriage. She suggested they go out with other couples; she pressed to host dinner parties. They used their joint savings to go to Paris over summer vacation. They made careful decisions about rugs and sectionals, what movie to see on Saturday night, whose families would host them for which holidays.

It wasn't enough. She wasn't full. Natalie was never, ever full.

They moved, first to Chicago, then to Ann Arbor, then to Minneapolis, to one half of the twin cities, because Natalie was restless again and Emmett refused to move to any place with a cost of living higher than anywhere they'd been before. He had family in St. Cloud and suggested Minneapolis, she knew, because he wanted children and wanted to be close to his parents and brothers and sisters when that happened. "When that happened" was how Emmett talked about procreation, as though it were as eventual as their next birthdays, their thinning hair and wrinkling hands, their deaths. Natalie didn't have the heart to tell him that the act of having a child — of conceiving, carrying, delivering, rearing—was something she could no longer imagine.

This was chiefly the result of being a teacher. All the time they were moving, she and Emmett were teaching: in public and private schools, the children of the wealthy, the super-wealthy, the poor and the destitute, the comfortable and the aspiring. But in every school and every ensemble she conducted, Natalie always had the same students. The same jerkoff percussionists who found it hilarious to ditch lessons and waste time in rehearsals. The same meek little third flutes, barely passing enough breath through their instruments to make them whistle. And the same phenoms, bright and bright-eyed, born full of talent, whom she tutored and praised and who always left her for something better. To them she was a yearbook signature, a souvenir, and she had come to resent all the hours of her life she'd given without hope of return. So for her it was too late for kids, even though technically, biologically it wasn't: she was only (ha!) thirty-five. It was just that she had already raised hundreds of children and didn't have the strength to raise another, one of her own — one who would leave as surely as all the others had, who would take what was left of her heart and everything else.

Now she loved her job and loved her husband in the same hazy, unexamined way. They were what she knew. They were the outward markers of a normal life, the kind of life, as a child, she'd never expected herself to live but had slid into sideways, by default, because it seemed safer. But filling herself with a normal life only ever got her a guilty conscience and this — this pain. This restlessness. This hunger.

She tucks her legs beneath her and pushes up from the bottom of the pool. When she breaks the surface, she laughs. Natalie isn't a good person. She isn't sure she's a bad person, either; most days it's enough to accept that she's a person at all. But today is not most days. Today she's swimming in a half-dead hotel, a ghost with a pulse, washing away everything about herself that isn't actually her. Today she's listening to the first good advice Viola Fabian has given her in years.

Get over yourself, Natalie.

She dives deep and opens her mouth and her eyes and fills herself up with cold blue water.

· · ·

Natalie's mostly dry by the time she finds him in the auditorium. She's already explored the dark concrete corridors of the basement, the laundry, and the kitchen, a cat burglar creeping from one nook to the next, taking mental note of all the exits and escape hatches. She sees a few people—kids from the festival, they have to be—laughing like jackasses as they run between each other's rooms. She wonders what Rabbit and Alice are doing tonight; she meant to check in with them at dinner, but they disappeared before she had finished serving herself. *Oh, right, Wink. Your tender young responsibilities. The reason you're here. Maybe you should have said hi before you went for that dip on the roof.*

They could be thoughts in someone else's head.

Instead of taking the elevator, she walks down the sweeping double staircase from the second floor to the lobby, holding her arms out for balance as she descends on quick, squishy tiptoe. A youngish man behind the front desk is reading a ragged paperback. He doesn't look up at her.

Down a short hallway, on the left, is a library with a green marble fireplace and overstuffed chairs that look like leather marshmallows, and another ballroom on the right, set up for the concert band. The neat rows of empty chairs and music stands have already seen one rehearsal. They stand slightly askew, littered with the particular detritus of young musicians: abandoned tubes of cork grease and vials of valve oil next to empty Mountain Dew and Fruitopia bottles, potato chip and candy bar wrappers.

She sees herself grabbing a music stand by the base and wielding it in a wide circle like a scythe, hacking and felling the neat rows. She'll hook a toe under the seats of the chairs and kick them on their backs, and when she's done with the chairs and the stands, she'll upend the conductor's podium; she'll heave the small wooden box over her head and launch it into the pile of rubble. What a beautiful racket she could make.

She's about to wrap both hands around the long thin neck of a music stand when she hears it.

A piano.

She follows the sound back through the lobby and into the auditorium and closes the double doors behind her. A thin man is sitting at a shiny baby grand in the orchestra pit, noodling on the keys with his left hand.

He doesn't know she's there. His back is half turned to the seats; he's hunched over the keys, rigid with purpose, scribbling on a piece of paper on the bench beside him. He's using the same hand to both play and write. As she approaches, quiet on her cat-burglar feet, she notices just how thin he is, how his body seems to be made of pickup sticks.

"Quit skulking about and have a seat," he says without turning around. He has an accent—English? "It's rude."

No: Scottish. Her shoulders fall and she smiles.

"I'm not skulking," she says.

He stops playing and turns around. He is pointed, bird-like, and undernourished, with dark eyes set deep on either side of a large nose, hair turning to salt and pepper around his temples. There's an extraordinariness about him, a strange, humming current. She moves closer.

"Where are you from?" she asks.

"The Westing School of Music," he says. "And you *are* skulking."

"I mean originally. Geographically."

"The planet Earth," he says. "You?"

She's close enough now to see his right hand, curled around the edge of the piano bench—or what's left of his right hand, at least. It's incomplete: only a thumb and first finger with three rounded stumps. Something triggers in her brain—the last line of a song, an old song. *Gimme your hands! You're wonderful!*

"Do I know you?" she asks. "You seem." She shakes her head. "Familiar." She leans against a seat in the front row without pushing it down. "I've seen you before."

"You're brand-new to me," the thin man says.

"Ever live in California?"

He shakes his head no.

"Indiana?"

No.

"Michigan?"

No.

"Minneapolis?"

"I'm quite certain we've never met." He smiles and leans forward. "I would remember."

Natalie has little experience fending off male interest (she's never been the kind of teacher teenage boys yearn for), but that doesn't mean she's lost the ability to tell when she's being flirted with. The thin man's interest is particularly obvious—obvious and entitled, as though he has little experience fending off female interest, but not from want of receiving it.

"I'm sure you would," she says. "They say I'm memorable."

"That you are. You're soaked to the skin and reeking of chlorine, for starters. The hell you been up to tonight?"

"I'm mostly dry. Now," she says. "You should have seen me when I first got out of the pool."

"Been wondering where the pool was hiding in this great gray beast of a hotel." He blinks rapidly. "Did you fall in?"

"Voluntarily. I was exploring this great gray beast of a hotel." She smiles, because she realizes she's still exploring, that this strange man is an extension of the hotel itself. Maybe that's what he reminds her of: they are both full of dark corners, odd places, possibly ghosts. "What are *you* up to tonight?"

"You know. Transcribing. Communing with the muse. Keeping dry." He rubs at his hairline with the eraser end of his pencil. "I'm with Statewide. I presume you can say the same."

She nods. "District chaperone."

"Oi, *liar*."

"Excuse me?" Natalie feels herself tilt.

"That's a lie, *liar*," he says gleefully. "You're a 'district chaperone' the same way I'm a 'conductor.' Let's not waste our breath. Who are you *really*?"

She lifts her head and looks at the thin man and feels more awake than she's felt in ages. She's been waiting for someone to ask her this question for months, for years, for half her life.

"I was a pianist," she says. Her throat catches. It's been so long since she's thought of herself that way, so long that it's barely who she is anymore.

"Thought I sensed a kindred." The thin man eyes her steadily.

"Who are *you* really?" she asks.

He smirks at her. He is so dark and wiry, a nerve stretched taut. So unlike Emmett, her sandy, smiling Redford of a husband. He holds up his right hand and wiggles the stumps of his missing fingers. "I was a pianist too."

"What happened?"

"Nibbled by a rabid piccolo player."

"Oi," Natalie says. "*Liar.*" She holds out her own hands. "Can I — see?"

The thin man pauses. Then he moves to the far left of the piano bench. Natalie accepts the invitation and sits beside him. He shows her what remains of his right hand — a thumb and index finger, a deeply lined palm, and three pink, puckered stumps where his middle, ring, and pinkie fingers ought to have been. He waits until she's sandwiched his hand between both of hers to wriggle the stumps, and laughs when she laughs.

"Most people run screaming when it comes to life," he says.

"Can you play at all with this hand?"

He shrugs. "Nothing like I *could,* once."

She passes his arm around her side and rests his torn right hand on the back of her complete one, her full fingers extending over the keys.

"How about now?" she asks.

She's surprised him. He tenses for a moment, and then slowly passes his thumb over hers. He whispers close in her ear. "Play when I press your hand, like this. It's slow and strange, so don't worry when it sounds wrong. It's supposed to be odd. It's supposed to sound like church bells in an asylum, or perhaps what bells would sound like to a man who's gone mad."

The fine golden hairs on the back of Natalie's hand prickle with the chords, which do sound, and not by suggestion alone, like the slow, sad chiming of bells warped by an unquiet mind. But for all the strange dissonance and rhythms, there is a clear, deep longing that builds in urgency and volume until it rings itself out, leaving only a minor echo hanging in the air. She feels the last flash of a desperate light pass between them. She knows it by taste, by feel, by name: it's a cousin to the fierce sadness that has been quietly devouring her for months. This strange man lost some vital part of himself, and then lost any hope that he might ever get it back. And *that's* how she knows him.

The auditorium swallows the last of the sound. They sit in silence, breathing, until the thin man jerks his hand from hers as though he's only just realized he's burning.

"Who are you," he whispers, "really?"

Natalie wants nothing more than to answer him truthfully, or, barring that, take him somewhere—to the swimming pool on the roof, where they can drown together in their sad shared electricity. But not tonight. Tonight she can still save him the trouble of knowing everything she is.

"No one," she says, and walks away.

8

Alice Sees the Future

EVERYTHING IS WRONG.

This is what was supposed to happen: Alice, on the first night of Statewide, was going to put on a cute top and sticky pink lip-gloss, use her eyelash curler, and go to someone's room for a party that would start as a bunch of cool people just hanging out, nothing major. Alice was going to drink someone else's cheap beer and flirt with enough boys to forget that Jimmy Kopek used to be her boyfriend. She was going to introduce everyone to her famous roommate, and then laugh with her famous roommate later about everyone she was introduced to. Rabbit was going to be at her side, eyes wide and shy, and Alice would be fun and make people want to know who she was. At some point after midnight, at the peak of the party, the three of them would decide (well, mostly Alice would decide) it was time to leave. There were two more nights to go, Friday and Saturday. Tonight was merely the prologue, the pitch, the promise of things to come.

This is what is actually happening: Alice, on the first night of Statewide, is sitting in her hotel room, in her pink pajamas since nine-thirty, stomach rumbling from not eating enough at that disgusting dinner. Her journal is open on the bed in front of her, but she can't bring herself to write anything. It would be too embarrassing for her posthumous memoirist to come to this chapter, after all the triumphant foreshadowing, and see *this* Alice Hatmaker—lonely and hungry Alice Hatmaker, her brother at a party that starts as just a bunch of cool people hanging out, nothing major, without her. While her famous roommate is God knows where and didn't think to invite her along. And the television in her room doesn't get cable, and the only station it can pick up with its stupid bunny ears is one that's showing reruns of *Matlock,* and Alice has seen enough movies and played enough lovelorn ladies in musicals to know what it means to be heartbroken, but still. Still.

She never dreamed it would hurt like *this.*

She never dreamed that "heartbreak" was a literal description of how it would feel, physically, when your boyfriend said he didn't want to be your boyfriend anymore. When you were left all alone, abandoned by your *twin* on a night you'd been looking forward to for weeks. Stupid Jimmy. Stupid Rabbit.

Heartbreak had once been a pretty sort of shorthand, a way to say in a single word that one felt sad and regretful, that one didn't want to talk about it anymore, that one wanted to eat a half gallon of ice cream and wear sweatpants for an entire weekend. But when Jimmy called—called!—and said they were over, *finito,* done forever, Alice felt the two sides of her heart leap from her body in opposite directions, one toward and one away from Jimmy, far away, as far as it could get, so he would never be able to say such things to her again. Her heart tore itself in half, ripping into two jagged hunks of meat straight down the middle, unable to function. Not for loving someone, not even for beating.

Her malfunctioning heart had been one of Jimmy's reasons for breaking up with her. "I know you don't love me. I know you can't," he had said over the phone. "Because you don't have a heart."

If only that were true. She can understand how Jimmy would think that she is actually heart*less,* but Alice does have a heart, and it tugs the wound a little wider every time she remembers her Jimmy in the beginning, how he used to pay attention and tell her jokes and kiss her. The way he'd look at her, smile spreading wider and wider, as she practiced her solos for the spring chorus concert—forever ago, last May.

The other reason was even more ridiculous. "You don't have any *room*, Alice," he'd said. "You don't have any room in your head for anyone or anything that isn't you. You're lost in your own wonderland."

Alice isn't entirely sure she knows what that means, other than that Jimmy Kopek is the kind of jerk who makes obvious jokes about her name.

She wishes the bag of blood and bones that is her body could turn to fairy dust and feel as light and charmed and perfect as she can imagine herself to be, as she is when she sings. She slaps her journal shut, and sticks and unsticks and sticks and unsticks the Trapper Keeper flap over the top. She is too heartbroken even to cry.

The door opens.

Alice sits up. She's so happy that someone is here, anyone, that it's impossible for her to contain her eagerness, and when she realizes it's Jill Faccelli—of course it's Jill Faccelli, who else would come back to their room this late at night?—it's all she can do not to leap at her like a Golden Retriever.

"Hi, Jill!" she says. She sits back on her heels and the bed squeaks. "How are you? How was dinner? I didn't see you in the banquet hall. I was looking."

"Dinner was fine. I ate with my mom."

"Is that what you're just coming from? From your mom's room?"

Jill squeezes her eyes shut as if she has a tremendous headache. "Yeah," she says. "We ate dinner for about twenty minutes and then she yelled at me for three hours. I am the single most ungrateful girl in the world, and I am *going* to rehearsal tomorrow morning, where I will apologize profusely, and I mean *profusely*, to both the *esteemed* conductor Fisher Brodie—do I have any idea who I've insulted today with my arrogance? *Do I?*—and to all of my fellow musicians, whose time I have wasted so selfishly." She kicks off her sneakers. She pulls off her socks, which she wads together in a ball and whips fiercely at the wall. "Then I'm going to stab myself with my own flute and swan-dive into the orchestra pit."

Jill stands at the foot of her bed and stares it down like a gunslinger. "Like this," she says. Spreading her arms out wide, she falls listlessly forward, face-first onto the bed. Her shiny dark hair fans out around her head like a pool of black oil.

"You can cry if you want to," Alice says quietly. "Or I'll leave. I'll . . . go in the bathroom and turn on the water if you want some space." This is actually the exact opposite of what she wants to do. Let Rabbit be famous for tonight, among his cool new friends at Statewide. Jill is the real deal, famous every day of her life, not for a single out-of-character stunt but because she is who she is. Alice wants nothing more than to know this other misery, so much more exotic than her own.

Jill turns her head sideways and looks at Alice. Her eyes are clear. "I don't feel like crying. I feel like . . . screaming."

"You can do that too. I don't care."

"You want to know the funny thing? I love *Afternoon of a Faun*. I would die to play it." Alice has no idea what this has to do with anything, but it's not the time for questions. "I would die to play it, I really would. But I resent—I hate—being told. Being manipulated. The way Brodie sprang it on us, I *hate* that. My mother does that . . . she's done it my whole life. That's all she's ever done. Soon as she realized there was something I could do well—really well, like, phenomenally well, freak-of-nature well—I never had a single choice of my own to make again. God forbid I try to make one anyway."

Now Jill's eyes change: they go from clear to too bright, too shiny, but they don't blink and they don't move from Alice's. "She calls it having tea," Jill says. "'Put out the teacups, Jill. Plug in the kettle. Get out the spoons and the sugar. Let's have a cup of tea and chat about everything you've ever done wrong, everything you're not good enough at. Everything you're ungrateful for, you stupid girl.'"

Alice doesn't understand. It's so beyond her own experience as a child, as a daughter and a human, that at first she thinks Jill is joking. But it isn't a joke. It isn't a joke at all. Jill blinks once and the brightness disappears from her eyes, as if it were never there.

"Tea is for little old ladies and the Queen of England," Jill says. "And my mother, when she wants to remind me what a piece of shit I am."

She should do something. Rush over and take Jill's hand? Hold her hair back and let her cry it out? She doesn't have much experience consoling others, real others with real problems not scripted in plays. Jill doesn't say anything.

"What's your dad, um," Alice stammers. "D-do you have a—"

"No," says Jill. "I'm the immaculate conception."

"I didn't mean." This is going from bad to worse. "I didn't mean to—"

Jill rolls on her back and stares at the ceiling. "I had a dad for a little while. A stepdad. He adopted me and everything. But he didn't figure out my mom until it was too late."

"What happened?"

"They say he killed himself."

"That's ... awful." Alice's arms instinctively hug her twisting stomach. "What do you mean '*they* say'?"

"You should ask Viola," Jill says. She exhales.

Alice wants to say she's sorry but can't form the words. They're not enough on their own; they're laughably not enough.

"Fortunetellers," she blurts.

"Fortunetellers?"

"Tea is for little old ladies and the Queen of England and fortunetellers. They drink tea to read the leaves. Ever had your fortune told?" Alice pads over to her dresser and reaches into the top drawer for a small packet wrapped in a purple silk scarf. It had once belonged to her grandmother; devout every day of her life, Gram would be scandalized to know her granddaughter kept her deck of tarot cards in the same silk scarf she wore to Sunday services.

"Let me tell you your fortune." Alice presents the cards, still nestled in the purple scarf, for Jill's inspection. Jill lifts her head slightly from the mattress to see.

"You know how to read them?"

Alice nods.

"You promise not to tell me if it's really bad news?" Jill smiles when she says this, so Alice thinks she must be kidding. Still, she crosses her index and middle fingers and traces an X over her heart.

"My deck has good juju. Happy mojo."

Jill sits up slowly. Her black hair falls over her face and she shoves it back with both hands. She is not just tired, Alice thinks. She is weary, a kind of weary there is no name or cure for.

"Check the towels. Between them." Jill points toward the bathroom and grins lazily. "I've got a treat for us."

The treat is a bottle of red wine on the linen rack above the toilet, secreted neatly in the pile of standard-issue hotel towels. Alice hands it to Jill triumphantly.

"And it's even a twist cap. It's almost like you've done this before." She sits opposite Jill on her bed and crosses her legs. "Too bad all we have are those plastic cups over by the ice bucket."

Jill shrugs, tosses the twist cap to the floor, tips the bottle straight up against her mouth, and pulls the wine into her body, desperately, like a marathoner emptying a water bottle. She is already flushed and glassy when she hands the bottle to Alice.

"Ahhhhh," she sighs. "I needed that. I really, really needed that."

Alice has been drunk exactly twice in her life. Once, accidentally, as a child: at a Christmas party thrown by her father's boss, she had consumed eight punch glasses of hot wassail by filling and refilling the one half glass her mother poured for her. No one knew she was drunk until they arrived at home, when she took two steps inside the door and vomited red wine and cinnamon all over the foyer—no one, that is, except Alice herself. She'd figured out she was tanked and had kept the knowledge warm and slow and fantastically secret. Rabbit, if he had been any older than ten, might have had a clue his sister was blitzed by the way she latched on to him, more octopus-like than usual. If he had liked the half glass their mother poured for him too, he might have been drunk himself.

The second time Alice had been drunk was much more recently: a little less than two months ago, on one of the last weekends in September, at a party at Eric Cole's parents' house—or rather, a party at the adjacent field. This was upstate New York; why party in a house when there's a perfectly good field nearby? Eric had graduated a few years earlier from Ruby Falls High. Alice hardly knew him, and, frankly, found the concept of Eric Cole—easily twenty-two, partying while his parents were out of town with kids still in high school—desperately lame. But everyone was going. "Everyone going" meant next to nothing to Alice, but it meant something to Jimmy Kopek.

Being drunk at Eric Cole's house was a completely different experience than downing eight cups of wassail in the fourth grade. People she knew from school, a mix of those she was sort of friends with and not at all friends with, stood around a dented silver keg, passing foamy beer to each other in red plastic cups. And that was kind of . . . it. Alice remembered how happy she'd been the first time she was drunk, how all she wanted to do was laugh and pull the world close. She felt none of those things here. She felt cold and awkward and sad that Jimmy was standing on the other side of the circle of beer drinkers, laughing with his friends on the soccer team. They'd been together for nearly five months, since last spring and all summer long, but it was strange now that they were back in school. Summer had been a blur of rented videos and movie dates and late-night pancakes at Perkins and marathon make-out sessions while her parents were at work, just the two of them, Jim and Alice, Alice and Jim. Once upon a time, all he had to do was look at her a certain way—bashful almost, without blinking—and Alice felt she was the only girl in the world. But now he was different. It was soccer season, and Jimmy had somewhere to be, something to do and talk about other than Alice. She left messages with his little sister, with his mother, but Jimmy didn't call her back. She finished her third cup of foamy beer and wondered why her stupid boyfriend suddenly found her so easy to ignore.

Jimmy hardly spoke to her; no one spoke to her, really. She wished she'd said something to Rabbit. Invited him. He probably didn't even know this party was happening (she'd told her parents she and Jimmy were going to the movies), but if Rabbit were here, at least she'd have someone to talk to. But no: she'd been right not to say anything. Nelson Hamm, doubled over laughing at something

Jimmy said, had given Rabbit a wedgie-a-week all freshman year. Alice rationalized that if she'd invited her brother, he'd feel obligated to come, curious to see if this time, this *one* time—it was senior year, after all, this was the stuff movies were made of—he would finally fit in. And in the end it could only be this way: he would be hurt by the assorted jerks and blank slates whom Jimmy insisted he was friends with, either by their outright cruelty or complete indifference.

Why was she here if Jimmy—or hell, *anyone*—wasn't paying attention to her? *She was Alice Hatmaker.* She had a world waiting for her, outside this town and these people, and her brother was her best friend and he was going to go away, he was going to go to a different college and leave her on her own.

Alone in a crowd of boring people.

Alice was drunk enough at this point to think that was *exactly* what the future held for her. It was also the first time she'd admitted to herself how soul-deep terrified she was of the possibility that her brother would choose to go to a different college. Alice had applied to only one school, early admission, and though technically she was still waiting for her acceptance letter, she knew she was going to the Westing School of Music in Rochester. Westing was the biggest deal outside of Juilliard; it had the professors and the connections she wanted. Rabbit was planning to apply to Westing, but then he'd also gone and looked at Syracuse. Binghamton. A little place near Buffalo called Freedom-something-or-other. He would cast a wider net. His catch would come in, and the tide would take him to newer lands, lands where his sister had never set foot.

And oh God—what if it wasn't just Jimmy, what if she *was* easy to ignore? What if Alice Hatmaker was a star only in her own head? What if Westing didn't want her? What would she do then?

She had to talk to Rabbit. Rabbit loved her. Rabbit wouldn't lie to her. Rabbit wouldn't leave her, ever, not if she asked him not to. Not if she asked him tonight, right now.

Alice ran down the hill in the dark to the Cole house. The beer drinkers had managed to start a bonfire and were now circling the flames. Their shadows threw themselves in front of her, blocking her path, but Alice plowed through them like a thresher. The house was in front of her. The house had a phone, and a phone could call Rabbit—a phone would bring Rabbit here in their parents' Taurus to pick her up, to take her back home where she belonged.

The wraparound porch creaked beneath her feet and the screen door squawked as she threw it open. She could hear voices in other rooms, but here in the kitchen she was alone. Tears of relief swelled in her eyes. She made a beeline for a cordless phone mounted on the wall over a small breakfast bar. She had the phone in her hand.

"What's your favorite scary movie?" a voice growled in her ear.

She jumped three feet forward, away from the growler—who was just stupid Eric Cole, lame, too-old Eric Cole, carrying a case of more shitty beer in his arms. In her fright, Alice had thrown the phone and it skidded across the floor, spinning on its back like an upended turtle.

"Shit," she said, and suddenly she was crying. Sobbing, real tears rushing down her face, dangling in droplets on the underside of her jaw.

"Hey, hey, it's okay." She heard a clanking that must have been Eric setting the case of beer on the floor, and then she felt his hands on her arms, steering her to a stool by the breakfast bar. "Hey, don't cry. I didn't mean to scare you. I'm not a psycho killer."

She cried harder. She howled. Eric wrapped his arms around her and turned her head to tuck it against his shoulder. Alice had always had problems hyperventilating—her body was naturally melodramatic, could escalate tears into a maelstrom of unstoppable grief in less than ten seconds—and she began to shudder and gasp for breath against the warmth of his T-shirt. Every inhalation calmed her down. He smelled like boy. Clean, end-of-summer boy, of sweat and grass clippings, cotton and hay. Jimmy Kopek, these days, smelled like shin guards and soccer balls, mold and McDonald's.

Alice inhaled one solid, strong breath. She sat back from Eric Cole and blinked bleary eyes gummy with mascara. She'd been wrong; he was not a boy. He had a day's worth of dark stubble on his face and a dimple on his right cheek like he'd been marked with a pin. He was looking at her intently, without blinking, as if she were the only girl in the world.

She kissed him.

He kissed her back, but in truth Alice had kissed him first. And she couldn't say why, really, except that at that precise moment it had seemed the only thing to do.

Jimmy Kopek didn't care about what she'd felt like. Jimmy didn't even care that all that had happened between Alice and Eric Cole was a single kiss nearly six weeks ago — a fairly substantial kiss that Alice felt bloom all over her body, but one kiss nonetheless. She never found out who told Jimmy. She never knew how he knew.

He just knew.

So it is with mixed emotions that Alice takes the bottle of red wine from Jill and seriously entertains the possibility of getting drunk tonight. Righteously, horribly, shitfacedly drunk.

The bottle is warm from Jill's grasp. Alice thinks of her brother out in the world without her, as he will be from now on, surely. She thinks of the boy Jimmy Kopek had seemed to be at first, how much he had loved her at the start, and how it broke her heart to discover how easily she could be cast aside. She thinks of Jill sitting in front of a cup of steaming tea she doesn't want to drink while her mother berates her, crushes her, breaks her, and she tips the bottle back and glugs until she needs air.

"So tell me about the future." Jill crosses her legs and faces Alice.

Alice has Jill shuffle and cut the tarot deck, tells her to choose six cards and concentrate. Jill *ommmm*s like she's meditating, and Alice laughs. Alice loves the feel of the cards in her hands, bigger than playing cards, still stiff after years of use and satisfying to lay flat with a little snap. She bought them at the occult bookstore in Syracuse, by the university, on Westcott Street, with money from her fourteenth birthday. The possibility that you could know your future, could divine it through something as simple as a deck of special cards, was too alluring for Alice to pass up. She wanted to know. She wanted to see how glorious it was going to be. She was a girl who liked to be prepared.

"We'll start with a simple six-card spread. Major arcana only. Those are the face cards, the cool-looking ones." She clears her throat. "Think of a question. A big question. Life-altering. Let it kind of soak into your brain."

Jill shakes her hair back and blinks rapidly, gazing at the ceiling. "Got one. What—"

"Don't tell me what it is." Alice smiles. "Just hold it. Keep thinking it. I'm going to play your first card."

Jill covers her eyes. "I can't look," she says.

Alice spreads the purple scarf over the bed between them and lays one card smack in the middle, facing Jill. It's the Chariot. "Interesting." The Chariot, which shows a man riding a chariot with a raised sword, indicates conflict.

"Are you going to tell me, or do I have to guess?" Jill whispers theatrically. She takes another long pull from the bottle. "Because I'm thinking that means I should steal a car and get the hell away from this place."

"It means struggle. Battle. War. This card is your current state, the current place from which you asked your question."

Jill raises her fist in the air. "*Vive la Jill!*"

Alice plays another card, crossways on top of the first. Her pulse lifts.

"Don't get freaked by this," she says. The card is Death. "I know it's a skeleton and ... pretty scary-looking, but Death—look, I pulled this card last night myself."

Jill rests the bottle upright on the mattress. "I thought you said your cards had good mojo."

"They do, they do—gimme the wine." Alice drinks. "Death doesn't mean death, like, literal death. It means change. Something new and different coming your way, which would be—it would be *good*, right? Change for the better?"

"Death would be a better change," Jill says. Her eyes flick.

Whether she regrets the sentiment itself or having expressed it aloud is hard to say.

Come on, deck, Alice thinks. *Give me something to work with. Give me something good.* Above both cards she places the Magician.

"This is good, Jill. This is great, actually. This card represents your immediate goal, the thing you're going to overcome obstacles to accomplish. The Magician is sort of a . . . not a trickster, but a smart guy. Like, a clever guy with a plan, with the will and creativity to carry it out." Alice has always liked the Magician. His face is young but his power—between the infinity symbol hovering above his head and the snake eating its own tail he wears for a belt—is ancient. Eternal. "When the Magician shows up, he's telling you not to hold back. To rise up to your full potential. To make your own future."

Jill's face hardens. She takes the wine back from Alice.

The fourth and fifth cards Alice plays, which represent the past, are the Devil and the Tower. This is officially the scariest tarot reading she's ever given.

"Well. Shit," says Jill, looking from one card to the other. "That can't be good."

Both the Devil and the Tower, unlike Death, are unambiguously not-good cards, and Alice, on the edge of buzzed, feels her poker face slide, slippery as the silk scarf on which she's laid them. The Devil is, well, the Devil, representing violence, bondage, an inescapable fate. The Tower, with its drawing of a stone tower struck by lightning and tumbling to pieces under a darkening sky, means catastrophe. Destruction. Calamity and unforeseen misery. Alice has never seen the Tower come up in a reading she's done for someone else, or for—

She swallows.

"No," she says. "It isn't good. But the Tower is facing me, it's upright from my point of view. That means it's my card. My fortune, not yours."

Jill takes another swig. "Cheers," she chirps. "At least we can be screwed together."

Alice breathes out. It doesn't make sense. The Tower may be facing her, but its position in the spread represents the past, and there *is* no great calamity or unexpected sadness—

Unless you count what happened with Jimmy. Or the possibility that her entire life up to this point has been one epic delusion of grandeur.

Every last hair up and down her arms stands on end.

"One more card. One more and we're done, I promise." How much has Alice really believed in tarot readings before this one? They've always been easy to accept, full of High Priestesses (wisdom, serenity) and Justices (equality, virtue) and Suns (triumph, success). She's never been in a position to swallow a difficult or sad past, present, or future, has only had to accept a mirror of the extreme fortune to which she's been born. Reading for Jill, Alice feels as though she's being teased by something dark and nasty, something that gets a real kick out of inflicting pain. "One more card," Alice says, and prays for good.

The final card is the Hanged Man.

"It's going to take him forever to die like that," Jill says, her voice flat.

The Hanged Man—a man with his arms bound behind him, hanging upside down from one foot, the other leg bent in the shape of the numeral four—is another misunderstood card, like Death: scarier than it looks. But still scary-looking.

"This really isn't so bad—"

Jill cuts her off. "And this card is the future, right? We've already talked present and past, so . . . I thought you promised not to tell me bad news." Her smile is slight.

"No, it isn't so bad—he's not *killing* himself here. The Hanged Man represents sacrifice and . . . and transition. Surrender to something new. I think—" Jill, visibly drunk now, has begun to pitch back and forth unsteadily. The bottle of wine wobbles in her grip. "I think you have every reason to think things will change, and—and get better."

Jill lets go of the bottle. It falls forward on the mattress and sloshes its remaining contents all over the cards, the bed, and Alice's pajama pants. For as much wine as Alice knows they've already consumed, there was still a lot left, and a lot of wine everywhere at once, all over her. She lifts her arms instinctively. A series of quiet "Shit! Shit! Shit! Shit!"s hisses out of her mouth, also instinctively; this is exactly what her mother does whenever there's a spill. This is bad, this is really, really bad—everything smells like wine, and there's no way they're going to be able to hide the smell if they don't clean it up immediately, because you *know* that Jill's mother is going to come back at o800 hours and make sure her daughter is up and ready to greet the day, to be penitent, or face another punishment— but Alice tamps all of that down, deep in her gut, for Jill's sake. Jill doesn't need Alice freaking out on her too. Jill knows better than Alice how bad this could get.

"Oops," Jill says quietly. Her face crumples. "Your cards. Your deck. Oh . . . oh, crap, I'm so sorry."

"It's fine—it's really fine, we just need to—strip the bed. Let's get this into the tub—" Alice can feel her heart rate rising. There's no way they can clean this up with those white towels in the bathroom. No way. They need paper towels, something absorbent and disposable. "Jill," she says, and looks directly at Jill Faccelli and sees not an incredible star, a phenom and a talent to be breathed in and envied, but a girl. A girl with very straight, very black hair. With sad dark eyes set deep in her face. Too young and too old at the same time.

Alice repeats her name.

"Can you get this bedspread into the tub while I go find a housekeeping cart? I'm going to get some paper towels to clean up with. Okay?" Jill nods. Her bangs almost cover her eyes, but Alice can see that they are filling with tears, real tears that might finally get the opportunity to spill.

"Okay," Jill says. "Good idea. Thanks." She looks away shyly when she realizes that Alice has ripped off her wine-soaked pajama pants and is reaching for a pair of jeans. "Thanks for the fortune," she says. She gathers the bedspread to her chest like a toddler massing her security blanket in her arms. "I think you might turn out to be right."

Alice sets the now empty wine bottle on the TV stand, makes sure she has a room key, says she'll be right back, and leaves.

She's gone five minutes. She can't have been gone longer than that, she knows she can't have—she finally found a closet at the far end of the hall with two housekeeping carts parked inside, fully stocked with toilet paper, fresh towels, every cleaning supply you could ever wish for. It couldn't have taken more than five minutes—eight, max—for her to grab three rolls of paper towels and quietly, barefootedly scamper back to their room. To slip the key in the door. To turn the knob. To step inside and shut the door soundlessly behind her.

And yet it was enough time for Jill to hang herself.

She is dangling a foot or so off the bed. Her feet are bare, her toes long and thin. Her feet are the first things Alice sees, because you don't expect to see feet at that altitude. They surprise her. Her eyes travel up Jill's legs, which are still in blue jeans, darkened here and there with purple-blue wine stains, and to Jill's stomach and chest, which is hidden behind a curtain of black hair, her hair dangling forward from her head, her head dangling forward on her neck. Rising above her like a yo-yo string is a bright orange rope—or it's not a rope, it's shiny and plastic-looking. It's an extension cord, an orange extension cord, and it's tied and looped around an old bit of pipe running across the ceiling. The pipe must have something to do with the sprinkler system, must be part of the hotel's efforts to keep its guests safe.

For the second time that evening, Alice at first doesn't understand. Her first impulse is not to scream or run or cry for help. She is merely stunned. She can't comprehend how Jill has managed to do this to herself.

"Jill?" she says.

Jill's body is swaying as though in a gentle breeze. The air is still; all the windows are closed. Her body, her long feet and legs and her skinny arms and her knobby red wrists, her pale hands and long fingers—her hands are so ordinary.

Death is the most ordinary thing Alice has ever seen.

Her body grasps the situation before her brain or her tongue. It is almost a surprise to her when her back hits the door, and when her clammy, vibrating hand closes over the knob. Alice is running down the hall, almost to the elevator by the time she finds her voice—or rather, her voice finds her own ears, already in the middle of a word: "—*lp!*" The one part of her body she trusts, the one part she knows is beautiful and strong, Alice's voice has betrayed her totally. She can barely get it to rise above a whisper.

She steps inside the elevator and presses L.

In the elevator's mirrors she sees herself, sees her own face, her own ordinary body. She understands, she is screaming now, when she bolts out of the elevator into the lobby, she is shrieking at top volume, "*HELP ME, SHE'S HANGING! HELP ME, PLEASE!*"

Alice tells the man behind the desk that Jill is hanging, Jill is hanging in room 712. The man makes two phone calls, the second to a person he's calling Hastings, his voice is wobbling, he's more upset than Alice. Alice sits on a chair in the lobby, her knees drawn to her chin, her arms wrapped around her legs, and her hands clasped over her bare feet. She tucks her head down and closes her eyes and feels herself begin to rock back and forth.

Later, she has no idea how much later, a tall man with a maroon bow tie, undone, kneels on the lobby carpet in front of her. He is balding but still could be described as sandy-haired, and his eyes are blue. They look kind.

"Can you describe what you saw, miss?" he asks her.

Alice swallows. She feels calmer; she has stopped rocking. How is this night even happening? "My roommate, Jill—I left the room for five minutes and when I came back she was hanging from a pipe on the ceiling. I didn't—oh *no*. I didn't even think to try and get her down, could I have done that? How would I have done that? Was there a chair? I don't—" Her head thrums.

"Are you certain she was hanging?" the kind man asks.

Alice nods. She wants Rabbit here, now. The pain of his absence is so horrible, so acute, she thinks she will be sick.

The man grimaces.

"The thing is, miss—Hatmaker, is that your name?"

Alice nods again.

"We didn't find your roommate, Miss Hatmaker. She wasn't in the room. She doesn't appear to be anywhere at the moment." He reaches into his pants pocket and pulls out a piece of paper, ragged on one side where it's been torn from a spiral-bound notebook. "All we found in seven-twelve was this. Do you recognize the hand?"

Printed in neat block letters — in black Sharpie, Alice catches the tang of permanent marker ink — are four words:

NOW SHE IS MINE

FRIDAY
NOVEMBER 14, 1997

Scherzo Agitato

9

Clear as Crystal

WHAT IS THIS?"

The girl is adorable. That's the only word to describe her, really: adorable. Eyes round and dark as a cartoon. A frightened fairy. She doesn't look a day older than thirteen, though she says she's four years beyond that; perhaps Hastings has forgotten what thirteen-year-old girls look like. Caroline, after all, hasn't been a little girl for a very long time.

"'Now she is mine'—what does it even mean?" the girl says, blinking at the paper he holds before her. She pulls the blanket he's given her up to her chin. "Where did you find it? I don't get it."

"We found it in your room. Rather, I found it." He nods sheepishly at Megan—Officer Sheldrake, she's Officer Sheldrake now, not just Megan whose brother Tim works in the kitchen. She's already berated him for not waiting for the police to investigate the room. But how could he wait? How could he, Harold Hastings, the face of the Bellweather, be expected to wait after getting Roger's phone call?

He'd been drifting off to sleep in 130, hands clasped over his chest, thinking he ought to change out of his good shirt, when the phone rang. At first Hastings thought he was having a terrible dream. "She says a girl hung herself, her roommate," said the voice on the phone. "In seven-twelve. I just called Chris"—the hotel manager, who was next to worthless—"but I knew you'd want to know."

"Who is this?" he muttered. "What are you talking about?"

"It's Roger at the front desk, Hastings. We've got a report of a dead body on seven. *Seven-twelve.*"

"You called Chris and me—what about the police? The paramedics? Get off the goddamned line and call them!"

Every part of Hastings woke up. He jammed his feet into loafers, his legs into the day's discarded slacks (realizing, mid-jam, that he ought to have done so in reverse order), and hustled out the door still buttoning his wrinkled white dress shirt, bow tie undone and trapped beneath his collar.

Hastings was the first to arrive on the seventh floor. Chris lived in town, about a fifteen-minute drive away, and the police and paramedics, whom Roger damn well should have called first, usually took about ten minutes to reach the Bellweather. The elevator doors opened on the seventh floor with their customary hollow *donk* and Hastings dashed down the hall. He knew he was awake, but it felt like a nightmare. A nightmare about the only thing he ever saw at the Bellweather that frightened him. He expected to find the groom and the bride in 712 exactly as he had years ago, only this time, if he was fast enough and lucky enough, he might be able to do something about it. He might be able to use those CPR courses he'd taken. He might be able to compress the groom's bleeding chest with a giant Ace bandage, to stand on a chair beside the bride and hold her up, taking her weight off that horrible orange cord and into his arms instead.

His heart was thumping painfully by the time he came to the closed door of 712. He felt dizzy. Hastings slipped his master key into the lock, turned, prayed, and stepped into an empty room. He tensed. He smelled alcohol, something fruity and cheap, and saw a green bottle on the edge of the television stand. The comforter was off the bed. Hastings found it in the bathtub, soaking in pinkish water—pink from spilled wine, not blood.

He opened the drawers of the dressers and found girls' clothes. He opened the closet doors and found two empty suitcases and two winter coats, a nubbly green scarf, one pair of yellow work boots, and a pair of grungy pink sneakers. There was only one set of toiletries in the bathroom, one toothbrush and one tube of toothpaste and one pink, daisy-spotted stick of deodorant. It felt as though one and a half girls had checked into the room. Beyond the contraband booze, there was nothing out of order. No orange electrical cord secured to the sprinkler system. No bride, no girl, no body swinging from the ceiling.

Hastings, rubbery with relief, collapsed on the unmade bed.

That was when he saw it. The piece of spiral notebook paper was taped to the back of the door beneath the privacy peephole. Hastings had left his glasses in 130 so he had to squint to make out the black block letters.

"'Now she is mine'?" he read aloud.

"It doesn't make any sense. You can't—I don't believe you," says the adorable girl. Her voice quivers. "I saw her. I saw her body. She was dead. She was hanging. Why won't you believe me?"

"Do you think your friend could be playing a joke on you?" asks Officer Megan.

"This isn't a *joke.*"

"Maybe not to you." Megan sighs. "Can you describe for me what you were doing prior to the incident?"

"We were, um." The girl rubs her nose with the back of her hand. "Hell. She brought a bottle of wine and we were drinking it. I was doing a tarot reading for her. She was upset and I was trying to distract her, you know. Make her feel better. Then she spilled the wine and I left to find paper towels. That's when she did it, while I was gone. That's when she—" She swallows. "I know what I saw. I don't understand how she could just vanish."

Her eyes spark.

"You have to talk to her mother," the girl says.

Megan takes a small notebook out of her hip pocket. "Do you know her mother's name?"

"Viola Fabian," says the girl, and Hastings stifles a cough.

"An address? Phone number?"

"Here," Hastings says. "Viola Fabian is here at the hotel."

Megan gives him a strange look. An incredulous look. As though this is one too many coincidences, even for her; as though Hastings doesn't remember catching her skinny-dipping with her prom date in the rooftop pool when she was the same age as this adorable witness.

"So let's go talk to her," he says.

"Can I come?" asks the girl. "I want to come."

"No," says Megan. "And neither can you, Hastings. I'm sorry. This is official police business, not a parade."

"But—"

"If there's anything to share, I'll share it."

"This woman's daughter has disappeared from my hotel. I have a professional duty to at the very least *speak* with her."

"Speak with her tomorrow," says Megan, and motions the other police officer over, away from Roger and Chris at the front desk and the cluster of young gawkers they've attracted. They look college-aged, at least. Hastings prays they aren't Statewide children who'll take this gruesome story home to their parents. "Thank you, Alice. We've checked out your room, so I don't see why you can't go back to it tonight, though I'm sure Hastings can find you a new one if you'd like."

The girl—Alice—unwraps the blanket from her shoulders and pushes herself up on the arms of her chair. "I want to go back and see for myself. Maybe you missed something."

Hastings would be impressed if his gut didn't tell him she was lying (or drunk or high or the butt of an elaborate practical joke). He wonders what instrument she plays, or if she's in the chorus. She carries herself like a little actress, chin out and head up, all pluck and defiance, even though she's exhausted and still frightened. Unless, of course, that's all part of the act.

"You let us know if you find anything," Officer Megan tells her drily. If he weren't irritated at being shut out of this investigation, he would have laughed. Megan always was a smartass. "Evening, Miss Hatmaker. Hastings."

Hastings escorts adorable Alice Hatmaker back to the seventh floor. She doesn't speak, but he can tell she's thinking. Thinking hard, brows pressed down, face screwed tight. Caroline would make that face over a particularly difficult crossword puzzle, as if the sheer act of concentration could will a solution into existence. Alice turns her key in the lock and steps into 712 without a moment of hesitation. It has to be a joke. A prank. The missing roommate and this adorable girl have to be co-conspirators in some grand plan to . . . to what? Rebel without cause? Create mayhem for mayhem's sake?

One bed is still unmade. Alice looks around before taking another step inside.

"Did you find the extension cord?" she asks.

"What?"

"Did you find the extension cord? That's what she used to hang herself. An orange extension cord." She's looking at Hastings, watching him closely, but Hastings barely knows she's there. All he sees is the bride, the orange cord a tight line connecting the dots of her head and the ceiling.

"What?" he says again.

"I am not lying." Alice is shaking now, or maybe it's Hastings who's shaking. Remembering and shaking. "*I am not lying.*"

He shoves one of his business cards, bent from the pocket of his rumpled pants, into her hand and tells her to call if she needs anything. "Anytime, for anything. If you need me, call this number or stop by my desk. Have a pleasant evening," he says, and leaves her standing in the doorway.

He remembers every moment of the night the Driscolls died. The day is fuzzier—until the end, the wedding was just like any other held at the Bellweather over the years—but he recalls walking through the lobby in the evening when one of the housekeepers, a sharp girl named Lily, who was employed there for only a year or two, appeared by his side, took him by the arm, and said three words: "There's blood upstairs."

They called the police and the manager, and with Lily still on his arm, dragging like an anchor, Hastings rode the elevator to the seventh floor. He smelled the gunpowder first. Then he saw the body in the hall. Bloody and sprawled as though he'd tried to crawl back into the room. Hastings recognized him as the groom—he'd seen him earlier in the day, grinning at the future unfurling before him, the future that now looked to be approximately fifty years shorter than anticipated. Lily was tugging at him, she wanted to go back downstairs, they shouldn't be here, it was a crime scene, they needed to wait for the police. Hastings shushed her gently. "I know what I'm doing," he said. "I read about police work all the time. Just don't touch anything. Notice everything."

There were splinters of wood strewn across the carpet. "See that?" he said, pointing. "I'm guessing he broke through the door. Probably shot with his back to it, so the force of his body taking the shot—and the shot itself—fractured the frame." He pointed again. "See how there's no blood here by the open doorway? That means he was thrown with force. Must have been a hell of a gun." Lily was crying soundlessly, fat tears running down her face. Hastings peered around the doorway, into 712.

The bride swayed from the ceiling. Her face was hidden by her hair.

"Hung herself," he said. His throat felt strange. He gulped. "Orange extension cord. Secured on the sprinkler system." He gulped again. "One glove on, one glove off, dropped on the floor. Also on the floor—shotgun. Murder weapon."

Lily's hands were clamped around his arm, tight as a tourniquet. "Harry," she was saying, "Harry, we need to go. You can't be here. Harry, please listen to me."

"Bed's turned down, our service. Mints on the pillow. Not used." His throat clicked. "Uhm." He passed a tongue that didn't feel like his own over papery lips. "We have to go inside, we have to see the whole—"

Vomit lurched up his throat. He ran down the hallway and made it about ten feet from 712 before depositing the contents of his stomach in a small pile on the carpet. He knelt. He pressed his palms flat, deep into the pile. His vomit was blue, and for a moment he was horrified before he remembered the blue-frosted wedding cake downstairs. It was the last thing he'd put in his stomach.

Lily was kneeling beside him, rubbing his back with the flat of her large, cool palm, and Hastings was mortified to discover himself curling up in her lap. *What are you doing?* he thought. *This is not right.* He knew Lily, liked Lily quite a bit, but this went far beyond what was appropriate between a fifty-something concierge and a twenty-something housekeeper. His body didn't seem to care. His body only wanted to feel the warmth of her lap beneath his head, the weight of her hand on his temple as she stroked his hair, the warmth of her breath as she whispered in his ear, "Harry, I'm here. I'm here."

He saw the shoes then, with his head in Lily's lap. Small reddish Mary Janes, one clamped tight in the dead groom's fist. "Shoes," he said to Lily, but Lily didn't hear or didn't understand, because she shushed him.

The next morning, she brought him a breakfast tray and the news that the police had traced the Mary Janes to a bridesmaid, a little girl of twelve who'd apparently seen the whole thing.

He recalled a little girl, a shy little girl checking in with her family. Mouse-like, her fingers closing over a butterscotch candy without once lifting her head. She did say thank you, however softly; he remembered that. Then he had seen her again, yesterday, walking through the lobby in a bright maroon dress with puffy shoulders. He had greeted her, told her she looked very nice, asked her to save him a dance. She met his gaze with serious dark eyes but kept walking. Her dress had been the color of the shoes in the dead man's hand. An exact match.

That poor, poor creature.

"Can I talk to her?" Hastings asked.

Lily looked stricken. "The family's gone. I saw them leave the hotel this morning."

"How can they leave town before the investigation is over?" Hastings was so confused. He was in a hotel bed, in a hotel room smelling of old smoke—room 130, the room he occasionally catnapped in. How had he gotten here, had Lily brought him? He was in his undershirt, his shorts, and his socks. Had she undressed him? His head hummed. It was hard to think, hard to hear. "It's a crime. Unsolved. How can the police let them leave?"

Lily sat on the edge of the bed and looked down at the coverlet. It was several generations behind the rest of the hotel's bed linens. "It's been ruled a murder-suicide. No investigation."

"But it makes no sense. They just got married. *Yesterday*. Why would you kill yourself and your husband on your wedding day?"

Lily was fiddling with a ring on her finger, on her left ring finger. An engagement ring. Hastings hadn't known Lily was engaged. Had she told him and he'd forgotten, or had it been a secret until now?

She shook her head. "I have no idea, Harry," she said. "No idea at all."

Hastings wraps both hands around his third cup of coffee since midnight. He drums the warm ceramic with his fingertips. Was it ever mentioned in the newspapers what the bride used to hang herself with? Even if it was, those papers were fifteen years old—those stories were written when the Hatmaker girl was a toddler. How could she have known? How could her roommate have known? Why did it seem like a message, a sign meant specifically for him?

He's back in 130, still wearing yesterday's clothes, bow tie undone and draped around his neck. It's five in the morning on Friday. Hastings looks at the calendar tacked on his wall, each month overseen by a different still from a film noir classic. Over the days of November in the year 1997, Barbara Stanwyck's perfect white face and black, black eyes stare at him. Today is the fourteenth. Yesterday, the day Alice Hatmaker's roommate hanged herself (or didn't) with an orange cord, was the thirteenth.

November thirteenth is their anniversary.

Hastings's heart stops. The preparations for Statewide and all the activity of yesterday—checking students in, shuttling them around, answering questions from parents and chaperones and conductors, and that girl, that strange blurry girl with the dog—had distracted him from the Driscolls' anniversary. He does the math. If they hadn't died, the Driscolls would have been married for fifteen years yesterday. What was that—not paper, not china. Crystal. Their crystal anniversary. They would have had children by now, surely; those children would be in elementary school, middle school.

Why does he do this to himself? Every year, on every anniversary, as though their deaths were an act he could have prevented, Harold Hastings imagines a new future for an unchangeable past. He tells himself it's the least he can do for those poor kids. He's glad, relieved to have only just realized this. It was hard enough to be around room 712 last night without knowing that history was repeating itself in every way, down to the date.

Hastings finishes his coffee and looks at his watch. Five. That's ten in the morning in Wales.

He dials Jess's number. She sounds sleepy when she says good morning.

"Yesterday was the anniversary," he blurts, and knows that Jess understands what that means. She waits for him to continue. "And it was like the damn thing was happening again. Some Statewide girl said her roommate hanged herself with an orange electrical cord in room seven-twelve."

"What?"

"Last night. Here, at my hotel. *Jess*. I wish I were lying but I'm not."

"Hastings—slow down, Hastings. Where are you?"

"Where?" He sniffs. "In my room, of course. I've been here all night, ever since *Officer* Megan Sheldrake told me to take a hike. She wouldn't even let me speak with the girl's mother. That's my *job*, that's what I do. I take care of the guests, and that includes telling them their daughters have disappeared."

"You need to calm down. You're scaring me a little."

He sees her sitting at her kitchen table, lightly touching her collarbone with her fingertips.

"Jess, I'm sorry. I've had a lot of coffee tonight." He laughs.

"I'll say. Start from the beginning. Tell me what happened."

"That's the thing. I can't tell if *anything* happened. Went up to seven-twelve, searched the whole place myself. Nothing there. No dead roommate. No live roommate either. It's the damnedest thing."

"Is she still missing?"

Hastings shrugs. "As far as I know. Megan spoke with the mother last night, who happens to be none other than Doug Kirk's replacement. If you'll believe that." He closes his eyes and presses a thumb against his eyelid.

"Who reported it? Do you think she might have been lying?"

Hastings smiles. His wife has been addicted to murder mysteries her whole life. It was Jess, in fact, who first introduced him to the particular pleasures of Raymond Chandler and Agatha Christie. Mickey Spillane. Of Columbo and Kojak, Poirot and Marple, Holmes and Watson. The tone of her voice shifted whenever she slipped into investigative mode, from sunny to crisp, clipped, and efficient. Sharp. He loved her best when she spoke like a private dick.

"Her name was Alice. Alice Hatmaker. Sounded like she was telling the truth. She seemed truly frightened. But I wouldn't put it past any of these kids to make this up. I only wish I could figure out why."

"Something's rotten in Statewide."

He laughs again. "Shakespeare you're not, dear."

"Have you gotten any sleep at all tonight?"

"No," he says.

"Then here's what you're going to do. You're going to turn off your brain and get some sleep. You're going to talk to the girl's mother, and then you're going to go to work."

"Aye-aye." He smiles. Jess always has a way of making the world crystal clear again. "That's why I call you, you know. You make everything make a little more sense."

She laughs this time. "Then we're both in trouble," she says. "Sweet dreams."

When he hangs up, the sleep he missed last night drags his eyelids shut and slows his breathing. He has always been a catnapper, but lately Hastings finds himself powerless to resist his own tiredness, slipping under an instant after he realizes he might fall asleep. He slumps into a fretful darkness wondering whether a horrible thing he saw fifteen years ago—the most horrible thing he's ever seen—was only the beginning of something worse.

10

Return of the Unremarkable Cupcake

INNIE SHOULD PROBABLY get off the elevator. She's been riding it up and down, lobby to upper floors and back again, since she got on at four, her own floor, about thirty minutes ago. In that time, she's shared the elevator car with three violinists, one cellist, and one tuba player. The hotel is full of teenagers carrying musical instruments. When she imagined her triumphant, ass-kicking return to the halls of the great hulking horror of her dreams, Minnie Graves saw wedding dresses. Orange extension cords. Perhaps a melee, a fight to the death, a fire ax chopping down a bathroom door.

She did not see band geeks.

A reedy boy in jeans at least three sizes too big, his waist cinched with a belt like a drawstring purse, smiles as he steps into the elevator on the eighth floor. "Five," he croaks. Minnie nods at him and presses the button. "Please." He smiles sheepishly.

"Big night, huh?" she says.

The boy's cheeks ignite.

Minnie tries not to notice when the elevator passes by the seventh floor. Thankfully, it does not stop. She focuses on the teenager instead, who may, in fact, be wearing a girl's top. The hem is loose, floaty; the collar is ruched like a peasant shirt. Just because she's never had a big night herself, a night big enough to end with someone else's shirt on her back, doesn't mean Minnie isn't familiar with the signs. She wants to ask what happened. Maybe some kind of strip string quartet.

The boy gets off at five and a woman gets on. No—a coiled, terrifying creature in women's clothing. She is tall, though she's getting the bulk of her height from horrifying-looking red pumps that make Minnie's arches ache in sympathy. Her hair is white and pulled back in a murderously tight ponytail. As soon as she's inside, she stabs the L and then the Close Door button and casts a glance at Minnie that might as well be a shiv jerked between her ribs.

"Gotta move faster than that, honey," this insane woman says.

It takes Minnie a moment to understand the woman thought Minnie meant to get off at five with the boy. Logical; not many people go joyriding in the elevator. Still, Minnie resents it. She knows she looks like an unremarkable cupcake. Fluffy, pale, round as a moon pie. But what Minnie resents most is this horrible woman's assumption (some would say reasonable) that if you are fat—and Minnie is fat, not overweight, not chubby, she is solid with *fat*—you are someone who Cannot Help Herself. Someone Who Will Defer. Someone Who Is Weak.

When the fat, in fact, is one of the few parts of Minnie that make her strong.

"Lady," she says, and pushes the emergency stop button. The elevator jiggles to a halt. "Do you have a problem with me?"

"Who wouldn't?" the woman says, eyes glimmering. "Now be a good girl and release the elevator, so I can get back to my life and you can get back to your collection of limited-edition Beanie Babies."

Minnie stares at the woman but doesn't speak. She steps close and pushes her belly into her like a sumo wrestler. Minnie moves with surprising speed and the woman, caught off guard, wobbles on those ridiculous heels. She tries to steady herself by placing a hand on Minnie's arm.

Minnie removes the woman's hand from her arm and twists her wrist backward with a sound like a fistful of uncooked spaghetti snapping in half. The woman makes a cartoon noise—*Auck!*—and slams against the mirrored wall to her right. She slides down to the floor, holding her wounded wrist to her stomach, and Minnie smiles.

None of this happens in real life, of course. But Minnie imagines it so vividly she finds it hard to believe actually doing it would be any more satisfying.

Minnie Graves, since the night of November 13, 1982, when she watched from the sidelines as two just-married strangers obliterated themselves, has lived almost entirely in her mind. She always had an active imagination—it was curiosity that drew her closer in the first place—but since that night, her mind has gone Technicolor. Surround sound. She has lived in stories and in movies.

Horror movies.

Minnie had witnessed real violence and now lived for the Hollywood version. Before that November, every time Mike would tell his little sister about the latest awful thing he'd watched with his friends, he'd done so only to torture her. Then what Minnie saw at the Bellweather changed everything about what she considered scary. How she felt about fear and what it meant to be afraid.

For weeks afterward, through Thanksgiving and into December, her family spoke quietly and walked on tiptoe. Minnie didn't smile. Minnie was afraid of everything—every closed door, every dark closet, every unexpected noise. Minnie didn't sleep through the night. She couldn't be woken without screaming, kicking, fighting for her life. Her doctor suggested introducing her to animals. "Take her to a shelter or a pet shop or the zoo," Dr. Ramble told her parents. Minnie could still see their faces, their exhaustion and worry for her carving every line and crease deeper. "Let her hold a bunny."

"Dr. Ramble is a kook," her father said in the car on the way home. "I think he got his degree at Wossamotta U."

"I'd like that," she said quietly. "I've never held a bunny before."

Their neighbors kept rabbits in a hutch in their garage, and must have been instructed not to upset poor little Minnie, because they brought her over to hold their pets with palpable solemnity. They all knew why she was there, including Minnie. If it was for her sake they were pretending she wasn't broken, they needn't have bothered; after all, she knew better than anyone just how broken she was. Beth, the oldest neighbor girl, pulled a squirming mass of dark gray fluff from the corner of the hutch and said, "This is Rocket."

Minnie's heart sped as the bunny approached. She didn't know what to do, how to hold it. Did you hold a bunny like a baby, not that she'd had much more experience holding babies. She was going to hurt it. She didn't know why she'd said she wanted to hold a bunny; its big back legs would kick and tear at her. But then Minnie was simply — holding the bunny.

Flat against her chest, nothing to it. The rabbit was warm and soft, softer than any of her stuffed animals, softer than her grandmother's mink stole, softer than anything she had ever held in her own arms. Beneath the cloud of its softness she could feel its heart beating like a mad butterfly, matching and then doubling her own heart rate. It was almost too ridiculous to believe, but there it was. The bunny was afraid of her. The bunny feared her, feared Minnie Graves. *Minnie Graves*, who was lately afraid of the whole entire world, possessed the power to instill terror.

She pressed her palm flat against the rabbit's back and stroked its fur until its heart began to slow. She didn't know which was more of a revelation, to have been granted this incredible power by a living creature, or to discover she had the ability to soothe the fear away. She pressed her face into the bunny's side and breathed in its woodchippy scent. It wasn't a miracle or a cure, but it helped.

By the following spring, the Graves family was breathing easier. Minnie, if she wasn't completely her old self, was at least sleeping through the night and not jumping three vertical feet at every odd noise. Mike and his friend Henry (she would develop a terrible crush on Henry in two short years, a relationship built around buckets of fake blood and that would never develop beyond *Hey, bye,* and *George Romero is a genius*) were monopolizing the Graves's new VHS player with a stack of tapes they'd rented from the Rite-Aid. Minnie was working on her social studies homework in the kitchen, half listening to her brother and Henry's murmured conversation.

She was memorizing the names and capitals of all the countries of Europe for a quiz on Monday. It was a Saturday evening. They'd had sloppy joes for dinner, Henry too, and she'd accidentally spilled her glass of milk and it had dripped into the table, through the cracks on either side of the leaf they'd had to put in because Henry was joining them. She remembered everything about that day: the map of Europe in her social studies textbook, countries the same pastel colors as Necco Wafers. Her mother had braided her hair that morning just for fun. The braid was draped over her shoulder and Minnie couldn't resist chewing on the end. She could still taste it, comforting, fibrous, weirdly metallic.

She had to pee. Walking to the bathroom, Minnie passed the doorway to the family room. Mike and Henry had shut off all the lights, and when Minnie turned, attention caught by the bright square of the television screen, her feet stopped themselves.

Minnie was in the Bellweather.

She was looking through the television *into* the Bellweather, looking down that long hotel hallway. At the end of the hall were two little girls in matching pale blue dresses and high white knee socks. Then they were on the ground, torn to pieces, legs and arms at ugly angles, blood on the walls. Then they were standing again, as pale blue as before.

She walked into the family room. Mike and Henry were sitting on either end of the couch with their backs to her. She stood behind the couch and watched and didn't breathe and didn't blink.

Henry noticed her first. Later Minnie would think that the seed of her crush had been planted when Henry noticed her before her own brother did. "Hey," he said, "hey, Minnie, you don't have to—"

Mike jumped off the couch. "Jesus, Minnie, Mom and Dad'll gut me. You have to get out of here."

"I want to see it," she said. "I'll tell Mom and Dad it's not your fault. I want to, Mike—I want to. I want to see it." Her eyeballs were dry. She wondered when she'd last blinked. On the television, a little boy—*Danny*, this must be Danny—was pressing his hands over his eyes. They covered his whole face. Then the picture and the noise stopped, replaced by a silent blue screen that hurt Minnie's eyes. Henry had turned off the tape.

"None of it is real. It's just a movie," Henry said. "If you don't want to see anything, you can always close your eyes."

Minnie sat on the couch between them. She pulled her legs up.

"Are you sure, Bug?" Mike said. "Are you really, really sure?"

"I want to see it," she said.

The Shining, seen at last, was horrifying. Wrong. Minnie didn't understand everything but she *felt* everything, every shrieking, grinding sound, every frame of every scene. When the tide of blood poured out of the elevator shaft and into the hallway, gushing over the chairs and tables and washing them away, Minnie's own blood roared in her veins. There were things in that movie she didn't know could be *thought* of, much less seen, much less made to happen.

She went straight to bed. She hadn't told her family, but she had been dreaming of the Bellweather every single night for months. The reason she'd ceased to wake herself up, shaking and crying, was that she'd become too tired to fight; the fear had won. She had accepted that, in her dreams, she would always be afraid. Then *The Shining*—and no other movie would have done for this first, critical dosing—inoculated her. She had been exposed to the fear that was eating her, slowly but surely, in the light of day; she had confronted it in her waking hours and was rewarded with a night of black, dreamless peace. When she woke up the next morning, a kind of rested she'd forgotten she could feel, Minnie at last knew how to train herself to survive in the world. She would spend the rest of her life pouring the fear out of her dreams and into scary movies.

Minnie grew up. She didn't have many friends, and certainly no best friends. She never had any boyfriends; Henry wasn't interested, and he was the only one she ever cared about. She slept through the night. Even though she remembered fewer of them, she was still dreaming horrible dreams; if woken mid-dream by an unexpected loud noise or by her mother, worried she would miss the bus, Minnie screamed and swung and scratched as hard as she had that first night at the hotel. Her family had learned to let her oversleep.

The list of new things that frightened her grew and grew. Being asked to dances. Regents exams. High heels. Unlocked doors. Driving tests. Failing driving tests. Garage door openers left in unlocked cars. Airplanes. Lyme disease. College applications. College. Dorms. The list of horror films she watched, again and again and again, kept pace. She poured her fear into *Night of the Living Dead*. Into *Halloween* and *The Exorcist*, *The Evil Dead* and *Alien*. She had nightmares on Elm Street and spent summers on Camp Crystal Lake. She watched Hitchcock and the Universal and Hammer horror films, but they didn't have nearly the visceral potency of *The Texas Chainsaw Massacre*. Mike and Henry, home from their first years at college, took her to see David Cronenberg's remake of *The Fly* for her sixteenth birthday. The movie — and Henry, whenever he gushed about the girl he'd met at school — broke her heart in a hundred places.

She got fat. She wasn't able to say when it started, somewhere in eighth grade, she suspected, around the time gym class began to feel like a circus sideshow, with her as the main attraction, but the sizes of her jeans, her tops, her bras increased with each season. At first it was another thing for her to be fearful of, but as her new size stabilized, she came to enjoy it. Her body had barely been hers since that November — it jumped, it flinched, it twitched at everything — but the fat was her own. It was armor. It made her feel solid, planted, like she could defeat anyone who crossed her simply by falling on them.

She got a two-year degree from the local community college, because her parents wanted her to, in biology. When Jennifer and Theo (he *was* still her brother-in-law, despite a few years when it was touch and go) came over for family dinners, they asked what she intended to do with her degree. Make a paper airplane, Minnie would say. Use it as a lobster bib. In truth, she had no desire to do anything. No desire for more school. For a job. No interest in making friends, or, God forbid, going on a date, being someone's girlfriend (someone who wasn't Henry), getting married. When Jennifer and Theo forced her, by their very presence, to consider that such lives were not only possible but in fact fairly commonplace, Minnie's stomach flopped like a dying goldfish. How could she be expected to participate in the world? The world was a terrible place. People hated each other. They killed each other. They shot each other on their wedding day, they hanged themselves and tried to— would have—

Minnie's brain shut down whenever she found herself wondering what the woman in the wedding dress had meant to do to her when she called Minnie closer to pick up her glove. When she called *Little girl. Little girl.*

She was twenty-five, fat, living with her parents, sleeping in the same bed, in the same room, surrounded by the same posters as when she had been that little girl: three orange kittens piled into a white wicker basket. And when she was a slightly older little girl, a little girl who'd learned how to vaccinate herself against the horrors in her dreams: the original theatrical poster for George Romero's *Dawn of the Dead*. Stacks and stacks of old issues of *Cinefantastique*. There were stuffed animals piled on her dresser, grayed with dust, and a towering bookshelf packed with every book Stephen King ever wrote. She was not happy, exactly, but not unhappy either. Mostly what she felt was safe, enclosed, a girl who'd opted to be locked high in a tower surrounded by a forest of deadly brambles, who would turn away any attempt at rescue with a curt *Not interested, get the hell out of my brambles* and a threatening wave with a roaring chain saw.

Enter Auggie.

The Graveses never had a family pet. And though Minnie improved after first holding the neighbors' rabbit, and her parents, giddy with relief, offered to adopt a rabbit, a cat, or a dog, Minnie had said no. She loved creatures, loved her power over them and their power over her, but the responsibility of ownership was unfathomable. The thought of her animal—her own animal—getting sick, being hurt, or dying was more frightening than anything she could imagine, scarier than balloons popping and being left alone in the dark combined.

Auggie showed up in August, the month from which he took his name, the dog days, hot and still, the air in their small lakeside town heavy and oppressive as a soaked blanket. Minnie was reading on the front porch, swinging lazily in the hammock her father had installed for his retirement but never used. Something caught her attention: a tiny, tinkling noise, the sound of dog tags jangling on a collar.

She set her book on her chest and peered into the distance. A dog was walking down the middle of the empty street.

The Graveses lived in a refurbished turn-of-the-century house on the main road of their small (and obnoxiously quaint — every summer weekend there was a festival named after a fruit) town in rural New York. They hardly had any traffic, but still, any traffic to be had was had on this street. The dog didn't seem to care. He might have been a mutt, but he was mostly Corgi, low to the ground with a proud little chest, Creamsicle coloring, and big fox-like ears, with a bright pink tongue that lolled happily from side to side as he took in his surroundings.

She frowned. She didn't recognize him, but the fact that he had tags meant he belonged to someone who was likely missing him, and wouldn't want him splattered in the middle of the road.

She had just turned to call the local shelter when another sound caught her: the low puttering chug of a semi. When there was a backup on the Thruway, tractor-trailers roared down her street as if it were their own personal highway. She couldn't see it yet, but it was coming.

"Hey, dog," she called from the porch. "Hey, dog, get out of the road!"

The dog, oblivious, continued to trot down the double yellow line.

Minnie pulled her T-shirt away from her sticky skin. "Dog!" she shouted. "Dog, c'mere! Hey!" The semi was getting closer. She stepped down off the porch and grabbed a twig from the front lawn. She whipped the stick across the street into the Hatchers' yard on the other side.

The dog stopped and tilted his head in the direction the stick had flown. Then he sat down in the middle of the road and looked straight at Minnie.

She could see the truck now, barreling up the street from the left. Maybe sixty, seventy yards away, closing the distance.

"Dog!" Minnie yelled. She clapped. "Get out of the damn road, jackass."

The dog pulled his tongue back into his mouth. He closed his eyes and lifted a hind leg to scratch behind his foxy ear.

Was he sick? Why the hell wasn't he getting out of the way? Minnie bit her lip. Her hands were clammy. There wasn't any foam around the dog's mouth, he wasn't charging, he wasn't attacking—

The truck was close. About thirty yards now, not far at all, but it wasn't blowing its horn. The driver hadn't noticed yet, hadn't seen there was something in the road, small but moving. Something alive.

"Dog!" Minnie was shouting now. Her throat was sore. "Move your goddamned ass!"

The dog shook his head, tags jangling and ears flapping cheerfully.

Minnie had two choices. She could stand on the edge of her lawn and watch as the dog was struck and killed. Or she could run into traffic and save his life.

Later she would describe to her mother how the dog had smiled at her, how his tongue rolled out and the black edges of his mouth pulled back in a friendly grin. What she didn't tell her mother was that, in the heartbeat before she ran into the road, she found herself unable to recall the last time a stranger had smiled at her, easily, like a friend she didn't know yet. It was funny to remember so clearly what was on her mind when so many other things were happening all at once—the truck's air horn finally blowing, Minnie flying out in front of the semi with a speed and grace that belied her earthly heft. She scooped the dog to her chest and launched herself across the other half of the street, turning in midair so that she didn't crush him, landing on her back and sliding across the damp grass of the Hatchers' yard.

The semi, horn blaring angrily, roared past without stopping. A snap of air rushing behind the truck ruffled Minnie's bangs.

She closed her eyes. Everything hurt. She had broken something. She had broken everything. All for a stupid dog who was probably rabid, who would be sinking his pointed white teeth into the fat of her neck in three, two, one—

The dog's tongue was everywhere on her face, licking her nose, her eyelids, her cheeks, her chin, her ears, licking excitedly, joyfully. Minnie laughed and the dog licked and licked. He followed her back across the street, empty of all traffic now, and climbed the steps of the Graveses' front porch as though he, too, were simply going home. His tags identified him as up-to-date with his vaccinations but contained no other information. No name, no phone number, no address.

"You're nobody's dog," she said, pulling gently on his silky ears. He made a friendly noise in his throat, not quite a bark, and pushed his nose against her hand.

"What are you going to do with him?" her father asked at dinner. "Do you want to keep him?"

Minnie shrugged. She hadn't yet told her parents exactly how she and the dog had been introduced. It surprised her how happy their little adventure made her feel. She couldn't believe she'd done it. "He must have a home. I guess try to find it for him."

"I think you should just keep him," he said, and finished off his beer.

In the end, after canvassing all the shelters and pet stores in the area, after posting *Found Dog* flyers across town and several towns over, Minnie did keep him. She named him August, Auggie for short, though it was sort of pointless to call him anything, since it took little time for Minnie to realize Auggie was completely deaf. She called him, instead, by opening food—his tub of kibble, a jar of peanut butter. He always came.

When she thought about Auggie getting sick, getting hurt and dying, a cold hand closed around her heart, but then she remembered saving his life. He was already a dead dog walking. The life he had now, with her, was *because* of her. He was a deaf canine soul, entirely in her hands, and he began to change her.

His care forced her to go to places she would never have approached, like the dog park across town, where people shocked her by not only engaging in friendly conversation but remembering her name, her dog's name, and the content of those friendly conversations upon later meetings. Strangers stopped them on their walks around the neighborhood. Auggie's vet appointments, grooming, and food were expensive. So Minnie got a job at the library, which had been supporting her voracious reading habit since middle school, and started freelancing with the local paper as a movie critic.

Six months after adopting Auggie, Minnie moved out of her parents' house and into a small apartment three blocks from the library. She went home to walk Auggie on her lunch breaks. At night she made them both dinner, they watched a scary movie, and then they went to sleep. Something began to stir inside, given breath and life by each tiny declaration of independence. Minnie found herself wanting. Desiring. Needing more than what she already had — more people in her life, friends. She began to daydream, to imagine other futures for herself. Living in a city, working at a university library, reviewing movies for a real paper. Meeting friends for coffee, going to the movies, dancing with someone interesting, someone with a comprehensive knowledge of the early films of Brian De Palma. What she imagined for herself was, given the scope of human possibility, tame; but to imagine it all actually happening to her was revolutionary. For the first time in her adult life she began to think of herself as unhappy. She was thrilled to realize simply admitting that she was unsatisfied, that she wanted more, didn't make her sad. It made her hopeful.

There was just one thing she had to do.

Minnie Graves needed to go back.

That's what all horror heroines did: they went back to the beginning. They returned to face the monsters head-on and defeat them for good. Ripley (albeit under duress) did it in *Aliens*. Nancy came back for the third *Nightmare on Elm Street*. Hell, Jason did it in *Friday the 13th, Part 2*—he returned to the place where he nearly died, where his mother was killed.

Not that Minnie Graves was Jason Voorhees; she wasn't going back to *become* the monster. In most horror movies, there is one girl, virtuous and tough, who makes the best of horrific circumstances by taking a stand. Minnie was that girl. The girl who survives. And it was time she started living.

She planned her vacation carefully. She asked the library for four days off around the middle weekend of November. She bought Auggie a red harness and stitched a big white cross on his back. "Well," she said to him, scratching between his friendly, broken ears, "one of us is handicapped."

On Thursday morning, the thirteenth of November, Jennifer and Theo's fifteenth anniversary, Minnie Graves tossed a suitcase she borrowed from her mother into the back of her parents' Lumina. She'd told her parents the library was sending her to a conference out of state. Telling them where she was actually going and why was both none of their business and too much their business. Her mother would never, ever have let her go back to the Bellweather alone.

She wasn't alone, though; she had Auggie. He climbed in the front seat.

"You'll be safer in the back," she said.

Auggie licked a spot on the dashboard that might have been a dried drip of Diet Coke.

"Yeah, I like you riding shotgun too," Minnie said, and backed out of the driveway.

The trip was uneventful. They ate lunch at a rest area. They stopped again, once they were off the Thruway and into the countryside, for Auggie to pee. When the Bellweather first came into view, Minnie felt nothing at all. It looked smaller than she remembered, even older, and much, much busier—full of kids, high schoolers with trombones and flutes and folders of sheet music. This weekend, her great homecoming, was also some sort of high school musicians' conference. Even without his working-dog camouflage, no one would have noticed Auggie in the tumult.

Minnie checked in. She got out food and water for Auggie and lay down on the bed in room 407, fully clothed, sneakers still on. She was here. She was back. She was ready, really ready, to face her past. Ready to defeat it.

She had been lying to herself all day.

She was terrified.

Minnie has been swimming in dread for about sixteen hours. Dread flavored the meatloaf (too salty) she ordered from room service. Dread gushed from the showerhead when she washed up before bed. That she hasn't bolted in terror from the hotel, running in a straight line out the door for miles across the countryside until her heart exploded and she fell down dead, is a miracle, because that's what Minnie's dread has been urging her to do, every second of every minute she's been back.

Minnie's dread put yesterday's clothes back on, put her feet in sneakers, and walked those feet into the elevator on Friday morning. It made her press L and almost made her step out into the bright morning light of the lobby. But it was Minnie's will that stopped her from going any farther. Auggie was still asleep at the foot of the bed. He is the one thing her dread has absolutely no power over. She will always go back for him. He will keep her here in the hotel, and keep her honest. When Minnie's dread said *Get out,* Minnie's will, for Auggie's sake, said *Make me.* And here in the elevator, will and dread cancel each other out.

Which is why she's still here—in elevator limbo, Minnie gets a break from being two things at the same time, each hell-bent on consuming the other. The car stops on three and two and opens on the lobby. The woman with the red pumps and the white hair and everyone else get out. Minnie stays inside and goes back up.

She sighs, closes her eyes, and leans back against the mirrored wall as the car rises. She wonders if, when she opens her eyes, she will be greeted by the reflection of herself at the age of twelve in that heinous bridesmaid's dress, her past reflected again and again, to

128

infinity, forever. Because she's in elevator limbo, this isn't horrify-ing but merely intellectually interesting. Maybe she's always been in this hotel. Maybe she left part of herself behind, the way Cinder-ella left her shoe, and she only has to find it to be whole again.

The doors open on ten and so do Minnie's eyes. A handsome boy—closer to a man, he must be twenty-one, twenty-two—with dark hair and tanned skin steps on. He is *Tiger Beat* material, im-possibly, boyishly cute. He nods at her.

The doors open again on six for a short boy with dark hair.

His eyes bulge and a gigantic smile parts his face like a curtain. He knows the other boy, the older boy, but not well—this isn't the easy reflection of old friendship, or even the cautious kindness of recent acquaintance. The boy knows him from across the room, from stories, from rumors his friends have told him. Minnie, on a normal day, fades into the background, but here she is completely invisible. The new boy has a crush on Tiger Beat, a life-killer of a crush, a crush the size of the former Soviet Union.

"Do I know you?" says Tiger. "Wait. Last night. You're the bunny boy, aren't you?"

Bunny Boy nods. He flushes. "Yeah. That's me. Last night, at the party."

"How late did you stay? Heard it got pretty crazed."

There is an awkward moment when Bunny Boy realizes he's still facing Tiger, grinning at him like a moony moron and holding up the elevator. He steps into the car and they stand side by side. The doors close.

"I was there until the end, I think. I guess it got . . . crazed." Bunny Boy is glowing with joy. Minnie is surprised the car doesn't spontaneously combust in a pop of gleeful light.

"So you haven't heard yet," says Tiger. He touches Bunny Boy's forearm conspiratorially, casually, but with artful intention. Tiger understands the power he has over Bunny Boy, and he is enjoying every second of this. "You haven't heard about the girl."

Bunny, distracted by the two square inches of flesh so recently indented by Tiger's fingertips, looks up. "Um, what? Who? What girl?"

"The dead girl," Tiger whispers, "in seven-twelve."

"*What?*" says Minnie.

Everyone in the car is shocked to hear Minnie's voice, including Minnie.

Tiger, slick, rolls with it. "No kidding," he says. "There were cops in the lobby last night. I saw 'em when I was coming back from the bar. They were saying some girl killed herself last night in room seven-twelve."

Is this a hallucination? This is not what she expected. None of this is what she expected. Not the band geeks. Not the constant dread. *Never* another dead girl in 712. She knew she had to return to the Bellweather before she could get on with her life, but she never—she couldn't—*it was supposed to be metaphorical.*

"Are you *sure?*" she says. Her voice cracks. "You mean to say a girl . . . in room seven-one-two . . . in *this* hotel . . . killed herself last night? On the night of November thirteenth?"

Bunny Boy and Tiger regard her with mirrored mixtures of confusion. Tiger's has a touch of don't-upset-the-crazy-lady, while Bunny Boy, more compassionate by far, is concerned. He leans closer to her.

"That's what they're saying," Tiger says. "What do you know about it?"

Minnie laughs.

At first it's a single, short bark, but the more she considers the question—*What do you know about a dead girl in 712?*—the more absurd, the more horrifying, the more hysterical her life becomes, and Minnie laughs until she doubles over, her stomach muscles contracting. Her face is wet and she understands she's crying with laughter, that she must be terrifying these kids—and then Minnie's knees and legs go out from under her and her back slips down against the mirror. When her big butt hits the floor, the elevator gives a little hop, and Minnie Graves is laughing louder and harder than she's ever laughed in her life.

The doors open on the lobby.

Tiger bolts, eager to distance himself from the insane laughing fat lady as soon as possible. Bunny Boy holds the doors open with one hand and shouts across the lobby that he needs some help, there's a woman . . .

His voice trails off. *Yes, Bunny Boy,* Minnie thinks, *how would you describe me?* After which she takes a breath and starts laughing all over again. She wishes Auggie were here. He can probably sense her distress; she can picture him hopping nervously at the door on his tiny legs. He hardly ever barks. The most noise he ever makes is a low sort of growl that means he's happy or hungry or has cornered a chipmunk.

Minnie howls loud and long enough for the both of them.

11

Alice in the Morning

OR THE FIRST time in her life, Alice has nothing to say. She wakes up Friday morning remembering, like a series of slaps, everything that happened the night before — Jill's story. The tarot hand. The spilled wine. Jill's feet swinging in the air. She grabs her Trapper Keeper and her pen but doesn't have words. Well, she has plenty of words, starting with WHAT THE FUCK, followed by I KNOW WHAT I SAW, AND I SAW HER CORPSE and THERE'S SOMETHING WEIRD ABOUT THE CONCIERGE, based on the blank look he'd given her along with his business card. But none of the words feel like they're ready to be written down, preserved for future generations. Whatever this is — and Alice has no doubt that this is a *this,* a thing, an event — it's still happening.

She cries in the shower, because it was all so horrible and Jill is gone, it's so horrible to be so young and dead for no good reason. Was there *ever* a good reason to be dead? Alice, blow-drying her hair, starts to cry again, because yesterday Jill had blown her hair dry for the last time without even realizing it.

Jill's disappearance, the fact of it, gnaws on her insides. A riddle she feels compelled to solve. How could Jill disappear herself—

how could she be both magician and charming assistant at the same time? Answer: she couldn't have. Answer: Jill had help. She didn't cut *herself* down from the sprinkler system. Which means it wasn't suicide. She didn't kill herself; someone hanged her and hid her. Someone murdered her. Alice has to find out what happened when the police talked to Jill's mom. She has to make them believe Jill was afraid of her own mother. She feels sick. Alice is the only one who knows the truth. The cops don't even think she's dead, let alone murdered. Why would they suspect her mother of a crime they don't believe was committed?

No one is down in the banquet hall yet. The breakfast buffet is still being set out. Alice watches as pans of milky-looking scrambled eggs and sausage patties the color of puddles are ferried from the kitchen, and feels conquered. She touches her throat. What time is rehearsal? Where is rehearsal again—what are they singing? Why is she here?

Her roommate was *murdered*.

She sits heavily in a chair at one of the empty tables and blinks back more tears. Why is she so weepy? It's not like she even knew the girl—not really; if she were still alive they wouldn't have known each other for twenty-four hours yet—but. But. There are no napkins on the table, so Alice blots her running mascara on the maroon tablecloth. All this crying has made her eyeballs feel too big for her face. She doesn't know how long she's been sitting here before other people begin to trickle in for a chance to be disappointed by the food. They wake her from her reverie, and when the first warming tray lids are lifted, the smell of grease and fat overwhelms her. Alice decides to skip breakfast.

She splashes cold water on her face in the hall bathroom and walks back toward the lobby. The concierge desk is unmanned. He must know what the cops found out by now. So where is he? When will he be back?

Someone shouts for help. Alice wobbles. It's happening again. There's been another murder. It's—

It's her brother's voice.

Rabbit is holding the elevator in the lobby, shouting for help, that there's a woman—

And then Alice plows into him, it's her brother, it's her Rabbit, it's the soul who was with her at the beginning. She locks herself around him. She doesn't speak.

"Alice, that—that hurts, Alice," he says.

"I don't care," she says, and squeezes harder, pressing her nose against his shoulder until it's squashed flat.

"Uh, help," Rabbit says, and Alice faintly realizes there is someone else with them: a woman on the floor of the elevator making odd keening noises that might have started out as laughter. She senses the woman standing up.

The elevator, annoyed at having been held open all this time, buzzes like an angry wasp.

"Rabbit, don't you dare leave me again," Alice says, just as she feels herself being pried from her brother by two strong hands on either side of her waist.

"You two know each other?" says a voice close by Alice's head. The other person, the woman from the elevator, is holding her up off the floor as easily as if she were a bag of mulch.

Rabbit steps aside and lets the elevator close. "She's my sister."

"Rabbit," Alice gasps, struggling weakly. "Rabbit, someone killed her. She's dead, someone killed Jill."

He squints and frowns. "What—"

"My roommate got murdered last night." The words and all the remaining fight in Alice floods out of her body in a single gush. She sags against her captor, who sets her down on her feet.

"I found her, I found her hanging." Alice's throat clogs.

"That's not funny," he says.

"No, it isn't," says the woman. "Are you telling the truth?"

Alice faces her. She's younger than Mrs. Wilson, overweight, wearing a gray sweatshirt and jeans, with pale skin and blondish-brownish hair in a messy bun. There's very little to hold on to about her. She's unfinished and hazy around the edges, except for her eyes, which are small and angry.

"I'm Minnie," she says. She gives an awkward half wave. "I was here—I was here fifteen years ago."

Alice and Rabbit look at each other.

"The first time this happened," Minnie says.

Alice can't believe she's still here. Still at this hotel, standing in the lobby as though a crazy stranger named Minnie *didn't* just tell her and Rabbit about a murder-suicide she witnessed fifteen years ago last night, in Alice's room.

She, Alice, should be calling the police. The papers. Her mother. She should be shouting to anyone who will listen: Hey! Here's your headline: CRAZY WOMAN RETURNS TO KILL AGAIN! FREAKISHLY STRONG, TORMENTED BY THE HORRORS SHE WITNESSED AS A CHILD! No *way* this was a coincidence, her showing up and having a fit the morning after a similar crime is committed, on the anniversary of the crime she witnessed. Minnie told them her life story right there in the lobby, down to the color of her bridesmaid's dress, and then, with another awkward little wave, she got back on the elevator because *she had to take her dog for a walk.*

"Are you hungry?" Alice asks her brother as soon as the elevator doors shut. "Do you want to get some breakfast and talk about how that insane woman killed my roommate?"

"Yes," Rabbit says.

They find a small table tucked in a corner of the banquet hall, away from the larger crowd. Alice's appetite has returned with a fury. The food doesn't look any more appetizing, but she doesn't care. There's a crazy murderer on the loose and she needs fuel.

"First I thought Jill's mother did it. But now I think *she* did it," Alice says, folding a sausage patty in half and biting off the end. "*She* killed Jill."

"How could she?" Rabbit's plate is similarly heaped, but he hasn't taken a bite. He looks at it despondently. "You were gone from your room for, what, a minute? Two minutes?"

"She could absolutely string Jill up in that time. The woman was *strong.*"

Rabbit pokes at his eggs with his fork. "It doesn't make any sense. Unless she's experiencing a total break with reality."

"*Ding.*" She slugs back her orange juice.

Now he's looking at *her* funny. Like he doesn't believe her, or doesn't trust her, or thinks she's going to hurt him.

"What?" she says.

"You're not doing so great with reality this morning either."

"Oh, I wonder why. Maybe because a psycho lady with beady little eyes hung my famous roommate off the sprinkler system with an extension cord last night. I mean, *right?*" She tears off a hunk of unbuttered toast with her teeth. "What the hell did you do last night?"

Rabbit examines his food.

"I mean," she says, "how was the party?"

Boring, thinks Rabbit, with three moments of total exhilaration. One: about an hour into the party—which largely consisted of people who knew each other too well, and whom he didn't know at all, drinking cheap beer and laughing at inside jokes—when the Tenor first came to the door. Two: a half hour later, when he overheard that the Tenor's name was Pete Moretti, that his *a cappella* club was from the University at Buffalo. And three: another hour into the party, after an exhausted Rabbit had given up hope of conversation with the Tenor in the crowd and was making a quiet exit, when he opened the door to leave and found Pete Moretti on the other side.

"Hey," said Pete. "Leaving so soon?"

"Uhhhh, no," said Rabbit. "Just getting. Um. Air."

"Good answer," Pete said, smiling as he squeezed by Rabbit to get back inside. Rabbit caught a whiff of something soapy and sweet underneath the funk of cigarettes and beer. He closed the door again, lost track of Pete, and ended up staying until midnight without once speaking with him again.

"Fine," he says to his sister the next morning. "You know. A party."

Alice nods slowly. She looks worn out, paler than usual, so pale she's nearly see-through. He feels genuinely terrible that, while his sister had been dealing with a hanged roommate, he'd been killing the night at a stupid party. Nursing a beer, which tasted gross. Waiting for the chance moment that came right at the end and that, when it came, he hadn't been able to seize. How hard would it have been, while Pete Moretti was brushing by him, to mention that his name was Bertram Hatmaker and he was (now, definitely) applying to the University of Buffalo?

And this morning, in the elevator. Again fate had thrown him a perfect pitch and Rabbit had swung and missed. Minnie Graves and her episode must have been fate's smack upside the head for being such a bozo. He can't even remember what they'd said to each other. Though apparently Pete knew who he was, had heard a story about the Bunny Boy. Rabbit flushes. Great.

There's nothing sexier than bunnies.

"What?" Alice asks.

Maybe now is the time. To tell her, to tell Alice about the gay stuff. Maybe it'll distract her from—all of this.

"Alice, so—"

"What do we *do*, Rabbit? We have to *do* something. No one is doing anything because no one believes she's dead. They think this is a stupid prank. But it isn't. She didn't kill *herself*, she was murdered, Rabbit. We should at least tell someone about the psycho dog lady, tell whoever's in charge—" She swallows a huge lump of sausage. "Have you seen Wilson anywhere? It's like she dropped us off and then poof. The lady vanished."

Now is not the time. "Haven't seen her," he says.

"What the hell do you *do* when shit like this happens? Brownies did not prepare me for this. You were a Boy Scout."

"Cub Scout."

"Are there merit badges for reporting murders everyone else thinks are pranks? Is there a way to force people to believe you?" Alice braces her arms against the table and goggles at her empty plate. "Where did all my food go?"

"You ate it."

"Right. So. Jill's dead and I should probably not be sleeping in the same room, because killer invisible dog lady is going to come back tonight with an ax. Can I stay with you? Who's your roommate? Will he care?"

Rabbit shrugs. "You can stay with me."

She exhales slowly and narrows her eyes at him. "You believe me, don't you?"

Rabbit looks down at his toast.

"Rabbit," his sister says softly. "Rabbit, please. Why would I lie about this? Why would I lie to *you,* of all people?"

He shakes his head. *Because you're an actress first and my sister second? Because it kills you when the world isn't paying attention?*

"A murder at Statewide," Alice says. "Nerdy concert camp full of nerdy musicians and their nerdy teachers—is it so hard to believe none of us are killers? Jill was a star. Jill, out of all of us, was *real,* Rabbit. You honestly think no one here would be jealous or crazy enough to wish she were dead? And that's not even counting the legitimate suspects. Deranged dog lady. Jill's own *mother.*" Alice pushes her fingers back through her hair. "You know, that's the difference between you and me, Rabbit. You believe people are basically good. I know it doesn't matter whether people are good or bad. It matters what they do, not what they are, and I know people are capable of doing more horrible things than you can imagine."

She's scaring him. He has seen his sister under many circumstances, she's dramatic, melodramatic even, but he has never seen her quite like this. This is manic, desperate, unhinged. He isn't sure if it makes him believe her story more or less.

"Alice, go to rehearsal."

She frowns.

"Right." She pats his hand across the table. "Thanks, Rab. I'm going to go throw up now."

"Bulimia is so '87," Rabbit says automatically. He's suspected this for a while now, he hates to say, but there it is. Maybe he should just blurt the gay stuff too. Maybe casually blurting bombshells minimized the damage from the blast.

"Oh, I'm not bulimic," she says with a dismissive wave. "I'm just freaking out. See you later."

She lied; she is bulimic, a little. Every once in a while, when her stomach felt too tight with food or before a big show, a concert, or an audition, throwing up took off the edge. It left her feeling alert, hungry, controlled, and at the ready. But today, after realizing that just going back to her room to collect her music or her clothes could be dangerous, it does absolutely no good whatsoever.

12

Declarations

FISHER RUNS INTO Viola Fabian in the Bellweather lobby. Physically runs into her, so that the paper cup of bitter goat piss the hotel is passing off as coffee is crushed against his chest when their bodies collide. He shouts—not only is the coffee toxic, it has been brewed to a temperature barely below scalding—"Gah, bugger!" and spreads his arms wide, flinging drips of molten pain onto the lobby carpet. While he didn't necessarily mean to direct the epithet at his collider, when he realizes it's Viola, he doesn't apologize.

"Hi, love," he says.

She makes no sound, but her eyes, and her nostrils, could not possibly be wider. A hot dark stain is spreading across the lapels of one of her trademark wool suits, but she makes no attempt to remove her jacket. Perhaps she's actually drawing power from the searing pain in her chest. No question, she was on her way to disembowel someone. Fisher can't help smiling. He has never slept with a more evil creature.

And yet, for all he knows of her reputation (scheming, conniving, backstabbing, resolutely amoral), she was never particularly violent in bed. If the rumors were true, and they usually were, she saved all her psychopathic behavior for the wider world of social interaction, manipulating colleagues shamelessly in the pursuit of getting what she wanted. *That* appointment. *His* grant money. *Those* concert tickets. *This* lover. *That* husband. It was as if, by the time she got what she set her eye on (in Fisher's case, the young Scottish piano prodigy with the tragically mutilated hand), she had no further objective, no further plan, and, again, in Fisher's case, no further interest. Which is why their brief affair suited them both. Over the course of two years, while he was living in New York, they saw each other at two conferences and four concerts. Every time they fucked. Then they returned to their respective homes.

"I heard you'd be here," Fisher says to Viola. "Just coming up from breakfast myself. Was late to my own rehearsal yesterday, if you can believe that. Now I've got to change my bloody shirt, so I'm going to be late again."

Viola smoothes her ponytail and tugs her suit coat down.

"Good to see you again, Dr. Brodie. I trust this will be the last rehearsal you're late for. Conductors are a dime a dozen."

"Ouch."

"Sorry, were you expecting a hug and a kiss?"

It's been a decade and a half since they last saw each other, and the lag is catching up to him. She is every bit as stunning as the first time she caught his eye, during an intermission at Lincoln Center: stark white hair, fine, harsh features, tossing back a glass of red wine. There was something chiseled-in-marble about her, classically unyielding, but Fisher senses a new shadow, a darkness pulled and stretched out of proportion. Viola Fabian has blackened. She is speckled with flecks of rot.

Maybe it's not Viola who's changed. Maybe it's him.

"Have you seen a girl with short dark hair? Name of Alice?" she asks. "I have a message for her. You know I'm running the show now?"

"That's what I heard. Congratulations."

She responds by smiling, brilliantly, and Fisher almost forgets the unease crawling up his spine. Her beauty cannot be unseen.

"Say, will you be at the reception tonight?" he says. "I'll buy you a drink."

"The drinks are comped," she says. "But yes. We should catch up. Because we are old friends who used to screw. Is that what you're thinking?"

"I'm not that old." *And are we friends?* "Mostly what I'm thinking is—" He pauses, thrown. Was she always like this? "Is everything all right?"

"Yes," she says. "So you haven't seen an Alice? Last name Hatmaker."

Fisher has no reason beyond instinct not to tell Viola everything he knows about Hatmakers—for surely Alice must be his valiant bassoonist's sister or cousin—but he holds his tongue. "No," he says. "Bad news? I mean, the message. Not that it's any of my business."

Viola smiles again. "It really, really isn't," she says. She gives his arm a squeeze and says she'll see him later.

Viola was one of his Unavailables—Fisher's preferred sort of lover, married, partnered, steadfastly independent, or otherwise engaged—yet she always stood out as something rather special. They met when he was twenty-one and on his own in the great city, though he'd been legally on his own for the past five years. Fisher was born in Edinburgh, but he spent his childhood on airplanes and trains and in hotel rooms. He was a textbook child prodigy. One day at the age of four, he sat down at the family's upright piano and played along perfectly to a song on the television; by the time he was six, he was performing in pubs and concert halls; by the time he was nine, a year after his beloved Auntie McDunnock died, Fisher had a recording contract and a full slate of concert bookings that left very little time for school or friends, for bicycles or films or birthday cakes, even. His mother and father, who were both semiprofessional musicians (and, until they began managing their son, accountants), had no intention of letting Fisher's mental and social well-being stand in the way of their good fortune.

The only person he ever felt truly cared for him was his mother's great-aunt, Clara McDunnock. He loved her more than anyone else on earth, including his parents and his three older sisters, who he thought were all a bit shite. She never asked him to play the piano for her. She never instructed him to do anything other than stand up straight and eat his vegetables, be nice to the cats in the barn and come in before it got full dark. Every summer the Brodies visited her in the country, Fisher's engagements permitting, and every summer, up to her last, he never left her side.

"Fisher," she told him on her deathbed, "I'm going to die in just a bit, and when I'm gone I want you to take a little something of mine. But you can't tell anyone. They're mine to give as I please, and you're not to tell a soul, understand?"

He nodded.

"I want you to take them and—" She coughed viciously, and Fisher felt close to death, right up in its face, for the first time in his life. "Take them and keep them safe and get yourself something beautiful. If it's really beautiful it will probably be useless, not good for anything, but that's just fine. It doesn't have to feed anyone or save lives or combat suffering and injustice, it just has to be beautiful. It has to stop your heart. And maybe its useless beauty will inspire you to go out and feed people and save lives and combat suffering. Or not." She coughed again. "That part's up to you."

Fisher was kneeling by her bed with his arms propped on the mattress, and he put his head down between them and burrowed his nose against her side like a dog already grieving for his lost master. He didn't want her to see him cry.

"Stay with me, Fisher," his Auntie continued, "and lock the door and don't let anyone in until you're sure that I've gone up to the Lord. And when you're sure I'm gone, but before you unlock the door, I want you to take those pliers over there—by the bookshelf, see?—and you're going to just pinch my teeth and slip them out of my old mouth."

Fisher raised his head. His Auntie smiled at him, a golden smile, with four golden teeth that she'd had planted in her mouth in the years between the wars. "Your mother," she went on, "is a loon, who married a loon, who begat three loons and a swan, love. You take what I want to give you, don't be squeamish now, I won't feel a thing. You take them and don't tell a soul, and you get yourself something beautiful."

Fisher was eight when he watched his Auntie die—peacefully, all things considered—and suddenly much, much older when, as instructed, he knelt in the bed beside her corpse and gently pulled her golden teeth from her mouth. He unlocked the door and ran to his parents' bedroom, finally allowing himself to cry, shouting that she was dead, she was dead, and when later his parents asked what the hell happened to her teeth, he could turn out his empty pockets and not lie when he said maybe they'd been swallowed. He just didn't specify down whose throat.

Another eight years would pass before Fisher knew freedom, and it was a terrible kind of freedom, the kind you arrive at because you've been left with no other options. He lost three fingers from his right hand. Ha: "lost" is the wrong word. He tore three fingers from his right hand, tore his own future from the rest of his life, while he was on tour in Germany. The German doctors, unable to reattach his middle and ring fingers, thought they could at least save his mangled pinkie. But Fisher, white with shock and blood loss and the realization that his hand was useless—for turning doorknobs, let alone playing the piano—told them to chop it off.

When his parents protested, he pointed out that he was sixteen, the legal age of consent in the marvelous country of Scotland, and would thereafter be taking complete financial control of his destiny. He had his newly autonomous fingers bronzed and delivered to them, tucked in a lovely potted fern. The hand that remained consisted of right index finger and thumb and three rounded stumps he was astonished to discover he could still wiggle. Fisher felt his phantom fingers for weeks, still felt them when he woke some mornings, muzzy from dreams of playing, playing, always playing the piano.

When he held his hand down to his side, it looked like a perpetually cocked finger gun. A child had brought this to his attention one day when Fisher was visiting London, purely as a tourist, something he'd never had the luxury of doing before the accident. He was riding the tube to the British Museum, hoping centuries of archeological plunder would distract him from his own modern troubles, when a little boy sitting across the aisle brought his hands together, pointed with both index fingers, and unleashed a hand howitzer. Fisher frowned at his destroyed hand and leveled it directly between the child's eyes. "Bang," he said, "you're dead," and got off at the next station, even though he was nowhere near the museum.

After that he moved to New York, where he studied music composition and conducting. Where he first met Viola Fabian. It's bizarre to see her here at the Bellweather, now, the morning after meeting another strange, intriguing Unavailable—as he's quite certain his late-night red-headed visitor will become. Maybe he's passed on. Maybe the Bellweather is some purgatorial soap opera where he can't help but stumble over lovers old and new alike. He doesn't quite feel up to dealing with both.

Fisher is so unsettled by the encounter with Viola that he's standing at the conductor's podium rolling up his sleeves before he remembers his shirt front is drenched with coffee. It's starting to cool. He smells slightly burnt. He's of no mind to go back to his room to change, now that he's here and his musical minions are gathering. He's pleased to see that most of them are giving him odd looks. Unpacking their music hesitantly. He's made them wary, on guard. He's woken them up.

Wary—that's how he felt in Viola's presence. As if he might be called upon to defend himself, bodily, from her at any moment. An awful lot can happen to change a person in fifteen years, though he's buggered if he can figure out who has changed more. Did Viola become evil? Did Fisher grow a conscience? He blanches—God, he hopes Viola doesn't try to sleep with him—then he laughs, because it may be the first time in his adult life that he's ever thought such a thing. But even if he weren't otherwise sexually fixated, entranced by the enigmatic new Unavailable in his life, to sleep with Viola Fabian at this conference would be . . . the only word that seems to fit is "catastrophic."

Fisher has been thinking of nothing but the red-headed pianist (save for his brief, recent encounter with Viola) for the past eight hours, waking and asleep. She crept through his dreams, skulking, silent. The mysterious red pianist and her hands: while she'd been lending her right, he'd been eyeing her left—ring finger banded, perfectly Unavailable. When she wrapped his arm around her and played the piano beneath his hand, Fisher had felt every atom in his body align, expand, vibrate with desire. By quick count, she was the thirteenth Unavailable; was she the one to which it had all been building? Could she be the last, the first he would fall in love with? How ridiculous it felt to think such a thing, and yet everything about her, about himself in relation to her, felt new. Different. Possible.

He snaps his head up.

"Right! Children! Welcome to another day." The orchestra, now full, gazes up at him with a hundred or so eyes, eyes that today hold more than blank readiness. There is interest, a hint of trepidation. Resistance. The girl at the timpani is tense, readied. Half the trombones are glowering. He scans the winds, marking the absence of the first flute, which is no real surprise, and locks eyes with his Hatmaker, with Rabbit. Rabbit gives a little jump but pleases Fisher immensely with a slight frown and a returned stare of equal intensity. The basses lean against their fiddles, hunched thugs. The cellos hold their bows like sharpened spears, and the violas look positively mutinous, which is confusing until he remembers tossing off a disparaging comment about violas yesterday. The violins are stiff, perched on the edge of their seats, eyeing, he has no doubt, the pulse of the carotid artery in his neck.

"You all look lovely today. I trust you slept well. Tracy Hazlett, Miss Timpani. What did you do last night?"

"Relearned all my music."

The orchestra ripples.

"Oi, liar," Fisher says with a wide grin. "I was here in the auditorium nearly all night and no one else came in to practice. Unless you've got some big drums in your room, Hazlett, you're lying."

She blushes furiously. Half the orchestra titters and the other half glares double and triple bloody murder at him. When he smiles again, he makes sure they can see all his teeth. He leads them through several warm-up scales, and, satisfied with their intonation (they are, without question, excellent, if slightly hollow), he cracks his fingers loudly.

"After yesterday's scene," he says, "I've been thinking. The other music I picked out originally, it wasn't all shite. Not *all* of it, at least. I hope none of you went and threw it out. I'd rather like us to go to war today." He registers a few panicked faces. "Holst. 'Mars, the Bringer of War.'"

A small hand snakes up from deep in the second violins.

"Oh, come *on*," Fisher says. "You actually got rid of the music? You threw it out? Who does that? Hatmaker, would *you* throw out your music because some raving foreign madman told you to?"

Rabbit's response is to stare back in silence. Fisher feels the temperature in the auditorium rise about twenty degrees. They are furious. They wanted him dead to rights before. Now that he's gone after their rabbity mascot, they just want him dead.

"Let's," he says, and lifts his arms.

"Mars" begins in the distance and marches inexorably forward on fifty plucked strings, on low, dark tones that gather and build until they are all assembled in one defiant wall of sound. The players are, in fact, spiking in and out of tune, but by the time the violins are slashing their bows across their strings and the French horns are sending out a battle cry, they are playing not with their heads or their hearts, but their guts. Their vital humors. They collapse together on a single note, a note that explodes like a bomb, and when they rise, wounded, they are mad as hell. The brass section takes up the banner of those dark carillons, rising higher and louder in the air as the campaign reaches a fever pitch.

Fisher holds the glory of all that noise in his open arms. He presses his face against the sound. Takes it into his lungs. Beauty, weightless and useless and the only thing he knows he loves, truly loves. He thinks of his Auntie. He thinks of her small gold tooth, the only one he has left, now a cufflink that he'll wear when he conducts Sunday's concert. And he brings his orchestra crashing down, bomb after bomb after bomb, until they are all standing, spent and wobbly, together and bleeding in the center of a rubbled crater.

He gives them a moment of peace.

"Now that," he shouts, "is *music!*"

There is a wave of relieved laughter. They sit easier in their chairs now, easier but no less alert.

"What you felt, the beast that swallowed you all and spat you back out, that is the great big bloody point of all this. If you learn nothing else from this bizarre and awkward experience—this gathering of strangers to blow into horns and pluck catgut—remember that you have the power to feel that. The power to create that. With your hands. Your breath. You are gods, children, and you can make war."

Rabbit's hair is a mess, his skin pale except for two spots of pink high in his cheeks. He looks as though he's been run over.

"Look at Hatmaker here. The boy is wasted." Fisher laughs. "Been to hell and back, have you?"

Rabbit nods. "We can make other things, too," he murmurs. "Not just war." He flicks his eyes up in the tiniest of challenges.

Fisher feels it like a barb hooked in his heart.

"Today all we're practicing is war," he says, the words sticky in his throat. "And later, sex, when we get back to our Debussy. From the top, basses. Bassoons. Describe the field of battle for us."

It is a far, far better rehearsal than yesterday's, all according to plan. Fisher has tried this tactic at other festivals—forcing these wunderkinder to recalibrate themselves, to open up to the reality of their own experience by being a complete and utter asshole to them—but the children at Statewide are the hardest nuts he's ever had to crack. The most in need of reprogramming. Which makes sense, when he thinks about it. When he thinks of himself, even younger than these kids fanned in arcs of chairs and music stands before him. *He* was the original dancing bear and organ grinder's monkey rolled into one. Music, the piano—everything had come easily, naturally. His gifts were a birthright he had never realized could be revoked until they were gone. Perhaps he would never have fallen in love with music so deeply if it had never been taken from him; would eighty-eight keys live in his dreams if they filled his waking hours? Nothing, after all, is more powerful than a love unrequited.

He thinks of the Unavailable redhead, of how she gave him music, if only for a moment, with her beautiful, whole hands. He cannot wait for rehearsal to end. He cannot wait to learn what other powers her hands might hold.

Rabbit is washing his hands when he sees, reflected in the bathroom mirror, a boy exiting one of the stalls carrying a French horn. Rabbit blinks. Yes, he is actually watching a boy exit a bathroom stall carrying a big gold horn. The boy steps up to the sink beside Rabbit, tucks the horn under one arm, and washes and dries his hands without a word.

If only that were the weirdest thing happening at Statewide.

Rabbit heads back to the auditorium, where the others are retaking their seats after a mid-morning break. Fisher Brodie is obviously mentally unbalanced, but there is something half magical about his lunacy. Again today, Brodie is playing with them as much as he is conducting—but he *is* conducting, and they, the orchestra, are *playing*. They played the *shit* out of that Holst piece. From the first read-through and spot rehearsals to a full performance right before break, every single time, Rabbit felt the hair on the back of his arms and neck shiver. His heart thumped. He had always identified himself as a pacifist (save for that one *fagott*-inspired fistfight), but this morning Rabbit wanted to tear someone's arms off. He wanted to throw on a breastplate and a kilt, smear blue paint down half his face, grab a sword—no, an ax—and run full tilt across a battlefield and fucking chop someone's head off.

Rabbit feels deeply weird, to say the least, about all of this.

About *all* of this. About his sister (his bulimic, manic sister?) and her missing (dead?) roommate, and the woman in the elevator, and Pete Moretti, the Tenor. He wishes his father were here. No—actually—no, he does not wish his father, or his mother, or anyone else who knows him is here, because here is the place where he might, just might, be brave and stupid and lit with hormones enough to kiss Pete. To kiss a boy. To feel it, finally.

All of this is running through his head—*kiss, Pete, kilt, ax, chop, Alice, death*—as he takes his seat, adjusting the leather strap hooked to Beatrice that he sits on. He sucks on his double reed. Kimmy sits down beside him with a toothy smile.

Brodie, looming above from the podium, cups his hands around his mouth and shouts to Rabbit, "Hatmaker! How would you like to be our new soloist?"

Rabbit's heart stops.

"Our fickle friend, Miss First-Chair Flute, didn't show up today. Her loss. Our gain." Brodie picks up a sheaf of paper and waves it in the air. "I thought she might still be in a snit today. You know how flighty first-chair flutes are. So I took the liberty of transcribing the solos in *Afternoon of a Faun* into bass and tenor clef for bassoon."

Rabbit feels every eye in the orchestra on him, and more than a few friendly smiles. They want him to do this. They want him to take the bait, show Brodie up. Does Brodie want that too? Or is he setting him up to fail, teaching Rabbit a lesson for his defiance yesterday?

"Stravinsky believed in the power of your tenor clef, Hatmaker. I think it's time we convinced Debussy. Pass this back, love, thanks." Fisher sends the music back through the orchestra.

Rabbit is floating somewhere above the stage, looking down on himself. Floating-Rabbit half wants him to do it, just *do it*—play the hell out of the piece, punch someone in the face, and then go find Pete and make out with him. The Rabbit sitting on the stage, however, holding his bassoon upright in one trembling, sweating hand, is grasping what it means to be terrified beyond the capacity for rational thought. He takes the music when it's handed back by the second-chair flute, who looks relieved.

Brodie's hand is neat and crisp. The notes are evenly round, the stems delicate. The staffs, clefs, and time signatures are calligraphic.

He can do this.

He cannot *possibly* do this.

"It's just for today, Hatmaker. Just for fun. I'm sure Miss First-Flute Temper Tantrum will come crawling back at some point. The question is, will we let her play?"

Rabbit's mouth opens before he can think.

"She won't be back," he says. "She's dead."

The entire orchestra goes silent. Rabbit feels the beat and then, half a beat later, realizes what he has done.

Whether he believes Alice or not, he's spreading her gospel.

"She's what, Hatmaker? What did you say?" Brodie leans closer, turning one ear toward him.

"I said she's dead," Rabbit repeats, louder.

"That's not funny," Brodie says.

"Why is that the first thing everyone says?" Rabbit's voice cracks. "Of course it's not funny. It's not a joke." And as he says the words, he believes them. He knows his sister. He knows she isn't lying. "She's dead."

"I heard—" A voice breaks behind him, somewhere in low brass.

"You heard what?" presses Brodie.

A blond girl peeks from behind her music stand. "I heard her roommate found her," she says, "and now her roommate's, like, catatonic with shock."

Rabbit frowns.

"I heard that too." A boy in a faded blue polo and pressed khakis—Rabbit can see the creases running from his knees to the tops of his loafers—raises his violin bow instead of his hand. "I heard the ASM is trying to cover it up. That this kind of thing has happened before. Like how at Disney World, they never report it when people die on the rides?"

"No," says Rabbit. "That's not what—"

A little cry goes up and is stifled, which of course has the opposite effect on the rest of the group. The orchestra begins to buzz and hiss, a balloon leaking whispers. Rabbit turns. It's Jennifer—tiny Jennifer Czerny, who was drunk at that stupid dinner with Alice last night. She's balancing her French horn on her lap with one hand and covering her mouth dramatically with the other. "You don't think," she says, her eyes wide, "it has anything to do with the ghost.

The woman who hung herself. The Bellweather Bride? And Rabbit, Rabbit, wasn't Jill your sister's roommate? Oh my God, is your sister—did your sister *find her?*"

Rabbit starts to formulate words, a response of some kind, but Brodie holds his arms out wide and shouts at them, "OI. *OI!*"

The silence is only temporary.

"Everyone *keep*. Your fucking wits about you," Brodie says. "Hatmaker. Answer me. Was the first flute your sister's roommate?"

"Yes."

"Did your sister find her last night?"

"Yes. Hanging from the ceiling. Then, uh—"

"'Uh' what, Hatmaker?"

"Her . . . body." Rabbit swallows. "Sort of . . . disappeared."

The orchestra ripples and Brodie shouts it back to silence.

"Are you, for your own obscure but surely logical-in-your-own-mind reasons, lying to me?"

"No."

"Where is your sister now?"

"In the ballroom. Rehearsing with the chorus."

"Whom did she tell about her roommate?"

"The hotel people. The concierge."

"And what did they do?"

Rabbit swallows. "I don't know," he says. "Called the police."

The orchestra is straining against itself. It wants to burst. It made war all morning and has now been thwarted from the promised release of sex. Brodie can feel it pulling away from him; Rabbit can see it on his face. He feels a little sorry for being the cause of all this, and, improbably, a little sorry he won't get the chance to play that solo after all. It's an incredible piece of music.

"Well, then. Everyone's done what they're supposed to do." He pauses. "What else, Rabbit. I can see you're dying to say something else. If you'll pardon the figure of speech."

"She was—" He clears his throat.

Floating-Rabbit and Rabbit-on-the-stage have merged back into one body. Rabbit, complete, knows he is standing on the edge of something large, already writhing with a life of its own. Bigger than he is, certainly, not remotely about him at all, and yet what happens next is entirely his doing.

"She was murdered," Rabbit says.

Statewide erupts.

13

Dangerous Girls

ASTINGS OVERSLEEPS. HE needed the sleep desperately, he knows this, and yet he's ashamed to have missed his first chance with Viola Fabian. It's ten-thirty in the morning when he finally inspects the glow-in-the-dark hands of his Baby Ben. The woman is probably up and gone, running a conference session or at least attending one. Hastings is unshaven, barely rested, and still wearing yesterday's bow tie, his knees and ankles aching prophetically. He stops by her room and calls her twice but gets no answer. With any luck, the story of the disappearing girl hasn't gotten out of control; with any luck, Hastings will catch her during lunch, in a manner timely enough to still be considered professional.

But his luck has left the building. By eleven-fifteen, when he rolls down to the lobby, the rumor is a living thing. Everybody knows about the dead girl. The kitchen staff, down to the new help brought in specially to work the festival, knows. The chambermaids and the check-in girls and the girls who push the vacuum around the lobby are blazing like firecrackers with every sordid detail. It changes every time Hastings overhears it. The girl was shot. The girl was stabbed. She hanged herself on the showerhead. She hanged herself out the window. She was dragged down the hall and the trail of blood disappeared at a locked door that hadn't been opened in twenty years.

He tells them to remember themselves, that gossip is totally inappropriate. What he really wants to say is *Don't you idiots know where you work? Don't you know every last closet, crack, and crevice of this hotel, and don't you know there is no door like that?*

He is straightening his bow tie with one eye on the clock — everyone will be recessing for lunch shortly — when the concierge phone rings. The woman on the other end doesn't bother introducing herself, but Hastings knows instantly who it is.

Viola Fabian. And she's screaming at him. About what a fool he is, what an incompetent moron he is to let the story spread all over the hotel. Now she wants to talk with the girl responsible, wants an opportunity to tell her, firsthand, what a miserable little shit she is. "Alice, her name is Alice," she says. "I met her yesterday afternoon. I interrupted when she and my daughter were conspiring. She's short. Dark-haired. Find her and *bring her to me.*"

Hastings finds he hasn't the words to respond to that request.

"Are you deaf?"

"Dr. Fabian, I insist — I insist that we meet in the Bellweather's front office. Behind the check-in desk. I'll find Alice and her chaperone and we'll meet there in, say, fifteen minutes."

"Ten." And she hangs up.

Helen Stoller, as always, included a copy of the concert program in the conference materials she sent to Hastings; he finds Alice's name listed under the altos in chorus. He hates to interrupt rehearsal, but he hates more to imagine what will happen if Viola Fabian is kept waiting. Alice knows exactly what she is being called away for. As soon as the door to the ballroom shuts behind them, muffling the excited chattering of the chorus she's left behind, she says, "It's her mother, isn't it? Her mother wants to see me."

Hastings doesn't like this one bit.

The lobby is full of children when they return; the orchestra must have ended its rehearsal early. An impossibly skinny man and a familiar-looking boy are waiting at the concierge desk—familiar because he must be Alice's brother, Hastings realizes.

"Are you Mr. Hastings?" says the tall man. He has an accent, and Hastings remembers Helen's prep packet: he's Fisher Brodie. Conducting the orchestra. Scottish child prodigy who'd destroyed his own career rather spectacularly, according to Helen's usual gossipy annotations. "Master Hatmaker here opened his big bloody mouth and I'd like to direct him in a slightly more responsible direction. We were told you're the man in charge."

"No," Hastings says. "She's coming."

"She's here," says Viola Fabian from behind him.

Hastings asks Sheila, at the front desk, to reach the Hatmakers' chaperone—call her room, stop by any sessions she was scheduled for—and politely invites the Hatmakers, Viola Fabian, and Brodie to step into the office. Viola immediately perches, half standing, against the wide aluminum desk Hastings bought secondhand from the high school when they refurbished their classrooms. Rabbit and Alice jostle together on the old couch, looking down at the floor, and Brodie sits on one of the couch's arms.

Hastings opens a folding chair and sets it by the couch.

No one speaks.

"Are we waiting for someone?" asks Viola.

"The children's chaperone. Sheila's tracking her down."

"I'd rather do this without witnesses." Viola smiles as if she's kidding. "Alice?"

Alice looks up at Viola.

"Do you remember what I said to you yesterday?"

Alice flushes. "You said I was nothing special."

"I did indeed. Nothing special." Viola shrugs comically. "How was I to know you would take that so personally? Or rather, how did my saying that grant you and my daughter the right to be such entitled little brats?" She nods at Fisher. "Oh, it's true, Fisher. When I stopped by my daughter's room during yesterday afternoon's rehearsal, I found her and this Alice. They were clearly planning something, at the time I had no idea—"

"That's not true!" Alice says. Her voice is a squeaky half laugh.

"But you admit you skipped yesterday's rehearsal, that you were in your room with my daughter. You admit we were all there."

"Yeah, but—"

"Alice. Dear girl." Viola taps a red-lacquered fingernail against her mouth. "As I told the police, my daughter is not dead. She is not." She exhales. "Dead."

Alice glares at her.

"Jill is troubled," Viola says. "She's an extraordinary girl, with an extraordinary amount of potential and promise. And pressure. She's difficult. She's dramatic. She *does* this."

"Hangs herself?" Alice says. "Then cuts herself down?"

"Oh, Alice," says Viola. "Shut up."

Alice's face roars with silent indignation. Hastings is beginning to believe her spunk isn't an act at all.

"Jelly is theatrical. She knows how to frighten people. She knows how to frighten me. Which I will ask you to remember: this is between my daughter and myself. Wherever she is, she's laughing at *me*. All of you—Alice especially—just happened to get in the way this time."

"There have been other times?" Brodie asks.

Viola nods. "She disappeared for an entire night in Tokyo, showed up the next morning stinking of Sapporo. I've lost her for hours at a time in New York, in Dallas. London. Boston. Los Angeles. She trashes hotel rooms like a coked-out rock star. Like a Manson. She's ripped up duvets and pillows, and written notes on the wall in sweet-and-sour sauce. 'Do not call police.' 'We have her.' 'You will pay.' Et cetera, et cetera."

"Sounds like a fun girl," Brodie says.

"She's a frustrating girl, Fisher." Hastings catches an odd note in Viola's tone, an overfamiliar note. "I honestly wish I knew how to make her take her life more seriously."

"She *does* take her life seriously," Alice says.

"Does? Not *did*? I thought you said she was dead," Viola says. "Come on, tell us where Jill is hiding. How did it work? Did she tell you this morbid story, or did she give you license to make something up? If the latter, bravo. You've a twisted mind hiding in your pretty little head."

"That isn't what happened. That isn't what I saw," Alice says. "I don't know how to make you—" She looks hard at Hastings, at Brodie, at her brother. "I don't know how to make you believe me."

Viola shrugs again. "You are free to believe me or to believe this girl. You can't believe both." She looks to Fisher. "What are *you* doing here, anyway? I only asked to talk to Alice."

"She isn't the only Hatmaker with a big mouth." Fisher sets his hand on the boy's back. "Her brother just about turned my orchestra inside out by telling everyone your daughter had been murdered."

Viola blinks. Then she throws her head back and laughs. Hastings finds nothing more beautiful than a woman laughing—even now, he can see and hear Jess, her eyes shut but her heart wide open, burning with life. Viola Fabian, no matter how cold she may be, possesses a certain beauty, an evil sort of glamour. When she laughs, for a moment you forget she has her cool and perfect hands wrapped around your throat.

"Jesus!" she says. "I asked the police to respect my family's privacy, but I didn't realize I needed to ask the same of my students."

"I'm not your student," says Alice.

"You're a Statewide student. You *are* my student. And you'll do as I say: you'll keep your mouth shut. You'll stop spreading disgusting rumors that have nothing to do with you."

"Is this the longest she's ever been gone?" It's the first the brother has spoken since the meeting began.

"She's been gone this long, and longer," says Viola. "But she's never missed a concert. Not that *this* concert holds a candle to any of the others she's played." She shakes her head. "I should have known she had some ridiculous plan to humiliate me. She was far too eager to tag along, after Kirk's heart finally gave out and Statewide came crawling to me."

Hastings stiffens. With every word that falls out of Viola's mouth, he dislikes her a little more. She is, as his mother would have said, a piece of work. Listening to her on the other end of the telephone was painful; standing in the same room with her is atrociously uncomfortable. She has blood in her eyes and violence in her heart. If she's correct that her daughter is alive, that this is an elaborate prank designed to hurt Viola, then Hastings can't say he blames her daughter one bit.

"As head of ASM," Viola says, "I could suspend you both from participating in the rest of the festival."

Panic glimmers in the boy's eyes even as icy resolve chills his sister's. Hastings feels ill when he hears her refer to herself as head of the ASM.

"Oh, come on, Viola," Fisher says gently. "Don't be cruel."

Viola grins. Hastings bends toward her in spite of himself.

"Don't give me another reason," she says, and pushes herself off the desk. When she leaves the room, shutting the door behind her, Hastings sways, woozy.

Fisher Brodie stands, sighing. "Word of advice," he tells the Hatmakers. "Keep your wits about you. Go to your rehearsals. Rehearse. Get low and stay low."

"Why does everyone believe her?" Alice says. "She's obviously lying."

"A good lie is only obvious to the person telling it," Fisher says.

"It's not right. Jill is—someone has to find her, we can't just—"

"You really don't know where she is?" asks Fisher.

"No!" Alice stands up. "Screw this. Come on, Rabbit."

Rabbit doesn't move. "I don't want to get kicked out," he says. "I think—I agree with Mr. Brodie. She seems." He licks his lips. "Dangerous."

"She is," says Brodie.

"Yeah?" Alice pushes past Hastings, heading for the door. "I can be dangerous too."

As soon as she's gone, Brodie laughs.

"Sorry," he says, covering his mouth. "I shouldn't laugh. It's just . . . I found that hilarious for some reason."

Hastings looks to Brodie, who looks to the Hatmaker boy, who looks back to Brodie, who looks back at Hastings. Hastings straightens his bow tie.

"In any case," he says, "lunch should be out in the ballroom any minute now. I hope the rest of your stay is . . . pleasant."

They all laugh, even though it isn't funny.

There were three places where Hastings felt most like himself, three places where he knew he belonged. Only one of them remains unchanged: standing behind the concierge desk. The swimming pool on the roof, beneath the beautiful glass dome, where Jess and Caroline used to spend their summer days, was the second. He would visit on his breaks and show up in his trunks after his shift. Jess, always with a book, some hardboiled detective story, double-glassed: sunglasses pushed up into her blond hair and reading glasses on her nose. Caroline would be pruney, exhausted, glowing from her own hard day's work of diving for treasure at the bottom of the pool, but she'd perk up when Hastings turned on the radio. There were speakers in the big potted ferns around the water. Hastings would wade into the shallow end and sing to his daughter, sing inside the echoes of Sam Cooke and Diana Ross and Dusty Springfield. When she'd float up beside him he'd lift her by her middle, she'd brace her foot against his thigh, and Hastings would call on every muscle in his arms, his legs, his entire body to propel his daughter up. He'd fling his rocketship daughter high in the air and she'd laugh until she fell, sucked into a terrific splashdown. Even now, even in November, the lounge silent and the pool full of nothing but water, Hastings visits and remembers what it feels like to be in the right place with the right people.

His third home was Clinton's Kill's Carnegie library, or had been when Rome Cohen was still the town's librarian. Rome and Hastings had been friends for . . . to tell the truth, Hastings had no idea how long he'd known Jerome Cohen. A long time. Too long. Rome was younger than Hastings, though not by much. They had grown up in Clinton's Kill knowing of each other, in the same way that all denizens of a small town are peripherally aware of one another's existence. Hastings had been a lifelong library patron—he had read every title in its mystery and crime section—but it wasn't until Rome began renting a room at the Bellweather from time to time, much later in his life, that the two men became more than generic acquaintances. The room was for entertainment purposes, Rome told Hastings as he tapped his American Express card on the front desk. Really, the room was so Rome had someplace to bring a woman after a date without having to take her to his own house, which was an uninhabitable nest of clutter. Hastings was oddly charmed by Rome's little assignations; they reminded him of the old days of the Bellweather, the days of illicit affairs and three-piece suits, summer flings, passionate trysts.

"What d'you know, Hastings," Rome would say while his date was barely out of earshot. "Who'd a thought a library would attract so much squirrel, huh?"

"You are a gentleman and a scholar" was Hastings's typical reply.

"You should come by! Oh, I know you're spoken for." Rome would grin. "I meant for the books."

And the bourbon, which Rome served in conical white cups he would order in bulk from some discount warehouse, cups you could never set down because of their pointed bottoms—the reason Hastings went home from the library several sheets to the wind more times than he would care to admit. The Carnegie was a beautiful old building, all cool classical stone outside and warm golden wood inside, with glorious tall windows that made him think of church. It had gone up in the early twentieth century, the fruit of Mr. Andrew Carnegie's grant money, when the idea that Clinton's Kill would become something grand seemed beyond dispute. The Bellweather had been built around the same time. Perhaps that's what had kept Hastings so fond of Rome, so loyal to him, despite all his peculiarities; they were men who'd outlived their ages, brothers fixed to the buildings in their blood.

But while Hastings would go down with his ship, Rome chose to jump. He was old enough for Social Security and had a nest egg, and he didn't want anything to do with computers. "They're coming," he told Hastings one night, neatly folding his conical white cup into a flat triangular spear. "The computers are coming and they're going to smother everything that's real."

The computers are here. Hastings has been to the Carnegie since Rome's retirement, but only to check out and return books. Today he has come to do research, and instead of the matte-gray window of the microfiche reader, he is staring into a cool shining television. The bright blue screen bulges slightly out of its square box of off-white plastic, humming weirdly, and if Hastings didn't feel it was of the utmost importance to discover just who is staying in his hotel this weekend, he thinks he would turn around and walk straight out.

"Do you need help, sir?"

The girl—Rome's replacement has only ever been discussed, between the two of them, as "the girl," though she is clearly well past girlhood—smiles pleasantly at him. "Are you looking for a legal document or a newspaper article?"

"Newspapers, please," he says. His hands hover instinctively over the tray of beige keys. He momentarily wonders what happened to his Underwood. It had belonged to his father; he wrote letters to Jess on it, once upon a time. "I'm looking for information about a woman named Viola Fabian."

The girl takes a seat beside Hastings. "Do you know how to double-click, sir?"

"Hastings," he says. "Please, call me Hastings."

She smiles. "Hastings. Place your right hand on this—" She indicates a plastic lump the size and shape of one of the hotel's fancy éclairs. "Have you ever used a mouse? It makes the arrow move on the screen. It's how you talk to the computer." He flinches to see the small white arrow move in tune with his own hand. How odd. How damned odd. "Tap your index finger twice when the arrow is over that icon—" He taps twice. Nothing happens; he's too deliberate, apparently. He taps again. Still too slow. And again, irritated, but this time the icon twitches and the screen goes from blue to white. He blinks.

"Now type the name you're looking for in that box, inside quotation marks," says the girl, who's taken charge of the mouse for him. A vertical line blinks on and off inside a tan rectangle. "This database is called LexisNexis. Right now you're searching literally hundreds of newspapers published around the world. How amazing is that?"

Hastings blinks again. A tiny hourglass spins in the middle of the screen.

"It is rather amazing, I suppose," he says. He would never tell Rome, but the girl is perfectly nice. The screen suddenly fills with lines of text. "Looks like we found a few things," she says. She does something quickly, too quickly, with the mouse, and he hears an even louder humming noise off to his left. She stands.

"The first printouts are free, Mr. Hastings," she says as she hands him several pieces of warm paper. "Let me know if I can help with anything else."

He nods and mutters thank you. He has never needed Rome Cohen and his library bourbon more than he does right now.

Rome hasn't booked a night at the Bellweather in well over a decade. Maybe longer. In retirement, Rome had blossomed into a misanthropic hermit who only ever let one person into his house. Hastings has mixed feelings about having been granted this dubious honor. Sometimes when Hastings visited Rome he felt he ought to bring reinforcements—the police, Sheila, compassionate-looking women at the Buy-Rite next to the gas station—to drag Rome back into the real world before it was too late. Rome would never leave on his own. He knew his house, every square inch, every scrap of information contained on every sheet of paper, every photograph and artifact and piece of junk. It was the only world he knew anymore, the only world he trusted, and Hastings never brought reinforcements because he didn't have the heart to take that away from his friend.

Rome's house was a two-story Victorian not far from the Carnegie, in the center of Clinton's Kill, about a twenty-minute walk from the Bellweather. Hastings is puffing clouds like a smokestack into the crisp November air by the time he raises his hand to the rusted door knocker. He didn't like the sky on his walk over, and it looks worse now. The clouds are too heavy. They've been predicting snow all week, but every forecast has gotten progressively more dire. His knees and ankles, achier now that he's been walking, do not disagree.

"Go away," says Rome, already on the other side of the door.

"It's me."

"I know. Go away."

"I'd like a drink, Rome."

"Who wouldn't."

"Rome, I just want to talk. Something strange is going on at the hotel and I—"

There is a series of clicks and snaps and clacks as Rome unlocks each of the eight deadbolts that run the length of the doorjamb.

"Get in here, putz," says Rome. "Of course something strange is going on at the hotel."

"What do you mean?" Hastings asks as he steps inside, cautiously avoiding three neat stacks of thick gray pharmaceutical manuals.

"Isn't this your annual pubescent orgy?" says Rome, already disappearing into a forest of musty objects. His house has a perpetual odor of wet paper and old coffee grounds. Hastings follows him past a disintegrating lawn chair, its seat stacked high with newspapers touting the inauguration of Ronald Reagan. What must have been Rome's mother's pie rack now displays thirty or more empty Big Gulp cups. A bowling ball bag. Books. Books. More and more books. Bloated, ruffled paperbacks and ancient hardcovers with split spines and textbooks with skewed covers, no covers, ripped covers.

Rome's trail ends in the dining room. At least, Hastings thinks it was the dining room, from what he remembers of the house in earlier, less cluttered years. A large wooden table, big enough to seat twelve or more, is covered with copy paper boxes and stacks of glossy magazines, save for one bald corner—the only open surface in the house, Hastings thinks. Rome points to a white wooden stool.

"Have a seat. I'd offer you that drink, but I'm not sharing what's left of the bourbon."

Rome's eyeglasses, which he broke years ago but never got repaired, are held together on the bridge with a piece of clear tape. He takes them off and polishes them on the edge of his cardigan.

"It's beyond teenagers running amok," Hastings says. "It's a woman."

"Isn't it always."

"Doug Kirk had a heart attack a few weeks ago. So this woman is subbing for him, running the festival this year, and she's—" Hastings sits on the stool and winces. His knees are swollen now, tender. "She's unlike anyone I've ever met, Rome."

"Describe. Don't leave anything out."

"Well." He loosens his bow tie. "She's probably in her fifties, early to mid. Striking. Long white hair. Lovely features—she's this side of gorgeous. But she's terribly unprofessional. Cruel. I watched her verbally attack a young girl, a student. The girl probably wasn't innocent, but still, you don't expect that kind of behavior in an arts administrator. When you're in a room with her, it feels smaller. You're drawn to her, you *must* pay attention to her. You want her to pay attention to *you,* and at the same time you're afraid to attract her notice. I've spent a grand total of thirty minutes in her presence, maybe less, and I can't stop worrying about her. She doesn't seem entirely human."

Rome rubs his chin.

"I came down here to look her up at the library, see what I could find. If I have a reason to be worried she's sleeping under my roof." Hastings flutters the handful of papers he received from the girl. "It's research by pushbutton these days. No more spooling, no more heaving great dusty volumes of crumbling newspaper around. Just 'double-click' and print." He shakes his head.

"So *that's* what you're doing down here," says Rome. "Fraternizing with the usurper."

"She's not the usurper, Rome. She was quite nice. And that's not the only reason I came. It's going to snow tonight; you know my standing offer."

Rome props his elbow on a pile of magazines. "You honestly think we'll be safer stuck in a hotel infested with hormonal morons?

I should offer to let you stay *here,* Hastings." He snorts. "Though I've half a mind to take you up on it this time."

Hastings blinks. "Are you serious?"

"You offered." Rome pushes his mangled glasses up his nose. "All these years, were you kidding? Did I just call your bluff?"

"You're going to leave your house? You, Rome? When was the last time you walked thirty feet from your door, let alone half a mile through town?"

"We can take the ATV. I keep it gassed up in case the Rapture comes." Rome snorts again. "That was sarcasm. But I do keep it gassed."

"Does it have a sidecar?" Hastings does not know what to make of this. He offered and he meant it, every time; it was due diligence to at least ask. Much as it occasionally depressed him, Jerome Cohen was, next to Jess, his oldest friend. His only friend. It was right to save him from being buried alive in his tomb of a house during a snowstorm, but he never, ever expected Rome to agree to it. Rome was the most dependable, unchanging, unmovable stone in his life, and if Rome is motivated to act, something is wrong. Something very queer is happening.

"Why, Rome? I'm not trying to discourage you, I'm legitimately curious."

"Because you're my friend and I know you're disappointed Doug Kirk's not here." Rome pushes at the taped bridge of his glasses and grins. "And because of that lady. Your mysterious research subject. I want to meet her."

"Why?"

"She sounds like a bona fide psychopath."

At the check-in desk, Sheila, ever the professional, doesn't blink at the sight of Jerome Cohen. She barely lets on that he's darkening the lobby, has set a ragged cardboard box of toiletries and clothes on the carpet. The only way to describe him, physically, is to say he is a dumpy little man, unpleasant and frayed, his meanness solidified by the compression of time. Mostly forehead, with white caterpillar eyebrows. He points a thumb backward at the front doors.

"I parked around the side. Hastings told me I could."

"He can stay with me," Hastings says, and Sheila cocks her head. "I'll get a cot from housekeeping." He waves his hand dismissively to say, *I know. Leave him to me.*

"Sure," she says, brows pulled together in gentle concern. Sheila is such a good kid. She started working at the Bellweather part-time in high school and came on full-time after her graduation last spring. Much as he appreciates her service to the hotel and to him, Hastings knows she deserves a life elsewhere. A life of fresh air beyond the confines of this moldy old hotel. This moldy old hotel that he loves, but that is collapsing around their ears. Who knows how many more years the Bellweather has in her. How many spring floods along the basement tunnels, how many summer thunder-storms and fall winds against the rattly windowpanes. And snow-storms — Hastings feels a flutter near his sternum. Now they're say-ing the storm is going to dump several feet of snow from Syracuse to Albany down toward the city, blanketing the Catskills. The roof has passed inspection, but Hastings can't help but worry about the weight of all that crystallized water. God forbid a warm spell follows the storm, but it could; it's early, not yet Thanksgiving. The glass dome over the swimming pool is still original.

"You're a peach, Sheila," he says, smiling at her. "I'll get set-tled and be back in a while. Call me if there are any other Statewide fires."

She frowns slightly but nods.

"She's a cutie," Rome says as he drops his box on Hastings's bed. "Didn't her mom used to work here? She looks familiar."

"Not her mother, her aunt. Don't put that disgusting box on my bed." Hastings catches his reflection in the mirror on the back of his door. Going over to Rome's always leaves him disheveled and dusty. He brushes off his sleeves and straightens his bow tie. Neat-ens his hair.

"So this is what it's like outside my house. Huh. Looks the same." Rome nudges his glasses and leans in close to Hastings's wall of crime clippings. "Same violence. Same nutjobs. Like I never left."

Hastings cannot argue.

"So where is she?" Rome asks. "Where's the mystery psycho?"

"I don't know."

"Yes, you do. You went to her room this morning."

"I know where her *room* is, Rome, but I don't know where *she* is. There are conference sessions going on all over the hotel. She's probably at one of them. Rome." Hastings squints. "Look at you. You're filthy."

"Haven't seen my shower since 1994. Well, I've seen it, but it's been full of home repair manuals. Are you asking me to bathe? Do I offend your delicate sensibilities?"

"Don't use my razor."

Rome shuts the bathroom door and turns on the taps. In a moment, Hastings hears him shrieking that he's *melting, meeeeeeelting!* Rome hasn't acted this spry, this jokey, in years. It worries Hastings. It feels slightly desperate, as though Rome's brain is sparking with nervous energy. Maybe he should have let Sheila book him his own room after all.

Frowning, Hastings considers the cardboard box that holds Rome's worldly possessions—at least those required for a few nights' stay, which Rome did not remove from his bed as requested. He drops the box on the floor and kicks it aside.

He takes the papers the girl gave him out of his coat pocket and smoothes them flat on his desk. The first article is from the *San Francisco Chronicle*—so she wasn't kidding when she said she was searching newspapers all over the country. He knows that this ability ought to fill him with awe, with wonder, but it makes him feel terribly small in a terribly large world.

The date of the article makes him feel even smaller, and older: 1969. A single article hidden in thirty years of news, and that computer found it in thirty seconds.

Hastings clears his throat and murmurs as he reads. "'Body of Local Man Found, Missing Since Concert. The body of Kevin Montrose, twenty-five, was discovered in Golden Gate Park on December twelfth by a park-goer's dog. Mr. Montrose appears to have sustained a head wound after a fall. His fiancée, Alison Bean, twenty-four, reported him missing on December second when he did not meet her following the concert as planned.' Graduate student at the San Francisco Conservatory of Music ... here we go: 'Montrose was last seen performing at a concert in the park the night of his disappearance. Viola Fabian, twenty-three, who accompanied the deceased on piano, was the last to see him alive. Ms. Fabian told investigators that Montrose asked her to deliver his trumpet to his fiancée, and that he would follow shortly. He was not seen again.'"

He looks up at his wall of news clippings. They are all sordid tales of victims, of crime scenes and criminals, of confessions and trials and technicalities. Yet they share an essential DNA, a circumstantial gravity—of course it was the boyfriend, of course it was the boss—and Hastings has trained his gut to recognize the signs. He knows that this story of Kevin Montrose, or rather, the story of his death and discovery, is the prologue to a longer one. So where is the rest? Was Viola ever seriously questioned? She must have been if she was truly the last to see him alive. The article reports that the police have not ruled out foul play, that the investigation is ongoing. Or was, thirty years ago.

Barbara Stanwyck all but winks at him from his calendar. *You know what that means.*

Whatever happened, she got away with it.

14

Big Dance Number

Bunny boy, *psst.*"

Pete Moretti the Tenor is standing on the other side of the dinner buffet from Rabbit, and he is talking to Rabbit, smiling at Rabbit—in fact, it appears as though Pete Moretti has *cut the line* in order to be standing directly across from Rabbit. They're reaching for the same tongs to grab a slice of grayish roast beef.

"What's your real name, by the way?"

"Rabbit." He feels himself blushing in the steam rising off the warming pan.

Pete laughs. "No, your *real* name."

Rabbit's face blushes brighter. "Bert. Bertram," he says.

"My middle name's Ernest. If it makes you feel any better." Pete flops a lump of mashed potatoes on his plate. "Want?" he says, and drops a scoop on Rabbit's plate.

"Thanks."

"Gravy?"

Rabbit nods and Pete smashes a dent in his mashed potatoes with the gravy ladle. "My *nonna* taught me this," Pete says. "She called it making lakes."

"Thanks," Rabbit repeats. Why oh why can't he think of anything witty to say? Why can't he be easy? Why can't he be cool? He grins moronically because he knows the answer to all these questions: he is too happy, he is too excited. This is too awesome to even pretend to be cool.

"What are you doing later, Bert?" Pete tosses him a roll. It hits Rabbit's plate and bounces into his mashed potatoes.

"Nothing yet," Rabbit says, "Ernie."

An easy smile slides across Pete's face and every one of Rabbit's internal organs turns to slush.

"Room ten-thirty-three. The Boys from Buffalo are throwing a party in honor of the dearly departed Jill Faccelli. It was going to be a search party, but who are we kidding, right? It's an Irish wake. Since you and your sister were so close to her, we'd love you to be the guests of honor."

"Yeah," says Rabbit. "Yeah, that would be fun." His mouth is saying the words while his brain is thinking that using Jill's disappearance, her theoretical death, as an excuse to get tanked is in horrendously poor taste. Then his heart is feeling Pete Moretti tap his elbow. His heart is hearing Pete say he'll see Bert later, whenever he wants to come up, they'll be there from eight on.

Alice goes nuts. Rabbit knew she wouldn't take the invitation or the party in the spirit it was intended; hell, he had a hard time himself, which is why he didn't tell her until they were back in his room after dinner. Even so, he had never expected her reaction to be so violent. She screams at him—no words, no accusations, just a long, high wail that terrifies Rabbit's roommate, Daniel (second-chair clarinet, concert band), who was already less than enthused that a third party would be sleeping on their floor for the remainder of the weekend.

"I'm going to take a shower," Dan says. Rabbit hears him lock the bathroom door from inside.

"How can you even . . . Rabbit, what's the matter with you? What those idiots are doing tonight is *gross*. And you want to be a part of it?" She takes hold of his arms and sits them both down on his bed. "I thought you believed me. I thought it meant something to you that a girl is dead. Now you want to dance on her grave? Is this 'getting low and staying low'? Is this how you pay your respects to a—a lost, sad girl, a girl you didn't even know—by drinking warm Coors? Making out with some skanky band geek? I mean, you went to a Statewide party last night, you know what they're all about."

The defiance Rabbit felt at dinner yesterday, the urge to tell his sister to take a flying leap, makes him sit up straighter. "You don't have to come," he says. "I'm not holding a gun to your head."

Alice crosses her arms. "I'm coming and you can't stop me. I'm going to remind them what assholes they're being."

"Don't you dare, Alice."

He is angry with her. Not just defiant, *angry*. Whatever happened to Jill, they can't *do* anything about it, so why shouldn't they enjoy themselves? For what purpose would his sister even *want* to go, if she's so morally opposed to it? Other than the same purpose Alice is always serving: her own. The constant desire to be the center of attention, the most important girl in the room.

Alice's eyes cloud. "Rabbit," she says softly, "what's going on? Why are you acting like—"

"Like what? Like how am I acting?"

"Like someone else," Alice says.

Because I am in love with a boy who might like me back, he thinks. *Because my heart is running the show today.* "I'm only me, Alice," he says. "If you're coming, let's go."

The Boys from Buffalo—or the BFB, as their matching homemade T-shirts proclaim—are already drunk when Alice and Rabbit reach room 1033: drunk and beatboxing, that deadliest of combinations. They are singing, harmonizing sloppily to "Groove Is in the Heart," which is cranked on a stereo in one of two suites connected by an adjoining door. It's barely nine and standing room only. It's going to be the longest night of Alice's life.

Well. Considering last night, maybe the second-longest night.

Someone hands her a beer—Coors Light, what else?—and Alice hands it off to her brother. Rabbit's head is nodding to the beat. He's grinning. He looks happier than Alice can remember seeing him in a long time, and she feels sick. This party is sick, these people are sick. The world is sick. When another beer is passed in her direction, Alice keeps it for herself.

She recognizes faces. Harrison Map, Violet, and Jennifer Whatever, from dinner yesterday, are perched on the heater that runs the length of the window, knees drawn to their chins. They're throwing their heads back and laughing wildly, and when they see Rabbit they wave him over. He joins them without a second's hesitation. When she sees one of the Buffalo boys, the gorgeous dark-haired tenor who was singing lead when they showed up at dinner yesterday, Alice squeezes her eyes shut. That moment was a million years ago. The Alice who saw that gorgeous boy is a changed girl.

Is what she feels or looks like important? Will she accomplish anything worthwhile before she dies? For she'll die just as surely as these other people, these strangers drinking Coors and rubbing up against each other, whipping themselves to a froth. She presses her back to the wall beneath the smoke detector and drinks her beer. *Look at all of us,* she thinks. *All of us singers and actors and musicians, all of us dreamers. All our lives, each of us hearing the same things: you're so bright, you've got such potential.* That's what she feels in this room — a dense, choking fog of human potential. It fills her nose and stings her eyes.

All we need is a spark.

The gorgeous tenor crosses to the window and joins the conversation with her brother and the kids from dinner. Through the milling crowd, Alice watches them. Violet is smiling; she is also gorgeous, Alice thinks. Alice finishes her beer and, like magic, another appears in her hand. These college boys sure know how to host.

Her brother is positively glowing, his cheeks pinked by beer. She loves her brother Rabbit — her brother Bertram. Bert, the good twin. The moral twin, the kind, quiet, smart twin, who's changing in front of her. She can't allow Bert to be compromised by this sick, perverted world. Alice needs him to stay Rabbit, needs to remind him that he matters to her. That there is such a thing as good, that Rabbit is good, that she'll never give up on good.

The song on the stereo in the next room flicks her head back like it's a silver Zippo.

"Hey, Rabbit!" she shouts. "Listen!"

The din of the party swallows her voice. She shoves her way to the window. Her brother is talking to the tenor when Alice grabs his arm and hisses in his ear, "Rabbit, listen to the song! Listen to what it is!"

"What?" he says.

"Oh, come on, you still know the dance. I know you do." Alice spreads her arms and backs up, clearing a small space. "We only spent an entire summer learning it."

She feels the tenor's eyes on her. She feels Rabbit's eyes, and Harrison's and Violet's and Jennifer's.

"Whitney Houston?" the tenor says. "When did this turn into my little sister's sleepover?"

"Rabbit," says Alice, "get *over* here." She box-steps and makes a vine to her right. There are overhead hand claps. A spin and a head tilt. A shoulder shrug and a shimmy. She closes her eyes and re-members dancing with her brother in the den, in front of the stereo. She'd begged and begged her mother to buy it for her, even though her birthday was a long way off, and then one Saturday night, after a particularly grueling week of doing all her regular chores *plus* wa-tering the flowers and the lawn, *Whitney* was waiting on her pillow. Listening to the cassette brought on a sensation of intense physi-cal joy that ran from her ears to her feet to her butt to the tips of her fingers. It *made* her dance. She had choreography for every song, but the steps for "I Wanna Dance with Somebody," her favorite by a mile, came to her on a wave of divine inspiration. The funny thing was, unlike almost anything else she ever did with her brother, she hadn't had to rope Rabbit in against his will. He'd been watching, interested, drawing a little closer with every passing minute. She fi-nally held out her hand to him.

"You've seen it enough. You must know it by now."

"I do," he said, and smiled at her.

He still does. He knows. Alice knows he knows.

Of *course* Rabbit knows. Of *course* he remembers every kick, every hip check, every spin his sister choreographed to Whitney Houston the summer they were seven, but there is no way in hell he is going to dance with her.

Not here. Not when he's seventeen, drinking in a room full of strangers. Not in front of Pete. Not when she's ground this party to a halt, when all eyes, as always, are on her. Alice looks at him. She's singing, wants to feel the *heat* with somebody. When she sings she can't fake it, can't hide herself, and he can see in her eyes that she's heartbroken, though he can't imagine what she could possibly be heartbroken about.

She hardly knew Jill. And Jill is—Jill can't *really* be dead.

The mood is changing. What was once a stand-around-and-drink party is beginning to jostle itself. Several girls behind his sister, watching her steps, have begun to copy her, and pockets of rhythmic swaying have broken out. Another Buffalo boy, dark, with a high little beer belly straining against his blue BFB T-shirt, appears beside Pete.

"Never fails," Rabbit overhears him say. "Want to get girls dancing? Play the first songs they ever loved."

"Shameless," Pete says. "But brilliant."

Rabbit tracks Pete's gaze to a short girl with her hands over her head, swinging her head lazily from side to side. She's a mass of hair, her face completely obscured, all bright blond waves and breasts.

Pete leans over to Rabbit and says, "She was looking over here. I think she was looking at you."

Rabbit's entire world slants. He nods vaguely and takes a slug of beer.

"I Wanna Dance with Somebody" comes to an end and something else, equally dance-riot-inciting, begins. Alice gives one final head flick, hair swinging, and deflates, exhausted. Defeated. She rubs her eyes. "Have fun," she tells Rabbit, and disappears into the dancing crowd.

Unlike last night, Rabbit heeds his natural impulse to go after his sister. He catches up to her by the door and taps her shoulder. When she turns, she doesn't look like herself. She looks like—Rabbit almost laughs, because the first thing he thinks is that she looks like their mother.

"Here's the, uh." Rabbit digs into his pocket. "My key, Alice."

Alice's fist closes over his room key. She looks up at her brother.

"Be good," she says. Then she does something she hasn't done in years. She pops up on her toes to kiss him on the forehead.

She leaves, shutting the door behind her.

She is so clearly, genuinely sad that Rabbit, good Rabbit, decides to follow her back to his room. To ask her. To talk to her.

Pete Moretti appears out of nowhere.

"I like her," Pete says. "She's perky." He raises his eyebrows. "Think next time you might introduce me?"

"I'm. I have to go," Rabbit says. He reaches for the doorknob.

"Me too. It's getting way too VH1 *Big 80's* in here for me." Pete crosses in front and opens the door for him. "Come on, my room's across the way."

Rabbit, if he had whiskers, would be twitching like mad. He feels his pulse throb in his temples. The hallway is mostly empty. He's surprised how well the noise of the party is muffled when the suite doors are shut. You could do anything in these rooms, these old, probably lead-lined rooms—play the drums, have crazy wild animal sex, shoot someone—and not a sound would escape.

Pete opens a door farther down the hall. "You smoke?" he asks. Rabbit shakes his head. "Well, you do now," says Pete.

His room looks exactly like Rabbit's. Two brown beds, fusty carpet, an ancient rabbit-eared television, and thick dark drapes. Rabbit's every molecule is alive. He has no clue what to expect, what happens next. Pete waves him into the bathroom, where he's already opened a small transom window, and once Rabbit is inside, Pete stuffs several towels in the crack of the door.

"I've been dying for this for hours," Pete says. "These traveling things stress me out. I miss sleeping in my own bed." Rabbit has seen enough movies to know that what Pete tips out of a metal Band-Aid box is a joint. He sniffs. Smoke makes him sneeze. "But they're footing the bill, right? Pretty nice of the state to put us up in this shitbox of a hotel just in time for a huge snowstorm."

This is peer pressure! At long last, Rabbit is experiencing one of those pivotal moments they warned him about in elementary school. He smiles, drunk on the adventure unfolding in this yellowed bathroom, because he is absolutely going to succumb to this particular peer's pressure. Pete lights the joint and inhales as he continues to talk. "I shouldn't complain. I mean, what else would I be doing this weekend? Going to a few parties. Smoking. Drinking. Might as well do it here instead of Buffalo for a little variety. If I were in Buffalo, I'd be studying for something or . . . think I have a paper to write. Art history." A cloud of blue-white smoke floats from between his lips. "You know how funny art history is, Bert? It's like, here's a stick man some French caveman drew on a wall. And here's a urinal some guy signed. Let's look at pictures in a dark lecture hall until we fall asleep." He passes the joint to Rabbit, cool as can be, and then kind of wrecks it when he says, "You know what to do?"

"I think so," Rabbit says. He holds the joint between his dry lips and slowly, gently opens his lungs.

His body contracts. First he coughs, throat scalded. He drops the joint on the bathroom floor and sneezes six times in quick succession, high-pitched, fussy little honks, the likes of which never failed to send his sister into paroxysms of glee.

It has roughly the same effect on Pete. He doubles over, holding his stomach, and slides down the front of the vanity to pick up the smoldering joint. "Are you allergic or something?"

"Smoke. Makes me sneeze." Rabbit snuffles, mortified. His head feels tight and balloony, but he can't tell if it's from the pot or the sneezing or the embarrassment or this guy standing not three feet from him. He is so confused by him. It *feels* as though Pete is interested. It *feels* as though he likes Rabbit. But what was that comment about the blond girl?

"I didn't notice the girl," Rabbit says. His brain feels slurry. "I don't ever notice girls."

"I did," says Pete. He inhales again and passes the joint back. "Try again?"

Rabbit tries again. It's awful, but at least this time he doesn't sneeze. When he exhales his eyes fill with tears and his shoulders loosen. "I thought you," he swallows. His tongue is wrong. "I thought you noticed me."

Pete doesn't respond for a while. They both lean against the vanity.

"I did," says Pete.

"You noticed me or you noticed the girl?" Rabbit rubs his nose.

"Can't I notice you both?" Pete turns, smiling. Rabbit feels the smile but doesn't return it. A strange, sharp sensation is beginning to squeeze his body. It's not the worst feeling in the world, but it isn't exactly pleasant either. He sits up straighter. Blinks. Sniffs. Suddenly his hands and arms and feet need to move. Have to move. Must move.

"Where's your roommate? Do you have a roommate?" Rabbit asks. "Is he coming back? When are you expecting him? Did you hear that?"

Pete sighs. Twin plumes cascade from his nostrils.

"Should've known," he mutters.

"No, really," says Rabbit. He stands up. The bathroom is too small. He paces anyway. "You don't hear that? I hear—it's like a little shuffle. Like *shuuuuurrrrrrffff*. Like the sound a door makes when it passes over carpet. You really don't hear that?" Shit shit shit shit shit. This is not what Rabbit wants to be doing, this is not what Rabbit wants to be feeling, but this *is* what he's doing and feeling, and Pete thinks he's a paranoid moron and maybe he is, maybe he's a moron but maybe he's right, maybe Pete's roommate is outside the door and will catch them and will wonder what the hell is going on, and if Rabbit has learned anything at all at Statewide, it's that everyone is watching him. Everyone knows who he is. And there are no such things as secrets.

"I have to go," he says.

"Okay." Pete sighs. "So go."

Rabbit kicks the towels away from the bathroom door. Pete's roommate is not outside in the room, they're alone. "See?" says Pete, suddenly close. "We. Are. Alone." His arms wrap around Rabbit from behind, around his middle, and it feels—Rabbit smiles—it feels good. "Unless you want to call your sister," Pete says, and Rabbit yanks himself away as Pete begins to laugh at him. It was probably a joke, it has to be a joke, but Rabbit runs.

-to-God, clinical sociopath. Look how she works the room. [char]arming. Magnetic. You pay attention to her. You can't *not* pay at-[char]ntion to her. Though she'd just as soon brain you with a shovel as [t]ake your hand." He shrugs again. "Or so I've heard. And she was [yo]ur *teacher,* you say? What was it she taught you?"

Natalie looks into her empty drink. "That I'm not any good," she [sa]ys.

"At what, darts? Skittles? Playing the washtub?"

"Fisher Brodie." God, but Fisher loves the sound of his name on [h]er tongue. She rolls the *r* in Brodie. "What do you know about her [d]aughter? Anything?"

Fisher sits on the stool beside her. "Flautist. First chair, orches-[t]ra. My orchestra, that's what I'm here conducting. She made a fuss [y]esterday, and today she didn't show. Supposed to have killed her-[s]elf. Hanged." He points up. "From the ceiling."

"That's a hell of a prank."

"Viola's a hell of a woman to have for a mother."

"Or a lover. What did *you* learn from her?" Their hips are touch-ing, one stool next to the other. He leans into her and Natalie presses back.

"To sleep with one eye open," he says.

"Valuable." Natalie finishes her drink. "Still, the world would be a better place without her." Her voice catches.

"Let's not talk about Viola Fabian," says Fisher. "If we eat din-ner with her, we'll be talking about nothing but. Let's talk about you, Natalie."

"You never told me what happened to your hand."

"Oh, it's not that thrilling a tale," he says.

"Why don't I believe you?" She leans closer. "Let's have another look."

Fisher holds up his right hand, thumb and index finger splayed. He turns it in midair so she can examine each side, and spreads the left to compare the two. His hands are steady, fingers slender, palms soft and lined. The backs are lightly freckled. The nails are neat, even tiles, and the tips are round and pink. He keeps his hands as

The elevator, a funhouse of blinky, twitchy Rabbits reflected in its mirrors, does nothing to ease his paranoia. He's shaking by the time he gets to his room on the sixth floor. He just wants to be in-side, curled into a ball, where he can sleep this shit off and get his brain back together.

"Alice!" he says. "Alice, open up!" He knocks. "Dan?" He knocks again, louder. With both hands. There is no response. Rabbit is ter-rified, alone and terrified, his heart higher in his chest than it has any anatomical right to be. The only thing he can think to do, the only thing that makes sense, is to sit down in front of his door. To wait right here, on the carpet, and not move, because eventually his roommate or his sister will come back and let him in and right now there is nowhere else he is meant to be.

15

Surprises

FISHER ENTERS THE hotel bar at twenty past five, grievously in need of a drink and a redhead. There are a handful of people clustered around the high-top tables and the bedraggled plush barstools. They look a little bored, a little lost; they have paunches and tired eyes, and when they talk, they talk with their hands. Music educators, always conducting. The bar itself is old and beautiful, wood burnished by hundreds of thousands of glasses and napkins and elbows. Is she here? She must be; she should be. Where is she?

Viola is at his side before he can blink.

"Fisher," she says. Her grin is tight. "I'm so sorry you got involved in my daughter's ridiculous bullshit. Let me make it up to you." Her fingers press into his forearm as she leans close. "I want to introduce you to someone I'm certain you'll enjoy."

It's her. It's his redhead, his new Unavailable, suddenly in front of him on a seat at the bar, hunched over a double old-fashioned that she's drained of everything but ice.

"Natalie," Viola says, and Fisher's heart pings at the revelation of her name. "I'd like you to meet Fisher Brodie. Old friend of mine."

Fisher feels his face smile. He hears her voice, sees her lips part and close again over the word "hello." He puts his insubstantial

right hand into hers and squeezes instead of sha[king]. [She] says, leaning in. "*Natalie.* How do you two—?"

"Natalie is a former student of mine. One of my [best.]" Viola smiles and places a hand on Natalie's back. [Is it imag]ination that Natalie's spine jerks up straighter. "Fi[sher and I have] been meeting on and off for years at things like t[his.] Conferences. Festivals."

Fisher's awareness may have been compromised [by the odd]ness of this unexpected pairing, but still, he notices [the room] has quieted. He can hear Viola too clearly. People a[re trying to] catch what she says. Viola must notice it too, because [she lowers her] voice and clears her throat.

"Excuse me for a moment." She turns to address t[he] crowd of adult conference attendees. "Everyone, ma[y I have your] attention?" Even from the back, Viola is commanding[. Her shoul]ders say *Listen to me, I am talking.* "I'm sure many of yo[u have heard] the rumors, the spooky stories making their way arou[nd] today. I cannot stress enough the importance of getti[ng this] straight. If any of your students speak of this to you, plea[se tell them] the truth. My daughter, Jill Faccelli, played a prank on m[e.] Just a prank."

This information has an immediate and puzzling effe[ct on Nata]lie. She stiffens, eyes widening. Fisher stands beside he[r] and she presses against him for balance.

Viola laughs low. "She's a bit of a handful. Not unlike he[r mother.] Now enjoy your cocktails. I'll be coming through the cro[wd." She] turns back to Natalie and Fisher. "Have dinner with me?" [ ] "I'd love to catch up with you both."

As soon as Viola has drawn safely away to speak with ot[her peo]ple, Fisher leans close to Natalie's ear. "How do you rea[lly know] her?"

"Like she said, she was my teacher," Natalie says. "How [do you] know her?"

"Casually," Fisher says, shrugging his shoulders.

"So you've slept with her."

Fisher smiles. "I think she's a sociopath, you know. A real[ ]

trim and tidy as he can, considering they are a constant reminder of what he's lost, and that they are just so damned ugly.

She examines them, her fingertips cool and dry against his skin. She turns them over. Bends them back and forth at the wrists, straightens and extends one finger at a time. Then she takes both his hands and presses them against her own, palm to palm. She threads her fingers between his, wrapping them over the top of his stumps, and squeezes.

"Beautiful," she says.

Fisher exhales slowly and Natalie smiles.

They talk of nothing but Viola Fabian at dinner. What Viola's been doing with her life. The jobs she's had, the concerts she's played, the prizes she's won, and the people she's met. She never once mentions her daughter, and everyone else at the table—besides Natalie and Fisher, there's an assortment of mousy teachers and turtley conductors from around the state—is too engrossed in her life story (or far too timid) to broach the subject. If Natalie weren't there, Fisher would press the point. But Natalie *is* there, and for the bulk of the meal, Fisher is delightfully distracted by the presence of Natalie's foot exploring his own like a nosy terrier.

From the waist up, arms casually resting on the table, Natalie is silent. Grave, even. Her still eyes never leave Viola's face. Her foot might be attached to another person's body, controlled remotely by someone else's brain. Fisher snort-laughs when Natalie, having managed to de-shoe him, tickles the bottom of his foot with her big toe.

The food is every bit as wretched as the other meals Fisher's eaten in the hotel, and he takes hold of Natalie's elbow as the table adjourns en masse. "I'm starving," he says. "Meet me in the lobby at nine-thirty. Think we can beat this storm they're all talking about and get a bite elsewhere." He looks down at her skirt, her sensible, professional heels. "I've got a bike. Dress for it."

She isn't just a bike, and when Natalie reappears at nine-thirty, he can tell from the spark in her eyes that Natalie understands this without having to be told. A year before Fisher met Viola Fabian, the year he turned twenty, he realized his inheritance by hocking three of his Auntie's golden teeth for a vintage motorcycle. The machine belonged to a man in Rockaway named Al Monte, who all but sobbed when Fisher climbed on it in his driveway.

His wife had persuaded him to sell her, Al told Fisher. "She just takes up space in the garage, and I never ride her anymore. But I still remember when we first met, when I first *saw* — I couldn't take my eyes off her."

Fisher knew the feeling, having only recently locked eyes on her himself. The ad tacked to the board in the student union — *Vintage Motorcycle For Sale, A Thing of Beauty* — had caught his eye, but nothing could have prepared him for the effect she would have in person. She was more delicate, smaller than he'd expected, designed for aerodynamic economy but perfect in every sense of the word. She was a *bike* — two wheels with spokes, two handlebar grips, the seat cushioned with springs like silver tornadoes. He would feel the road *through* her, feel the road in his knees and legs and hips. All her gleaming guts were on display, coiled, waiting to be released, purring with the naked promise of speed and flight, of becoming something greater when they yielded to each other. She could give him her power, and he could give her his will. Useless, magnificent, and beautiful, the motorcycle fulfilled his Auntie's dying wish — which, Fisher now understood, had been a wish that he know the freedom that comes from loving something for its own sake. She was a Triumph, a Bonneville, the same bike beloved by the likes of Steve McQueen. He named her Bonnie.

It took several years for Fisher to shake the feeling that he had stolen another man's true love, that he and Bonnie were carrying on a torrid motorcyclic affair, which may have explained why he'd slept with no fewer than twelve married and otherwise Unavailable women. He'd enjoyed the women, but he knew he'd never be faithful to anyone but her. Sometimes he wondered whether he might have led a different life, if he hadn't had the parents he had, or hadn't sat at the piano just to show off — an impulsive stunt that had remade his life in its own image. The thought terrified him, that he could be anyone other than who he was, because who he was allowed him to love, fiercely and freely, the only things in the world that mattered: his motorcycle and his music.

His life had only recently begun to trouble him.

He could trace his unease to an early-morning phone call that woke him two weeks ago. On the other end was the ASM secretary, Helen Stoller, calling on behalf of Doug Kirk, a man Fisher knew well, from having conducted at several local ASM festivals, and liked well, because Doug always traveled with good booze. Apparently, Kirk—who had slurred such Scotch-enabled true confessions to Fisher as "Hanging around all these teenagers makes me hornier than a toad," and "Don't you ever want to smack 'em in the face?"—was in a coma.

Helen was beside herself. She was calling to inform him of the situation, she said, and to ask if he had any suggestions about who might serve as an interim head, even though Helen and Fisher both knew the responsibility would naturally fall to Kirk's second in command. Viola. Which was the real reason Helen woke him, voice pinched and high—because she hated Viola Fabian, didn't trust Viola Fabian, and there was a small, insistent whisper inside her that said Viola was to blame for Kirk's heart attack.

"It doesn't make sense, Dr. Brodie," she said. "I know he was taking his pills. I picked up his refills, for Pete's sake. And that *woman*. This is just what she wanted, you know. She wanted to be in charge. Am I crazy? I honestly don't know which would make me feel worse, being crazy or being right."

It was common knowledge that Helen Stoller was in love with Doug Kirk, had been for decades, and now her devotion had blossomed into a kind of tender paranoia. Fisher, half awake and oddly touched by her hysteria, assured her she was neither crazy nor right. *These things happen,* he said, wishing he hadn't smoked so many fags the night before, wishing his voice sounded as gentle and genuine as he meant it to be. He asked that Helen deliver his good wishes to the Kirk family. Then he hung up and rolled under the covers, intent on falling back to sleep. He was an adjunct at the Westing School of Music in Rochester, and his first class of the day wasn't until the afternoon.

Teetering on the edge of a dream, he wondered if he'd ever loved or been loved by anyone so deeply as to inspire delusions of conspiracy.

Then he had a vision. He saw his body laid out before him, his bare, thin chest in the foreground, his long legs and feet receding to the horizon, and his heart burst out of his flesh like a bladder full of black paint, splashing warmth across his face. He lay supine and watched his body for days, his blood congealing as the sun rose and fell in the world outside. He closed his eyes, and when he opened them again he saw his toes pressed against the cold steel of a morgue drawer, and when he blinked, cold silver gave way to the hot brick walls of a crematorium. He burned. He felt hot and cold but he could not move and could not cry out. He dreamed of no others, no witnesses, no mourners, no morticians or undertakers. No one touched his body. It propelled itself through the stages of death as it had through life, of its own accord, alone.

He got out of bed and took Bonnie for a ride.

In retrospect, he wishes he hadn't done that. If he hadn't gone immediately from that horrible dream to the comforting thrum of Bonnie, he wouldn't have subconsciously created a bridge between them—ever since that dream, every time Fisher Brodie climbs on his motorcycle, he remembers how he died.

His redheaded pianist, his Natalie, is the cure for this memory. She is dressed entirely in black—black coat, black turtleneck visible beneath her collar, which makes her skin look white as bone and her hair bright as fire. A perfume of anger and desperate sadness follows in her wake as she crosses in front of Fisher to appraise his bike from all angles. He couldn't fix her if he wanted to. He only wants to know what made her the way she is, what he can do to help her forget. He suspects it has everything to do with music, like everything else in his life. In her life. Their lives.

"This is yours?" she says. Her words float out on a cloud of breath. "She's beautiful."

He nods. "She is indeed." He hands her his helmet but she shakes her head.

"Clearly," she says with a half smile, "you don't pay much attention to the weather."

"*Clearly,*" he says, "it's never as bad as they say it's going to be."

"Don't come crying to me when you can't get home on Sunday," she says.

They are the last words spoken between them for an hour. He climbs on and helps her up behind. She locks her arms around his waist, leans her body fully into his. Turns her head to the side and presses her cheek to the back of his shoulder. Fisher smiles. They ride through the dark of Clinton's Kill, past a convenience mart, a gas station, a bar, and old, old houses in various states of restoration and dilapidation. Bonnie purrs rhythmically, comfortingly. As soon as they arrive in town, they're out of it again, out on the black roads, the black and empty roads that are theirs and theirs alone. Fisher opens the throttle. The air rushing over them is freezing, but every part of Fisher is warm. He unzips the top of his jacket. The sky, when he rolls his head back to look, is shocking, open, scattered with stars like shining grains of salt. His lungs fill with bright air that tells of distant fires and coming snow. Natalie moves against him, resettles, squeezes him tighter. She slips one cold hand inside his jacket and holds it over his heart.

The roads cut through open fields, through woods. An occasional lone house peers from a hill in the distance. Fisher and Natalie fly. He thinks of his Auntie. He knows this is exactly what she would have wanted for him. To fly. To be free. Free but not alone.

In the middle of nowhere — they've driven through several nowheres, and this is definitely the very middle — Fisher pulls Bonnie into a gas station. The pumps are empty. A single car, a greenish-blue Neon, is parked beside the station mart.

"Why are we stopping?" Natalie's voice is ragged. She hasn't let him go.

"Didn't I promise you a bite?" he says, turning around and pointing at the mart. "I'd kill for a Ho Ho."

After the dark of the roads, the fluorescent lights inside make his eyes water. He wipes them with his thumbs. Natalie has already found the rack of Hostess products, single-serve, cellophane-wrapped fruit pies and custard-injected pastries that Fisher, who had never had such gloriously terrible foodstuffs before coming to the States, frequently craved. Not that there was a dearth of gloriously terrible foodstuffs in Scotland; his parents just didn't believe in having them in the house. And since most of his life in Scotland had been spent under his parents' roof, his parents' management and control, he had had to go to New York, to university, before being exposed to the delights of Hostess and Little Debbie. She tasted like liberty.

"Ho Hos for you." Natalie tossed him a packet. "Cupcakes for me. Twinkies for . . . because. Anything else?"

"Think that covers it." Fisher cannot look away from her. Her pale face has gone lavender in the cold and wind.

"What? What are you staring at?" she says, smiling, turning a deeper purple.

"You should get out more," he says.

"So should you."

The boy behind the counter—and it is a boy, he can't be older than twenty—sets aside a paperback novel with a woman in a lion skin wielding a comically giant sword on its cover. *Back to the Moons of Venus,* Fisher reads, upside down, squinting.

Between beeps from the cash register Fisher hears it. A tiny click over his shoulder.

"Whoa," says the boy. He backs into a wall of cigarettes, hands up, palms out.

"Get the cupcakes," says Natalie. "Now."

"What—" says Fisher, and turns. Natalie is standing behind him holding a gun, pointing it at the poor nerd behind the counter, the nerd squeezing his eyes shut so hard his face looks folded.

"Nat—"

"Shut up and get the cupcakes," she says. Her eyes are even brighter than they were. They are dancing, they are singing in her face. "Get the Ho Hos. Come on. Come *on*."

Fisher doesn't think. He grabs all three snacks and Natalie

laughs at him and it's automatic, he laughs back and he hears the bell above the door chime as they tear out of the store. Everything is instinct. He shoves the snacks in the inside pocket of his jacket and climbs on the bike. Natalie climbs on behind him and grips his middle. He guns it and they're gone, back on the black, anonymous roads, and Fisher's heart is beating, beating. He wants to shout. He wants to laugh. He wants to crash his bike into the closest ditch and dig a hole and die there. He wants to take Natalie back to his room, *now,* and kiss her, touch her, make love until they both turn inside out. Natalie is shaking. Fisher is shaking. No matter who started it, they're both shaking, they're both laughing, they're both thrilled to bits.

They ride in silence. Fisher doesn't know what to do other than head back to the Bellweather. The hotel's great middle tower is dotted with lit windows and the lobby glows, but everything else is dark. Fisher pulls his bike partway up the main drive, just hidden in the shadows, and cuts the engine. They sit there together, breathing hard. Natalie squeezes him tighter with each exhalation.

"There weren't cameras," she whispers. "I checked. Of course I checked."

"It is real? The gun."

She swallows. "Yes." Then she laughs. "Yes, it's real." She lets go and Fisher feels his ribs open up.

"Can I have my cupcakes now?" she says. She strolls around to the front of the bike, facing him across the handlebars.

He has never seen anyone look more beautiful. More alive. And God, all the saints and his Auntie McDunnock preserve him, Fisher has never felt more alive than he does tonight with Natalie. The stars and the air and the wind burn, and Fisher burns with them.

He climbs off, dropping Bonnie's kickstand. He reaches into his jacket and shows Natalie her cupcakes, smashed flat in their cellophane pouch. Cream oozes white through cracked chocolate.

"Is that my fault?" she asks, grinning.

She reaches for the cupcakes. Fisher pulls her close, his hand around her waist for a change, and kisses her.

He can tell she's surprised, though she shouldn't be. Her lips are dry from the wind, but her mouth is hot, and shut. She pushes Fisher away and frowns, on the verge of words. He can hear them already: *I'm married. I'm sorry. I can't do this.* The Unavailables have been different in every respect save for their words, and he has always known, before tonight, the most convincing rebuttal in each circumstance. Humorous: *You're married? Well, that makes one of us.* Inductive: *There's nothing to be sorry about. I'm the one who ought to be sorry, I'm the one who brought us here—though I didn't get here alone.* Logical: *Can't and won't are two entirely different things.*

Then Fisher remembers whom he kissed, and who, without another word, is kissing him back.

The snow comes quietly in the night and covers everything.

It starts around three in the morning. Hastings is awake, but he isn't looking out the window; he doesn't see the storm rushing across the fields of Clinton's Kill, a wall of tiny points of white light. He doesn't see the wind pressing the high grass flat or bending the low branches on the trees. Snow falls in thick, silent sheets in the darkness, transforming the cars and hedges into earthbound clouds, frosting the houses like Victorian cookies.

Hastings, unable to sleep for Rome Cohen's snoring, feels the storm in his knees and ankles and wrists as surely as if it were snowing in his room. So many terrible storms have battered the Bellweather, but she has borne them all with style. No one claims to remember how the hotel got its name—for all Hastings knows, it was a spelling error on the original deed—but he has always considered it a good omen. The worse the weather, the more inviting the glowing lights of the tower. The higher the drifts, the more they covered the patches on the foundation. Snow was kind to the Bellweather. It blurred her edges and made her beautiful.

Imagining how his hotel will sparkle in the morning, Hastings almost forgets to worry about the several hundred square feet of glass roof and several hundred souls sleeping beneath it—almost. Then he worries that his only friend in the world is an antisocial nutjob, that the love of his life left him to live on another continent,

that there is a murderess and a (possibly) dead daughter somewhere in the hotel. In *his* hotel.

Hastings's thoughts bury him until he can no longer hear his
bunkmate's snoring. Hands curled around old brown blankets, he
joins Rome's one-man chorus.

16

In the Dark

WELL, THIS WAS unexpected.

Natalie tucks the covers between her shoulder and chin; she is warm and snugged tight. The other side of the bed looks impossibly empty without Fisher. She can hear him splashing at the bathroom sink and wishes he would hurry up and finish his story. He has been telling her, finally, how he lost his fingers. So far the tale has involved several German barmaids, a game of Russian roulette, and a dragon. She suspects he has taken some liberties.

Sex, now *that* she had expected. Natalie knew sex was where they were heading when he kissed her in the dark outside the hotel. No, earlier. When she climbed on the back of his bike. At the time she thought, *Of course he drives a motorcycle. With one and a half hands. In a blizzard.* Wasn't the man you have an affair with required to be the opposite of your spouse in every respect? Emmett drove a Toyota Camry with antilock brakes. Was short and a little stocky. Taught science. Had ten fingers.

Since the break-in, sex had become something Natalie knew she ought to do but could never truly commit to, like going to the gym regularly, eating fiber, reading the classics she'd missed in school. She thought she'd simply lost her taste for it, the way she'd lost her taste for everything else. But tonight, here in this hotel, here with Fisher, she felt differently. (Ha ha, of course she felt differently; Fisher wasn't her husband.) Sex might have been a foregone conclusion, but it was suddenly *interesting* to her again.

Natalie hadn't been able to let go of his tattered hand as they crossed the quiet lobby. There was a youngish man at the front desk reading a book, and she'd thought of the kid in the gas station. (She can't believe she held up a convenience store. For Hostess cakes. She is an armed robber, on top of everything.)

In the elevator, she had pressed the button for the sixth floor.

"Are you on the sixth floor too?" she asked Fisher.

"No."

"What kind of girl do you think I am?"

"I've no idea."

They got off at six.

"Fair warning," she said, opening her door. "You know I'm armed."

Fisher practically leapt on her as soon as she shut the door, the latch passing over the strike plate with a cold metal clap. Her first instinct was to laugh at the ferocity of his approach; it was charming, youthful, like something her high school boyfriend would have thought would blow her mind. She stumbled back on the bed hard enough to bounce, and then she did laugh, and something shifted deep inside her. She didn't know Fisher, not really, not the way she'd known her other lovers, and yet she knew she was safe here with him in the dark. She couldn't be hurt, not by him.

The sex was fast and desperately fun, and when it was over Fisher fell against her in a jumble of marionette limbs. After a long silence that began to feel more awkward with each exhalation, Natalie cleared her throat.

"Well," she said, "now that *that's* out of the way."

That was hours ago. Hours and hours ago, hours spent talking. Telling each other stories, their own and others'. It was easier to do in the dark, in a strange room that was home to neither of them, where there was nothing to hold but each other's version of the truth. Her belly is sore from laughing; Natalie has laughed more in the past three hours than she has in eight months. It tires her, it wears her out, she is exhausted but alive with desire. To share. To tell. To confess. He wants to know exactly who she is. He wants to hear her whole story, her entire ugly truth, and she wants to tell him.

That she never saw coming.

The bathroom door opens in a bright flash. Fisher's profile burns itself on her retinas for an instant and vanishes as he turns off the light. He climbs into bed and presses his knobby feet against her shins.

"Ice! Ice!" Natalie shrieks and kicks him away. "You are made of ice!"

"Now, where was I? Right. Dead drunk in Germany. Sixteen and angry." He props himself on his elbow. "And very stupid, because I honestly thought my life was over. All I could imagine for all the years to come was more of the same. More of being herded, poked, and prodded, told what to do. More dancing when instructed to dance. I could barely comprehend what I was doing, let alone what I was *capable* of doing, of becoming, if I had the bloody chance to grow up. I was so tired of everything, and so very drunk and stupid, that I looked down into my third stein of horribly delicious German beer and wanted to smash the world. I thought if I broke my life, it would at least be my choice. It would be my doing. So I started with the man sitting beside me at the bar."

He holds out his half hand and flexes it.

"I punched him in the ear. Landed well, since he wasn't expecting it in the least, which made me want to punch him harder, and again, and finally he got tired, picked me up and tossed me over the bar like a twig. Into one of those big mirrors, you know, that they have behind bars, so you can see how sorry you look getting pissed? Shattered. I held out this hand to sort of—I don't know. Stop myself? Don't remember much of it, just the feeling of flying and how cold the mirror was when I punched it. After that . . . glass becomes crunchy when you break enough of it. I was sticky. There were sharp little bites all over my arms, my neck. Could have been worse. Could have died, if he'd thrown me harder, if I'd cut my throat, if they hadn't rushed me to hospital. These two"—he wriggles his middle- and ring-finger stumps—"I dropped on the floor of the bar. A kind German doctor took care of the pinkie."

Natalie brings Fisher's hand to her mouth. She kisses his palm and presses it to the side of her face.

"Your turn," he says, rubbing her cheek with his thumb.

"My turn to what?" she asks, as if she didn't know.

"Your turn to share, love. See, I've been trying to figure what in the world could make a seemingly sane, professional woman of your caliber hold up a shop for a cupcake."

Natalie blinks. Blue fire flickers up her spine.

"Does it have to do with our mutual friend?"

She blinks again. "In a manner of speaking."

"So you're saying there's a concrete reason. You have a sob story of your own."

"It's not a sob story."

Fisher frowns. "Didn't mean anything by that."

"You could say Viola was the beginning. And the end, in a way."

"Once upon a time," Fisher says. He turns on his back and spreads his fingers in the air, framing the scene. "There was a brave young peasant girl named Natalie and a wicked queen named Viola." He looks at her sideways. "Am I close?"

She doesn't respond.

"Natalie?" Fisher says quietly.

Her throat is full of everything. Everything she never even told Emmett. She tried to. She *tried,* she really did, in the hospital that very night. She had the whole truth all lined up in her mind, and then the first things Emmett said when he saw her weren't ques- tions—*What happened? Are you okay?* Instead he fed her statements, facts she didn't have the heart to argue. *What you did was self-de- fense. That was the bravest thing anyone could have done.* And so she felt worse, sick down to her soul, and silent.

"Viola poisoned me," she says. She pulls the sheet up to her chin and stares straight ahead. "She took the first thing I loved, the best part of myself, and she crushed it. I've never gotten over it. My heart broke and I never figured out how to fix it." She takes his hand.

"This is your last chance, Fisher. You can tell me right now you don't want to know and I'll shut up."

"Don't you dare," he says, and in that moment Natalie loves him more than she's ever loved anyone.

"Last spring." She licks her lips. "Last spring a man broke into my house. Our house. On a Sunday night, after I'd gone to bed."

She closed her eyes and smelled, not popcorn or Old Spice or any of the things her husband normally smelled like, but cigarettes — *Emmett was smoking again?* — and she opened her eyes and saw the man. She didn't know who he was at first, thought dreamily, *Who is this? Do I know this person?* He was young and had a thick reddish beard spotted with acne and red-purple dents under his eyes. He was sitting on the bed with his back to her but had turned around at the sound of movement, his face half lit from the street outside.

Natalie's first thought was *What an idiot, he's going through Emmett's bedside table, all the jewelry is in mine.* Her second thought was *Shit, oh shit,* because she had just remembered that in Emmett's bedside table, hidden in one of those jokey hollow books, was a revolver, the .38 his father had given him. Because you never knew.

She woke up instantly. She dove across the man's lap, desperate to beat him to the gun. The man, to his credit, quickly realized the situation was out of his control and rolled off the bed. Natalie threw the hollow book on the floor and wrapped her cold fingers around the gun, and her thumb, thinking for itself, cocked the hammer.

"Get out," she growled. "Or I will shoot you."

He looked so young. He could have been one of her students.

He —

"Hollis?" she whispered.

Ed Hollis turned several shades paler than he already was.

Ed Hollis, who graduated two years before — or would have if he hadn't gotten kicked out in the spring of his senior year. Ed Hollis, a burnout, a loser, the kind of kid who was never in band but whom Natalie knew anyway, because you *always* knew kids like Ed Hollis. The ones who had to start shaving in the seventh grade, who were taller than their teachers, who were in and out of detention, as if it were an actual class, for bringing knives to school.

She officially met Ed Hollis in the band room one day after the final bell, where he was beating the holy hell out of the school's drum set.

"Hollis!" she shouted at him, out of surprise more than anything else, and he immediately brought his drumsticks down with a clatter. "Ed Hollis, is that your name?"

They had never spoken before. He had bright blue eyes and ruddy cheeks, and looked genuinely shocked at having been caught. Innocent, almost. He passed a nervous tongue over chipped front teeth.

"Yes, ma'am," he said. "I'm sorry, I was just . . . drumming."

"Are you staying after with another teacher? Do you have a permission slip?" Of course he didn't; he was Hollis. Hollis didn't ask permission for anything.

He shook his head. "No, I'm sorry, I should have—I should have asked, I know, but. You see, I need to practice. And I can't practice at home, my ma has to sleep during the day."

"What are you practicing for?"

"Ryan and Mike and me, we're starting a band. I'm the drummer." Ryan Paulson and Mike Lucas, also burnouts, also losers. His tribe. "Would it be okay if I—sort of—practiced after school a few days? I know I should have asked first. I'm sorry."

How could she refuse him? She was keeping him safe in her band room, off the tough suburban Minneapolis streets; or more like, she was keeping the Minneapolis streets safe from Hollis. "Tuesdays and Thursdays," she said, and wrote him a permission slip to take the late bus.

All that fall and into the spring, every Tuesday and Thursday, Hollis came to the band room and smashed the shit out of the school's drum kit and never improved, not one tiny bit. She offered him lessons. He halfheartedly listened and went right back to beating the snare, the toms, the bass into submission. He said they were a punk band, but when she tried to talk to him about the Stooges or the Sex Pistols he met her with a blank stare. The only time he didn't look blank, in fact, was when he was pounding on the drums; then, and only then, he looked almost content. Controlled. The drums were doing something for Hollis, something real, something he needed, and as obnoxious as it was to listen to it every Tuesday and Thursday, Natalie let him play.

Hollis's band booked their first gig that spring at an after-prom party. He added Wednesday to his practice rotation and began to talk to Natalie, constantly, incessantly, about what his life was going to be like when he was famous. He'd shout over the drums that he was first going to move to New York, just live in some shithole apartment, and they'd play all night long in shithole clubs until they got discovered, until they got found, and then it would be nothing but beer and girls and money, and more girls.

Natalie began to find everything about Hollis tremendously irritating. Pathetic. This seemed like a perfectly natural reaction for a sane person to have to seven straight months of noise, of crimes against drums, with an added bonus of delusions of grandeur.

As quickly as it had begun, everything ended. Natalie wasn't even supposed to be at school, but she stopped by on a Saturday afternoon to pick up her plan book and caught Ed Hollis stealing the drum kit. The rear doors of the band room were propped open and he had a snare drum and a hi-hat, one in each hand. He froze, as though, once motionless, he might blend into the pale yellow cinderblock walls.

"Hey, Miz Wilson," he said eventually. "I swear I'm just borrowing it. For the gig tonight. I'll bring it back tomorrow, I promise."

"Hollis," she said, "you don't get to do that. You don't get to steal—"

"Fuck that," he said. "Sarah Reinhardt's tuba belongs to the school. She takes that home and you don't call *that* stealing. How is this any different?" His voice was the voice of an angry adult. For the first time in months, he frightened her.

"It's different and you know it," she said firmly.

"I'm taking it anyway. I need this. I won't get famous without—"

"You won't get famous, Hollis," she said. "Period."

"Yeah, I know, I need some fucking drums."

"The drums have nothing to do with it. You won't get famous because you aren't any good," she said, and she didn't regret it. Not then. "You're a fucking terrible drummer, Hollis, so put the kit down and get out of here before I call the police."

Every part of him—his arms, his hands, his face, his eyes, even, it seemed, his hair—went slack. He dropped the snare but tossed the hi-hat at the nearest folding chair, where it made a deafening crash. "Fuck you," he said, and ran out the propped doors.

She doesn't know what he was officially suspended for, though it wasn't for attempted robbery; she didn't rat him out. She probably should have. He might have gotten some kind of help. He might have turned himself around, might have graduated.

He might not be standing in her house, in her bedroom, trying to rob her two years later.

"Miz Wilson," he says flatly. "You live here?"

"Yes, Hollis." This is absurd. "Obviously." She holds the gun down at her side. Her arm quivers.

"Was that your husband downstairs?"

Oh no. Oh no, Emmett. "What did you do?"

Hollis shrugs. He looks sick.

"Hollis, you don't have to—you don't have to do this." Whatever this is, whatever he is planning to do.

"How else am I going to make some money?" He frowns. "I'm a fucking terrible drummer."

Hollis steps closer, and Natalie is terrified. This feeling, this bright, whirling, too-alive feeling is terror, and she knows it; she's never felt it before, but in her oldest, most animal brain, she recognizes this moment for what it is. Hollis is an arm's length away, but he's staring at her from across two years—two years that might have been different if she'd have let him take that drum kit, just for the night, he meant it when he said he would bring it back. Or even if she hadn't let him take the drums, if she had let him go on believing he was any good at it. If only she'd let him keep the thing that he loved, the one thing in his whole rotten world that made him feel like himself, that made him feel special.

He slaps her, hard, right across the mouth.

Natalie tastes warm salt as her teeth pierce her lip. She knows what comes next. She remembers this scene. She played it once herself, with her own teacher, only Viola didn't know the second blow was coming. And Viola hadn't been holding a handgun.

It was self-defense, all right.

"He was me," she tells Fisher. "I was Viola. And before he could take another swing, I shot him in the chest."

SATURDAY
NOVEMBER 15, 1997

Allegro Furioso

17

Alice, the Next Morning

LICE CAN'T MOVE. She really . . . can't move, and it's
dark, and holy shit, she's tied up.

Her wrists and ankles are held tight against the arms
and legs of a chair with heavy bands of cloth. She tries
to scream but there's fabric, soft and rough at the same time, in her
mouth, on her tongue. It absorbs her spit. It tastes like soap.

The floor growls.

Alice freezes. She's been kidnapped and now she's going to die.

She opens her eyes wide and blinks, but the dark doesn't get any
lighter. Is she blind? How did she . . . what's the last thing she remembers? *Think, Alice, think.* The party. She remembers leaving the
party, a little buzzed, sad about her brother, hugely disappointed
with him and with herself for not being able to get to him, get him
out of there. He knows that dance. He *loves* it. Won't he feel like an
asshole when his sister's dead body is discovered. Bet he'll wish he
danced with her *then*.

She has to pee. It must be morning.

The floor jingles. Dog tags. There's a dog in the dark with her, a
guard dog, probably a Doberman, a starved, fed-a-diet-of-human-
flesh Doberman, he's going to tear her throat out. *Oh God oh God.*

Think.

After the party, Rabbit's key in her hand. She started to go to her brother's room but—she changed her mind. She was half drunk. She was pissed off. She wanted to sleep in her own damn pajamas. She went back to her own room instead, the room she shared with Jill. Alice was afraid of nothing and no one. Not evil moms. Not psycho dog ladies.

Light slices through the black, through a crack in the door. She can see she's in a closet. Wooden hangers dangle above her. There's a half-size ironing board mounted on the far wall and an iron, strangled with its own cord, lying beneath it. At least she's still in the hotel.

A dog, a fat little fox of a dog, is sitting in the corner next to the iron. He tilts his head, opens his mouth, and smiles an idiot smile at her.

Alice remembers everything.

She went to her room, yes, she went to 712. She was brave with beer. If Jill's killer came back, Alice was in the mood to give her a piece of her mind. She had shoved her own key in the lock and turned the knob and the room looked like she and Jill had never been there. No stink of cheap wine. No pinked sheets wadded beside the sink, no rosy waterline in the tub. The wine-rippled tarot cards she'd spread to dry on the bathroom floor that morning were all missing. Two coats hung in the closet, two suitcases beneath. Both beds were neatly made.

After everything—a murdered, stolen roommate, a condescending concierge, her nonbelieving brother transforming into a frat boy before her eyes—after all of that—

They turned down the room as if nothing had happened?

Alice sat down hard on the closest bed, on Jill's bed, and cried noisily, desperately, choking herself with her own breath like an exhausted three-year-old. But crying wasn't going to be enough. Crying alone wasn't going to ease the feeling of having been so thoroughly erased.

She stood up on the bed, the mattress elastic beneath her sneakers, and bounced. She bounced again. She bounced harder until she was jumping, grunting with each landing and shrieking as she sprang up, thrashing that mattress and box spring to pieces. Then she howled in animal rage and leapt to the second bed.

The crazy dog woman must have been there the whole time, must have been sleeping or lying silently on the small strip of floor between the second bed and the wall, but to Alice the woman was not there, and then the woman was *everywhere,* red-faced and shouting, arms flailing, hands clenched in fists flying through the air. Alice's legs jellied in shock. As she collapsed to the mattress, the woman punched her in the face so hard, so fast, it was the last thing Alice knew for eight hours.

The crazy dog woman. Minnie.

Alice is going to die. She allows herself a tiny whimper.

She hears a door open. "You can just give it to me," Minnie says, which is Alice's cue to go bananas. She struggles in the chair, which is too heavy to move, too heavy to knock against the wall or into the closet door. She hollers damply through the cloth in her mouth. The dog whimpers in sympathy and trots over, head-butting her shins. It's weirdly comforting, but Alice is in no mood to be comforted.

The room door closes again. She droops, defeated.

Minnie flings open the closet doors and smiles at her.

"Breakfast is here!" she says.

Alice shrinks into the chair. Her eyes gush tears in the sudden brightness. She looks down and sees she's been tied up with hotel linens, her wrists with pillowcases, her legs with towels.

"Oh, sorry." Minnie reaches in and gently removes a washcloth from her mouth. Alice coughs. Too late, she thinks she ought to have tried to bite her. "I didn't want you to accidentally wake me up again. I kind of lose it when that happens. Like last night, when you found me — you woke me up. I feel awful about your eye."

"What about my eye?" Alice croaks.

"It's pretty black."

The left side of Alice's face wakes up with an epic throb.

"Please untie me," she says.

"Oh, sorry about that too. You smelled like beer and I was afraid you'd ralph in your sleep and choke on it, and I wanted to make sure you were propped upright. Let's see, what else are you probably wondering about . . . You're in the closet because I didn't want room service to get the wrong idea." Minnie smiles a shaky smile. "You know there's something like thirty inches of snow outside today? And it's still coming down? We can watch the news while we eat."

Alice shakes her head. She's so hungry she's dizzy. Or maybe she's been drugged. Minnie is going on about the breakfast she ordered—she didn't know whether Alice was a vegetarian or a carnivore, so there's pancakes and waffles and fruit and bacon and sausage patties, and aren't sausage patties *better* than links, somehow?

"I like patties," Alice murmurs.

Minnie squats, wrapping both hands around the front left leg of the chair, and Alice and her chair are dragged out of the closet in a straight line. The room service breakfast tray is nestled in the sheets of an unmade king or queen bed. She sees a fork and a knife, and on the small desk beside the bed, stationery scattered across the surface, an uncapped pen. Alice peers at Minnie and imagines having the chance to stab her with something.

"Why are you looking at me like that?" Minnie says.

"How am I looking at you?"

"You're looking at me like you think I'm going to kill you. If I were going to kill you," Minnie kind of laughs, "I'd have done it by now."

"If you *weren't* going to kill me, you'd have untied me by now."

The dog yawns squeakily.

Minnie flushes. "I know. I *know.*" She sits on the bed and the breakfast wobbles beside her. A drop of jostled OJ rides down the outside of the glass. "How about I untie one hand so you can eat?"

"I have to go to the bathroom," Alice says angrily. This woman, however dangerous and crazy she may be, might be bullyable. She sure looks like a pushover. "Who the hell do you think you are? What gives you the right to treat me like this?"

"I told you who I am. My name is Minnie. And I believe you about your roommate. I believe she's dead."

Alice's heart stops at *I believe you.* Her mouth doesn't. "That doesn't give you the right to tie me up in your closet!"

"I know." Minnie stands up. She's overweight, but beyond that, she's tall, and Alice truly fears that this giant woman will hurt her. She's certainly strong enough. She's certainly *crazy* enough. "I know what I did is just about the least okay thing to do, under any circumstances, to anyone, but I didn't know—" Minnie frowns and looks down at the dog, who is wagging his tail and smiling his idiot canine smile. "I didn't know what else to do. I need help."

"No shit."

"I need *your* help." Minnie locks eyes with Alice. "To prove there's something going on here, someone or some*thing* bad here in this hotel—that it isn't just us, we're not nuts and this isn't our fault. When I was a little kid, what I saw here broke me. And I grew up around the broken parts but it wasn't the right way to grow up. I'm all twisted and weird inside and I'm sick of bad dreams and horror stories. What happened here doesn't get to dictate how I spend the rest of my life, or how you spend the rest of yours, and it's no coincidence, us meeting last night in the room where it happened. *We are the girls who survived*. We are the girls who saw something awful and lived to talk about it, and now we have a chance to join forces and *beat it*. We can win. We can *win* this time, not just survive."

Minnie looks away.

"I don't want to hurt you. I would never hurt anyone on purpose," she continues. "And now that I've said what I needed to say, I'm going to untie you and you can decide for yourself what you want to do."

Alice's heart beats all over her body. In her temples, her fingertips. Blood pulses into her ankles and her arms when Minnie loosens the linens binding her to the chair. She flexes her toes and rolls her wrists.

Minnie laces her fingers together and sits on the edge of the bed. The outside of Minnie—unassuming as oatmeal, from her dull, messy hair to her ORANGEMEN sweatshirt to her holey athletic socks—is a perfect disguise for the angry, avenging little girl Alice now sees inside. She's just the sort of person Alice needs: someone who has a history with this hotel, someone with nothing to lose, and, most important, who believes her with dead seriousness.

"What do you propose we do?" Alice asks.

"What do you mean? Oh, hey, have some breakfast. It's getting cold." Minnie hands her a plate of pancakes. "There are some packets of syrup around here too—ah. Here they are."

"I mean, I'd love to find out who killed Jill. It's just a little . . . overwhelming." Alice tries to sound nonchalant. "Can I have a fork?"

The dog has stopped grinning and gazes longingly at Alice, as though she holds all the keys to all the happiness he might ever know.

"Auggie loves pancakes," Minnie says.

"His name is Auggie?" Alice presses the pad of her thumb over the fork's tines. Fairly sharp.

Alice tosses the dog a small square of pancake and he snaps it out of midair. For such a friendly-looking creature, his teeth are white and wicked as a wolf's. She can't believe she's doing this. Here she is, brave, stupid Alice, stringing her prime suspect along while she arms herself with forks, acting as if they're going to form some sort of grand crime-fighting, mystery-solving duo in the hopes that— what? Minnie will slip and incriminate herself? Minnie will crack and murder Alice too?

Alice has no idea what she hopes for anymore. Not for Minnie, not for Jill, not for Rabbit, and least of all for herself. Ever since that stupid field party, when she realized her brother would leave her and she ended up kissing Eric Cole, Alice has been on autopilot. She swims through one day and the next and the next, like a salmon pushing mindlessly upriver, biologically instructed to ignore the current, to look neither left nor right, to press on. But now Alice has reached open water and she has no idea what to do but swim in a small circle.

"What were you doing in my room last night?" Alice asks. This sudden episode of philosophy fills her with questions. "How did you even get in?"

"Picking a lock is surprisingly easy." Minnie grins. "You'd be surprised."

"But what were you *doing* there?"

"Sleeping. I have nightmares—that's why I wake up swinging if you disturb me—and, I don't know, I was kind of hoping being back there, sleeping, maybe having a nightmare in that room, would cancel everything out. Erase and reboot me. It seemed like the scariest possible thing I could do, trying to fall asleep in *that* room, especially after what happened yesterday."

"And you did fall asleep."

"Auggie helped. He snores. It's soothing. Like one of those noise-maker alarm clocks that let you fall asleep to rainfall or ocean waves or crickets. It's the most peaceful thing, watching his belly rise and fall. He'll curl up right here"—Minnie places her hand flat to her side—"like a really big cat. And that's how we get to sleep."

"How old are you?"

"Twenty-seven." Minnie pops a bite of bacon in her mouth.

"Ten years older than me."

Minnie shrugs. She reaches for another strip of bacon.

"What did you dream of," Alice asks, "when you were my age?"

Minnie's hand stops, hovering over the breakfast tray. She sighs. "I don't remember. But I'm sure they were all bad."

Alice has never been a particularly compassionate person. Her drama directors were constantly dinging her for not connecting to a character's "truth," whatever the hell that meant. She could belt their songs into next week, but apparently that wasn't enough to make people care about what happened to a character, wasn't enough to make people believe a character was real. "Nancy is trapped," Joe Shipman, who directed the Ruby Falls production of *Oliver!* when Alice was in the tenth grade, told her three nights before dress rehearsal. "She knows she's trapped—she's trapped in poverty, but more than that she's trapped in love with a bad man, a rough man, an evil man who is going to kill her, and she knows it. She knows it and she can't do anything about it. How does that make you feel?"

Alice, wearing her bright red barmaid's costume for the first time and more than a little in love with the incredible things it did to her chest, shrugged. "Sad."

"Listen to the *words* you're singing." Joe's hands always spoke louder than his voice. His two clenched fists shook with suppressed emotion. "Nancy believes this brute needs her, even though she knows he treats her terribly. He's violent. She's afraid to show him how much she cares. That isn't love, but it's the only love she has. And the way *you* sing it—Alice, you sing it like Nancy thinks being trapped like a rat is the greatest thing that's ever happened to her. You sing it like it's 'Don't Rain on My Parade.' If you were trapped like Nancy, how would you feel?"

"Pathetic," Alice said, running her fingers up and down the corset boning. She remembers Joe Shipman frowning at her and saying that would have to do, that she certainly had talent but wasn't living up to her potential, and no one other than Joe said a damn thing to her about her supposed inability to portray the gravity of Nancy's predicament. Further proof that Nancy's predicament had nothing to do with Alice's potential.

But it did. It does. It has taken Alice almost two years to see it, but finally she gets it, her mouth full of room service pancakes on a bright Saturday morning, watching the local news, which Minnie has turned on. Everything is about the storm—how many feet of snow fell, how many more are yet to come—and as the anchors drone on and Minnie watches, rapt, cutting dainty pieces of sausage patty for her own breakfast, Alice imagines what it would be like if she were Minnie. If she had witnessed a murder-suicide as a child. If every night she had nightmares so awful she woke from them ready to fight for her life, and the only time she knew peace was while watching her dog sleep. If the only way she could ask for help was to tie a stranger up in a closet.

Alice doesn't think it's the stress or the hunger or the fact that she still has to pee. She thinks the tears pooling in the corners of her eyes are evidence of her first truly compassionate experience. She feels fuller, brighter, like she's been given an extra note on the upper and lower ends of her vocal register. This is what Joe Shipman meant when he said she could never be a great performer if she didn't learn to empathize: you simply couldn't understand all the shades, variations, and intricacies of human experience until you felt them for other people. *Through* other people, regardless of whether they were real or made up. And you had to let those feelings stay with you, change you, before you could use them as part of your own paint box.

"I'll help you," Alice says, wiping her eyes with the back of her hand. "I don't know how or what we'll do, but I'll help you. We'll do it together."

Minnie turns from the television. "Really? You mean—are you crying?"

"No," says Alice, mopping her now runny nose on her sleeve.

"You're crying." Minnie, smiling, looks like she might cry too. Auggie props his tiny front paws on Alice's knee, and when she leans closer, he licks her teary cheeks.

All of the stitches holding Alice's heart together disintegrate. Whether it's true compassion or Stockholm syndrome hardly seems to matter.

18

I Want to Believe

RABBIT IS UP, watching the sun. He can see it on the edge of the horizon, out his bathroom window, casting pale, perfect light. The world glows blue. Nothing has touched it since the snow began falling. Not a dog, not a deer, not a soul with a shovel or a snowblower. The land, blue-white and shimmering, is floating. Rabbit feels himself bouncing on the balls of his feet, as though the hotel has been set adrift on a sea of Marshmallow Fluff.

He isn't sure why he's having a religious experience looking at snow this morning. He's seen a lot of snow in his life. He's sledded through it, made balls and forts and men with it, shoveled it and brushed it off cars. Snow has dripped down the back of his neck, melting off trees; snow has given him frostbite, trapped against his skin under the wrists of puffy winter coats. Snow is a given, a fact of life. When snow isn't serving a purpose—providing material for balls, forts, and men, or canceling school—it's a pain in the ass. Until this snow, this morning. This strange blue and white morning after a boy named Pete came on to him—*a boy named Pete came on to him,* for real, for REAL, Rabbit is remembering something that *has actually happened to him*—is a new morning, a new world with new snow. It belongs to Rabbit. Whatever he may have done, however painfully stupid he may have acted the night before (he's quite sure, as soon as he turns away from this beauty, he's going to remember every idiot thing he did and said), Rabbit knows he can start over.

It's been seven years, but Rabbit remembers this feeling.

Every summer growing up, he took swimming lessons with his sister at the community pool, ostensibly to get out of the house but truthfully because their mother had a morbid fear of her children drowning. She'd never mentioned this fear directly, but Rabbit and Alice had independently come to the same conclusion. It made sense: her own brother David had died at twelve when he hit his head on the underside of a floating dock on Oneida Lake, at the vacation home the twins' grandfather still owned but never visited. Rabbit and Alice hadn't been given the full details. Possessing only the barest outlines gave the story a fairy-tale quality, as if it had happened to some other family, in some other, made-up world. (*Once upon a time, there was a boy who drowned.*) Forced swimming lessons every summer vacation were, then, less a paranoid remembrance of their forever-unknown Uncle David and more a boring waste of time.

Until the summer before fourth grade, when Mattie DeLuca showed up poolside. Rabbit, at ten, had never had a real crush. He liked plenty of kids at school, but his social default was always his sister, who adored having a sidekick. There was one girl, Kelly McCallister, who was always leaving notes and trinkets in his desk, who had invited him to her birthday party, in fact — which turned out to be Kelly, Rabbit, and three other girls from school who did nothing but giggle themselves into fits while Kelly and Rabbit spun each other around, blindfolded, to pin the tail on the My Little Pony.

Kelly clearly thought he was her boyfriend after that, though Rabbit didn't spend any more time with her at school than anyone else, so he didn't understand how she'd come to that conclusion. He didn't mind her, not really, and he even tried to kiss her once just to see how it felt, during recess on a cool spring day. They were tucked neatly in the shadows behind the high steps of the gymnasium's rear entrance, the concrete damp and clammy with dew. The gigglers had seen them disappear and had formed a loose barrier from the rest of the playground—"So we can be alone," Kelly had whispered to him—and Rabbit thought, *Well, here we go,* and moved in with pursed lips. Kelly hadn't been expecting it. She made a squeaky noise and pulled away, then closed her eyes and darted her head like a cobra, planting her lips on his with a loud smack. Rabbit assumed it would get better after he hit puberty, though he remembered doubt tugging at his heart as he looked at Kelly, her cheeks coloring with the thrill of it all. His first thought was *I'm sorry.*

And then came Mattie. Mattie DeLuca, with his toothy white grin and his dark eyes, his city-cool attitude, his skinny brown limbs. Rabbit noticed him immediately, backflipping off the side of the pool exactly like he wasn't supposed to. They were in the same swim group and frequently paired because of their heights. Mattie took to Rabbit right away, saw him as the perfect straight man, which he was, thanks to years of his sister's grooming. They played pranks all summer long. They stole the lifeguard's trunks from his locker and taped them to the edge of the tallest diving board like a flag. They filled his whistle with peanut butter. Rabbit distracted their instructors while Mattie unwrapped a Snickers bar and tossed it into the kiddie pool. None of the staff, who had known Rabbit for years, believed him capable of being Mattie's sidekick, and Rabbit was so madly in love with Mattie DeLuca that he barely noticed he was irritating nice people he'd known practically since birth. Rabbit Hatmaker was a good kid to the very core, but around Mattie, *he just didn't care.*

He didn't know it was love—that this, not Kelly McCallister's smacky kisses, was what Rabbit would feel in his heart—until the final week of lessons. A radio was set up poolside while they had free swim. Rabbit was acutely aware that his friendship with Mattie had an expiration date of five days. There was no way he could persuade his parents to drive him in to Syracuse to hang out with Mattie—not the kid who'd famously been a pain in the ass all summer. And there was no way he could persuade Mattie to visit him in Ruby Falls, because who wanted to go out to the sticks? There was no mall, no movie theater, so what the hell would they do? And while he was wondering what they would do together if they were left to their own devices, The Bangles struck.

The radio was tuned to the local pop station and the song reverberating in the openness of the pool was "Eternal Flame," but Rabbit wouldn't know the title or the artist for years. He would know it only as the song that revealed to him what he felt for Mattie De-Luca—that it was love, romantic love, the kind they write poems about. The kind Hallmark sells every Valentine's Day, the kind that makes people do crazy things. His heart was beating; he wanted Mattie to understand. Did he feel the same, or was Rabbit only dreaming? All other sounds diminished, all splashing and echoing voices fell away, and Rabbit heard the words *I don't want to lose this feeling.*

This was him. He loved Mattie. He wanted to touch Mattie and hold him. He felt his heart would crush itself, would collapse with the intensity of everything he wanted. He had been hanging on the edge of the pool, kicking his feet behind him, and he pushed himself under to try to even the pressure. The song was far away but still playing in the world above, and Rabbit didn't know whether to laugh or cry. The pool swallowed both.

Rabbit closes his eyes to that memory and breathes in the cold promise of a new and waiting world. When he opens them, the sun is that much higher, the sky that much lighter. He shuts the window and catches himself in the bathroom mirror, and remembers every idiot thing he did and said the night before.

What is *wrong* with him?

There's a knock on the door.

"—a minute," he says. His voice is a crackle. He turns on the faucet and scoops cold water into his filmy mouth. He smoked pot. Lamely. He ran away. And when he got back to his room, he couldn't get in because he gave his key to Alice—

He opens the door. His roommate, Dan, is on the other side, rubbing his eyes.

"Have you seen my sister?"

"Have you seen the snow? It's insane."

"Did she come back here last night?" Rabbit asks. "How did I get in?"

"I let you in when I came back from the vending machine." Dan shrugs past him into the bathroom and shuts the door. "I have no idea where your sister is."

Everyone at Statewide has been called from breakfast into the auditorium—everyone except Jill Faccelli and Alice Hatmaker. If Rabbit was worried when he woke up, he has now reached an absolute zenith of anxiety. He can't stop blinking. His head swings back and forth, back and forth like a pedestal fan, as he scans the crowd, hoping the doors will open again, praying he'll pick out Alice's dark bangs and eyes from the sea of faces.

He should never have let her go back to her room alone last night. Not when there was a killer prowling the hotel, which Rabbit believes now without doubt. Not when Alice was already sad about something she wouldn't share with him. The first thing Rabbit will do when he sees his sister again, after making sure she's not hurt, after giving her a hug, is tell her the truth. He'll find a quiet corner and they'll sit down and he'll tell her he's gay and that will be the end of *that*. That will be the end of lying. The end of pretending, the beginning of being. He's wasted too much time, he's wasted *seven years*. He will never forgive himself if, after seven years, he's one night too late to tell the truth about himself to the one person who matters most.

She does matter the most. He knows it. She was there at the beginning, she'll be there until the end. Even now, when she's gone, Rabbit can feel that his sister exists. That he will see her again.

He jiggles his leg so violently against the seat in front of him that the sitter turns around and tells him to freaking cut it out.

The decibel level in the auditorium is incredible. Rabbit overhears worries about the snowstorm (are they going to be able to leave tomorrow?) and the concerts (what maniac parent would drive into a state-declared winter weather disaster area to hear them play?), gossip about who made out with whom the previous night (are you *kidding?*) and, more than any other topic, about the Bellweather Bride's fifteen-year thirst for souls.

"I'm telling you, it's the Bride. She's a ghost. She's walking these halls and she killed that girl, and now we're all snowbound here with a ghost who's pissed she got shot on her wedding day," says the girl sitting next to him. Rabbit has never met her, doesn't even know her name. She shivers theatrically. "*Jeez.* Freaky. You believe in ghosts, right?"

"No," lies Rabbit.

"Whatever," she says. "Where's the fun in not believing in ghosts?"

"Ghosts don't kill people."

"How do you know?"

"She didn't get shot," Rabbit says. "She hanged herself." He feels sick just saying the words. He can't say them without feeling his own throat tighten, crushed, squeezed by rough rope.

"What?"

"You said she was pissed she got shot on her wedding day. She didn't get shot. She shot her husband, then she hung herself."

"Look who knows everything."

Rabbit blinks. "I'm sitting somewhere else," he says.

He finds an empty seat in the front row, which is a better vantage point to scour the crowd for Alice, to confirm that she's nowhere to be seen. He sees everything else: kids staring at the ceiling, gray foam headphones over their ears, wires snaking to unseen Discmans. A nervous girl with a violin in her lap, running her fingers up and down the strings the way a little kid strokes a blankie. Girls in shapeless sweatshirts, curly hair swept back with mismatched plaid scrunchies. Statewide hookups—he can spot them a mile away— couples with too-red cheeks, faces smashed together by the urgent knowledge that this, and only this, weekend will be the entire span of their great love. Bleary-eyed teachers gripping disposable cups of coffee, so exhausted by the prospect of being trapped in one building with several hundred teenagers that they can barely look at each other, let alone discuss it.

Rabbit also sees things he can't possibly see, flashes out of the corner of his eye: Pete the Tenor, sitting a few rows back, smoke wisping up from another joint. He sees his mother and father, toward the rear on the left. His mother is knitting one of the green and red slipper booties that have, without fail, shown up in his stocking every Christmas morning, and his father, like Rabbit, peers around furtively. Is he searching for Alice too? How does he know? How does he know Rabbit failed to look after his big (by three minutes and twelve seconds) sister?

They're ghosts, surely, and Rabbit absolutely believes in them. There are things in the world, strange machinations of physics and chemistry, queer intersections of biology and theology, that Rabbit hasn't the slightest interest in assuming he'll ever understand or be able to solve. They're simply there to be believed in, and Rabbit is a born believer. He wants to believe. He has always thought of life as pregnant with possibility—a freak twister or a wardrobe the only thing separating him from another world—so ghosts, spirits, aliens, and supreme beings coexist within Rabbit with ease. There's a kind of beauty in accepting the possibility, if not the plausibility, of everything imaginable.

Rabbit has a much, much harder time placing his faith in other people. With the unknown world, there's nonetheless a form, a shape, an internal consistency. With other people, there's an illusion of expectation; there are rules of decency, of kindness, yet you still never know what you're going to get. Whom you can trust. Who's a nice guy coming on to you, and who's a nice guy coming on to you to mess with your head.

Which is why he finds it impossible to believe in the Bellweather Bride. To accept that the ghost of a suicidal woman would take the life of an innocent girl in the same manner as she'd taken her own—it didn't make sense. The generalities of belief are, of course, always easier to swallow than the specifics, but it's more than that. It didn't make *sense* for a suicide to return as a murderer—well, she'd killed her husband, but she *shot*, not hanged, him. Rabbit now believes that there is a real live *human* murderer on the loose, stuck with all of Statewide, bound together by snow. The Bellweather Bride is real, but she isn't a ghost. He might have met her in the elevator yesterday. She might be named Minnie.

"Everyone—please, everyone—your attention, please."

No one gives the woman in front of the stage any notice. Rabbit recoils when he recognizes Dr. Viola Fabian. Dangerous Viola Fabian; he's more than happy to take Fisher Brodie's word on the subject. He can see the tendons in her neck tensing from twenty feet away.

"—your attention—" Dr. Fabian clears her throat. "HEY." She sucks in a breath.

The look in her eyes makes Rabbit's chest freeze.

"SHUT UP!" she shouts.

The auditorium stills.

"Thank you," she says mildly. "First of all, I would like to extend the sincere apologies of the Association for School Music to all of you, students, musicians, educators, and so on. For the first time in the history of the festival we have decided to cancel Statewide. Yes—" She holds her hands up over the immediate murmuring. "Yes, even though the conference is already half over. The . . . severity of this storm took us all by surprise, and now it's simply too dangerous for travel to or from the hotel. We will not be holding our concert for the public tomorrow. You will, however, all follow the schedule as planned, including the performances, and you are welcome to attend those performances in which you are not playing. We hope the roads will be clear enough to send you home in the evening. If the snow stops sometime soon, that is."

The auditorium has an air of mutiny, made righteous with disappointment. It buzzes and hums. Someone boos from the back. He catches words: *Stupid. Are you kidding? Fucking lame. Why me? Why my senior year?*

"This is bullshit!" An anonymous girl's voice rises above the din. "Statewide sucks!"

"Oh, grow up," Dr. Fabian says. "It's time to tell you a hard, uncomfortable truth that your parents, your guidance counselors, your big brothers and sisters, the movies, television, and the entire world is keeping from you." She clears her throat and the disgruntled buzzing quiets. "You." She points into the crowd, at no one, at everyone. "You're not stars. You're more talented than some, true, but you're not *that* good. One less concert makes no difference to ninety-nine percent of you. Who did you think was going to be in the audience, two hundred talent scouts? How about two hundred mommies and daddies." She smiles. "Your musical 'skills'—in the real world, you will have to give them up. If you don't want to starve or prostitute yourself, *you will give them up*. If you ever truly loved them, you'll carry a hole in your heart, a little hole you'll never be sure how to fill. The process of growing up is accepting that *this is life* in America. Your dreams are already over, already being lived by other people. If you don't grow up, if you don't accept this, your time on the planet will be a long, painful, dissonant drudge—living paycheck to paycheck, taking odd jobs to support your music, your dreams, your silly ambitions—until you die."

Rabbit looks to his right and left. No one is reacting; no one knows *how* to react. He doesn't know whether to hide under his seat or throw up.

"Don't listen to her!"

All heads whip around and Rabbit sees Mrs. Wilson—Mrs. Natalie Wilson!—standing tall, straddling the seats with one foot planted on a cushion in each row, and he laughs when he realizes Fisher Brodie is sitting beside her, his arm wrapped around her leg for balance. It's the first time he's seen her since Thursday, and those missing two days have been good to her: her hair hangs loosely in curly red waves and she's smiling, gleaming with flint in her eyes. She points at Dr. Fabian.

"Don't listen to her. She's miserable and she's trying to take us down with her." Natalie grins. "It doesn't have to be that way. It doesn't have to be like that. She'll eat your heart with a smile on her face, so DON'T BELIEVE HER!"

For the first time all year, Rabbit likes his teacher.

Natalie is full of life. *Full,* of life, of heat, burning like a small sun. It wasn't just the sex, though the sex was good (and good sex always had a way of making her feel that she would never die). It wasn't just that she'd confessed to a soul who wanted to listen. *I killed a man,* she said. *I killed a boy, my student, twice. Once when I told him he wasn't any good, and again when I shot him.* Fisher's eyes grew wide enough for her to see the whites around his irises, but he didn't speak. He didn't flat-out deny, as Emmett had, the possibility that there was anything at all for her to feel guilty about.

Fisher opened his arms and held her.

Natalie is light, air and light.

And these *kids* in the auditorium. When she first walked in, Fisher's cool knuckles brushing lightly against her arm, she felt them all around her, pulsing, purring. They were gorgeously, impossibly young. New. She hasn't felt anything around young people in years—not hope, not pride, not anger or hatred—not before Ed Hollis, and certainly not after. Now they were coals, hot glowing coals, and Natalie walked through them, over them, across them, and radiated.

Until Viola's diatribe struck a match across her breastbone.

"Don't believe her!" she shouts again. She wobbles on the seats and Fisher tightens his grip around her leg. She smiles. She waves and wobbles again. She has to tell them. She has to tell them the truth. "My name is Natalie. I'm a teacher now but I used to be one of you."

They're staring at her goggle-eyed. Like any minute she'll rip off her shirt and run around the room twirling it over her head.

"Viola Fabian was my teacher when I was your age." Viola is still at the front of the auditorium, frozen, waiting. Natalie stands straighter. "She gave me that same speech, more or less, when I was eighteen years old. I believed her. I believed every word."

"Mrs. Wilson, please sit down," says Viola firmly. "This is unnecessary."

"She's not completely wrong. That's the awful part. It's hard, right? It's *hard* to have a comfortable life, to be secure, to succeed, whatever that means, when you're a good musician. It's hard if you're a *great* musician." She catches a blond girl's gaze and the girl's eyes dart away, frightened as fish. "But being perfect is not the point. Playing first chair, getting into that conservatory, winning that solo—none of that is the point of playing music."

"Then what *is* the point?" says a boy's voice in the back. The auditorium ripples and Natalie smiles.

"Excellent question!" she says. "Maybe the point is that it's good work. You get better, you learn. If you're lucky, the point *becomes* that you're good at it." She's dizzy. Hot. It's warmer up here, eight feet off the ground, that much closer to the auditorium lights. "The point is that it might open a part of you that's always been closed. The point is you might make yourself heard. You might reach someone. You might find you have a beautiful and terrible—you have a power." Something is happening to her. Fisher—she feels him standing up beside her, bracing her. "We make music to—to find each other in the dark. And I have to believe the point is that we don't—we don't ever stop calling out—"

She sways. Her vision clouded with heat, Natalie sees bright eyes, bright young things, watching her. Hanging on her open mouth. Then she sees Viola, two red cheeks framed with a smeary white halo of skin and hair.

"And this woman." She blinks. She stabs her thin finger at Viola. "This woman would leave you lost in the dark forever. This woman is—" She tries to swallow. Her throat shudders. "This woman is evil," she says.

Viola's eyes open as wide as Natalie has ever seen eyes open. They yawn into twin black pits and Natalie, leaning over, falls in.

A voice. A hand on her cheek. *Natalie. Natalie, wake up.*

More voices, louder, shouting. She's being held, squeezed. *Natalie. Natalie, say something. Come back.*

She can't. She lets herself be lifted.

When she opens her eyes she sees the ceiling and all those hot lights, a blurry glow, those round recessed lights that flicker when intermission is ending, but the show must be over because they're applauding—

No—

That's the blood flooding her ears. Her brain feels so far away.

"Maybe next time," says a voice, "we should have a little breakfast before we fight the power."

She's sweating. Breathing with her mouth open. Panting, almost.

"It was a lovely sentiment. Really." Fisher's lying on the floor beside her. When she rolls her head, she hits his. "A poetical antidote. You fainted, love. *Shoom.* Straight down into my arms like a sack of flour. Ever done that before?"

"Yes," she says, emptying her lungs. "In high school." Filling them. "In the shower."

The world is wrapped around her head like a towel, muffling sound, warping light. She has to loosen it to bring herself back. She has to breathe.

"Where are we?" she asks.

"Orchestra pit."

"Where did everyone go?"

"Away. There was a lot of tittering and shouting and then our friend Fabian told everyone to take themselves elsewhere."

"She did that." Breath. "For me, huh?"

"Yes," says Viola. "I did that for you."

She hovers into Natalie's field of vision like an evil eclipse, a white-haired moon blotting out the starry ceiling. Natalie stops breathing.

"That was entirely unprofessional, *Mrs.* Wilson," Viola hisses. "I would say I can't believe it, but I can. Jesus, you haven't changed. You still think your pain is the most important thing in the world, don't you?" And she nudges Natalie in the side, just below her ribs, with the tip of her shoe. "Fisher, move her—I don't know. Wherever. Stand her up in some corner. And get on with your rehearsal. Your precious little bastards can't wait out in the lobby forever."

Viola licks her lips. "You make a cute couple," she says.

19

Connections

W E NEED TO start with facts—what we know, everything we know, from the beginning." Alice holds a
can of Diet Coke up to her face, rolling it slowly over
the swollen red lump beneath her eye. She doesn't
wince, but Minnie does. Minnie has a terrible feeling that she's
contributing to both the delinquency and the malnourishment of a
minor; from the vending machine near her room Alice has already
consumed two Cokes and a late-morning buffet of Combos, Dori-
tos, and peanut butter Ritz Bits. "The beginning is you."

"The beginning is me?" Minnie points a finger at her chest.

"Yes, you. Walk me through everything you remember about that
night."

Minnie's face says, *Do I have to?*

"Yes," says Alice. "You have to. I'm sorry."

Minnie leans against the headboard and closes her eyes. She
has never stopped hating to remember. She looks at her lap. Alice,
sitting in one of the wingback chairs with her feet propped on the
mattress, snaps open her soda, rapt.

So Minnie tells her story, again. Jennifer getting married. Running away from the reception. She neglects to mention the bruise

on her sister's back, but she covers the flying groom, the blue cummerbund, the smell of metal, the bride in the air, calling her closer. How the groom told her to run, and she ran.

"Did you know them?"

"No," says Minnie. "It was a murder-suicide, so we weren't involved in any kind of criminal investigation. Last month, after I booked this trip, I did some digging at work, at the library. All I found was a short notice in a tiny local paper about two deaths at the Bellweather, a man and a woman, last name Driscoll. The way it was worded was weird, kind of gossipy and apologetic at the same time—'unfortunately discovered hanging,' I remember that phrase. 'Mrs. Driscoll was unfortunately discovered hanging from an orange extension cord,' something like that." Her arms prickle.

Alice tilts her head to the side, reminding Minnie so much of Auggie that she stifles a laugh.

"Huh?" says Alice. "What's so funny?"

"Nothing." Minnie can't help it; she laughs out loud. "Nothing's funny."

Alice squints at her, and Minnie laughs again because this is all so ridiculous, so improbable, and because, with one eye almost swollen shut, Alice's squint is hilariously lopsided. She is going to prison after this weekend—Minnie is, not Alice—or at the very least into some kind of protective psychiatric custody. None of it looked good: lying about where she was going and why. Booking specifically on the anniversary. Even Auggie's fake working-dog getup.

But the pièce de résistance was assaulting and kidnapping a stranger. A young girl, a minor, probably. For a while in her teens, Minnie had had a particular fear (ironically enough) of being kidnapped. Learning how to pick a lock seemed the least she could do to prepare for that horrifying prospect, so getting into 712 had been a snap. She didn't want to stay long. She didn't want to mess up the covers on the beds, even. The safest, snuggest place in the whole room was the narrow channel between the far bed and the wall, and there Minnie lay, her sweatshirt pillowed beneath her head, her heart beating like a kettledrum. Auggie close and warm on her side. Two Dramamine pills dissolving in her bloodstream.

Fall asleep, she sang to herself. *Fall asleep, Minnie. It's just a room. It's just a room. It's just a roo —*

She was in her parents' house, alone. There was no air. The anniversary clock under its dusty glass dome did not swing or spin or tick, and neither did Minnie — she wasn't blinking, her heart wasn't beating, she was stuck in space. She stood facing the front door, which was wide open, the screen door propped. She heard high heels clicking on the flagstones.

The bride's shoes thumped dully on the wooden steps.

Mrs. Driscoll stands just outside the door and smiles at Minnie. Her face is fat with death. A deep purple line runs from ear to ear beneath her chin, and she holds a bouquet of vicious red roses at her chest.

"Hello again, little girl," Mrs. Driscoll says.

The roses are bleeding.

Minnie is stuck and Mrs. Driscoll steps into the house and then — then —

Oh God, thank God, she can move her arm, she can stand, she can swing —

She was still asleep, still dreaming, technically, when her fist connected with Alice's face. She was half awake when she saw a stranger slump backward on the bed, unconscious, her own trembling fist held high. Only it wasn't a stranger. It was the girl from the elevator that morning. The girl whose roommate hanged herself.

Minnie would like to blame it on the drugs — and it was true they had fogged her decision-making — but the real reason she threw the girl over her shoulder and ran out of 712 was because she was afraid to be alone. Even unconscious, here was a soul who would listen, here was the only other person in the world who knew how it felt to see a body hanging in this hotel room. She was Minnie's mirror, and Minnie couldn't bear to leave her behind.

"I have to be honest with you," says Alice. "When I met you yes-

terday in the elevator, you jumped to the top of my list of suspects."
She pauses. "You're still there."

Minnie shrugs. "That's fair," she says, and then, a little wounded,
"The top? Really?"

Alice nods gravely.

"Am I still?"

"Maybe . . . maybe not the top," says Alice.

"Who else is on the list?"

"Jill's mother. Her name is Viola Fabian. She's in charge of the
festival. Jill was afraid of her, legitimately afraid, and not in an
'I'm going to be so dead' way. In an 'I'm going to be actually dead'
way." Alice shakes her head. "I've met Fabian twice. She's a colossal
bitch."

"But is she a murderous bitch?" Minnie reaches down to feed
Auggie a Dorito. "What do you know about her or about Jill? I
thought we were still in the gathering-facts stage."

Alice tucks her legs beneath her and hugs herself. "Her name
is—was—Jill Faccelli. All I know I learned from reading magazines
and articles and stuff. She's super-famous. As music prodigies go,
at least. Traveled all over the world. She plays the flute."

"Have you heard her play?"

"You know," Alice says, "I never have," and the twist of her mouth
tells Minnie that this realization makes her stupendously sad. "We
were roommates, random roommates. Right before she disappeared I was telling her fortune. Doing a tarot reading."

"Ooh, neat. I've always wanted to do that."

"Well, if I ever get my cards back—they're missing. Housekeeping took them or threw them out when they turned over the room."
It still bothers her, clearly. "Her reading was all over the place.
Scary and awful. Then she spilled some wine and I left the room to
get stuff to clean up. When I came back she was—"

Alice's eyes lose focus.

"Um. She was—"

"I know," Minnie says softly, and when Alice meets her eyes they
both understand. They have decided to trust each other. For whatever that's worth.

Minnie pushes herself off the bed. "I want to go on record as saying this mystery is probably not nearly as complicated as it appears. That said, I've got an idea."

"Are we going somewhere?" Alice asks.

"Yes," says Minnie. "Detecting."

Sheila briefed Hastings as soon as he arrived (early, but he could tell his presence was appreciated) on which staff had either spent the night on a folding cot or braved the elements on snowshoes, sleds, or snowmobiles that morning. She fell into the latter category, she told him with a glimmer of pride. Statewide would apparently go on as planned for Saturday, but the musicians would be performing only for themselves and the Bellweather staff on Sunday. Sheila dropped her voice to tell him, impishly, that there'd been some sort of outburst at the morning assembly, that one of the teachers had had a fit and climbed up on the seats to yell at Viola Fabian.

"About what?" he'd asked, incredulous.

"An old grudge or something." Sheila bugged her eyes. "She called Fabian *evil*. Can you imagine?"

Hastings caught himself before he could nod. "And the girl. Her daughter. Has she turned up yet?"

Sheila shrugged. "Not that I know of."

He hoped Viola Fabian's daughter was as eerily resourceful as her mother, that she wasn't hiding out in the games shed or the tiny golf clubhouse, someplace without heat. He asked Sheila to send one of the grounds boys to check. Just in case.

Now, if it weren't for the constant apocalyptic chatter on the radio at reception (this was apparently the worst storm in fifty years) or the occasional whine of wind against the front windows, Hastings wouldn't know it from any other Statewide Saturday. He rather enjoys weathering storms at the hotel, snug in the one place on earth he feels safest and most needed.

In the quiet, his mind drifts back to the strange case of Viola Fabian. He flattens the printouts from the library on his concierge blotter. The first is the article detailing the mysterious death of

Kevin Montrose. The second is an obituary, also from the *San Francisco Chronicle* but barely two years old.

ALEXANDER BRIAN FACCELLI. April 18 at the age of 62. After a long career at Microsoft, Mr. Faccelli dedicated himself to serving his local community. Neighbors say they will miss his infectious laugh. He is survived by his wife, Viola Fabian Faccelli, and a beloved step-daughter. Burial will be private. In lieu of flowers, donations can be made to the Muir Woods Volunteer Coalition, c/o the National Parks Conservancy.

Viola is a widow? Of course she is. He sees her through a soft-focus lens, pale and lovely as death, tears glistening like melted snowflakes on her lashes and cool white cheeks. Lips black, the corners turned up ever so slightly; she's a merry widow, if she's any-thing. The beloved stepdaughter must be the still missing Jill. The grounds boy had snottily informed him that no one was currently or had been in the clubhouse or the shed for months. Hastings invol-untarily raises his hand to his heart. A monstrous mother, a dead stepfather. No wonder she ran away, poor girl.

The rest of the articles are fluff. A profile of mother and daugh-ter, manager and child phenom, describing young Jill as "tremen-dously gifted, otherworldly, grave." A caption for a missing pho-tograph, an image the computer didn't have on file, that referred to "Viola Fabian and student," and a short accompanying article about a series of youth concerts and recitals in San Francisco. Has-tings scans the text for familiar names: Marcus Bellman. Casey Mc-Gregor. Viola Fabian, again. Natalie Wink. He curses the computer, the all-knowing machine with its brain full of holes. These names mean nothing. They're too old, too far away. If only he could see the picture. The blank page sneers at him.

The final piece is another pictureless caption, but a bit more helpful:

On hand at Lincoln Center, L to R: Frances Hallowell, Viola Fabian, Fisher Brodie

He'd sensed something between Viola and Fisher during that bizarre scene in the office: an overfamiliarity, a closeness that went beyond the professional. Of course it was natural that they knew each other—the Statewide circle isn't *that* large, especially at a certain level—but Hastings's gut had told him it went beyond that. The year on the caption is 1980. So they've known each other for nearly two decades. Fisher had called Viola dangerous. What did he know about how dangerous she could be?

Hastings glances across the lobby at Sheila. She stands with her hands clasped behind her back, shifting her weight from foot to foot. What had she said about the morning assembly? Someone—a female someone—had yelled at Fabian. About an old grudge. He pulls out the Statewide packet he keeps at the concierge desk and flips until he finds the master participant list. He's looking for a Frances. A Casey. A Natalie. He's looking for an echo from the past. The first Casey he finds, he circles with blue ballpoint. Then he finds another—no. He shouldn't be looking at the students, they're too young. There are fewer participating educators and chaperones. He circles a single Natalie, a Natalie Wilson of Ruby Falls Central School District.

Ruby Falls.

He flips back to the student participants. He runs the pad of his right index finger down the list until he finds them. The Hatmakers . . . also of Ruby Falls.

Hastings stands up straight. His eyes hurt and he rubs at his brow. This has to mean something. Natalie was Viola's student. Natalie's student was Viola's daughter's co-conspirator. An old grudge, an old wound. Drops of sweat bead at his hairline, moisten his upper lip. He has to talk to Jess. He has to tell her what he's found. She'll know what kind of sense to make of it.

He's about to ask Sheila to keep an eye on his desk when two people approach. He recognizes them both. One is Alice Hatmaker, with a swollen black eye; on anyone less pugnacious, he would wonder how she got it. Standing beside her is the blurry girl, the large blurry girl who checked in with her dog on Thursday.

"Hello," says the blurry girl. For a woman who occupies so much space, her voice is tiny, soft, the voice of a young girl.

"Hello," he replies. "How may I help you?" He nods at Alice. "Hello, Miss Hatmaker."

"Hey," Alice says. She thrusts her chin up. "What did you do with my stuff?"

"Pardon?"

"What my sister is asking—"

Sister? But Alice has a brother, a brother named—he scans the program—Bertram.

"My sister had a very special item stolen from her room." Hastings simply can't help himself: he stares at the girl. He knows her. *How?* "It's a terrible violation of privacy to have your belongings stolen from a hotel room."

He nods. "I agree," he says. "I—I'm so sorry. I will absolutely make this right. Could you describe what was taken?"

"My tarot cards," Alice says. "They were a gift from my grandmother. Who *died.*"

"Cards? A deck of cards?" Hastings asks.

"Not just a deck of cards, a deck of *tarot* cards. I've spent a lot of effort making them *mine,* you know, that's how tarot works. They were in my room when I left yesterday morning and they were gone when I came back at night. Someone from housekeeping took them."

Hastings blanches. "I assure you, no one on my staff would ever steal."

"Well, someone from your staff is the only other person with a key." Alice crosses her arms over her chest.

Hastings inhales a long breath through his nose. "What about your roommate?" he says, though he knows precisely how the girl is going to respond.

"My dead roommate, you mean? Jesus!" Hastings flinches; he has never gotten over all these young people cursing, especially the girls. "How many times do I have to tell you? She is dead. Dead girls don't steal."

"But you must admit, the fact that the cards are missing suggests—" He waves his hands in the air. "It suggests she may not be dead."

"Sir," says the other girl, her supposed sister, "Alice is a bit upset." She puts a hand clumsily on Alice's shoulder. Hastings looks from one girl to the other. When he saw Alice's brother for the first time, he knew beyond a doubt they were related. These girls look nothing alike.

These girls are lying to him.

"Alice, honey. Can you give us a moment?" The big girl nods and Alice rolls her eyes way, way back in her head and walks away. "To tell you the truth, she's upset about the cards but she's *really* upset about the girl. About Jill. Is there anything else you can tell us? Any news? What about her mother?"

Hastings gathers the papers on his blotter without looking away from the girl's face.

"You're not her sister," he says.

She looks away. "No," she says.

"Who *are* you?" And as he says it he knows exactly who she is: Alice's missing chaperone. Natalie Wilson, née Wink, of Ruby Falls Central.

"I don't know what you're playing at," he says, taking a step forward, "but this is my hotel. These are *my* guests staying under *my* roof, and if we weren't in the middle of a blizzard I would throw you both out this instant." It's so obvious now, it's so clear: his gut has been telling him not to trust her from the minute she checked in. At first it had felt like déjà vu. But it was never recognition, it was *pre*-cognition. She was trouble. She was the trouble at his Statewide, the cancerous ghost in his hotel. With her milky forgettable face and her unfixable gaze and her *dog*—wherever the hell he was, whatever the hell part he played in this ridiculous charade.

"I don't know what you think—" she says.

"I think you are a liar, Mrs. Wilson."

The look of exquisite confusion on her face is almost enough to convince him of her innocence. Then he remembers Alice, the little actress, and wonders if they aren't sisters after all.

232

"I think," he continues, "that you had better go back to your room and not cause one more second of trouble. Not for me, not for my staff, not for any one of my guests. Am I being clear?"

She nods.

"Good. And now that I have your attention, I must—I do not *understand* you. Why would you use—why would you exploit such a terrible tragedy to—to what end, exactly? What is the point of all this? Of covering for Jill and terrorizing her mother, of questioning me as though I had anything to do with it? When Doug Kirk was here—when Doug Kirk *returns* as head of Statewide, he won't stand for this . . . this bullshit." The curse surprises everyone within earshot, most of all Hastings himself. His voice isn't his own. It's far away and tight and five times louder than it ought to be, rising with every word. "This tawdry, disgusting plot of yours makes me ill. Do you want revenge? Do you want justice? Do you want to know peace, after whatever hell you believe Viola Fabian put you through? You're not going to get it from me. You're not going to find it here. It hasn't been here for a long, long time."

"Mr. Hastings, please." Her eyes look so kind and sad. They can't possibly be telling him the truth and he hates them for it. "I never meant. *We* never meant to—"

"Who gives a good goddamn what you meant."

Then Sheila is at his side. She isn't speaking, she's taking his arm. She's leading him back behind reception, to the quiet of the office with the door shut. The world is quiet. The only light is on the desk. Hastings, who can barely stand to think anymore, sits on the couch and watches the clock on the opposite wall. The second hand sweeps the face clean, remaking one minute after another, after another.

20

Accelerando

I

FISHER WAS THIRTEEN when he decided to run away. He was in New York—not for the first time, but for the first time as a teenager. Around the age of twelve, life had begun to feel like a knife in his side: sharp and insistent, a constant pain that couldn't be ignored, and never more so than when he'd been booked to perform in American cities. New York cut him so deep he wanted to lie down and die. Life was larger here, dirtier and busier. Fisher had a vision of himself disappearing into the crowd that surged to meet him and his mother whenever they crossed the street. New York was the only place she physically held on to her son; she grabbed his arm as soon as the walk sign flashed and didn't let go until their feet were safe on the opposite curb. Gorgeous young girls on their way elsewhere, businessmen in crisp pinstripes, students with ratty hand-knit stocking caps, old toothless men who looked like they were crossing the street simply to have something to do, all touched Fisher, brushed by or banged into him, and each time they did, if not for his mother's fingers locked around him, he thought he might stick to them like a piece of lint and be carried away.

He had hated his life for quite some time. New York when he was thirteen was the first time he considered he might be able to change it.

Fisher Brodie, fantastic teenage prodigy from across the bloody great Atlantic, had been invited to perform with the New York Philharmonic during its regular season. He was an add-on, a treat. Tickets to see him didn't come with the normal season subscription. "You're extra," his mother cooed. "Special!"

Nothing about the performance felt extra or special to Fisher. He walked onstage, bowed to the conductor, played Chopin, stood and bowed to the audience, played more Chopin, stood and bowed, and then left the stage. He had done the exact same thing in San Francisco a year earlier and would do the exact same thing in several months' time in London. The only thing special about this performance happened when it was over, after they took a taxi back to their hotel and Fisher's mother realized, as the elevator doors were closing, that she'd left her gloves in the cab.

"I'll go check," he said, and darted out of the elevator.

It hadn't been a thoughtful gesture. It had been pure instinct, and Fisher didn't recognize it for what it was until he was standing at the curb, the cab he'd shared with his mother long gone, alone. He was never alone. And now he was alone in the greatest city in America, at eleven o'clock on a Thursday night. He had twenty U.S. dollars in his pocket, no sense of direction, and no other chance but this. He could disappear. Right now, tonight. This city would swallow him. He would never have to perform if he didn't want to; he could play whatever and whenever he wanted. He would never hear his mother and father talking as if he were sitting in another room. (They didn't speak to him so much as around him, and always, always about him.)

His sisters would never smack him or call him names or trip him when he walked down the hall; his mother would never shout "Mind his hands!" as though it were perfectly all right for them to break every other bone in his body. He could meet people who had no idea who he was, who might like him in spite of what he was. *He* had no idea who he was, outside this life. He could find out. Tonight.

Thoughts of his Auntie's golden teeth in their lozenge tin, squirreled beneath his mattress back home, gave him a moment's pause. They were valuable. It would be stupid to run away without them. Then again, it would be stupid to not run away when he had the chance, because who knew when he'd ever have the chance again. It was late January and unseasonably warm, but Fisher didn't have the proper wardrobe to withstand a winter on the streets of New York. Was that what he was thinking—that he'd scavenge and scrounge? Sleep under bridges? What if he got frostbite, what if he lost his ears or his toes or, God forbid, his fingers? Would that honestly be any better than the life he was living now?

Yes.

Maybe.

He looked down the street to his right. The road glowed, full of orangey-yellow cabs and red taillights like hot coals. The hotel was on a corner. A crosswalk led across the street, its white ladder lines beckoning him to climb to the other side, to another life. The walk signal glowed and Fisher's breath fogged the air before him and the signal began to blink and then it was red and Fisher was not going to run away. He was only thirteen and didn't know where to go.

His mother was waiting in the lobby when he came back. She had been watching him through the glass entry doors. She knew— she always had a way of knowing—and she gave his arm a good hard squeeze as they walked side by side to the elevators, looking like any other mother and child made unusually close by the circumstances of their lives.

Fisher, grown, an adult conductor, remembers her words as if she'd spoken them on the telephone last night; as if she weren't dead and buried somewhere in Scotland; as if, after emancipating himself three years after that night in New York, Fisher ever saw his mother again.

"Good lad," she said. "It's a nasty old world out there. You wouldn't like it."

Fisher still wonders whether he would have all ten fingers if he'd run away when he had the chance. When he had the *chance*—that was the key. He knows he can't do anything about what wasn't done, just as he knows it would be equally foolish to pass up the opportunity to run, should another present itself.

Natalie is another chance. Fisher cannot believe she is real, that she is an actual person. For the first time in his life, he is in love.

He has never felt so necessary to another person, or so in need. The ability to forgive—and he did forgive her; he had no idea he had such capacity for forgiveness, but there it was—Christ, it was an intoxicating kind of intimacy. She'd confided the worst thing she'd ever done in her life (and it was horrible, all right), but all Fisher could feel was gratitude that she'd thought him a worthy confidant. He, placed in a similar situation, could've done the same thing and would've felt like the same piece of responsible shit as she overwhelmingly did, but he didn't dare tell her; she didn't want to hear that. She didn't want to hear words of any kind on the subject. She only wanted to be heard and to be held, and Fisher only wanted to listen and to hold her.

And they were so alike, so similar, so mangled in their own peculiar ways. Twinned. When he woke up beside her, the last thing he expected her to do in an hour's time was leap up on her seat to rain fire and brimstone on Viola Fabian. Fisher had felt drunk (and inspired—it could have come straight from his own de-brainwashing playbook!), and he wasn't doing anything more than steadying her leg, hugging her thigh, and pressing his face against her to stop from laughing out loud. She's traumatized, overcome by guilt. She's unstable and violent and broken, and he hasn't any illusions of saving or fixing her. He only wishes to be with her, to spend the rest of his life knowing her, reflecting her. Running with her. Away from this hotel. From this world.

He bounces to the conductor's podium, lighter than air. "Right, everyone! What a lovely start to our day, eh? Nothing wakes you up like a little drama." Fisher hasn't felt like this . . . ever. This is love. His heart could be made of spun sugar.

The orchestra looks sluggish and perturbed, which is reasonable considering they're trapped here in the middle of a storm and have just been told there's to be no audience for their concert. Well, no audience but one another. Fisher claps his hands to get their attention. "Oi, lovelies! Remember when I made that disparaging crack about your mums and 'Jupiter'? I was lying. Again. Hope you kept your parts."

In truth, he hadn't been lying; before today, before he was in love, Fisher hadn't given two shits for that movement of *The Planets*. It was all happy bouncy violins and syncopated brass and big swells of sound and chirpy little woodwinds, and it was enough to permanently put you off your lunch. But today he's in love. He finds he has more patience and goodwill than he knows what to do with.

"Mars," he says, "brings war. Venus, according to Holst, brings peace. And Jupiter? Jupiter brings jollity." He clears his throat. "Lah-de-fuckin'-dah Jupiter. Aren't we adorable."

He catches Rabbit's eye. He feels very protective of his Bunny Boy, and in a sudden and unexpected blush, eager for his approval. His sanction. Hatmaker's nerve—his resistance to Brodie's attempts to railroad him in that first rehearsal—was the first delight of this weekend, this increasingly astonishing weekend, and if Fisher were superstitious, he would feel he owed the boy a tithe. A sacrifice in grateful recognition of having reaped such fortune. He hardly ever felt Scottish—though Fisher's ancestors may have come from just outside Glasgow, his personal homelands were the antiseptically welcoming Hiltons and Marriotts of the world—but perhaps there was a drop of old pagan blood in his heart after all.

Rabbit, who's been working his double reed around in his mouth, moistening it, neatly affixes it to the end of his bocal and meets Fisher's gaze expectantly.

"Let's be jolly," Fisher tells them. He raises his hands and they're off. It's every bit as obnoxious as he remembers. Rising and falling eighths in the trombones, the theme scampering like a drunken leprechaun from violins to winds to brass and then, like an overly obvious joke, a pompously grand countertheme rising from the horns. Fisher has always hated clowns. From childhood, he'd found them smug and unfunny, and it makes perfect sense that he's always disliked this movement, because "Jupiter" is, essentially, the soundtrack to a massive clown orgy. *Oh ho-ho,* say the violins, *aren't you a naughty jester! What,* chirp the clarinets, *you want to put that pie where?* Despite his candy-floss heart and head full of Natalie, the music begins to grate, and he's thankful when the flutes stumble over their own twee feet. They've never recovered from the loss of Jill Faccelli.

Fisher calls a halt.

"Egh," he says. "I've got clown all over me. Flutes, you've got to—what's the word. You've got to be disgusting. Revoltingly cute. You should be pretty good at that, being flutes. From the beginning."

After the flutes, Fisher rehearses each section of the orchestra in turn. When he brings them all together again it's almost flawless, wound tight as a music box, and he feels it pulling the edges of his lips back in a manic grin as it rolls cheerily along. Yet he's unprepared when the first third of the piece quiets and the middle section begins.

He knew this, the *andante maestoso,* was coming. He has conducted *The Planets* several times before, after all. Fisher is a relatively sloppy conductor, technically speaking, but he isn't entirely unprofessional; he'd studied the scores in the weeks leading up to Statewide. He knows that "Jupiter" is divided into three sections—the first and third are quick and cheerful, *allegro giocoso,* the essence of jollity (which Fisher finds hard to believe is actually a word). The middle is not silly. The middle is not syncopated. After some leftover tootling in the winds, the middle begins with strings moving together as one sonorous beast, slowly, majestically. The theme is restated, picking up winds and brass and percussion. It soars higher and higher until all the orchestra is reaching the same climactic phrase, released from gravity for only a moment, and gently falling back to earth.

It is a hymn, a prayer.

It's the sound of several dozen souls singing the same song, and Fisher isn't leading them. Fisher is one of them, part of them, his skinny arms swooping of their own accord. The middle doesn't end so much as pause thoughtfully; more ridiculous merry bullshit is coming, but this feeling, this true joy, is always there. The winds make a halfhearted attempt to leap into the final clownish act, but no one is ready to move on quite yet. Fisher looks out at the orchestra, at his Bunny Boy, whose eyes are peaceful slits. At the bright-eyed blonde resting her cheek on her violin, breathing through her open mouth. Third-chair trumpet, who never looks forward, not when he can help it, is looking straight at Fisher and smiling. This has never happened before, not in any group Fisher has ever played in or conducted, this true synchronicity. They all felt this. Together. Music passed through them all and made them different.

And Fisher is transformed. He is things he has never been before: in love. Part of this orchestra, the way a nose is part of a face. The man who dreamed he died in his bed and burned, alone, is comforted. The young idiot who knew exactly what he was destroying when he punched a stranger in a German bar, who remembers how warm and comforting his bloody hand felt, is forgiven. The teenager who stood on a corner in New York and didn't run. The boy who pulled his Auntie's teeth from her mouth, who slept in all those hotels, bowed to all those conductors, heard all that applause and felt nothing nothing *nothing* — is alive.

Fisher's broken heart only needed twenty years of music, one motorcycle, one Natalie, and one student orchestra to mend itself. He's mad with joyful feeling, with the surety of knowing just what he needs to do. He can remake the world with a single sentence: *Run with me, Natalie*. It rhymes; of course it rhymes, it's a song. It's the song of Fisher Brodie's life, the song he's waited a lifetime to sing.

Don't wait, he wants to tell them. *Don't wait. Use your hands while you have them.*

Instead, he asks, "Who wants to play that again?"

The orchestra is a field of raised hands, gorgeous young wrists and palms and fingers fluttering, rippling like sweet spring grass.

II

"Toss me the bears?" Minnie asks, and Alice flings her a squishy bag of gummies, their bright paws pressed desperately against the cellophane. Unlike Alice, she hasn't eaten anything since breakfast. She hasn't had the stomach or the heart.

"I am a *bad* detective," she had muttered to Alice after Hastings blew up at her — Alice, who was still doing her bad-cop/disgruntled-sister act on the other side of the lobby. "I think we broke him."

"I think he did it." Alice pushed the elevator call button. "Or maybe he didn't do it, but he *knows* something. He's *hiding* something."

"He called me Mrs. Wilson. Does that mean anything? It *does*." Alice's eyes had widened.

"He knows something we don't." Alice gnawed on her fingernail. "Hey," she said, stage-poking Minnie with her elbow, "we make a pretty good team."

Then why do I feel like such an asshole? It was a good question Minnie felt would be almost mean to ask: the Robin to her Batman was giddy, pink with the excitement of their little adventure. Were all teenagers so heartless? No—it wasn't heartlessness, not really. If Alice were heartless, she wouldn't have agreed to help Minnie. It was more like . . . a willing suspension of disbelief so total, so consuming, it occluded all ethical and moral realities. Minnie frowned as they stepped back into her room.

"Say—say Hastings and Viola Fabian *are* in cahoots. Now we've tipped him off. Now he suspects us of knowing the score."

"Now he suspects *Mrs. Wilson,* you mean." Alice tossed off a dazzling stage grin. "This is the *best*. This weekend is—" She faltered, her face falling as she remembered everything this weekend was turning out to be. Not heartless after all; melodramatic, ridiculous, and a little selfish, but not heartless.

"Who knows what the hell this weekend is," Minnie said. "Want to watch some TV about the storm?"

They watched the news, which wasn't promising—the blizzard had slowed but was predicted to dump at least another foot and a half on them before it ran its course—and then they watched *Days of Our Lives* and *The Bold and the Beautiful,* and all the while Alice talked about her classes and the school musical she was rehearsing and that she'd die to get cast in a soap, not that she didn't have grander aspirations, but lots of actors got their start there, there wasn't any shame in it. Minnie started to feel less like an asshole and more like eating a handful of gummy bears.

Friends! Other people who weren't your relatives! Who weren't four-legged and nonverbal! Minnie, before, had always been terrible at making friends. She had little interest in getting to know other people, and when she tried, she had some kind of horrible inverse friend radar. She was guaranteed to say hello to the one person in the room who had no interest whatsoever in saying hello back.

After Auggie, her brother Mike is probably her closest friend, which is sort of pathetic, since she can't remember the last time they spoke. Once, she would have counted Henry as a friend too, but Henry moved to the West Coast after college and she doubted whether Mike, even, still heard from him. She had, in recent months, considered picking up the phone, calling information in San Francisco, and tracking down the Henry Wattersmiths (how many could there be?), but of course she'd never been brave or stupid enough to actually do it. What would she say? *Hi, Henry. I know you were just nice to me because I was Mike's kid sister, but the only time I was happy as a teenager was when we were watching scary movies together.*

Alice is unlike anyone Minnie has ever met, let alone tried to make friends with. When you look in her eyes they fix and look back instead of darting off to another corner of the room. She opens to people. Minnie folds in like an envelope; Alice erupts like a self-exploding piñata. She's easy to be with, provided you don't mind the constant chatter, the non-sequitur song cues, or her total lack of an indoor voice. Maybe this is what it would have been like to have a sister, a sister who wasn't already grown up, moved out, and married by the time Minnie was ready for all-night candy binges and video marathons, for hand-me-down trashy romance novels with the juicy parts dog-eared at the corners. Minnie crosses her feet at the ankles and leans back on the bed against the pillows, chewing a green gummy bear.

"I have to take Aug for a walk," Minnie says over the next commercial. "Want to come?"

Taking Auggie for a walk in a massive blizzard amounts to thirty shivering seconds in the shoveled semicircle outside the front doors, just long enough for him to do his business, and for Minnie to note Hastings's absence from his post and feel both relief and embarrassment. The rest of the walk is a leisurely stroll through the hotel, up and down the tower.

They're just getting into the elevator to return to the fourth floor when Alice says, "So this may come out of nowhere, but I've been thinking. I have to talk to someone about this and you seem like a really neat person, Minnie. I know you think you're a big fat weirdo"—Alice stammers, which is enough to let Minnie know she didn't mean to call her fat, not like that—"but you're not. You're cool. And you're older and you've dealt with some crazy stuff in your life, and I—the future terrifies me. It scares me so much I've been daydreaming about dying young so I don't have to deal with it. That's screwed up, right? The only thing I've ever worked on, the only thing I love to do is sing and act and be a ham, and if I can't spend my life doing that, then what the hell was the point of learning to love it? I'm not totally worthless otherwise, I can write an essay and I got a 1440 on my SATs, but it's the thing I do *best*. It's the work that I love, and what the hell am I going to be good for if I have to spend my whole life doing something else? What if letting my dream die makes me all bitter and angry and cranky—and if I never get to do and be the thing I love, how will anyone ever see me, or know me, or love *me?*"

The elevator doors close. Minnie doesn't push any of the buttons and neither does Alice.

"What do you do—you said you work in a library?" Alice flutters. "Do you like it?"

"Mostly it's shelving, reshelving, checking books in and out, helping people find what they're looking for. Yeah, I like it fine."

"Is it the thing you do best?"

"You know," Minnie says, "I'm kind of the last person in the world to be giving advice about the future, considering I've been stuck on pause for so long. But—"

This is what it's like to have a little sister. A super-talented, super-dramatic little sister.

"I have no idea what I do best. I haven't figured it out yet. So you're one step ahead of me. You're one step ahead of a lot of people, I think. I can tell you to worry about a broken heart when it breaks and not before. And maybe try not to drink so much caffeine."

"There's something else too," Alice says. "I'm a twin. My brother has always been the good twin, the sweet and kind and smart one, and so I've always been the bad twin, the loud and funny one who would probably run her own saloon if the Gold Rush were still on, and I am so afraid of who I'll be when Bert isn't there to remind me what my better self, my best self, is made of."

This last sentence falls out so quickly and so softly—Alice barely whispers it—that Minnie almost makes the mistake of asking her to repeat herself. All it takes is one look at Alice to see what this admission has cost her. That's what this torrential freak-out is about: Alice is horrified at the prospect of losing her grip on the most essential things in her life—her brother, her talent, her self—in the seismic shift known as life after graduation. She can't imagine who she'll be on the other side.

Minnie presses the button for four and the car falls. "I don't mean to laugh," she says, unable to stop herself from laughing, "but you don't strike me as the type to peak in high school."

She opens her arms and Alice falls in. It's extraordinary to hug a person who desperately needs one, especially when she's in so desperate need of a hug herself.

The elevator opens on four. Auggie is rumbling from the lowest point of his belly before Minnie has even turned her key in the lock and heard the tumblers click. He darts into Minnie's room the second the door opens, tags jangling merrily, and attacks the intruder with both barrels of puppy kisses. If Minnie were using her best friend as a guard dog, she would be terribly disappointed.

The young woman sitting in the desk chair looks very familiar, but Minnie doesn't place her until she sees a threadbare maroon blazer tossed across the desk, the same maroon blazer that all the staff at the front desk wear.

"You," the woman says over the bright music of Auggie's tags, "had better explain yourselves."

"You're from the front desk, right?" Alice says as she shuts the door. She holds out her hand. "My name is Alice Hatmaker. This is Minnie—"

"Graves, yes, I know who you are. That's how I found your room. What I don't understand is why you're hurting a sweet old man." She gives Auggie one final, gentle push away and crosses her arms over her chest. "Mr. Hastings is like a grandfather to me. What is your *deal?*"

Minnie stands up tall, having just realized she's probably the oldest person in the room. The front-desk girl looks much, much younger without the maroon blazer. She has sloppy highlights, and her feet, out from behind the desk, are stuffed into bright green sneakers. Her ponytail is held back with a purple scrunchie. She might be even younger than Alice.

"I can't tell you how awful I feel," Minnie says, "for distressing him. We honestly had no idea he was going to get that upset. We were just trying to get a handle on." No, that wasn't right. "I wasn't trying to do anything this weekend but—"

"Survive." Alice juts her chin defiantly. "Solve the murder of Jill and the mystery of the Bellweather Bride."

The girl pauses, then looks from Alice to Minnie and back again, and says, "You're kidding."

"Minnie here *saw* it, you know. Minnie was just a kid when it happened, but she saw it and she came back for answers. Who was the bride? Why is she still here in the hotel, claiming more victims?" Alice works the room, playing to the cheap seats. "Or, if it isn't the bride, who's celebrating the anniversary of her death with murder? Could it be—"

The girl holds up both her hands. She looks at the carpet and purses her lips and suddenly looks much older than either Alice or Minnie. "My Aunt Lily used to work here. In housekeeping, before she moved to Buffalo. Sometimes I'd come with her when she picked up her paycheck, and Mr. Hastings always had a little something for me. Piece of candy. A new postcard from the gift shop." She lowers her voice. "'Good afternoon, Miss Czeckley—checking in?' He was nicer to me than either of my actual grandfathers ever were, both of them combined. He treated me, my Aunt Lily, he treated everyone like we were special.

"She *knew* the bride, my aunt. They were friends. Lily was there the night everything happened. She saw what you saw, Minnie. Unless you're lying about that too."

Minnie's knees dip and she sits heavily on the bed. It squeaks.

"It's not a ghost story," the girl says. "It's not a movie or a mystery or this big crime to be solved. It's just a sad thing that happened. The bride, who I guess had never been all that normal, found out during her wedding reception that her husband was, you know, *with* another girl, was planning to run away with her, that he'd gone through with the wedding because he didn't feel he could stop it. So she stopped him with a shotgun and hung herself from the sprinkler pipe in room seven-twelve. My aunt was one of the first to find the bodies, my aunt and Mr. Hastings. Only Mr. Hastings wasn't just the concierge that night."

"What do you mean?" asks Alice.

"He was the father of the bride."

"The father," whispers Alice, "of the *bride*."

The girl nods. "They used to live in a big old house in town — Hastings and his wife and daughter. He's still on the payroll, but it's not like we really need a concierge in this dump anymore; we usually have about five guests in the whole freaking place. But he was friends with the manager back then, and everyone felt so awful about what happened that they let him move in for a while, and he just kind of . . . never left. He still goes to his old house sometimes. I can always tell when he's been, because he comes back all dirty, like he's been dumpster diving. I'm afraid to see what the place looks like. He's so —" She rolls her eyes and taps her forehead with her fingertips in a gesture that can only mean cracked. Broken.

"My aunt told me his story when I started working here. She wanted me to know — she wanted someone to know, to understand Mr. Hastings. To look out for him. He doesn't have any friends. Aunt Lily told me he used to be tight with this old librarian geezer, but then *he* died and left Hastings all his junk. He isn't dangerous crazy, just sad crazy. You'd think he'd want to be as far away from here as he could get, but I don't think he has anywhere else to go. He's totally alone with a house full of someone else's garbage. Sometimes I—" She swallows. "I probably shouldn't, but sometimes he calls the front desk just to, like, chat. I can tell he thinks I'm someone else— he calls me Jess—and I kind of just go along with it. He's lonely. He's always been so nice to me, and Aunt Lily asked me to take care of him, and it's so freaking boring at the front desk otherwise. That's not so awful, right?"

She looks from Alice to Minnie and back to Alice, as though someone closer to her own age will be more understanding. Will forgive her for an act that, admitted to others, suddenly seems the exact opposite of her stated intent.

Minnie's chest is so tight she can barely fill her lungs.

She remembers a butterscotch candy in a crinkly wrapper. A tour of the hotel that was offered but never taken (squash courts—what were *squash* courts?). A bow tie. *Save me a dance,* he called across the lobby. All her other memories from that first weekend at the Bellweather—all this time she thought the home horror movie she could never stop screening in her mind was a perfect recording. The whole picture.

This is why she came back. This is why she's here at the Bellweather. When the bride killed her brand-new husband and herself, she took more than Minnie Graves's childhood. She took most of her own father's heart and mind.

Minnie was never the only survivor.

III

Rabbit presses Play. His Discman purrs to life in his hand, and he sets it down on the carpet. It hums beside his leg, a happy bee. A second later, Weezer fuzzes and buzzes angrily in his ears, moaning that they're tired of having sex (so tired). Rabbit stretches his neck. He isn't tired of having sex (you'd have to be having sex to be tired of it), but he is tired of *thinking* about sex. He is exhausted of thinking about sex, thinking about how he wants to have sex with other guys and feeling as though he has to *explain* this to people. He closes his eyes.

He's been over all of this a thousand times in his mind. He doesn't know why he's going over it again now, especially since there are way more important things to be worrying about, like: his still-missing sister and the fact that she has his room key. He's waiting outside his own door, hoping Dan doesn't decide to go straight from rehearsal to dinner. He should be looking for Alice, canvassing the Bellweather for her, but he has Beatrice to consider. He can't leave her alone; he doesn't have the money—or more important, the heart—to replace her if she's stolen. So all he can do is sit here and wait, and hope, and listen to the CDs tucked in the pouch of his sweatshirt.

And relive that rehearsal. There simply isn't any room for fear in his heart or his head after that. It was the best rehearsal of Rabbit's life. There wasn't much to compare it with—when he thinks of performative bests, they seldom occurred during rehearsals—but Rabbit has never felt so wholly connected to other people, to sound, hell, to a long-dead composer, as he did onstage that afternoon. They were all floating on that tremendous sound they made, floating and then flying, and they'd played it again and again, like kids getting off and on and off and on a rollercoaster until they were dizzy and pukey with joy.

And Fisher Brodie—Rabbit loves him. He's cruel and temperamental, disrespectful to both the music and the players, and whenever he really gets talking, all Rabbit can hear is Groundskeeper Willie. But he can't deny that Brodie has squeezed something unexpected from him this weekend, something rebellious and alive, just as he can't deny that sometimes Brodie sounds more like Sean Connery than Groundskeeper Willie, and that every low-slung vowel and purring *r* ignites a tickle in the bottom of Rabbit's stomach as if he's swallowed a cricket.

So yes: fine. It's true. Rabbit's crushing heart has revealed a talent for multiplicity.

But what he feels for Brodie is deeper than what he thought he'd felt for that maddening, terrifying Tenor. It's truer. It's closer. After they played the *maestoso* middle of "Jupiter" for the first time, from twenty feet away, over the heads of the flutes and the second-chair violas, Rabbit watched a light come on behind Fisher's eyes, a light Rabbit hadn't seen all weekend, a light that probably hadn't been on in years. The light came on and Brodie remembered himself, and Rabbit loved him for not caring that it happened in full view of the orchestra. He let them see him, all of him. Let them see that he was lonely and frightened, barely more mature than the teenagers he was conducting, with no more idea what he was going to do with himself for the next fifty years. He was humbled. Grateful. He couldn't have been more naked if he'd stripped down to his pale hide right there on the podium. Rabbit felt naked too—felt that they were all naked—but he didn't feel any shame. He felt a warm kinship with all of his fellow players, and a loving awe for the man who brought them together.

Pinkerton isn't cutting it, isn't speaking to him, isn't telling him anything he doesn't already know. He flips through his travel CD wallet and snaps the first disc of *Mellon Collie and the Infinite Sadness* into his Discman instead. A hallway is the essence of limbo, he thinks; it isn't where you came from or where you want to go, but rather the place you're stuck if you don't have the key to the right door. (Or to any door.) He feels left back, left nowhere, and all he wants is to act. He wants to *change,* he wants to change his life. He wants to be brave, wants to climb up on a chair and let the truth rain down the way Mrs. Wilson did. He wants to be as naked and unashamed as Fisher Brodie. His Discman beeps cheerfully as he skips to the second track.

A wave of violins crashes into his ears and Rabbit grins wide between them. The song pours into him, pounding over guitars and a military drum—through his head, down his neck, roaring into the cavern of his body and pushing all the way out to his toes before pulling back to crash into the next swell. He has liked "Tonight, Tonight" since he first heard it, but now, vibrating with love and possibility, Rabbit takes the song into himself and hears it as his very own. It sounds like the edge of something new, something strange and beautiful and happening now in his life. *His life*. Rabbit, to-night, believes the impossible is possible.

He listens to it four more times before Dan finally shows up. In those few minutes, he notices tiny but definite changes. His heart is beating faster. His neck is looser, his shoulder, elbow propped on his bassoon case, feels softer. Even his clothes seem different. It's as if before they were wearing him, and now he is wearing them. What the *hell* happened today? Was it just the great rehearsal? This new bloom of affection for Fisher Brodie?

Rabbit watches his roommate walk slowly toward him up the hall. He doesn't know what's coming, but he isn't afraid. The future is going to be his.

IV

Natalie's in love with the bartender. As soon as she entered the ball-room, she saw what looked like a rugby scrum in the far left cor-ner—mostly college-age kids flashing licenses and stuffing them in their back pockets, surrounding a man in a black vest. Still bleary from a nap that had turned into four hours of the best sleep she's ever had, at first she thought the bartender was a mirage.

He may as well be; he's magic. He had a glass of red wine wait-ing for her the first time she pressed through the crowd, and he has continued to have glasses of red wine waiting for her every time she drains one and requires another. She feels like a jerk because she doesn't have money to tip him, but the bartender doesn't seem to care. He's younger than she is, with a burnt-orange widow's peak and sleepy brown eyes, and he can flip two bottles of booze, one in each hand, like a Hollywood gunslinger. When she approaches he says, "Hello, dear," and when she leaves he says, " 'Til we meet again," and this is how Natalie finds herself hammered by the end of dinner.

And why not? What *isn't* worth celebrating? Fisher listened, he knows everything, and he's still here! She stood up to Viola! She threw that monster's words right back in her face! Fisher's hand on her leg holds her down, teasing, but not really. He peers at her between slitted lids as if he's lost a contact lens or she's become too hazy to see. He's been looking at her like this ever since he came to collect her for dinner. She'd been half awake, still dreamy, when he knocked violently on her door.

"Hi," he said, and kissed her, pushing her back into the room. She lost her balance but he caught her in both arms. "Feeling better? Did you eat lunch?"

She propped her chin on his shoulder. "No. I mean, yes, feeling better. No to lunch. So tired."

Fisher set her firmly on her own feet. He held her face in his hand and a half and tugged playfully on the flesh beneath her eyes with his thumbs. "Look a little peaky still." His own eyes were twitching, laughing, dancing. He had something to tell her. She could feel a tremendous confidence pressing itself against his throat, his tongue.

"How was rehearsal?" she asked.

"Terrific," he said, grinning wildly. "By far the most—I really don't have words. I don't know what happened. The kids got religion. It was an absolute orgy. An orgy of gorgeousness."

She led him over to the bed and gently pushed him backward.

"Oh, fine," he said. "If you insist."

"You're not worn out from your—" She grinned. "Your student orgy? You know I could get you fired for just *saying* that."

He propped himself on his elbows. "Natalie," he said.

"Fisher." She nudged his knees apart and stood between them, her own knees pressing against the edge of the mattress. *Go on, say it. Say what you came here to say.*

"Run with me."

"Run?"

"Yes."

"With you?"

"No, with that other guy."

He reached for her. If he'd held out his left hand, she might have been fine; she might have been able to take it without thought, without consequence. But Fisher reached for her with his right. He held out the most broken part of his body, and Natalie understood what that meant.

"Run with me, Natalie," he said again, his voice thinner.

She took his torn hand in hers.

In the moment, it hadn't felt like a promise or a lie, though of course it was both.

Now Natalie licks her wine-purpled and plumped lips and curls them at the corners. Everything, absolutely everything in her fucked-six-ways-to-Sunday life, feels fine with wine. There's nothing to worry about, nothing to *do* right now but sit on this old hotel chair and lean against Fisher and make mashed potato mountains and smile a secret smile, because in her handbag is her gun. Right where it belongs. Natalie is drunk and armed, ready for anything, ready to push her precarious life all the way over the edge as the circumstances demand.

She has to stop kidding herself about the gun. She has to stop pretending she doesn't understand why she wants it around, why she needs it, why she tucked it into her purse tonight while Fisher was washing up. This is the truth: she is the gun. It's the phantom instrument of her dark little heart, the anger she's always been afraid of, the power she didn't want to claim.

Get over yourself, Natalie.

A blast of sound. Behind her. Her hand jerks, knocking the last few drops of wine from her glass. It's those collegiate *a cappella* jackasses, singing Queen. The evening's entertainment has begun. If only the ghost of Freddie Mercury would return, back to the Bellweather for one night only, with a Russian assault rifle. *That* would be entertaining.

She pushes away and up from Fisher, who makes a halfhearted attempt to either go in her stead or prevent her from going at all, and makes a beeline for her magical bartender. Natalie is an incredible drunk. She's been an incredible drunk all her life, meaning she can be drunker than a hobo riding the rails but never give the impression of being more than slightly tipsy. Alcohol focuses her attention, her brain, her motor skills, and her balance to a fine point; she walks a tightrope of complete control. In the days and weeks following the break-in, she drank excessively every night, but it wasn't until Emmett opened the mostly empty liquor cabinet that he discovered the full extent of her self-medicating. She felt even more guilty, and poor (Natalie only drank the good stuff, unless she was at Statewide and it was free), and thereafter settled into a new, self-administered treatment plan for Coping with Having Murdered—

There's that word.

She could live as a blank. Blankness was a sustainable kind of existence. She could walk a tightrope of total absence and control. She has been walking it for months now, until this weekend.

Natalie's left heel wobbles in the carpet's pile. The collegiate jackasses, in four-part fratty harmony, ask her to open her eyes. Look up to the skies and see.

This weekend will end. They're stuck here under an avalanche of snow now, yes, but this is upstate New York. An avalanche is nothing. The hotel will be plowed out, freed. They will go home. She will go home. She will see Emmett, the man she married, and she will have to say something to him about this weekend. What could she possibly say?

Unless. Unless she actually *does* run away with Fisher.

She needs more wine. More wine more wine more wine.

Goodbye, everybody, the boys sing. I've got to go.

"Hello, dear," says her magic bartender, and Natalie can barely look at him as she grabs the proffered wine and bolts it down. He has another waiting by the time she hands him the empty glass. The singing boys are the same college boys she saw bellying up to the bar earlier. Alcohol would explain the swagger in their voices. Alcohol, and the girlish squealing that punctuates their every hip shake. She detests them. Their youth scrapes against her skin.

Fisher pats her leg when she returns to the table. The boys are scaramouche-ing and fandango-ing with gusto. Everyone—girls and boys and teachers—is laughing at their cheerful vulgarity, and by the time they attempt the guitar solo using only their lips and tongues and vocal cords, Natalie has decided. She isn't going home. She can't. She fills her mouth with wine. Emmett deserves—well, let's not pretend the decision was made based on the needs of another person. But Emmett *does* deserve a wife who doesn't treat him as Natalie has treated him.

So she'll run. The question now is whether she'll run with Fisher. He meant it when he asked; she doubts he's ever asked anyone the same question with the same gravity. She can imagine what it would be like to run away with him. When she thinks of climbing on the back of his bike and never seeing the Bellweather, never seeing her students or her band room or her house or her husband ever again, relief drops down over her shoulders, heavy and rich as a fur cloak. What she finds she can't quite imagine is where Fisher will take her. Where she could tell him to go. What will happen when they get there, and after that, and after that.

She loves him. He listened. He wanted to know what she'd done, who she really was.

Fisher rests his hand on her leg and looks at her sideways. His eyes glow. He is *in* love with her, and, good God, there's a difference.

The rest of the program drifts by like fog. Viola speaks briefly. She seems subdued, as though she's misplaced some of that old Viola Fabian zeal, and Natalie gives her own back a mental pat. Viola thanks the Boys from Buffalo for their spirited rendition of "Bohemian Rhapsody." She congratulates the students of Statewide's class of '97 for being so passionately committed to their music. A florid man in a tweed coat is introduced next, and he takes the podium to drone on about his personal musical journey. His eyebrows are enormous, so monstrous and distracting that Natalie is unable to pay attention to anything else, and when she hears polite applause, she is surprised he is finished speaking.

But not nearly as surprised as when every light in the ballroom winks out. There is a moment of confused silence, then cautious murmuring, and then there is nothing in the world but DUNNNNN DUN DUN DUN DUN DUNNNNN DUN DUN DUN DUN DUNNNNN, otherwise known as the most famous bars Andrew Lloyd fucking Webber ever wrote. Natalie isn't sure whether she's ever been this drunk in her life, but even so, this can't possibly be happening, can it? Fisher nudges her in the direction of the ballroom doors, which have opened to reveal the kitchen staff wheeling in carts of flaming dessert.

The flaming dessert—once extinguished, it appears to be an institutional form of Bananas Foster—is mediocre.

"Really," says Fisher, "all it ever had going for it was its ability to make an entrance."

"The grownups got alcohol." She licks caramel off her spoon. "The kids got food on fire."

"The grownups got food on fire *and* alcohol," Fisher says. "We win."

As last meals go, it is at least memorable.

Viola takes the podium again to remind everyone of Sunday's schedule—the concerts will go on as planned, without an audience—and to thank them, once again, for their patience with the storm. The snow, for the moment, has stopped falling. With any luck, they'll be able to return to their homes late tomorrow evening or early Monday morning. The crowd claps restlessly. They are tired of rehearsing; they're ready to go home. Yet there's a dull sort of electricity in the air—tired but alert, half cabin fever, half aching sexual tension. This could be their last evening in the Bellweather together. Tonight is the night for star- and school-district-crossed lovers to seal their respective deals. And there are still ghosts and lost girls to find, before everyone returns to the other lives that are waiting for them beyond the snow.

But the old life that's waiting for Natalie will wait for her forever. Tonight she picks herself up and walks herself and her gun toward another life entirely. And if she has any unfinished business, she had better take care of it now.

"Be right back," Natalie whispers to Fisher.

She bobs her way across the ballroom. She doesn't recognize the man Viola is chatting with. She hovers, not caring whether she's being rude.

Eventually Viola excuses herself and says, sharply, to Natalie, "May I help you?"

Natalie opens her mouth.

She is going to vomit. She closes it again.

"Natalie—oh, Natalie. *Look* at you." Viola takes her arm and gently leads her toward the rear of the room, behind a large screen set up to corral students and diners more cozily in the center. "Are you drunk? How did that happen? Sit down, sit down."

Natalie plunks heavily into a chair. Her purse slips from her hands and hits the floor with a dead *thunk.* There are stacks of extra chairs against the back wall, leaning towers of seats, beside a door with a shiny silver crash bar. There's no breeze, but the door itself radiates a cold that cuts through the red fuzz in her brain. She fills herself with wonderful cool air.

"Oh, Natalie." Viola's voice is soft and sad. She brushes Natalie's hair back off her face. Tucks it neatly behind her ears. She pulls Natalie closer, and before Natalie can help herself she wraps her arms around Viola's middle and holds on tight, as though she were clinging to a tree trunk in a hurricane.

I'm— Natalie's head pounds.

Viola rocks her for a little while, letting her hold on.

"Miss Wink," she says.

Natalie half laughs. The words are wedged at the base of her throat, pressing hard against her voice box, getting closer to being said. *I'm sorry I hit you. I'm sorry I hated you.*

No, I'm not.

"Shhh," says Viola. "It's okay. Let it go."

I'm sorry I let you in—

"Get it all out." Viola pats her on the back, a little harder than necessary.

Natalie squeezes her eyes shut.

I'm sorry I became you.

"Now stand up straight." Viola peels Natalie from her middle. "Let me look at you. Dammit. You grew up. When did that happen?"

Natalie feels weak, almost too weak to stand, but Viola is pulling her up and—

Jesus, she's drunk.

And hot. Blood ignites her face. Again she feels like she's going to throw up.

"Can we open—" She shrugs at the door. "So hot."

"Great idea." Viola smiles luminously.

The white of her teeth stuns Natalie. For the next three seconds, everything stuns her. The blue darkness outside the door. The sensation of pressure from behind, of her center of gravity shifting forward. The biting cold as first her knees and then her hands break through the icy crust of a sloping snowdrift.

The innocent *snick* of the door closing behind her.

She shivers from shock and cold and sick. "Viola," she mumbles, "let me back in," even though she knows she knows oh shit *she knows* Viola will never do that. She pushes herself up out of the drift and wraps her raw red hands around the handle, but the door is locked, of course, because—

Viola is trying to kill her.

Natalie buttons her cardigan up to her throat, but a few extra buttons are hardly going to keep her from freezing to death, are they, and then she laughs, because wasn't this what she really wanted, an end to the life she was living, a new beginning? She tumbles back into the drift and it catches her cozily, an easy chair of snow. She's so tired. She's so tired and so drunk and so amused by the sheer poetic ridiculousness of her life that she hardly hears the tiny voice asking whether she's sure she really wants this. Natalie looks up at the dazzling deep black of the sky and the stars—there are hundreds of stars, hundreds of pinholes punched into the night—and gasps with delight, with awe.

Whatever will she do with the rest of her life?

Scream until she's hoarse, bloody her hands pounding on the door in vain? Or turn her gaze up up up to the awesome face of the universe as a blanket of snow pulls itself tight around her?

She looks up. She sees not a new life but a whole new world.

21

Solo Viola

W HAT A NIGHT! Viola presses the button for the sixth floor. Wink was so drunk, so out of it, just as pliant and spineless as ever. But it wasn't just Wink, oh no—everything was working in harmony, all the players knew their parts. The teachers at Natalie's table, disgusted at her drunkenness. The bartender, who had no qualms about over-serving an obviously inebriated person. That administrator from Poughkeepsie who'd been so rudely interrupted by Natalie, waiting to speak with her old mentor, waiting and hovering and swaying. Natalie's exhausted weepiness ensured she'd give up the second she figured out the door had locked behind her. That little priss might have humiliated her this morning, might have gotten her to bleed once upon a time. But all Viola had to do was wait. All Viola ever has to do is wait.

Circumstantial symphonies have arranged themselves around her all her life. Kevin Montrose, that arrogant, sloppy soloist, always coming in half a beat early, tripped and hit his head on a rock. The dreadfully happy, tragically unobservant Alex Faccelli sprinkled poison over his morning grapefruit of his own free will. They were accidents, perhaps lightly orchestrated. It isn't fate or luck; Viola doesn't believe in either. It's a kind of harmonic concord. Viola is the center of gravity, the point around which all revolves, and when she sees her opportunity, her advantage, she takes it.

She all but trots out of the elevator and down the hall to her room. The snow is easing. The plows, if the news is to be believed, are out on the roads and will work through the night and tomorrow afternoon, clearing the way for parents to arrive by early evening. It's unfortunate that they'll miss the concerts, but it would be cruel to keep the students any later, after such an exhausting ordeal.

She's going to have a cup of tea and call it a night. The light is on in her room, which is strange, but not so strange that Viola thinks about it for longer than the half second necessary to convince herself she must have left it on. She kicks off her pumps, curls her toes into the carpet. Her stockings come off next. She has always loved the feeling of taking off stockings, the fleshy satisfaction of thighs and hips released from compression.

Doug Kirk loved to watch her take off her stockings. "I can see it in your face," he'd said, "the exact moment you feel free," and he'd smile lazily at her because he thought he was wooing her with poetry. Poor Doug Kirk. Father of four, two boys and two girls, dual sets of twins, blond and brown-eyed, and Viola, since the last time she saw Doug Kirk, has forgotten everything he ever told her about them. He talked about them constantly. He loved them. If she were the kind of person who felt things, she would feel bad that not one of Kirk's four children was likely to have their father at their championship games, their graduation parties, their weddings, their whatevers. Thankfully, Viola Fabian is the kind of person who feels nothing at all.

That's not entirely true; Viola does feel certain things. She feels eyes on her when she walks into rooms. She feels hunger when she hasn't eaten. She felt Doug Kirk's lust—naked, stupid, and starving, throwing off heat like a bonfire in a bad suit—the first time they met. He asked her how she'd heard about the position. She replied that she'd seen it advertised in the most recent Association for School Music newsletter. He wanted to make sure she knew it was mostly administrative in nature, that there were conducting opportunities but she wouldn't be performing—and she witnessed, plain in his eyes as his sentence trailed off, the first time he imagined her naked. She assured him she was looking for a part-time position. She had just moved from California with her daughter and needed a job with a freer schedule to accommodate Jill's busy travel calendar. He said he'd be in touch after they'd made a decision, and she slid her business card across the desk and said he should be in touch any time.

Three days later, three hours after he called to offer her the job of ASM liaison for western New York, two hours and forty-five minutes after she accepted, Viola sunk her nails into Kirk's back in a hotel-motel north of the Thruway. Viola felt Kirk's dry fingertips on her skin. She felt Kirk's dumb desire, once satisfied, glow even brighter. She felt hungry, because they'd met under the pretense of lunch and ended up sleeping together instead.

Fabian had been sleeping with Kirk for nearly two years, on and off, before she got bored, which was something of a record for her. It was probably because Kirk, relatively speaking, had power. As the head of ASM, he oversaw programming and festivals and solo competitions for every music program in every school district in the state of New York. He scouted at Statewide; he could make young careers with a handpicked scholarship, a glowing letter of recommendation, and an assured acceptance at Westing or any of the other top conservatories in the country. Viola was drawn to power. It belonged to her, was her natural right, and it was only a matter of time and circumstance before she possessed it. Her job as ASM school liaison afforded her a certain degree of power—she chose which schools hosted which regional competitions and festivals, which conductors led which ensembles—but the time had come to move up. Viola Fabian was ready for her promotion.

Two weeks before Statewide, she'd asked Kirk to meet her at that first hotel-motel, the place they met after she accepted the job, because she had something important to discuss with him. Kirk had been every bit as discreet and adept at handling their affair as Viola; his wife, a bland woman Viola had met on many occasions but whose face she could never quite conjure, would be genuinely shocked to discover she'd had an unfaithful husband for twenty months. Viola sensed that Kirk was beginning to fear his family's discovery of their relationship. His children were becoming teenagers, and the anxious fog of puberty pervading his house had triggered his conscience. He accepted her invitation with a reserve in his voice that told Viola her instincts had been correct. Her timing was perfect. This would be the last time.

She would daydream about it again and again.

Kirk knocks on the door, two short raps, a pause, two more. Viola opens it and puts her arms around his neck before he's inside. He stiffens and shuts the door with a hurried kick, after which he melts against her. He knows this is the last time too—the last time he sees Viola Fabian like this, pale as the moon, white-haired and red-mouthed, warm to the touch but cool behind her eyes. She refreshes him, Kirk says, like a glass of ice water on a blistering day. Viola tells him that's the nicest thing any of her lovers has ever said to her. He asks what else they've said, and she replies, smiling, *"You bitch. You have no right. You have no heart."*

Kirk's eyes change.

I have us on tape, she whispers into the hollow of his collarbone. She sees her words vibrate through his chest and curl like a serpent around his heart. *I've recorded every second we've ever spent together. I have your home address and I have an envelope. I want your job. Give me your job.*

Kirk's skin pops with sweat. His face is gray.

You can't be serious, he says. *You can't mean that.*

I want your job, she repeats. *Give me your job.* She smiles because it's funny, because it doesn't make any difference whether she has the tapes or not. Kirk is trapped by the mere possibility. Viola stretches, satisfied as a cat, and rolls away across the cooling sheets, wondering which would be more fun: for Kirk to submit, terrified, and hand over his job, or for Kirk to call her bluff and find out it's anything but?

Kirk's entire body is gray now, the color of overwashed cotton.

You're a monster, he wheezes, and pitches face-first to the floor.

That last part—the part where Kirk falls, the muscle of his heart crushed to pulp by her words—didn't actually happen in front of her. Doug Kirk made it back to his car, to his office, before being felled by the massive coronary that put him in the hospital bed where Viola Fabian saw him for the last time.

Taking what was hers—namely, Kirk's job—was more complicated than she'd thought. So she is interim head of ASM, *interim* as negotiated with his secretary, Helen Stoller, because Helen has been carrying a torch for Doug Kirk for twenty-five years and refuses to believe he will never wake up again. Viola knows better. Helen called her in a frenzy the day after his heart attack, clucking and squawking that Dr. Kirk was in the hospital, in a coma, and with Statewide coming up in two weeks—

"Are you asking me to run the whole fucking festival?" Viola said. She almost laughed out loud, picturing Helen Stoller's fat face stunned into silence. Stoller was stubborn—she wouldn't give up on Kirk until he'd been cold in the ground for six months—but Viola bullied her for a thousand dollars more than Kirk would have been paid. That took some of the sting out of being named *interim* head, not head. And she could wait. All she ever had to do was wait.

She tugs the elastic out of her ponytail. Her hair, her scalp, her face—it all relaxes. She sits on the edge of the bed and rolls her head back and forth, side to side. Blood throbs in her temples.

Viola pushes her head back, stretching her neck as far as it will go, and sets her teeth.

She needs that tea.

She walks barefoot to the bathroom and fills the electric kettle from the sink. She snaps it into its base, presses the little red switch with her index finger, and sets the tin of loose Earl Grey beside the kettle. Then she opens her train case. Inside are two silver spoons, two matching white teacups and saucers, and an old baby food jar, one of Jill's, filled with sparkling white sugar.

She's been trying very hard not to think about her daughter. Not to waste any more effort or time or anxiety on Jill. She looks at the twin cups and saucers and spoons, at the tiny jar, its label long gone, the only feature identifying it as having once held food for her child a word, GERBER, in blue on the lid. She grabs one spoon, one cup, and the sugar, and sits down at the desk.

Viola knows she's different from most people. She suspects that most people, people who talk about feeling sorry or concerned or worried, aren't lying the way she has learned to do, or at least they're not lying in quite the same way. She used to ask other people to describe how it felt to be those things, to feel regret or sadness on another's behalf. Her curiosity was genuine.

Her bafflement even more so—other people spent so much time worrying, fretting, coddling each other, and to no discernible end. It was a tremendous amount of energy wasted, energy that could have been better spent doing, winning, getting. It made them weak; it made Viola, blessedly unburdened, even stronger. Her clarity, her strength, her freedom from sentiment—they were her talents, the gifts she alone could give to the world. Experience had taught her that very few people were qualified recipients. Natalie Wink, for instance, had been an unmitigated failure.

Then there was Jill. Viola remembers the moment she understood she was going to have a child; she remembers writing a list of pros and cons for terminating the pregnancy. She remembers grasping that to have a child, to be a mother, would afford her a power unlike any other, potent and ancient, physical proof of her ability to create life. But the best reason for keeping her was this: a child of her own, born of her blood, would surely be able to accept Viola's gifts.

In the beginning, she thought she might feel love for Jill, that the physical experience of carrying and bearing a child would transform Viola into one of those Other People. Thankfully, in time she realized this feeling was just another kind of lie, the kind she was familiar with, a lie that everyone else expected to be true as a matter of course. She performed as a mother must. She hugged her child, wiped her face, fed and clothed her, and gave her treats. When Viola thought of her daughter, she thought of the word "useful." Jill was an extraordinary machine, an instrument perfectly tuned. She gave Viola status, entrance, access; she could be controlled and handled, molded and made to execute. Viola assumed that her daughter was exactly like her, free from the too-human tyranny of feelings, until she found her crying in her bedroom one day. Jill was no older than five or six, disconsolate because they were making Father's Day presents in school.

"I miss him," Jill said.

"How can you miss him?" Viola asked. "You never even met him."

Jill sobbed harder. Viola, for the first time, felt what might have been sadness. Her daughter was not like her. Her daughter was one of the Other People, and would not be able to appreciate what her mother had to offer.

This did not stop Viola from trying, again and again, to teach her.

She twists her hair into a rope around her finger and lays it flat over one shoulder. The kettle is starting to whistle. Viola scoops a teaspoon of Earl Grey leaves into her diffuser. It clinks against the side of the china.

Doug Kirk, before his heart exploded, called her a monster. She pours hot water over the diffuser and calm settles into her bones. She wonders whether Jill would have said the same thing—that she is a monster. Jill had said many horrible things to her over the years, had called her many names, though she can't remember whether "monster" was ever one of them. From Kirk, it was a wayward arrow, a shot that didn't hit the mark. Coming from Jill, it might have felt like a compliment, an admission of understanding. Viola would finally know she had taught her something after all.

Viola closes her eyes, letting the steam open her pores. She unscrews the lid of the baby food jar and digs out a teaspoon of sugar.

22

What Hastings Saw

A PHONE RINGS.

Hastings knows he's dreaming. It's one of his elastic dreams, the kind he can half control, so he chooses to ignore the phone and focus on the Scrabble board in front of him instead. Jess kept a Scrabble board out at all times. Their games would last for days without their ever once sitting down opposite each other. CENTURY would greet him late one afternoon when he came in with the mail. He would play YOUTH off the Y, and the next morning, shuffling to the kitchen to make coffee, he'd notice that DOUGHTY had sprouted around the H. He didn't truly believe Jess was leaving him until the day he walked into the living room to see SWIMMER dangling, unplayed-upon. He'd never suspected it would be their last word.

This board in his dream is empty save for six tiles. He reads them and they don't make sense. He fiddles with his bow tie. The phone continues to ring.

Perhaps if he squints—he can make out a W. An A. A K.

And suddenly Jessica Mills Hastings is sitting across from him, palms down flat on either side of the board. When she opens her beautiful mouth, Scrabble tiles fall from her lips and he hears them as letters, he hears her chanting, she's saying—

Hastings is awake. Rudely, painfully, and the damn phone is still ringing.

Where the hell is Sheila? Where the hell is *he?*

His back is sore. Well, no wonder, he's been napping on the swaybacked couch in the front office. This couch has been at the Bellweather almost as long as Hastings. The phone on the desk is ringing, the manager's phone. That's why Sheila hasn't answered it. Sheila's out front, Sheila doesn't hear it.

Hastings clears his throat and straightens his tie. It takes much longer than it should, but he gathers himself and pushes up from the sofa. The phone has been ringing forever. It must be a worried parent, or maybe someone from the town with an update on the plowing. Life—here, in the present moment—is coming back. It's all coming back, and when Hastings presses the cool plastic handset to his ear, he almost sounds like himself.

"Hello, Bellweather Hotel. Hastings speaking. How may I be of—"

"Mr. Hastings! Mr. Hastings, it's Helen Stoller. Doug Kirk's assistant from—from Statewide?" Her voice is wobbly and far away. "We've spoken before. Many times."

"Yes, yes, of course. How are you, Ms. Stoller? And how is Dr. Kirk?"

Helen Stoller is silent. Hastings wonders how badly the storm has affected the phone lines, if she's been disconnected, until he hears the unmistakable sound of crying.

"He died," she says. "He was awake briefly this morning, he came out of the coma, but by the afternoon he was gone. I'm so sorry, I'm so sorry to be telling you this. I'm so sorry that this happened. He has young children, you know." She swallows, and then continues icily, "If you could please convey this information to Dr. Fabian. I've been trying to reach her but she's not in her room. She must be at the banquet still."

The banquet! What time is it? Has he slept through the banquet? What on earth is wrong with him this weekend?

"There's no real protocol for . . . how to handle this. And the *timing,*" Helen Stoller says. "Fabian just needs to know, that's all. She can tell people however she sees fit and we'll figure out the details next week. When you're plowed out, that is."

"I expect that shouldn't be long now." His mouth is cottony. "I'm terribly sorry to hear about Dr. Kirk. He was a gentleman and a great supporter of this festival. And . . . a friend."

"That's so kind of you," says Helen, before choking on a sob that Hastings has little doubt will turn into a full-fledged wail as soon as the connection has been cut. It isn't until he hangs up the phone that he realizes why Helen is so very sad: Viola Fabian is now the head of Statewide. *That beastly woman is now the head of Statewide.*

Hastings shudders but gets on with it. He straightens his sleeves and cuffs, tugs the wrinkles out of his jacket, and nods curtly at the boy at the check-in desk, he can't remember his name, who barely looks up from his paperback when Hastings emerges from the office. It is nearly nine. He tells himself he'll have ample time to feel embarrassed about wasting the majority of the day—not to mention missing the entire banquet and speaking program—*after* he's found Viola Fabian. Students and teachers are still milling in the ballroom, but dessert has long since been served. He asks one of the girls tidying up an empty table if she's seen a woman with long white hair, and is rewarded with a sympathetic shrug.

"Did everything go well tonight? Do you think they enjoyed their meal?" he asks.

The girl shrugs again.

"The dessert—did the kids like the flambé?"

"I guess," she says.

Hastings has been an absentee concierge. He's let them down. He's wasted the precious time he has with them, this time that he waits for all year.

The elevator ride is excruciating. The hallway seems to double in length as he approaches Viola Fabian's door. He knows how he'll say it—simply, just the facts—but he has no idea how he'll do so without betraying his own bitter disappointment at the pall that has hung over this particular Statewide.

He looks at his feet. He lifts his hand to knock.

The door is not quite closed.

"Dr. Fabian?" he calls. "Dr. Fabian, are you in there? I have an important message for you." He knocks lightly on the open door, which swings in under his fist. "Dr. Fabian, is everything all right?"

Hastings peers into the room. Fabian is sitting at the desk, her back to the door, head down on the desktop. Her white hair, released from its ponytail, trails over the edge like a frozen waterfall.

He calls her name again, at full volume this time, and when she doesn't respond he walks into her room. His eyes capture everything: the electric teakettle plugged into the wall, burping little clouds of steam. A teacup perched on its side. A small puddle of brown tea. What looks like a glass baby food jar full of sugar.

Fabian's face is tilted forward. She is looking at a piece of white paper tented on the opposite end of the desk, in front of an empty chair. He doesn't know she's dead until he reads the note. Printed in neat black capitals, in familiar permanent marker, are the words NOW WE ARE FREE.

Rome is waiting for him in the hall.

"Hastings," he says. "We have to talk."

Hastings pulls the door of Viola Fabian's room shut with what he hopes is a respectful click. He unplugged the kettle but left everything else as he'd found it. He needs to call the police. He needs to leave the scene untouched. He needs to figure out how he's going to tell them about any of this without sounding like the complete incompetent he is. Jill's death *was* a murder, he can see it as clear as a banner headline: FABIAN MURDERS DAUGHTER; CONSUMED WITH GUILT, TAKES OWN LIFE.

It had a pleasing shape. A logical symmetry. It ate its own tail.

But Viola Fabian would never eat her own tail. It didn't make any—

"Hastings, look at me," Rome says, and physically stops Hastings with a hand on each shoulder. "We have to talk about Caroline. About me. And Jess too."

Hastings exhales angrily through his nose. "I have work to do. Where the hell did you come from, anyway?"

"That's what we have to talk about. Listen—listen to me."

He shakes Rome away and walks double-time to the elevator. He calls the car and steps inside, and when he turns, his gaze traveling the length of the hallway, Rome has vanished.

Hastings is suddenly terrified.

He's sweating. His shirt feels sticky beneath his jacket.

A girl. A girl. A daughter in his arms on a dim dance floor. She should be happy but she's sad.

The elevator ascends. Hastings's lungs spasm with short, shallow gasps. He sees an unfinished Scrabble game. Pink and purple flowers on a casket. Bright blue bunting in the small ballroom. Bright blue cummerbunds. Bright blue frosting rosettes on the cake. He remembers dancing at her wedding. He remembers Caroline in his arms, his changeling, secret daughter, surprisingly light in that giant confection of a dress, smiling at him, pressing her warm forehead against his shoulder and humming along to Frank Sinatra, swinging together, singing. Rockies crumbling. Gibraltar tumbling.

He never talked to her. He never stopped her. He never knew her.

She didn't let him save her.

And he would have, *he would have*. She didn't even need to ask.

(But apparently she did.)

His bow tie is trying to strangle him. He works a shaking finger under the knot and pulls and he presses two burning tears from the corners of his eyes when he thinks of his daughter's throat, of that horrible purple line on his daughter's long throat, of that horrible red mass on his son-in-law's chest. Purple and red. Not bright blue.

The elevator hovers and stops moving. The doors open.

23

Found

"Y OU JUST MISSED HIM. Literally. By, like, ten minutes." The kid behind the front desk bobs his neck, flicking the hair out of his eyes. "He'll probably be back. He's always here."

Minnie drums her fingers on the counter. "Do you know where he went?"

"Dunno. He was moving pretty fast." He rubs his forehead with the spine of his book. "He always walks like he's got something important to do, so it's hard to tell when he actually does."

She looks over at Alice, sitting on one of the lobby chairs and leaning over to pet Auggie's belly. They'll have to wait. There's really no other option. And all because Minnie herself had insisted on waiting—on ordering dinner from room service, getting all the background they could from Sheila, and not rushing into a confrontation with a fragile old man. Minnie felt more than compassion for him. She felt responsible, as though it was her duty, hers and hers alone, to ease his suffering.

The more she found out about Harold Hastings, the worse she felt for him, which was another reason to wait. The last thing in the world he needed was a pity party—this from someone who had been a walking pity party for the balance of her childhood. Minnie suspected that all she and Hastings needed was each other: someone who had been there, whom they could talk to about that night without saying a single word, who would never begin a sentence with "You poor," followed by an invocation of a baby sheep. It had been ridiculously hard to talk about it with her parents and her pro-bunny therapist. But to have no one to talk to at *all* was unfathomable, horrifying, and, at least according to Sheila, Hastings was utterly alone. His wife had been killed in a car accident. His daughter had killed her husband and herself. His only friend had died and left everything he owned to Hastings, piles of junk he had to deal with. He had no other children, no other siblings, no other friends. He didn't even have the same coworkers, the ones who had known daughter and wife and Hastings in better times. The management was new. The chambermaids and kitchen and grounds crew had turned over several times since. He was a relic, a leftover.

He was a ghost.

Auggie nose-nudges her foot when she takes the sofa seat opposite Alice. Minnie's become acclimated to the idea of Hastings, to the memory she forgot, but she's as sad and anxious and jumpy as ever, on the verge of tears, of screaming, of running way the hell away. Alice makes a fist and a face that would be tough if she weren't so cute. *Solidarity, sister.* You can do this.

But what, really—what the hell does Minnie think she can do? How arrogant is it to think that *she* can be of use to a stranger with serious mental problems? Let's be honest, she's a cliché: an overweight girl seeking solace in stories, finding catharsis in movies, who would be pretty if she just took off her glasses, stopped referring to her pet and herself using the first-person plural, and went to the damn prom. It's way too late for the prom. She has to believe it isn't too late for everything else. But what can she possibly offer him? And why does she feel that she's the only person who can offer him anything at all?

Auggie rights himself with a puppyish grunt and presses his forehead flat against her shins.

"Good dog," she says, and rubs his silky ears.

Alice leans back in her chair, fingers laced, twiddling her thumbs.

Three people cross the lobby. Or rather, two walk while supporting a third between them, and they're so quiet and focused on their mission that Minnie's first instinct is to look away. There's nothing to see; nothing to do with her, at least.

The youngest turns so Minnie can see his face.

"Is that your brother?" she asks Alice.

Alice was obsessed with the superpowers that came with being a twin. These powers, strictly speaking, did not exist, but that didn't stop her from flexing her end of the muscle. On long car trips, she'd close her eyes, scrunch her face, and whip her head toward her brother.

"What number am I thinking of?"

"I don't know."

"Yes, you do. Think. *Receive,* Rabbit." She'd laugh. "Adjust your psychic rabbit ears."

Rabbit played along with her in the beginning—seven! thirteen! one hundred and eight and a half!—but it got pretty annoying after the hundredth wrong answer. He had a bit of a sixth sense about his twin, but that had less to do with parapsychology than with the fact that they lived in the same house, went to the same school, were raised by the same two people. Rabbit would have loved to believe his sister could speak to him using only her mind. He hated to think that she might, in fact, be able to do just that, that it was *his* mind that had faulty wiring and could neither broadcast nor receive. He'd tried sending messages to her, silent but strong shouts from the bottom of his brain—*Hello, Alice. Can you hear me? Thirteen. Blue. P.S. I'm gay*—but she never responded. She never gave any indication that she heard a word he thought.

So when he saw her in the lobby, Mrs. Wilson's arm heavy on the back of his neck—how could she be so heavy, she was *skinny*—when he saw Alice's face peering out from behind one of the high-backed chairs, the force of what he felt, what came at him from his sister, almost knocked him off his feet.

I love you.

She didn't speak. She sprang out of the circle of chairs and ran to him. He was so happy to see she was safe and to know that she loved him that Rabbit almost forgot he was dragging his semiconscious chaperone through the lobby, and how he came to be doing so.

It happened at the end of dinner. The very end—dessert had been (flamboyantly) served, and most of the people at his table had gone back to their rooms, but Rabbit, still high from rehearsal, still convinced the future was coming at him like a locomotive, was ready. He had to find his sister, had to find her tonight.

Fisher Brodie leaned in beside him.

Rabbit tensed. The table was empty now, Brodie hovering over him with both palms flat on the tablecloth. He looked fidgety.

"Hello, Hatmaker," he said. "Have you seen a redhead?"

"Uh." Rabbit blinked. "Yes."

"Oh, right, sorry—an adult. She's a teacher. Natalie—last name starts with a W."

"Wilson?"

Fisher frowned. "Yes."

"You were sitting with her this morning, in the auditorium. She's my conductor. My teacher, back home."

"She's *your*—" Brodie sniffed. "Well, naturally. Right, so, have you seen her?"

Rabbit shook his head. "Not tonight."

Brodie was more than fidgety. He was, as Rabbit's grandmother would have said, downright agitated.

"Listen, Hatmaker. I'm only telling you this because you're a decent sort. Our friend Mrs. Wilson had quite a bit of drink tonight and has gone missing. I called her room but she wasn't there."

He knew her room; *Rabbit* didn't even know which room she was in. He fought back the blush threatening his face.

"I am," said Brodie, "concerned."

"Me too. My sister—I can't find my sister Alice either. If I help you, will you help me? Find them both?"

"How many people has this bloody hotel eaten?" said Brodie,

more flippantly than Rabbit knew he felt. "But that's the spirit. Lend a hand."

"Should we tell someone?"

Brodie shook his head. "Not yet."

They searched for a full twenty minutes. Rabbit recognized plenty of people milling around. Some of them said hello to him, smiled as though they were old friends who hadn't met for the first time two days before. (Was this how it felt to be popular?) When they asked whom he was looking for, because he was obviously *looking,* he brushed it off. Someone, he said. Just someone.

Brodie, who'd had just as much luck, met him back in an empty main ballroom. The last of the hotel staff were clearing tables, changing soiled linens, stacking chairs. It made Rabbit feel even more anxious, like the scene of a crime was being dismantled before all the evidence had been collected.

"We can split up the upper floors," Brodie said. "I've not been beyond my floor. I don't know what's up there." He shrugged.

"Should we tell someone?" Rabbit asked again.

"Not yet," said Brodie.

"I think we should tell someone," said Rabbit.

Brodie glared at him. Rabbit glared back.

Rabbit watched as two of the staff collapsed a screen on the edge of the ballroom floor and carried it off. Behind it he saw chairs stacked in tall rows against the wall, beside a fire door.

There was a dark object on the floor next to the door. Rabbit squinted.

"Purse," he said, pointing, and Brodie was off. He reached the door just before Rabbit and pushed it open. There was a blast of frigid air. Rabbit saw his teacher cradled in the snow, eyes closed, lips blue. She looked dead. Frozen. And he didn't do anything but stand there and look at her.

She opened her eyes and looked back.

"Ish," she said, or something like it, and Brodie was already scooping her out of the snowdrift, dragging her back into the warmth of the hotel. Rabbit slammed the door behind them. He picked up her purse, which was surprisingly heavy, and slung the single skinny strap across his body. What happened next happened quickly and silently. Brodie took one arm and Mrs. Wilson extended the other and Rabbit, called, rushed to her side. She was *cold,* cold like a steak straight out of the refrigerator. He pressed his warm self against her side and they began walking. Through the ballroom. Toward the lobby.

"Can you walk at all?" Brodie asked her.

"Ish," she said again, and her face twisted. "Oo assed oo." *Who asked you.* "Oo ave ee nnyayy." *To save me anyway.* She made some huffing noises that might have been laughter.

"Glad you kept your sense of humor."

"Oof."

"What?"

"Ool."

"What?"

"Esus ucking eist."

Rabbit was struggling to keep Mrs. Wilson upright. Struggling to understand just how well Brodie and his teacher knew each other. Struggling to grasp how much this night was going to teach him, and how much of it he didn't want to know.

Which was when Alice found him.

He doesn't let go of Mrs. Wilson but he does stop moving, and pulls Alice in so that the four of them, Brodie, Mrs. Wilson, Rabbit, and his sister are collapsed together in the middle of the lobby in a group hug.

"What the f—" Brodie says.

"Alith," Mrs. Wilson sort of groans.

"Alice," Rabbit says, but it's doubtful anyone can hear him over Alice's chattering—something about the concierge, and being kidnapped, but it turned out fine and Minnie didn't do it, she wasn't the killer, she was a cool person and so was her dog—and for the first time in a long, long time, Rabbit doesn't wish she would shut up.

"I was worried," he says. "Why didn't you—" And then he remembers how he acted at the party, how he didn't dance, and feels like a jerk.

"I'm sorry," Alice says. Has she ever said this? Has she ever said she's sorry to her brother? "Are you wearing a purse?"

"Hank oo," Mrs. Wilson says in his ear. "Eed eye urse." *Need my purse*. And then her body dips, a bead of sweat rolls down from Rabbit's hairline, and the severity of the situation reasserts itself. His sister may be safe, but Mrs. Wilson is weak and cold, and what the hell was she doing out in the snow?

Fisher yells to the guy at the check-in desk to call 911, that this woman has been outside in the cold for God knows how long and is suffering from exposure, and Mrs. Wilson dips again, reeling on her feet, and puts her mouth next to Rabbit's ear and says, "Ake me oo tha ool."

"The what?" he whispers.

"The." She licks her lips clumsily and presses them together. "Puh."

"The pool," says Rabbit. "She wants to go to the pool."

Mrs. Wilson goes limp with relief. "Yes," she says clearly.

"Where is the pool?" he asks Alice, because she's right in his face and she usually knows everything, but this time she shakes her head. "The pool?" he asks louder, and catches the eye of the guy at the desk, already on the phone. He points up.

"Uh," says Mrs. Wilson. "Uh. Oof."

"She wants to go up to the roof," Rabbit tells Brodie, who is shouldering the bulk of Mrs. Wilson's weight now. She curls against him, into him.

"Take me. The puh. Ool." She presses her face into Brodie's shoulder. "Leeze."

"She says please," Rabbit translates, and Brodie looks at him first with frustration, then anger, and then, a thousand times worse than either, with fear. Brodie . . . likes her. Cares for her. He might even be in love with her. He knows it's stupid to take her farther from the lobby, farther from the coming ambulance crew, but he's going to take her wherever she wants to go because he loves her.

"Go," says another familiar voice. Rabbit turns, and confirms it's the voice of the psycho fat lady in the elevator, the psycho with the dog, who must have been sitting in the lobby with Alice. "Go to the pool and I'll send up the EMTs."

"I'm coming with you," says Alice to her brother.

So they go up.

The pool on the roof is magnificent. Fisher isn't paying attention to anything other than Natalie, chilled in his arms, drooling with cold, yet he can't help but notice the ornate tile, the brilliant sapphire circle of water, the warm green fronds all around. It's close and humid, thanks to the domed glass ceiling. He understands why she wanted to come here—or rather, come back here, for this is surely where she was before she went to the auditorium on Thursday night—but he wishes he could see the stars. All he sees when he looks skyward is glass and metal ribbing and the gray underside of many feet of snow. He knows they're on the roof but it feels tomblike, low, insulated, and dim. The only light comes from the pool itself, from blue bulbs ringing the edge beneath the surface.

He would have taken her anywhere she asked, just because she asked him, but dear God, he wishes she hadn't chosen here. It's the kind of place they seal you in for eternity.

Fisher is massively unprepared to save anyone's life. He has no idea what to do for exposure other than dial 911, and he's done that already, so if anyone else has a suggestion he's not going to object. He's glad Hatmaker is here—that two Hatmakers are here. His lucky Bunny Boy, doubled. That has to be a sign. He would rub Rabbit's head if he thought it would bring him any more luck than he's already entitled to, which is a frightening prospect, considering he's entitled to exactly zero.

"How much luck do you have, love?" he mutters as he steers Natalie closer to the water.

"Oo much," she says. "Not enough."

Rabbit and his sister bring over a stack of stiff white bath towels.

"Dr. Brodie," says Alice. "Hi, Dr. Brodie. I think you're supposed to—how do I say this without sounding . . ." She claps her hands. "If you want to be nude under the towels with Mrs. Wilson, that would be fine."

Rabbit freezes. Even his eyes stop moving. It's fucking hilarious.

"Skin to skin. That's how you treat hypothermia, right?" Alice says. The twins—they must be twins, did Fisher notice this before?—are an optical illusion when they stand side by side. They share the same pert noses and round eyes, only Alice's make her look like an especially girlish boy, and Rabbit's, a boyish girl. Fisher looks at one and is reminded of the other, at least until they open their mouths.

"Come on," says Alice, "we're all adults here."

"Oo you ahnt oo geh me *ired?*" Natalie slurs, and then makes weird breathy noises that must be laughter. "Don't have hypo. Ermia. Need to move. Help me walk."

She's already stronger, thank God, though Fisher still has to exert the lion's share of effort to keep her upright. They walk around the pool. At first her steps are halting, but they grow stronger, surer, her breathing deeper and more regular. "Blood," she says. "Need to move my blood."

"*Why* did you go outside?" he hisses. He hates that it sounds like he's attacking her, accusing her of something, but he can't help himself. Fear has made him raw. The Hatmakers sit quietly on the other side of the pool, too far to hear her response. "How did you get there?"

She pauses. Looks at him. Her cheeks are streaky with red, burned by the cold.

"Viola," she says. "Pushed me. Tried to kill me."

"I'm serious."

She closes her eyes slowly.

"Me too," she says.

"That isn't funny."

More of those awful laughing sounds. "Why does everyone *say* that?"

Brodie hugs her close, though she doesn't need all that much support anymore. He can feel her righting herself, holding her weight over her own feet.

"What happened?" he whispers. "Please, please tell me."

"Karma." She leans her head against his shoulder. "What I deserved."

"You didn't deserve to—"

They're ten feet from the Hatmakers, ten feet from making a complete circle around the pool, when Brodie notices the man. He's sitting behind the kids at what looks like a small cocktail table without an umbrella. There's a hole in the middle, a dark hole where the umbrella stand would go, and why Fisher focuses on this first and not the gun in the man's hand must have something to do with his brain's capacity for shock. He saw the gun in the man's hand and Natalie's open purse, lying on the other side of the table where one of the Hatmakers must have set it down, and Fisher's brain said, *Nope, not seeing it—let's focus on the round black hole five inches from the gun, the round black hole that's missing an umbrella.*

And the man? An older man. In his late sixties, early seventies, give or take a decade. Light hair, light complexion. Wearing a collared shirt, reddish bow tie undone and dangling, a dark rumpled blazer like the one the desk clerk who called the ambulance was wearing. It's—oh God, what's his name? The concierge. The man he reported Rabbit's confession to, the man who called the meeting with Viola and Alice. He looks so different tonight, Fisher didn't recognize him at first. His eyes are wrong. They're almost as black as the hole in the middle of the table.

The man holds the gun in his right hand, lightly, resting both hand and gun on the tabletop. His finger is on the trigger, but from the look on his face Fisher isn't sure he knows who or where he is, let alone what he's holding.

"Don't panic," he whispers into Natalie's red hair. "The man sitting behind them has a gun and I don't know why."

He expects her to tense, to pull closer, but she acts as though she hasn't heard him. They continue their slow movement forward.

Fisher locks eyes with Rabbit. *Don't turn around but there's someone there. Don't turn around.*

Alice turns around.

She does so easily, as if she's been expecting to see the concierge sitting behind her at poolside, holding a gun, all along.

"Mr. Hastings," she says. "Hello. I'm Alice. Do you remember me from earlier? I'm sorry if we upset you. Minnie and I, we didn't mean to."

"I remember," he says. His voice has no color.

"Minnie wants to help you," she says. "I do too."

"I remember," he repeats, and licks his lips. He lifts both arms theatrically; Fisher's pulse responds in kind. "I remember," he says, "when they used to come to this pool with their families. Pink bathing caps with white daisies for the girls, little black flippers and goggles for the boys. The *noise* in here! Shouting. Splashing. And I remember when they'd bring up their wives and their girlfriends, never at the same time, of course, for a late dip under the stars. Considerably quieter. We used to have a little bar over there in the corner to make cocktails. We'd find paper drink umbrellas floating in the water in the morning. They got stuck in the filters."

Fisher and Natalie stop moving. They stand side by side at the edge of the water, close enough to Rabbit that Fisher can grab him and dive for cover. If they dove into the pool, would that be stupid or brilliant?

"Tell me more," Alice says.

"She loved it up here. She was a swimmer, a great swimmer. There are speakers hidden in the bushes here—you'd never find them, very cleverly placed. I'd turn on the radio and I'd throw her high into the pool. Like a cannonball. Like a rocket. Splashdown! I can still hear Sam Cooke, that song about having a party. Having a good time with my baby. How he'd echo in here. In this room." He looks up at the dome. "She was happy here."

"I can see why."

"Why," says Hastings, and the blackness that had started to recede from his eyes seeps back in.

Alice senses it too. "Tell me more," she says again. She's turned all the way around in her chair, chin resting on the top of the back, like a little kid would think to do. "Tell me more about what you're—"

"She was happy. She was my. Daughter." Hastings's brow crumples. "Why would she ever? Why would anybody ever?" He looks directly at Alice. Whatever—whomever—they're talking about, Fisher can only guess, but the specifics of the conversation don't matter. What matters is the feel of it, the color and the tone, and even Fisher can tell that they've encroached on something darker. Angrier. Redder.

"She felt betrayed," Alice says quietly. Fisher hears the first tremor in her voice. "Her brand-new husband was going to leave her. For someone else."

"Well, I knew *that*," Hastings snaps. "We all knew *that*. Not before, of course, but after. After, it came out right away. Lily knew. Lily told me."

Alice swallows. She looks eerily pale in the blue-green light.

"That's a *reason*. It's not an *answer*," Hastings says. He looks down at his hands, one shaking, one holding a gun, and stands up swiftly, knocking over his chair. "It doesn't tell me *why*," he shouts. "Hurt him. Humiliate him. Hurt him worse than he hurt you—go ahead, Caroline, go ahead, I can understand that. I can almost understand why you killed him. I can understand *wanting* to kill someone."

Pinpricks of cold sweat pop all over Fisher's body. He looks down and sees he's gripping Natalie's hand, squeezing it white.

"But why did you leave me?" Hastings cries. "We were the only two left. We only had each other. Why did you take yourself away?"

Hastings jerks his head upright and now he's looking directly at Natalie. Fisher feels her accept the weight of his gaze. Her body finally tenses.

Hastings shuffles closer. He never takes his eyes off Natalie as he skirts Rabbit, motionless in his chair. He is no more than five feet away now. His face is wet, with sweat or tears or both. He shines in the dimness as though he's made of melting wax.

"You," he says. His voice is a rasp. *"You're* Wink."

"Yes." She nods once.

"You did it." His gaze flickers from Natalie to Fisher and then rolls back to take in the Hatmakers. "You all did it. I don't know how. Or why." He shakes the gun at them, forgetting again that it isn't just his hand. "But you did it."

"Did what?" Fisher asks.

"Murder," says Hastings.

"Yes," says Natalie, quickly, gently. Fisher feels her body draining, melting beside him, while his own hide bristles with panic. "Yes, I did."

Hastings hasn't heard her, thank God. "*How* is what I don't understand," he continues dramatically. "Indulge me. *Alice*. Walk me through your master plan. Did you hang her? Was your brother cutting her down while you ran for help?"

Alice is shaking her head in terror. "Mr. Hastings. Please, please listen."

"Did the kids kill the girl, and the grownups kill her mother?" He cocks his head. "It was the timing that gave you away. You had to do it in pairs. I got there so quickly both times, there was no other way." His head tilts so far to the side that he's practically resting his ear on his shoulder. "I was. I was there. I was there in the same room where Caroline . . . and just now, I was there again."

He looks at Fisher.

"What did I do?" Hastings asks.

Fisher has no response.

"Oh my God." Hastings looks down at his hands, at the gun. "Oh my God. What did I do?"

Slowly, more steadily than Fisher would have thought possible, Hastings raises his right arm, the hand holding the gun turning inward at the wrist.

"No." Natalie's voice is a whimper. "No." Stronger now. "Mr. Hastings, no."

"What are you—" says Fisher.

"I'm the murderer," Natalie says.

"*Natalie*," Fisher says.

"Why?" Hastings asks. The gun hovers, his arm begins to lower. "What gave you the right?"

Natalie is trembling. Fisher squeezes her hand hard, harder, even as she loosens her grip.

"Please," Fisher says. He has no idea what he's praying for. "Please—"

"Nothing," Natalie says. "Nothing gave me the right. I took it."

"That is not," says Hastings. He closes his eyes and shouts, "An ANSWER."

"I know." She blinks.

What are you doing? What in holy hell are you doing?

"Please give me an answer," Hastings says. "An answer. I just need an answer."

"There isn't any answer," she murmurs. "There's only me and what I did."

The flatness of her voice is what triggers him. Fisher becomes elemental desire—desire to cover, to shield, to fold himself around this person whom he loves, to make with his body an impenetrable shell. It doesn't matter that Fisher's body will never protect her from anything; it doesn't matter that he could die if Hastings fires. None of that even occurs to him. None of that is relevant. What Fisher does next is a reflex of the heart.

Still holding her hand, he takes one pivoting step between them, facing Natalie, with his back to Hastings.

It happens like this:

Natalie looks at Fisher. She looks over his shoulder.

A cannon rips through him.

Fisher lands in the pool.

Cold.

Pulled. Under.

He's been shot.

No—

He hasn't, he hasn't been shot, he's been pushed.

Natalie pushed him out of the way.

24

Lost

BOWIE FLOATS. He hovers above her. A high cloud of red hair, a blue and orange thunderbolt splitting his face.

A breeze ripples across his surface and Natalie knows she's lying on her bed at her parents' house, her single bed with the afghan her aunt knitted when she was born, and Bowie is floating above her because he's tacked to her ceiling with red pushpins. Everything as she left it. Her bookshelf, there to the left, with its complete set of *The Chronicles of Narnia.* Her dresser drawers half closed around purple and red and green lumps of cotton and corduroy.

Natalie calls out—for her parents, her sisters, Uncle Kevin—and her voice sounds distant to her own ears. Sound is all funny. She can hear a faint pulse, a beat like an irregular heart, but nothing else. No doors opening and closing, no faucets turning on or sofa springs creaking when her father throws himself down on them. She peers out the window at the end of the upstairs hall. Her street is there, but it isn't the street she saw the last time she drove through, years ago; the house on the far end that some crazy idiot bought and painted canary yellow is still the dark green she grew up with. All of the cars in the driveways are American, except for one lone VW bus parked at the curb.

She knows that car. That car belongs to the Paoluccis' son. He put a bullet in his head in the eighties.

A bullet.

Natalie turns from the window and walks downstairs, pausing on the landing, fighting the urge to lie down and hang her head over the top step. The house of her childhood opens to greet her. The brown and orange braided rug on the living room floor, the orange and tan plaid curtains. She can smell a faint whiff of smoke, but no one answers when she calls out again. Memories break over her. Every object, remembered or forgotten until this very moment, warms her face like an open flame. She is overwhelmed by the solidity of every detail. Someone (*I did it, it was me*) has drawn a smiley face in the dust on the television screen. The wallpaper in the front room, a pattern of tan and brown and yellow, is hideous to look at, but when Natalie presses her palm flat to the wall she's afraid she'll burst — with — it isn't sadness. It isn't regret.

Longing. She longs to feel as she felt in this house. She longs to feel possible.

Something is missing. Something isn't here and she has to find it. Her mother's car keys — on a lanyard, I made this lanyard at summer camp last year, purple and green — sit in a lumpen clay dish her mom threw at a class at the Y. Natalie takes them.

The street is as deserted as the house. No cars drive by. No mailmen, no kids, no adults, no dogs or squirrels or sounds other than that strange music, that pulse, faint but louder. It isn't coming from the house after all.

The car—! She laughs out loud. The family Nova waits for her in the driveway, shining copper-gold in the light. She learned to drive in this car. She hit a mailbox in this car. Ran right over the curb and dented the front fender on a street-corner drop box, and then sped away because it was an official post office box, it was government property, what she'd done was probably a federal offense. Natalie had been alone, freshly licensed. She told her parents she'd been hit in a parking lot.

So began her criminal history.

Her side burns.

Every street is empty, empty and silent. No birds, even. The music gets steadily louder — she's following it, homing like a carrier pigeon — and the day is bright and beautiful and wrong. She can't explain herself in this place or how she came to be here, any more than she can explain the sensations crawling through her body. Now she feels loss; she feels as if she's leaking. She has to gather herself. She has to fill the hole.

The Nova takes her to her high school. The music is loud now, but she still doesn't recognize it. There are no words, no verses, no themes. There are only tones. Chords. Deep sliding sounds and that beat, that thudding beat that presses itself tightly around her head. The parking lot is empty. When she puts her bare foot down on the gravel, she feels music vibrating up her leg. Natalie didn't dislike high school. Sometimes she played piano for the chorus, as accompanist; she played in the pit for a few school plays. This high school isn't quite her own, though. She wasn't a student here.

She was a teacher here.

The music is in the auditorium lobby. It rolls out like warm breath, lifting Natalie's hair from her shoulders. The auditorium is dark except for the stage. Her feet are cold and clammy, and almost slide on the worn rust-colored carpet as she starts down the aisle. The air rumbles. Her breastbone thrums sympathetically.

The stage is so bright she has trouble looking at it. There's a mussed bed on stage left, pillows and blankets on the floor, and a dresser on stage right, and at center stage is a piano — *her* piano, her mother's mother's piano, which is exactly what she came here to find. It shines in a tight white spotlight.

The music stops. Her ears throb in the sudden silence. Natalie, barefoot, slip-slides down the silent aisle to get to her piano.

Her side aches. She holds her hand to her side, presses and holds.

It hurts but she braces both palms on the edge of the stage, pushes up, and swings first one leg, then the other, and she's shaking, shaking she's so excited. It's here. It's all still here, waiting for her to play it. She can feel the keys beneath her fingers already. Natalie twists her hair and throws it over one shoulder and sits on the piano bench. Her mother's mother's piano is a warm red-brown, always cool to the touch, its shiny surface scratched by the everyday traffic of children and house pets. She lifts and pushes back the lid, smiling at its brassy ALDWIN decal (the B is long gone; her sister Laurie picked at it). She closes her eyes. Her fingers know where to go. They sit on the white keys, waiting, home. She presses down and for a moment it's hers again, the first sound she fell in love with, the first chord of "Life on Mars?" But that's all there is. No second sound follows the first. The keys stick. They feel gluey.

Natalie opens her eyes to see blood rising between the keys, rich red blood pooling around her fingertips, and she is too afraid to scream, too afraid, even, to move.

"Play," says Ed Hollis. He's crumpled by the dresser on stage right, where he landed after she shot him. His head is curled tight toward his belly, like a shrimp. "Play it anyway," he says again.

"I'm sorry," she says to Hollis. "I'm so sorry, Ed. You didn't deserve —"

"Play it."

"I can't, it's full of blood."

"It always was. That's why you fell in love with it."

The keys are a shiny red lake. She can't bear to disturb the surface.

"Play it."

Natalie closes her eyes.

She presses her fingers into the blood and finds the keys underneath. They move. Full of blood, the keys move fluidly. The music, the pulse, returns, and Natalie plays along with it. *Listen,* says Hollis. He must be sitting beside her now; she can feel his weight on the bench, but she can't open her eyes. Not yet. *Listen harder.* She remembers how it feels to play. To play with your whole body, your fingers, your wrists, your forearms and elbows and shoulders, your neck and your head, your legs, your feet. You are an orchestra entire. Your fingers are each a single instrument, your hands a section; point and counterpoint, melody and countermelody, concord and dissonance are born, sustained, resolved in your body. In your head and your heart. In the space behind your bellybutton: a flicker, a flutter. Each chord she plays rises. Her hair lifts from her shoulders. Her hips, her thighs, her legs straighten slightly as she floats away from the bench. The only parts of her still tethered are her hands, her fingers on the keys, and when Natalie finally does open her eyes, she and the piano are suspended in midair, upside down. The world falls away and in the perfect black she is weightless.

A drop of water splashes on her face.

She hears voices.

She's back in her bedroom, miles from the stage, from that high school, it's the night she killed a boy and Natalie has only just dropped the gun. Hollis flew. He was so close when she shot him that he flew back as he fell, and now he's slumped against her dresser. That night, the night it happened, she sank to the floor where she stood. She crouched, trembling, and watched Hollis die from the other side of the room.

Another drop of water. She's being rained on, but she blinks the rain away.

Her bare knees sink in the carpet pile as she crawls over to Hollis, the boy she shot, the boy who would have hurt her, she has no doubt, if she hadn't. It was self-defense. It will always feel like murder. Because how can she blame him? How can she look at him and not see herself?

"Hollis," she says.

His lips part on a bubble of spit. His head droops.

She gathers him in her arms. He curls tighter, smaller, pressing his head into her chest, and when he shudders she holds him as close as she can. This boy with his shaggy blond hair and fine-lashed eyes. His chipped-tooth grin. Whose future she took. She will hold this boy for the rest of her life.

The rain is chlorinated. She spits it out.

Someone is crying. Or laughing, she can't tell, but she feels terrible. Her side. Some animal took a huge red bite out of her side.

288

Her eyes focus. Above her is Fisher Brodie. He's sopping wet, dripping pool water all over her, and laughing and crying and saying what might be her name. She places her hands on either side of his feverish face and pulls him down, pulls him closer, pulls him to herself.

SUNDAY
NOVEMBER 16, 1997

Grave e Cantabile

25

Only One Afternoon

THE YOUNGER COP brings Alice a paper cup of coffee. She doesn't have any hands to take it, because one is holding Auggie's leash and the other is gripping her brother. She isn't sure she'll ever be able to let Rabbit go.

Rabbit takes the coffee and thanks the cop shyly. Maybe he was bringing it to her brother all along.

The cop sits on the chaise opposite them and rubs his eyebrows. He looks tired. He should be; it's one in the morning. The only reason Alice's eyes are open is the adrenaline spiking her blood like punch at the prom. She wishes they weren't still here at the pool. She hates the smell. Chlorine and dirt and blood, she swears she can smell the blood pooled by the water's edge, brighter where it traveled along the white tile grout. It smells metallic and awful. The older cop is the same woman who spoke with Alice on Thursday night, who didn't believe Jill was missing. Alice can see her sitting on the other side of the pool, behind a bank of foliage. She's talking with Fisher Brodie. More like, she's murmuring calmly as Fisher weeps.

Alice leans against Rabbit's shoulder.

"This shouldn't take long," the younger cop says. "Normally I'd take you down to the station, but I don't think we'd all fit on the snowmobile." A weak smile. "I'm Officer Hockster. Would you state your full names?"

"Alice Louise Hatmaker. And this is my brother—"

"Bertram Hatmaker," Rabbit finishes. He takes a sip of coffee.

"Could you please describe what you saw here tonight?" Hockster looks from Alice to Rabbit. "Take your time. I know you're upset."

Alice shuts her eyes. She's never going to be able to erase that part of her brain. Poor old Hastings with a gun, his hand shaking, all of him shaking, and then his eyes when Dr. Brodie stepped in front of Mrs. Wilson: blank. Totally blank. Alice turned around in time to see Hastings's entire expression—confused, angry, afraid— slide right off his face. Her first thought was that he'd had a stroke. He was *gone,* washed away like sidewalk chalk in a thunderstorm, but his body moved as though it had been waiting for this moment all his life. His arm rose. His finger squeezed. The sound. The *sound* in that room, bouncing, echoing, jamming itself into her ears. Alice had been watching Hastings and not Dr. Brodie or Mrs. Wilson, so when she turned to see Brodie flailing in the water and Wilson flat on her back, not moving, she was more confused than anything. A dark mass began to spread from Wilson's right hip, and Alice watched it without grasping what it was, what it meant, or how she felt, other than freezing cold. It's only now, gathering herself in front of Officer Hockster, that Alice knows she felt sick to the bottom of her soul.

"She." She clears her throat. "She was standing next to the pool—"

"Not facing it?"

"No, she and Dr. Brodie were standing sort of . . . parallel to it. Mr. Hastings was very upset. At first it was like he was talking to his daughter, do you—know about her?"

Hockster nods. Alice wonders if he's from this town, if he not only knows about but knew her.

"I was trying to calm him down. I'm afraid he got worse. I had no idea he'd—" She swallows. This isn't your fault, Alice. Stop making everything about you. "Then he sort of . . . accused us."

"Of?"

"Murder," says Alice.

"Did he say whose murder?"

"He was really confused," Rabbit says. "But I think he meant the girl who disappeared."

"Faccelli, right?" Hockster makes a note.

"He made it sound like someone else was dead. Then he acted like he thought maybe *he'd* done something."

"Did he say what he meant by that?"

Rabbit shakes his head. "No," he says, lifting his eyebrows and his shoulders in a full-body shrug. As he does this, he squeezes Alice's hand, and Alice realizes they are not going to tell Officer Hockster that Mrs. Wilson said Yes. Yes, she was the murderer. At first Alice thought Wilson had been playing along, just as she had, trying to calm Hastings down. But it didn't sound like playing, and her face—Wilson's face didn't look like playing. Alice doesn't understand, and doesn't really want to.

"What happened next?" asks Hockster.

"Dr. Brodie stepped between them," says Alice, "to kind of . . . shield Mrs. Wilson from Mr. Hastings and . . . I don't know. Hastings was angry, and I think it spooked him. He fired."

"She pushed him in the pool," Rabbit says. His voice catches. "Then went down. Hastings sort of shouted." Rabbit raises his hands to either side of his head, at his temples, in demonstration. "Held his hands up like this and the gun went off again. Firing up. I heard broken glass."

"Must've hit one of the panes in the dome." Hockster makes a note in his book. "Is that when Rin Tin Tin came in?"

"Yes," Alice says, brightening. "Minnie—Minnie Graves?—and the ambulance crew were just getting off the elevator. Auggie—that's her dog—he came tearing in and made a beeline for Hastings, jumped up against his legs, and knocked him down. Probably wouldn't have taken much at that point, he was so shaky." The sound of the elevator doors opening and the sudden sight of Minnie and several strangers carrying a gurney had immobilized Alice, and she had stared, thunderstruck, as Minnie's dog bolted for Hastings.

Alice reaches down to give Auggie's ears a gentle rub. He'd only been being friendly. He's lucky he wasn't shot.

"So the EMTs show up for a gunshot wound instead of exposure. For the same person." Hockster grimaces. "And Hastings at this point is on the floor—"

Auggie had been all over him, licking his face, his hands, barking happy little barks.

"Where was the gun?"

"In the pool," Rabbit says. "Hastings must've dropped it. Minnie followed her dog and kicked it into the pool."

"And where was Brodie?"

"Dr. Brodie was out of the water," says Rabbit, "doing CPR or something on Mrs. Wilson. I saw him pound her chest with his fist. The EMTs had to drag him off her."

"It was horrible." Alice is about to say more but can't. Brodie soaking wet looked like a drowned, skinned cat, and he was shouting over the EMT's shoulder to Mrs. Wilson. Screaming. *Don't go. Don't go. Don't leave me.*

That was when Alice grabbed her brother's hand. She hasn't let go since. Not when the EMTs got Mrs. Wilson up on the gurney and into the elevator, not when Minnie had to pin Brodie's arms behind his back to keep him from following, not when Rabbit, flushed, turned to his sister and said that they had to get help, had to call the police, and the Hatmakers in tandem rushed to the hotel phone to call the guy at the front desk. She didn't let go when Fisher Brodie, eyes glassy, grabbed her brother by the arms and said, *We have to go too, you have to help me, come with me,* and Rabbit didn't say anything but walked him to a chair and told him to sit down and wait, and Brodie did as he was told. And she didn't let go when she noticed Hastings and Minnie on the floor together, side by side with their backs against an overturned chaise, Auggie lying with his head on Hastings's lap.

They waited and she held her brother's hand. As the events she had just witnessed began to thaw from the quick-freeze of shock, she felt their hands grow warmer and sweatier, and their grip on each other tighten. The cops came and took photographs, and the gun from the bottom of the pool, and Hastings. Minnie went with him, leaving Auggie in Alice's care. That left the Hatmakers and the dog and Officer Hockster. Dr. Brodie and the policewoman. A pool of blood.

Alice inhales. When she exhales it's as if she's letting out all the breaths she's ever taken.

"Would you like me to call your parents?" Hockster says. Alice straightens. Her parents. The world outside the Bellweather. Her life outside this strange hotel and this horrible room. She shakes her head.

"How old do you think we are?" Rabbit asks. It doesn't sound bratty coming from her brother; it sounds like a genuine question.

Hockster could be twenty or he could be thirty-five. He has the kind of face that will look like a boy's until it becomes an old man's overnight. It's the kind of face her father—their father—has. Alice does wish their parents were here. Not that they could do anything. Not that they could take any of this back, make it better, or fix it. The desire to defer to a higher power is an old habit, and a powerful one. She wants to take everything she's seen and felt and pass it off to someone older, wiser, someone designated for that kind of heavy lifting, who will take her in his arms and tell her not to worry. Not to think about it anymore. To go back to sleep.

"Older than you look," says Hockster. "And older than you were this morning."

Her name is Officer Megan Sheldrake. Rabbit likes her immensely. He likes her salt-and-pepper hair and her tendency to smile with her eyes instead of her mouth, the casual way she rests her knuckles on her hips, and the manner in which she tells Brodie to calm the fuck down, sir. She uses those exact words, and her tone is so warm and gentle that Fisher Brodie, pinwheeling and despondent, calms down.

Rabbit is numb. Everything that happened tonight—how could he possibly have been a part of it? Not a guilty or responsible part, but still, he was a member of the cast. He, Rabbit Hatmaker, who admittedly had been playing fast and loose with his comfort zone all weekend, had witnessed a shooting. A shooting and possibly a murder. His eyes sting. He can't think about it. If he thinks he might have seen Mrs. Wilson get killed, he's not going to be any use to anyone.

And he wants to be of use, desperately, to Fisher Brodie. Officer Sheldrake can tell, which is another reason he likes her so much. She approached Rabbit and Alice after their cop, Hockster, finished his interview, with a request. Would they feel comfortable taking Mr. Brodie back to his room, making sure he got rest and wasn't left alone? "I don't think he's a danger to himself or to others," she said. "Otherwise I wouldn't ask. He's just tremendously upset. Exhausted. And he likes you both a whole lot. He wouldn't stop talking about *you*. Rabbit this. Rabbit that. By the way, what's your real name?"

"Rabbit," said Rabbit.

"It's Bert," said Alice.

He doesn't want to imagine what this night would've been like if he'd had to go through it alone. He doesn't ever want to let go of his sister's hand.

"Only if you feel comfortable." What Officer Sheldrake said next clinched it. "He doesn't seem to have anyone else."

"Mr. Brodie, sir," she says now, shaking him gently. Rabbit and Alice stand on the other side of the poolside ferns, watching, waiting for Officer Sheldrake to bring Brodie out. "Mr. Brodie, you're going to have to calm the fuck down, sir."

There is a long pause.

"The Hatmakers are going to take you to your room."

"No," he says.

"You can't stay here."

"Not my room. Any other room but my room."

Alice nudges her brother. "I have Minnie's key," she whispers. "Minnie and Auggie's room. I'm sure she wouldn't mind."

"What's wrong with your room?" Officer Sheldrake's cop sense is obviously tingling.

Rabbit bends toward the conversation.

"Nothing." Brodie sighs. "She's there."

"Officer?" Rabbit says. "We have another room we can take him to."

She looks at Rabbit, eyes narrowing, thinking. "It's a hotel. There's nothing *but* other rooms," she mutters. "Okay. Up, sir. Let's go. I'll leave you in the care of your friends, at least until tomorrow morning. Don't leave the hotel. Don't do anything but take off your shoes and lie down on a bed and rest." She pats his back. "We'll be in touch."

Brodie, standing now and halfway visible through the ferns, stops suddenly. "You'll call if you hear?"

"You aren't her next of kin."

"She's our chaperone," Rabbit says. He walks around the foliage and stutters over his next words, because Fisher Brodie is a wraith. What was once his conductor, his insane, magical conductor, is a jumble of dark clothes wrapped around sticks, with hollowed-out eyes and blood-smeared cheeks. Mrs. Wilson's blood. "She's responsible for us, so can we be responsible for her?"

Officer Sheldrake looks Rabbit up and down.

"Room four-oh-seven," Alice offers.

"Take care of him," says the cop, and Rabbit, still holding on to his sister for dear life, takes Brodie's elbow with his free hand. The four of them, Rabbit, Alice, Brodie, and Auggie, make the short journey from swimming pool to elevator to the fourth floor in silence. Rabbit realizes how tired he is, how wonderful it would be to lean against the elevator's mirrored walls and close his eyes and not open them for a very long time. The room—Minnie's room, which his sister walks into as nonchalantly as if it were her own—is more spacious than the one Rabbit's been sleeping in. Stacked on the desk are room service trays, rinsed dishes, and silverware. The room smells of French fries and garlic. There is only one enormous bed.

"I slept in one of the chairs last night," Alice says. "They're not bad."

"What are you talking about?"

"It's too long a story for right now. Help me with these?"

Fisher sits on the end of the mattress, docile as a kicked dog, and

Alice and Rabbit untie and ease off his shoes. He falls back on the bed, feet still on the floor, and closes his eyes.

"Are you asleep?" Rabbit asks him.

"Yes."

"Good." He doesn't mean it. Fisher looks like a corpse.

"He looks—" Alice says, and shakes her head, mouth hanging open. Rabbit squeezes her hand in his and lifts it to his mouth for a kiss—a quick kiss that astonishes and pleases them both. They let go of each other at the same time. His hand is red and cramped and he can still feel her there, like a phantom limb. It isn't a super-power, twin or otherwise. He knows what his sister is feeling because he's her brother and he's feeling it too.

She sits beside Brodie while Rabbit runs a fresh washcloth under the hot tap in the bathroom.

"Dr. Brodie? Are you asleep?" he asks again.

"Yes."

"If it's okay with you, I'm going to clean up your face." Rabbit crouches on the other side of the bed, opposite his sister, and takes Brodie's silence as permission. Rabbit thinks of his mother. How she would wrap her hand in a cooled cloth and press it against his hot forehead, his cheeks, his throat. This is kind of like that, only the cloth is beginning to turn pink with blood and he can feel Brodie's beard prickling his palm, Brodie's breath tickling his wrist. He traces his fingertips across Fisher's brow, rubbing softly into his thick eyebrows. Tilts his chin gently to clean beneath his jaw. Alice watches him; he can feel her watching him, and if he betrays a certain tenderness that goes beyond compassion, he doesn't care. He couldn't care if he wanted to. He's beyond that. All that matters is finding his Fisher again beneath this mask.

He rinses the washcloth in the sink, but it's going to be pink forever.

Fisher is split down the middle. Cleaved. Crushed. His head— his head isn't his head, it's a watermelon that's been worked over with the claw end of a hammer. Every part of him throbs, aches, or burns. His eyelids smart. His fingers pulse, swollen. His throat is raw meat.

But that's only his body, the bag of blood and bones his mother carried and bore, struggling physically out of a sleep deep as death. His brain starts the critical systems first, all the moving bits and pieces, before it turns to recent memory. And when Fisher, on waking, remembers Natalie, the world stops. All the bodily pain he feels is tamped down by the memory of what happened to Natalie. What *did* happen to Natalie? He stepped in front of her, she pushed him, she was bleeding, unconscious by the time he pulled himself out of the pool — he still smells of chlorine, he reeks, he's going to be ill — he remembers pounding on her chest, not that he knows how to do that sort of thing, but he's seen enough movies and it was the only act he was capable of at the time. Beating her heart. She opened her eyes, yes, he remembers that. She opened her eyes and she reached for his face and pulled him down, pulled his face down against her neck. The rest is a bit blurry. He was shouting. They were pulling him away. Then they took *her* away — good, good, she wasn't dead, at least not then — and the next thing he remembers is speaking with a woman in a uniform, a rather nice woman, a bit thick in the middle but comforting, a voice like warm brandy.

Then: Hatmakers.

Fisher doesn't have the strength to sit up. The spirit is willing, the flesh dead weight. All he can manage is lifting his head off the pillow. Well, he's still here. Here in this fucking hotel. He's wearing the clothes he wore to dinner last night, and someone has thrown a pilly tan blanket, hotel-issue, over his lower half. His shoes are off. He smells maple syrup. Girl Hatmaker is eating pancakes from a tray on her lap as she watches closed-caption television in the corner of the room. She's wearing a black skirt, black stockings, and a white blouse, because it's concert day, and as ridiculous, insane, as it sounds, the show must go on.

" 'lo," he croaks.

Girl Hatmaker turns.

"Hello," she says.

"Time is it?"

"Just past eleven. Do you want some breakfast? We ordered a ton."

"We?"

"Me and my brother. Rabbit." She swallows her pancakes. "He left a little while ago."

"Is he coming back?"

She shakes her head and stands, smoothing out her skirt, and stacks her breakfast tray with the others on the desk. She brings an untouched one to the bed, hooks her fingertip through the hole in the metal cover, and removes it with a flourish, and the sight and the smell of all those eggs, all that bacon, all that sugar and fat and grease, make Fisher's stomach turn itself inside out.

"Toast?" she says. "We have that too."

He shakes his head. No food. No food ever again.

"I know it's a really stupid question," Girl Hatmaker says, "but how do you feel?"

"Like shit."

"So you feel how you look," she says with a small smile.

God bless Hatmakers.

"I have some things to tell you," she says, tentative now, and Fisher's innards seize.

"Tell me."

She bites her lip, pauses, and finally sits calmly beside him, tucking her skirt around her legs. "The police stopped by this morning. You slept right through it. There's . . . a lot. Are you ready?"

He isn't. He nods.

"First: Dr. Fabian committed suicide last night."

"What?"

"She poisoned herself. They found her this morning when the hotel staff tried to tell her about everything else that happened."

"*What?*"

"They wouldn't tell me any more than that. I guess maybe they think she killed her daughter, and then herself, out of remorse. Guilt."

"Viola doesn't have a remorseful bone in her body. Didn't." He shuts his eyes. How can Viola Fabian, of all people, be dead, and how can anyone think she would kill herself? He has to tell Natalie. He has to tell her Fabian's dead, the wicked witch is dead, and then he remembers what Natalie told *him* last night while they were walking around the pool. That it was Viola who'd shut her out in the cold. The pieces are in front of him but they won't fit together.

"Do you think Hastings had anything to do . . ." Alice trails off.

"No," he says, because he honestly doesn't.

She seems incredibly relieved to hear this.

"What else is there?" he asks. "You said there was a lot."

"Okay, second: Mrs. Wilson made it through the night. She woke up this morning."

He makes a small noise in the back of his throat, a helpless, happy noise.

"She doesn't want to see you." Girl Hatmaker blushes and looks away.

"What?"

"She told the police, who told me to tell you." She still won't look at him. "That she doesn't want you to come to the hospital."

"Those are two different instructions." Fisher's head buzzes. Ears ring. This isn't happening. This isn't happening. He died last night, he died and woke up in hell. "Does she not want to see me *at all,* or does she not want me to see her in hospital?"

Girl Hatmaker shakes her head. "I don't know," she says. "I don't—the exact words Officer Sheldrake said were 'She doesn't want to see him.' I don't know how much room for interpretation—"

"The hell do you know?"

She recoils. "I know she's married. I know she got shot. I know I'd do what she told me." Girl Hatmaker fumes. "There's more."

"Get on with it."

"It didn't come from the police, it came from my brother."

"Old Bunny Boy." He grits his teeth.

"It's an invitation, asshole. They found another conductor for the orchestra, and the concert starts at noon. He said he has a surprise for you, a treat. To make you feel better. And FYI, I think he's kind of in love with you, so if you disappoint him, if you for one second do not give my brother the respect he deserves, you'll have *me* to answer to. I am the *bad* twin. My selfish guts are my ruling planet. If you cross or hurt someone I love, I will come down on you like a fucking house of bricks. You think *this* is a world of pain?"

The last thing Fisher wants to do in the face of this beautiful young creature, this teenage avenger, is laugh, but he can't help it. His mouth splits open in a smile and he laughs. Because she's young. Because she's right without knowing how right she is. The world is nothing but pain. By the time she's Fisher's age, she'll be used to it.

"Remind me what your name is," he says.

"Alice," she says.

"Right, right, Alice and Rabbit. I remember. What did you come here for? I mean *here,* Statewide."

"Chorus."

"May I hear? Would you sing for me? Angel of music and all that." He knows he's being a prat, but he can't stop.

"No," she says. "Take a damn shower."

The heat and the steam of the shower feel incredible, wonderful, amazing, spectacular, all the adjectives in the world, until suddenly the world is slipping through his brain and he smacks his forehead against the tile. The blow brings him back. He spins the knobs all the way to freezing and then, and only then, is Fisher truly awake for the first time. He plots. He plans. After this concert, he's going to dig Bonnie out of the snowdrift where she's waited out the storm. He's going to ride to the hospital, no matter what condition the roads are in. He's going to find Natalie's room (I'm her brother, her mailman, she's the love of my life) and kneel by her bedside and tell her he meant it, he still wants to run away, with her and only her. He doesn't care what she's done. He doesn't care that she didn't want him to see her like this. He wishes she had let him take the bullet. He wants to be with her, run with her, and he'll wait. He's already waited a lifetime to find her; he'll wait the rest of his life.

His legs are rubbery. Fisher has to take Alice's proffered arm and running commentary (you should've eaten, even toast would have helped) to make it to the elevator, which is already full of kids in black bottoms and white tops. Some of them are orchestra kids. He recognizes the shape of their violin cases before he recognizes their faces. What have they been told? That he came down with food poisoning? That he had a seizure? They are too afraid to ask him face-to-face.

It's ten to noon when they enter the auditorium, which is half full of teachers and musicians from the concert band and the chorus. Alice leads him down to empty seats in the front row, and when the kids in the orchestra notice that he's arrived, they break out in a rumble of orchestral applause, pounding the stage with their feet. They smile at him. Some of them hoot and wave. He doesn't wave back. He looks straight ahead, at the podium, at the black tuxedo–panted rear end of his replacement. It's the same guy who's conducting the concert band—Ralph something. Fisher can't remember.

The concert begins. They play the Holst. They play well. Then they play the Handel and the Mendelssohn, all the shite he told them to throw away on the first day, and even though Fisher's mind is on Natalie, on his plan to get to Natalie, he can't help hearing how good they sound. How alive. Alice keeps shooting him sidelong glances. His face is still, stiller than his heart, which stirs more with each piece, and he knows he's being a stingy git but he doesn't care. The music is nice (it's better than nice, it's good—it's true and good), but it isn't going to help matters. It isn't going to change anything.

"We have one more piece to play for you today," says Ralph the replacement, turning to address the crowd from the podium (who does that, how déclassé). "It's something of an experiment. I can't say how Debussy would feel about certain liberties taken, but I certainly hope he'd respect our good intentions."

Debussy?

Ralph whatever lifts his baton.

A bassoon takes flight out of the orchestra. The only sound on the stage, the only sound in the auditorium, is Rabbit, playing the flute solo that Fisher transcribed into tenor clef after the departure of Jill Faccelli. The solo swoops dizzily, sweetly. Fisher never believed he'd hear this. Never thought Rabbit would play it. He'd transcribed *Afternoon of a Faun* for fun, just to kill time, because something about Rabbit on that first day had moved him, and he thought, *Why not, have a go*. The strings dance alongside Rabbit, teasing him, pushing him around a bit. There should be a harpist, but of course there isn't—this was a lark. This was never supposed to be performed. On flute, the solos are lovely; on bassoon, they're haunting, lonely, sounds in search of something larger. The effect is so beautiful Fisher's face gives up and synchs with his heart. Out of the corner of his eye he catches Alice smirking and doesn't begrudge her a thing.

He sits closer to the edge of his seat.

Faun is dreamy. Slow and sensual, with loopy flourishes and high held chords and a constant driving insistence that there's only ever one afternoon, only one now. He told them on that first afternoon, when Jill Faccelli pitched her perfectly timed fit, that it was all about sex. The chase. The climax. Well. Yes, but—but. He covers his mouth with his fingertips and closes his eyes. Fresh green grass. Wind and warmth on the back of his neck. He can't believe he missed it earlier when Alice said that her brother was in love with him. He'd heard her, but he didn't piece the information together with the half memory, half dream of Rabbit cleaning the blood off his face last night. This performance is a second expression of that devotion. Fisher opens full eyes. The music slowly unwinds, folding itself up gently in its own arms. There is only ever one afternoon, and it ends. But one afternoon can hold so much beauty and so much love.

26

Songs for Two Voices

INNIE HANDS SHEILA her room keys and her credit card. It's not yet nine a.m. For the second time in her life, she's scurrying out of the Bellweather as fast as her legs will carry her.

"Do you know where he is?" Sheila asks. She sets Minnie's Visa neatly in the manual card imprinter and rams the shuttle back and forth with the flat of her hand. She doesn't meet Minnie's eyes when she returns the card.

"They took him to the hospital."

"The one in Clinton?"

Minnie nods. At least that's where they told her they were taking him. Hastings had barely been able to sit upright at the state police station, had been muttering and leaking tears and then shouting about Rome, telling Rome to get the hell away from him, to leave him alone. He needed clinical observation, not a cold cell where he could sleep it off.

Minnie signs the credit slip. Her hand aches. Why the hell does her hand—oh, right. Hastings. Hastings had squeezed her hand all the way to the police station, had let go only when they had him fingerprinted. She flexes her fingers. She makes a fist and considers popping Sheila in the face, but hands her the signed slip instead.

"Thanks, Erm—Ermin. How do you pronounce that?"

"I'll see you at the hospital later," Minnie says, and Sheila looks away.

The roads are passable. There's a mound of snow down the median, but it was harder to extract her car from the Bellweather lot—Auggie howling along with the radio as Minnie dug out all four of the wheels—than it is to drive through town. By the time she thinks to do so, it's too late to catch one final look at the hotel in her rearview. She's never going back to the Bellweather again. There's no need. All the ghosts are coming with her this time.

She's glad she was able to say goodbye to Alice. And to her brother, though they'd really only just met. The twins were dozing in her room, contorted over the chairs because the tall, skinny man who'd been thrown in the pool, the man with the woman Hastings shot, was passed out in her bed.

"Did you guys have a nice sleepover?" she asked. Not funny, Minnie. "Just came to pack my things. And get Auggie. Hi, boy." Auggie pressed his forehead against her shins and whined. She told them as much as she knew about Hastings. They told her as much as they knew about the woman who'd been shot. They sat in silence until Alice (of course), her voice strengthening above a whisper, said, "So this weekend. Right? What the hell was *that?*"

Minnie grinned at her.

She shook Rabbit's hand. She was in the middle of thanking Alice for taking good care of Auggie overnight when Alice, eyes glistening in the murk of the room, skinny guy sleeping blissfully on, rushed toward her with arms wide open. "Thank you for listening to my bullshit," she murmured, sniffling into Minnie's shoulder.

"It's not bullshit," Minnie said. "Try not to worry too much about the future. Or the past." She patted Alice's back. "Pay attention to the people around you." Look at you, Minnie Graves; big sister. "Also, do as I say and not as I do."

Auggie had yipped a little when Alice closed the door, but he was back to his natural state of happy oblivion now, riding shotgun on the way to the hospital with his tongue lolling out. Minnie rubs his ears every time they come to a stoplight. He howls when the Bee

Gees play on the radio, like he always has, though she'll never know if this is a complete coincidence or if Gibb falsetto is the only frequency her deaf dog can discern. But that's Auggie's only real mystery, other than where he came from. Minnie knows her best friend. She knows his excited bark from his anxious bark, his I'm-hungry whine from his I-have-to-go-out whine. When he rolls on his back, he wants to be rubbed not on his belly but on the top of his head, and she shares his belief that the pizza delivery guy simply must be given a hero's frenzied welcome every time. She's given him food and shelter, walks and tossed Frisbees; he's given her courage and strength by first giving her unconditional love. She never had to ask for it. It came into her life. All she had to do was trust it.

Which is so much harder than it sounds.

The hospital looks an awful lot like the little community hospital where her Grandma Harris passed away, the spring before her sister's wedding, before she had ever heard of the Bellweather: off-white walls with gray-green tile, long corridors that lead God knows where. When she finally finds the psychiatric unit, she doesn't want to lie, but the truth is too complicated, so she says she's his granddaughter.

Hastings is diminished. His face is as gray as the walls, as dull as the linens tucked around his thin body. Without his smart maroon jacket and his bow tie, he looks like what he is: an old man, bled out and lost. His wrists are tied down with wide cloth restraints. Minnie sits beside him and slips her hand into his.

That first afternoon he doesn't even look at her. She can't stay long with Auggie out in the car, but she stays as long as she can.

Rabbit has to find Alice. Where could she have gone? She was just here, in the auditorium with Fisher Brodie, and the orchestra and he—Rabbit glows—only just finished playing *Faun*. The orchestra has left the stage and Rabbit's packed up Beatrice; they couldn't have gone far in that time. He bounds up the auditorium aisle, elastic with joy. He. Can't. Believe. He did that. It had occurred to him in the shower, out of nowhere—he really ought to play the solos Fisher transcribed for him. It would be just the thing to rally his conductor, to get him up on that podium. Then he actually saw Fisher, sunk in the middle of the bed, colorless and hollowed. Fisher would not be conducting again, at least not today.

"You have to tell someone." Alice hugged her arms over her stomach. "Whoever you can find. I'll stay here with Aug."

So Rabbit left Fisher with his sister and the dog to seek out the closest Statewide-associated adult he could find and deliver the message that his chaperone had been shot. His conductor was comatose. He wanted to play *Afternoon of a Faun* on a bassoon.

Which was more improbable, that he'd had the idea or that they went for it? Considering the concert band conductor was kind of a kook and the fact that it was a glorified rehearsal instead of a concert, it was totally plausible all around. The performance was far from perfect, not even in the same neighborhood as perfect, but it had been so full of feeling Rabbit doesn't know how he's still standing, why he isn't collapsed in the corner, disintegrated by bliss.

This is why. This is *why.* This is why he plays, why he loves, why he listens. It isn't even a high—a high is too low—it is synchronicity with the universe. Physical proof of the three-part harmony between body and soul and song, all three living, dying, resonating. He needs to find Alice and they need to celebrate. This soaring sensation that he is part of a greater symphony is the antidote to the mortal vertigo he feels when he closes his eyes. When he closes his eyes he sees Mrs. Wilson on her back in a glossy pool of blood. It's mostly black, the blood—it isn't red like you'd expect, it shines on the edges and swallows the light in the center, and one of Mrs. Wilson's knees lifts her skirt like a circus tent and there's a rip in her stockings that starts at her bent knee and disappears under the dark of her skirt. Blood surrounds her right hand, fingertips submerged.

Don't think about it.

The lobby is loud. Schools of students swim against one another, orchestra heading for their rooms, concert band heading for the auditorium. Did Alice stay inside to listen to the band? No, she wouldn't do that. She wouldn't head back to the room they'd slept in, either, since Minnie turned in the keys when she checked out this morning. The weekend is slipping through his fingers, scattering before it's finished. It isn't time yet, he still has questions, he can't find his sister—

The Tenor bashes into his shoulder.

Rabbit rocks back on his feet, swinging his bassoon case wide and grazing another kid in the thigh. Pete the Tenor—the college guy, the *a cappella* guy, Rabbit has to remind himself—of all people, Pete is the one in the crowd who runs into him. They both stop. Pause.

So awkward.

"Hey," says Rabbit.

"Hey yourself, Bert." Pete smiles and Rabbit remembers why he fell. His knees go buttery. "Heard you were looking for me."

"Huh?"

"Well, you found me."

"What do you mean?"

"Weren't you running around looking for someone last night?"

"How'd you—how'd you know?" He *doesn't* know. He can't.

"I hear things."

Rabbit readjusts his grip on his case, which jostles against his leg. So . . . this guy. This guy's always going to be the first guy you sort of almost made out with, with his dark skin and white teeth, floppy brown hair tucked under a Yankees cap and curling around the tops of his ears. This guy you literally saw across a crowded room, who made time stop with his voice and his dark eyes, who looks a little like you imagine your first crush grew up to look like, who rocks a Macchio vibe in 1997. He's always going to be the first guy who singled you out and talked to you, who breathed down the side of your neck. This ordinary, exactly-as-expected guy is no one to run from. Or run to, frankly.

"I gotta go," says Rabbit. "See you."

His room door is propped open with a pink sneaker.

"Never gave you back your key," Alice says when he steps inside. His roommate, onstage with the band, has already packed his bag and set it neatly beside his bed. He wonders what kind of weekend

Dan's had, that he's so ready to leave. Rabbit ought to feel like running, like getting the hell away from this crazy place, but he doesn't yet. He has one more thing to say.

"You made him cry," Alice says.

Rabbit sets his bassoon down. "Fisher? Cried?"

"Not like great wailing sobs, but his face was wet. I think that's why he didn't stick around, he had to go collect himself. He told me to tell you, ahem"—Alice continues in a Scottish accent—"that he was quite moved. That you're bloody talented. That you should apply to Westing, if you haven't already." Sadness flits across her face. "I told him you had. That we both had."

College! Rabbit plunks down on his bed. Suddenly he can't wait to go to college. To go away again, away from home, and make his life in this wider, wilder world. College had seemed like such a remote idea, an intellectual inevitability, but now it feels like a real thing, an actual thing that will happen, with hot plates and highlighters and no one to answer to but himself. He'd applied to more schools than Westing—unlike his sister, Rabbit never thought of the future as a predestined line—but hadn't felt that special zip you're supposed to feel. You'll know, they said; you'll know what feels right. Now he feels Westing deep in his gut.

"We should have talked about this before," Alice says. She sits on the bed opposite. "We can go to the same school or not. I mean, if we both go to Westing, I'll stay out of your hair, we don't have to be attached at the hip or anything. Not that you need my permission, but you should go wherever you want. I know it's pretty self-centered to say this, but don't you dare base your decision on me in any way. Don't go to Westing because you feel obligated to follow me. And don't go someplace else just to avoid me."

"Thanks." He wrinkles his nose. "You thought that? That I would choose where I went to school because of you?"

"No," she says, grinning down at her chest. She looks at her lap and blushes, and Rabbit gets it.

"I won't leave you," he says. "I can't leave you. What if I ever need a kidney?"

That gets her to laugh.

"What if *I* ever need a kidney?" she says.

"We've got four between us. That should be plenty."

She takes a breath. Then she looks straight at him and asks if he's gay.

His ears pound with blood.

"Hurm?" he says automatically, looking down. The carpet is brown and orange.

She switches beds and sits beside him, and thank God, because it's easier when he doesn't have to look straight at her. "I asked if you were gay," she says. "I don't know—if I'm wrong—I just. Got a feeling."

"Okay."

She kind of laughs. "*Okay*," she says, drawling. "If you are, I mean. It's okay. It's fine. I don't care. That's not true—it's really not my business, but I do care. I care about you."

"Okay."

He's boiling. He's sweating and freezing at the same time. He grabs her hand.

"I won't tell anyone," she says.

Now he's falling. Falling.

"Unless he's hot." Alice balances her chin on his shoulder. "Then you better believe I'm going to tell him about my brother."

"That would be okay," he says, and they both laugh, high, a little hysterical, and Rabbit throws his arm around Alice and they squeeze each other until Alice says, "You know what I feel like doing?"

"What?"

"I feel like dancing."

"But there isn't—"

"Like I don't know every word of that song. And like you don't know every step." She clears her throat and hums.

He does remember every step. Every turn, every jump. She might be wearing her black and white clothes, but Rabbit expects Alice will skip the chorus concert this afternoon. This is her performance today, here in this ugly old room, in this dilapidated hotel, her voice strong and young and beautiful. She stands in front of Dan's bed, he stands in front of his own. Step forward. Step back. Step side, repeat. Shoulder rolls, head flicks. They look at each other and know, as they knew when they first taught each other this dance, to leap on their respective beds at the same time, to leap back to the floor, to grab each other's arms, to spin. Rabbit closes his eyes and hears his sister singing in the darkness. She's singing for Whitney Houston and Julie Andrews, Eponine and Eliza Doolittle, Auntie Mame and Maria, for every part she aches to play. She's singing for herself at seventeen, for herself at seven—she's singing for their past and their future. She's singing for him. Her voice opens and Rabbit hears nothing but music, inside and out, nothing but the songs they were both born to live.

Natalie opens her eyes. The world is made of light.

A soft beep keeps the time. It's her heart, given an electronic voice. Even though it seems every square inch of her body hurts, she smiles. It's kind of nice to hear your heart outside your body, gently reminding you of its existence. She wiggles her toes. Rotates her feet. Rolls her head from side to side across the pillow. Takes a long, deep breath.

The light has a strange quality, a sensitivity—too clean, too new. A New Year's Day sort of feeling, and Natalie, aching, her right side stiff with bandages and stitches (but no bullet—that went clean through), knows she has every right to call this the worst hangover of her life. And yet it feels like the *best* hangover she's ever had. The most earned. The most . . . deserved. Less like a hangover than a karmic feedback loop, closed. Like she's on the other side of a collapsed wormhole, a stargate leading from that other life, that not-life, that place where even the air felt as if it could hurt her.

Jesus, morphine is *awesome*.

She giggles.

Her arm itches under the IV adhesive. She stares at her forearm as fine reddish hairs spring up around her tape-puckered skin, her own fine reddish hairs, her own forearm, her own skin.

Every sound, every smell, every color and texture rubs against her ears, her nose, her eyes. There's a curtain to her right, tan with light blue stripes, and she can hear her roommate snoring. The air reeks of alcohol and plastic. There's a droopy flower arrangement on a table at the foot of her roommate's bed, several days old, mulchy and ripe. It's so much. It's so real. She's going to cry. She's so real she's going to cry.

She remembers the cops as though they visited her in a dream, but she knows it wasn't—it was here in the hospital, only this morning. A youngish man and an older no-bullshit sort of woman, she forgets their names. She remembers a brunette wearing scrubs dotted with purple and blue pansies, her nurse apparently, leading them in, asking Natalie if she felt up to answering a few questions.

"Yes," Natalie rasped. Her voice was stuck. "Do *they*? Because I'm not sure what happened either."

This was not entirely true. The drugs made it easier, but she knew she was going to tell a fuzzy, no-charges-to-be-pressed version of events as soon as she woke up, as soon as she remembered the look on that man's face. That old man with the dangling bow tie who *knew* her, who looked into her and knew she was a murderer. Who shot her deliberately but also accidentally, and didn't deserve to have his future taken away from him, however much future he had left, for what Natalie knew hadn't been an act of malice or violence or even self-defense but of brokenheartedness. A twitch born of pain and frustration that had granted him a flash of second sight. Not that she really believed in that, but still. Fisher saw the Natalie that Natalie wanted him to see; the old man saw Natalie as she really saw herself. In gratitude for his honesty, Natalie had no wish to subject him to any further torment than he was already subjecting himself.

Viola, however—she was a different story.

"Viola Fabian left me for dead outside in the snow," she said, "as payback for humiliating her. She's my former mentor. She's psychotic. And yes, I want to press charges."

The cops glanced at each other but did not ask about Viola again.

"It was my gun," she said. Best to drop the bomb. "How's that for irony?"

"*Your* gun? Why would you—do you have a permit to—"

It was very funny, the way they took this information. They became all perked ears and narrowed eyes. Notes were scribbled down. *It doesn't mean anything,* Natalie wanted to tell them, *other than that the universe has a sick sense of a humor and a love of symmetry.*

He was confused, ranting, very upset, she told them. I'm sure he didn't mean to hurt anyone. Fisher Brodie spooked him, that's all. The old man was raising his arm to fire so I pushed Fisher into the pool. I got hit. I'm lucky.

"Have you seen him today?" she asked. "Fisher?"

Not yet. They were heading to the Bellweather next.

"Tell him not to come here." Her voice was stuck again. "I don't want to see him."

The nurse in the pansy scrubs is back. She comes quietly around the corner as though she's sneaking up on a frightened kitten, and when she sees Natalie's eyes are open, she smiles shyly.

"Hello, Mrs. Wilson. How are you feeling?"

Natalie glances at the fat IV bags floating above her like water balloons. "Super-awesome," she says.

Her nurse grins. She's so young she could be one of Natalie's students.

They all could be.

"It's not any of my business." The nurse blushes. "It really isn't, I know, but I just couldn't help overhearing." She twists her hands. "What you did was brave."

Natalie stares at her.

"You pushed someone out of the way of a bullet. And *took* it. The way you told the story this morning, I knew you didn't think you were a hero. But you are." Her eyes are bright. "You should know that." She smiles again, satisfied with having done precisely what she came to do. "I'll be back in a little while to take your vitals."

She's gone.

Natalie wants to call after the nurse, to ask whether it makes her more or less heroic that she took a bullet for the man with whom she was committing adultery. Though she didn't think of it in those terms, she didn't—she really didn't think at all, in the moment, other than *Fisher, what the hell are you doing, get out of the goddamned way* — and then —

She's certain that someone has called her husband, notified her next of kin. That was her head's reason for asking the police to tell Fisher to stay away. Because Emmett was surely en route, and Emmett was a good man who didn't deserve any of this, least of all having to share the space around his wife's hospital bed with her lover. What he deserved was the truth. Natalie intends to confess everything she's done this weekend, every crime she's committed and with whom, and whatever happens after that, happens. She hadn't promised fidelity lightly. She knows what she's done and how she's betrayed him, but it would be a lie to say what happened between her and Fisher had been trivial, a fling, a nothing. And that's her heart's reason for telling the police she didn't want to see him — she wasn't ready to say goodbye to those four days in the Bellweather. She wanted to be brave and wise, the Natalie who climbed up on chairs and told an auditorium full of kids not to make her mistakes; to feel known, forgiven, the Natalie that Fisher fell in love with, for just a little longer.

She can't imagine never seeing him again, never knowing what he does, where he lives, who else he becomes, and yet she can't possibly imagine the kind of life they would have together. Though maybe that's all life ever is. Unimaginable, until it's happening to you.

She takes another long breath. Right now, here in this hospital bed, in the space between lives, Natalie allows her conscience to let go. To lay down the weight. To see how it feels to forgive herself, just see how it feels.

She's lucky. She lived. She could even be called a hero.

Just for one day.

Fisher knocks on his door. Three short taps. The *Do Not Disturb* hangtag bobbles on the knob.

She opens the door an inch and steps back into the shadows. Fisher hasn't spent more than twenty-five consecutive minutes —

the time it takes to shower, shave, and gather clean clothes—in his room at the Bellweather since Thursday evening, but someone has. Room service trays are stacked on the desk. The bedclothes are rumpled, the pillows piled in a tower five high. She throws herself into the big armchair by the window and twists sideways, kicking her legs over one of the arms. The shades are all drawn. The only light creeps out in a slice from the bathroom.

Fisher doesn't have time for this, not if he wants to get to the hospital before Natalie's husband does (they're certain to call for him, if they haven't already). And yet he finds he can't move. He has to say something.

"Did you do it?" he asks the girl in the armchair.

Jill Faccelli flattens her mouth.

"What do you mean?" she asks. "Do what?"

Fisher frowns. The suspicion has been coalescing in his brain all morning. Ever since Girl Hatmaker woke him with the news that the police found Viola Fabian dead, Fisher's subconscious has been churning. Viola Fabian would never kill herself. Not that she didn't have the mettle (she most assuredly did), she just wasn't the type. And Fisher is one of two people in the world who knows that the theoretical motive is horseshit. For one thing, Viola Fabian could never feel guilt. For another, her daughter is alive and well and her mother had nothing to do with any of it.

Jill cut her hair yesterday, poorly, using a pair of sewing kit scissors and Fisher's electric clippers. The better to disappear into a new life, she told him. She looks like a kewpie with mange.

"Your mother is dead," Fisher says. "I'm sorry to be the one to tell you."

Jill's expression doesn't change. She stares at him. This, in Fisher's mind, is proof enough.

He sits heavily on the bed. He should have known. Well, he did know. As soon as he saw the postcard in his mail slot at Westing, tucked between a staff memo and a guitar catalog, missing both postmark and stamp, he knew something out of his control was in motion. But it was too, too intriguing to resist. In black capital letters, on the reverse of an image of the sun setting over the Statue of Liberty, were the words DR. BRODIE, I NEED YOUR HELP. I WILL FIND YOU AT STATEWIDE. I HAVE NO ONE ELSE.

It wasn't signed. His first thought was that it was a bizarre joke, a prank played by one of the more immature Westing students, but there was something about that turn of phrase—I HAVE NO ONE ELSE—that struck him. *Me neither,* he thought. *Aren't we a pair.*

And then Jill Faccelli knocked on his door after dinner on Thursday night. He had to look through the peephole twice before he accepted that, yes, the prodigal hothead who'd stormed out of his rehearsal was standing in the hall with a small black bag over her shoulder, shuffling her feet, arranging her expression into a mea culpa. He opened the door.

"Yes?" he said, naturally irritated and not hiding it.

The penitent face vanished.

"I told you I'd find you," she said. "I have no one else, Dr. Brodie. I need your help to run away."

Fisher had a password. A trigger phrase buried in his subconscious that unlocked uncharted corners of the person he knew himself to be, and Jill had spoken it aloud: *I have no one else. I need your help to run away.* He knew it was probably inappropriate, or at least highly frowned upon (Jill was only fourteen, definitely one of the youngest children at the festival), but he invited her into his room without a second thought. She nodded crisply, stepped in, and dropped her bag on the desk. Fisher saw the scuffed tips of a pair of sneakers and what might have been several changes of clothes.

She explained that she needed a room to hide in while she waited for the festival to end. Her mother had terrorized her for years, she said, and she couldn't stand another second of it. Viola, if she wanted, could pretend to be normal, to be nice, even—Jill had seen her charm people as often as intimidate them—but she never kept it up for long. And she never bothered to pretend with her daughter. Jill's life was *her* life, Jill's music was *her* music, and Jill was afraid she would lose one or both of them if she stayed a minute longer. There was no way she was going to the police. Best-case scenario, she'd end up a ward of the state. Worst case, Viola would murder her for the embarrassment.

She wasn't kidding. Fisher believed her.

"She talks about you," Jill said, her eyes trained on his face. "She thinks you were brilliant and threw it away. That you had too much of a good thing too young."

Fisher grimaced. "Ouch," he said, because she'd hit the mark so squarely.

"I knew you'd know what it feels like to be trapped. And I hoped you'd help, because you also know what it means that this is the only chance I'm going to get."

That's why he was in the auditorium late Thursday—he'd given his spare room key to Jill, who was planning to disappear that night. He had no idea she was going to vanish herself so melodramatically; only later did she show him the false noose she rigged from a length of climbing rope, the orange extension cord she'd used as a prop. Jill had done her research on the hotel. She'd used all her powers of persuasion, all the considerable gifts she'd inherited from her mother, to come to the festival, to finagle a booking in the infamous room. She was a crazy opportunist, maybe just as crazy as Viola, but she was a bloody mad genius and deserved a chance to be free.

The only thing she hadn't counted on was Fisher and his stunt with *Afternoon of a Faun*. She stormed out of rehearsal not because she wanted to create a scene (though in retrospect it worked out rather well for her), and not in protest of Fisher's disrespect for his players. She ran out because she was furious with heartbreak. It was a final sign from the universe. A sort of cosmic *are you really sure you want to do this?* She could stay through the festival, she could abandon her escape and play the solos, those famously gorgeous solos for flute. Or she could prove she really, really meant it and abandon the music instead.

She chose flight. There would be other solos.

He let her lie low. He'd deliberately kept out of her way, insulating himself with plausible deniability. He spent all of Thursday night in the auditorium, stayed in Natalie's room on Friday, and with the Hatmakers in whoever's room *that* had been last night. He'd tried not to even think about her, about the runaway minor he was sheltering in his room, but there was something about Jill Faccelli that tugged on him. That harmonized with every cell in his body. She *was* him. He could give her the chance he never took. In hindsight, such an undertaking would have required more responsibility and involvement, and a bit more supervision.

"Was that your plan the whole time?" he says. "Or did you seize the opportunity when it arose?"

She kicks out her feet, knees hinged over the arm of the chair. Right foot, left foot, right foot, left foot.

"I don't know what you mean," she says. "I didn't have anything to do with it."

"Where were you last night?"

"Where were *you?*" She raises an eyebrow.

"Getting shot at. If you must know," he says.

Her legs stop moving. "Did anyone die?"

"Morbid little squirrel, aren't you?"

She grins fast without thinking and snuffs it out. But Fisher has seen it, and God help him, in spite of everything, it makes him smile. "No. A man went mad and N—a woman was shot. I got tossed in the pool. Enough chaos even for the likes of you."

He leans in closer.

"You ought to announce your presence to the police. But I'm not going to turn you in," he says. The words are as much a surprise as the sureness: he isn't going to turn her in for committing matricide, and he can't say why, but he *knows.* He knows he'll protect her; he knows she isn't a danger to anyone now that Viola is gone. "I just don't like being played a fool. You could have told me."

"You would have stopped me."

Fisher holds up his mangled hand, index finger pointing at the sky. "Ah-ha," he says gently. "I knew it."

Even in the gloom, he can see her face has gone the color of tomatoes.

"You would have, though," she says. "You can say now that you wouldn't, but only because it's done. She did it to herself, anyway."

"How do you mean then?"

Jill frowns. She looks about six.

"I found it under the sink two months ago. It looked like sugar, but I knew it couldn't be, because it was under the sink in a plastic baggie, hidden behind the Drano. I asked her about it and she said that's all it was, just sugar, but she took it away from me, so I knew she was lying. I'd already kept some before I even talked to her, and I brought it with me because—I don't know. Once I got away I was going to have it tested. I thought I might be able to prove she killed Alex." She blinks. "He would never, ever have killed himself. He was . . . he was a really good person."

"Good people commit suicide all the time, love."

"He adopted me." She sniffs. "He was my friend."

"Still doesn't mean anything."

She sticks out her chin. "He was going to take me camping near Muir Woods. We had tickets to see *Les Mis* when it came to the city. We had *plans*. And he would never have left me alone with *her*. Alex married my mother because he loved her and thought she loved him. I thought she was pretending like she usually did, but she was just so *good* at it with Alex. She sounded different. Better. Happy. It was the best I'd ever seen her pretend and I wanted it to be real, so I let her fool me too. Maybe it was real. Alex was pretty rich.

"But after a while, like always, she stopped pretending and it was too late for everyone. She hated him, because he was so—so nice."

"Come again?"

"He was kind and rich and normal. He smiled at babies and gave money to charity. I think at first she thought he was interesting, you know, the way a scientist thinks a bug is interesting. And then one day they wake up and realize they're married to a bug so they squash it. It didn't help that he was so nice to *me*. He paid more attention to me than to her, and after a while I paid more attention to him. She didn't like that at all.

"For a long time I've known she was—wrong, but I thought there wasn't anything I could do about it. And then I *did* get away from her, everything was going so well this weekend, and I had an idea to . . . test her. If it was really sugar, like she said." She sniffs again. "She would've passed."

She hugs herself. "Anyway, it's over," she says. "I don't have to worry anymore and neither does anyone else."

322

She rakes a hand through her weird thicket of choppy hair, back to front, faster and faster, and Fisher can see how bright her eyes are. She's trying not to cry. He never once saw her mother cry. Jill's tears have to be real; Fisher can feel them. He's so relieved, relieved for her, to see that she doesn't have her mother's pathological coldness, or at least she has this bit of empathy as an offset. Was lack of empathy a genetic trait, dominant or recessive? Perhaps she inherited the tears from her father.

Fisher's chest tightens like a fist.

He isn't going to the hospital.

Natalie doesn't want to see him anyway.

His electric clippers are lying beside the bathroom sink, which holds a few stray hairs Jill missed cleaning up. The bin, however, looks like someone threw away a black wig. He rinses the clippers and pushes the door open wider. Light falls on Jill's face.

She squints. Her eyes are set deep on either side of a rather large and thin nose.

"Come on, then," he says.

She sits on the toilet lid and Fisher holds her head in his palms. He tilts her skull forward, measuring the relative length of the patches on her head. "It's going to be short," he says, "if you want it to be even." She nods at him in the mirror. Then her eyes turn down at the corners and he watches two very real-looking tears pop from beneath her lids and race down her cheeks.

"It'll grow back," he says. "Don't worry, squirrel."

She rubs her nose on the back of her hand and sits up straight.

"I'm ready," she says.

Fisher adjusts the clipper and passes it once, twice, three times around and over and through her hair. She has a nicely shaped head, full as an egg. Fuzz rains down on her shoulders and her lap. He only knows how to give the haircut he's been giving himself for years, short on the sides and back, tapered at the neck. Her hair is soft but very thick.

He would be blind not to see it. He would be blind if he looked at her, with his own haircut, his own eyes, and his nose built finer and younger, and didn't recognize them as variations on the theme that's been watching him in mirrors his entire life. She hasn't looked up from her lap, and Fisher is terrified of the moment when she will. He feels so damn shy all of a sudden, so old and stupid and ashamed that he never saw this coming. That he never knew. That he never knew she existed. Later, he thinks; later I'll feel anger that Viola never told me. Later I'll feel used, surely. But right now all he feels is naked and far too aware of time, how much has already passed, how much there might be left him, and her—and how all of that time she will live knowing what she's done. Knowing where she came from and how she escaped. Knowing whose child she is.

Did Viola ever tell her?

Did she plan all of this because she knew?

He wants to give her the benefit of the doubt, wants to trust what he's been given. He places his ragged right hand on her shoulder.

"Right, then. We can go to a professional when we get home," he says. "If you'd like."

Jill looks up, first at herself, then at Fisher. Her face betrays no surprise. There is something there, something bruised but alive that doesn't want to let go. That may, in time, grow into a kind of love.

He has to trust it. He has to.

"Thanks, Dad," she whispers, and places her hand over his.

27

Hatmakers Descending

IDE BY SIDE, suitcases and bassoon in hand, the Hatmakers step into an empty elevator. Rabbit pushes L and the doors slide together.

Alice wishes she were a little happier. Well, she *is* happy— she's thrilled to bits about her brother, both that he trusted her enough to confide what she'd begun to suspect when he tucked his conductor into bed, and that she *totally* called him out. So to speak. And yet she can't help but feel an undertow, a nasty, nagging feeling that she's running away. She's a shitty detective, leaving the mystery unsolved. She's abandoning Jill.

No one's telling the truth. No one's saying *anything*. After the orchestra finished playing, the conductor asked everyone to connect with their chaperones. The roads were plowed; they were going home. There'd been no guidance on what to do if your chaperone had been shot. No one said anything about a missing girl or a missing concierge or the crime scene tape all over the swimming pool or the policewoman in the lobby or Viola Fabian, dead.

Thunder rumbles from above.

"What's wrong?" Rabbit asks.

Alice shrugs. "Oh, nothing."

"Liar," her brother says.

"I'm *starving*. Aren't you starving?" It's been hours since break-fast. They split a bag of Combos from the vending machine but that seems like hours ago too. "How long do you think we're going to have to wait for Mom and Dad?" Rabbit had called their parents from the room phone but only got the answering machine. Alice heard their father's voice blaring through the handset, saying he's sorry he missed their call, leave a message and we'll *callyarightback*. They had to be on their way to the Bellweather to rescue their kids. Right?

The car jostles as they pass the fourth floor.

"That's not what's really bugging you," Rabbit says.

"Gee, I wonder what else it could be." Alice slips her hands in her coat pockets and nudges him with her elbow. "It's not like every single thing that's happened since we got here has been batshi—"

There's something in her pocket.

Her fingers close over a stack of stiff, rippled papers. Even as she's pulling her hand out of her coat, even as she's opening that hand, she doesn't allow herself to believe it. It's too good a trick to hope might be real.

She's holding her missing tarot cards. The top card, warped and pink with wine, is the Magician.

"Oh my God," Alice says. How did she do this? *How?* She turns to her brother. "Rabbit. Rabbit, look, holy shit, *look what it is.*"

"What is—"

"It's the exact opposite," she says, "of a suicide note."

Something lands with a soft plop on the roof of the elevator car.

Again.

And again.

"Do you hear that?" says Rabbit.

The thunder is closer.

"What the—" Alice says, and a jet of cold chlorinated water caves in the elevator's access panel and punches her in the back of the head.

Thank God the doors open at just that moment, because the water is coming and coming and Alice is drenched, soaked through to her underwear already, her jeans are pulling off her hips, her wool winter coat is pressing her shoulders down, and she can think of no other reaction so she's laughing hysterically through chattering teeth. She hears a splash as Rabbit drops his suitcase. Water falls in a flat curtain across the open doors, a sheet of rushing, freezing cold hanging between them and the lobby. People are shrieking, fanning out as the carpet blackens under flooding pool water. Of course it's the pool. She knows this. She doesn't know how, but the pool has collapsed and is draining from the top of the hotel. The elevator doors frame a watery window on the lobby and Alice stares in shock. Potted ferns tip. Students scream and run, violin and French horn and saxophone cases held high over their heads, suitcases left behind to float on the tide. Some slip and fall and pull others down with them. A boy running with a tuba case trips and scatters a cluster of kids like they were bowling pins. The entire building shakes and an enormous gout of water pours into the lobby from Alice's right, setting a small sofa adrift and knocking two girls off their feet. Alice hears them grunt. One of them bashes her head against a sconce and leaves a bloody smear on the wallpaper.

She's cold. She can't move. Water pours all around her. Her teeth are clacking together, actually clacking she's so cold, and she laughs again because this is *really* happening.

The elevator doors are closing and she'll be trapped in here and the water won't stop, she'll drown, it was all true, it was all leading to this, the cards tried to warn her, she should have listened. Temperance. The Star. Death. Images of water jugs, a pool, a scythe, meaning harmony, optimism, change, *fuck that*—fucking tarot meant *water*, meant pouring pool water and literal death. Oh God, of course—this was inevitable, this was written in the cards and the stars and all those swimming lessons as a kid, fed by her mother's fears that weren't fears but premonitions. She was warned. She was warned and she ignored it, and this is her curse come true.

Rabbit grabs her hand.

Her other hand closes over her tarot cards, over the message Jill left just for her. She realizes she doesn't care how Jill did it; it's enough to know she did. It's enough to know that magic is possible, and what magician worth her salt tells you her secrets anyway? She squeezes her brother's hand, her other, better self, and they both howl with laughter, with rage and defiance. Because they aren't going down like this. This diseased old hotel doesn't get to take the Hatmakers down with it.

Alice lets Rabbit lead. Clutching his bassoon case to his chest, he hurls himself sideways through the doors and pulls her out behind. He lands with a grunting squelch on the lobby carpet. Alice lands on top of him, rolls off, and hits the ground with a noise like a wounded squeaker toy.

The roar of the water fades to a rush, a trickle. A drip. It's quiet for half a second. Someone shouts, swears. Alice hears crying. She's wet through, freezing cold. Her shoulder is jammed and her neck is funny where she rolled onto her backpack. She felt something give inside — her Trapper Keeper, probably, giving up the ghost at last. She looks to her left and sees Rabbit, blinking water out of his eyes, his lip split and bloody from having smashed his bassoon into his face. But they're whole. They're safe.

Alice grins.

"Rabbit," she gasps. Her voice is wobbly when she says, "Rabbit, we did it. The Hatmakers broke the curse."

AND AFTER

H E JERKS AWAKE. He barely has control of his thoughts. He has no idea where he is, or even who he is, but one sensation cuts clean through, strong enough to pierce the drugs: relief. Relief like a sigh of the soul.

He wishes the girl were still sitting beside him. He doesn't know when she left. It could be hours, it could be days.

He closes his eyes again and sleeps without dreaming.

She comes back the next Sunday with a small aloe plant — not flowers, not a balloon, nothing that tries too hard to be cheery, but something green and growing and alive — and a book. He doesn't look at her. For some reason he's afraid to, afraid to see in her eyes what she sees in him. She pats his hand and reads the book. She comes back the next Sunday and reads, but the week after that, without telling her, the nurses put him in a wheelchair, then a van, and take him to another hospital.

"You'll tell the girl?" he says to the man helping him into his new bed. "You'll tell her where to find me?"

The man isn't very reassuring, but the girl gets the message, and she shows up the very next Sunday, albeit a little later than usual. His new room isn't as nice as the old one. It's grayer. Still, she pats his hand and reads her book and he thinks next week, maybe, he might feel up to looking at her.

There are red and green and yellow paper chains draped in the halls and taped to the nurses' station on the Sunday when he finally speaks to the girl. He asks her what she's reading.

"Agatha Christie," she says. He's looking at her. She's very pretty. Her face is bright and open as a little girl's, though she's clearly much older than that. "Would you like me to read it to you? Out loud?"

He has a roommate at this hospital, a little mouse of a man whose name is Teddy. Teddy lifts his head and croaks, "Hell yes. Please."

Despite the fact that these are his sentiments exactly, Hastings resents that his roommate is speaking for him.

So the girl reads him Agatha Christie and Raymond Chandler. Hastings sits up straighter. In late January he's allowed to start shaving himself again, and snaps leaves from the aloe plant the girl brought him whenever he nicks his chin. She comes every Sunday; if she can't come Sunday, she comes Saturday. She reads him P. D. James and Dashiell Hammett. One day, he asks if she's his daughter.

"No," she says softly.

"But I do have a daughter, don't I?" he says. He knows he does. He remembers small shoes, shiny Mary Janes. He remembers a wedding dress, remembers dancing with a young girl in a wedding dress. "I know I do." He shakes his head. "You aren't her, though. I'm sorry."

"It's fine, Hastings," she says.

That night, a man comes to him in a dream. Or maybe it isn't a dream. It feels very much as though he's awake, but it's dark, well past visiting hours, and there's a funny man, balding, chubby, glasses held together in the middle with a piece of tape, sitting in the chair where the girl normally sits.

"Hi, pal," says Rome. "Miss me? Just kidding. I'm always here. Say, listen. You know you completely lost your mind for a while there? I mean completely, Hastings. Trust me when I say you don't want to know."

But he does want to know.

"Nope, you don't. Not yet." Rome looks around the dim room, the old-fashioned hospital beds, the dreary linens and curtains. "So this is what your tax dollars were paying for, back when you were a taxpayer."

"It's not so bad."

"It's not so great either."

"The girl makes it better."

"The girl, the girl, the girl." Rome rubs his expansive forehead with his thumb. "You know who she is, Hastings? I'll give you a hint. She isn't Caroline."

Caroline.

"Seen *her* lately? *She's* your daughter. She's the girl in the wedding dress," Rome says, and slaps a palm on each knee. "Well, it's been a gas. See you."

Hastings wakes up and the man is gone.

He doesn't tell the girl when she comes that week, but he does ask her to bring him a notebook, preferably college ruled, the next Sunday. He wants to write some things down, to keep track of the days. She does, and he's doing his best to transcribe the particulars of his conversations with the man named Rome—he's had several more since that first one—when he has a sudden, vivid memory of the last time he ever saw his wife.

He was standing behind his concierge desk. She was heading out the door, waving farewell to Caroline. Mother and daughter had been planning in the small ballroom, imagining where the flowers would go, how the tables might be set up for the reception. Now Caroline was staying behind, would get a ride home with Lily. Jess didn't turn to wave at him. He was sure it wasn't intentional; she was preoccupied with the wedding. In his final memory of her, she is pushing her way through the revolving lobby door, the strong late-afternoon sun lighting up the chamber like a shining carousel, transforming fingerprints into stars and comets. In ten minutes' time, the same sun will blind a man in a pickup truck, and when he roars through an intersection, he will T-bone Jess's two-door coupe.

When he looks up, he hears a quiet rustling in the hallway.

He puts down his pen. Beyond the circle of brightness cast by his book light, the room is dark. It's late, around the same time that Rome typically comes. The rustling sounds like curtains, like fabric or petticoats.

"Jess?" he whispers.

And then he sees Caroline standing at the door of his room. His Caroline, his daughter, his strange lost little girl, translucent.

She isn't wearing her wedding dress but he can hear it when she walks, the rustling of layer upon layer of white fabric. She's in jeans and a green cable-knit sweater he can picture her lifting out of a brightly wrapped box, shedding sheets of tissue paper as she holds it aloft.

"Caroline," he says.

"Hello." Her voice is an echo. "Rome told me I should come. That you were lonely." She sits in the girl's chair and hugs her own arms. "I'm sorry I didn't come sooner."

Hastings shakes his head. He hasn't seen Caroline in such a long time. She's so young. She *was* so young.

They sit in silence.

"Could I have—" He frowns. "Why did you choose to—"

Caroline laughs. It's a cold dagger in his belly.

"I can't tell you," she says. "You won't ever know."

"Was there anything *I* . . . could have. Could I have helped?"

She shrugs. "I don't know," she says. "I told Rome this was a bad idea."

"Please don't go," he says. "Please stay. I don't know why I even asked those questions. I know I can't expect you to answer them. I suppose I can't expect them to have answers."

"Everyone was leaving. I missed Mom. I missed her so much. I was supposed to be in the car with her." She lifts her eyes to his. "I could have saved her."

When Hastings wakes, he discovers he's written three pages of conversation between himself and his daughter. His daughter who murdered her unfaithful husband, who killed herself in shame and rage, who let her mindless pain and guilt animate her. The girl, his girl, whom he couldn't save.

The next day, Hastings starts writing something else. Something new. One doesn't spend a lifetime reading detective stories and not harbor a few fleeting fantasies about becoming an author of them. He has never tried writing like this before, writing fiction. It is fun. He likes how it fills his mind and his days. He's writing a mystery, of course, and it begins with the horrible discovery of a body hanging in a hotel room. It looks like a suicide, but his detective hero — or heroine, rather; Hastings finds himself writing about a young woman — suspects there is more to the story. His girl detective seems to have existed before Hastings ever thought to put pen to paper, and he finds it is the easiest thing in the world to conjure her. She is tall. Quiet, with bright, shrewd little eyes. She is a librarian. She is constantly being underestimated, which, of course, she is just as constantly using to her advantage.

He works on a first chapter for three weeks before he's ready to share it with the girl, who does him the honor of reading it slowly and carefully. It's spring. She asks if he'd like to take a walk with her. He's left his room occasionally, but this is the first time outside really *feels* like outside. Hastings is freer simply breathing the air. The girl takes his arm. He's grown unsteady during his time at the state hospital, weaker and unused to movement, but it feels marvelous to have a friend by his side on a bright spring day. They sit in the sun on a small stone bench.

"Hastings," the girl says, "what do you remember?"

He inhales. "Everything, I think. I remember working at the Bellweather for years and years. My daughter was married there. She died there, on the same day."

"What else?"

"I remember *you*," he says.

She hadn't been expecting that. "Me?" she says. "Who am I?"

"You're that little girl," he says, and leans down close. "I am so sorry you saw what you saw."

She hadn't been expecting that either.

"They found you in the stairwell," he says. "And now here you are, all grown up. You dropped your shoes in the hall outside seven-twelve. I remember how shy you were. How you thought squash courts were where we grew the hotel's vegetables. And how *serious* you looked in that flouncy red dress. I'm sorry to say that I never learned your name."

She laughs a shaky laugh.

Minnie's full first name is Ermingard. She's never talked about it with anyone she didn't have to, anyone who didn't already know. Ermingard. Who the hell names their little girl *Ermingard,* other than her Germanic great-grandparents on her mother's side and her own mother and father? "Minnie" had always been a better alternative (not saying much), but when Hastings asks on that gentle April day, when she steps back and sees herself exactly as she is, Minnie realizes she's wearing a name two sizes too small. It doesn't fit. She's still big physically, sure, but Minnie was the name of a scared little girl, a girl too terrified to grow up, a girl who lost herself in horror stories because they were safer than the real world. It was Ermingard who ran into the street to save a dog. Ermingard who returned to the Bellweather to face her fears. Who visits her fellow survivor every Sunday, a man who remembers her only as that scared little girl.

"Ermingard," she says. "My name is Ermingard Graves."

Hastings smiles at her. "What an unusual name."

"Thanks," she says, and it's the first time she's ever meant it.

It's been six months since November. Six months, and in all that time Hastings has never given any indication that he remembers her from those four days at the Bellweather. That he remembers what he did. That he shot a woman—a woman who declined to press charges, so it's unlikely he'll ever *have* to remember. Though Ermingard will help him, if it comes to that, just as she'll tell him his beloved hotel is closed, abandoned, the land for sale, but only if he asks. No one from the grounds crew shoveled the roof or the glass dome over the lounge, and as that November Sunday warmed, the dome broke, dumping five feet of dense melting snow into the swimming pool. It would have flooded just the lounge if the pool, old and heavy and out of code, hadn't cracked.

The Bellweather is dead. Drowned.

She knows all of this because of Alice, who e-mails her at least once a week. Alice is convinced that the second shot Hastings fired that night, the shot that went wild, hit the roof. Broke a pane of glass and started a chain reaction. Ermingard may one day tell Hastings his hotel is closed, but she'll never tell him he may have struck the fatal blow. Or maybe she will, when he's strong enough. He might find it poetic. He might be inspired.

"Do you want me to bring you another notebook?" she asks. "You're almost to the end of that one and your story's just getting started."

Hastings shuffles his feet beneath the bench. "Now that you bring it up, dear, would you be so kind as to bring me my old Underwood? It's in my house somewhere." He pauses. "Though perhaps it would be easier for you to find a new one."

"Sure, Hastings," she says. Her parents have an electric typewriter that they never use, now that they have a computer. They won't miss it. She could take it with all the rest of her stuff in the move. She and Auggie are renting an apartment in Syracuse so she can work on a degree in library science at the university.

It was Mike's idea to go to SU, to move—well, Mike thought of it first, but Ermingard made it happen. She talks with her brother all the time now, almost as often as she e-mails with Alice. They talk about everything—their parents, their sister, and their asshole brother-in-law. They talk about what happened when she was little and what happened last November. Mike is the only one in her family who knows the whole story behind her visits to the state hospital, also in Syracuse, every Sunday. Not that she's keeping it a secret or anything. They know she goes, and they've noticed how she's changed. How she stands straighter. Smiles more often. She isn't Minnie anymore.

"Ermingard Graves," Hastings says slowly. He narrows his eyes. "You may have noticed my story is missing a critical element. My detective doesn't have a name. May I borrow yours?"

For years, Ermingard Graves has existed as barely more than a ghost, a spirit haunting herself. At last she is here in the world, the one girl who survived. But she isn't alone.

She doesn't trust her voice, so she nods and takes his hand.

Acknowledgments

For all the players who made this book possible, I am eternally grateful — starting with my agent, Bonnie Nadell, who is awesome, not least because she introduced me to Andrea Schulz. Thank you, Andrea, for loving this book, for seeing it so clearly, and for being so much fun to work with. My thanks to all the wonderful people at Houghton Mifflin Harcourt, especially Larry Cooper, Chrissy Kurpeski, Patrick Barry, Michelle Bonanno, and Liz Anderson. I'm indebted to Michael Mercurio and Cathy Weiskel for sneaking me behind the scenes at a Boston Youth Symphony Orchestra rehearsal; Steve Lay, my motorcycle consultant; Ron Clarke, who taught me to fire a handgun on Mother's Day; and Kate Estrop, Tom Dodson, and the lovely folks of the Boston Writers' Meetup and at *Printer's Devil Review*.

Thanks are due to my MGH family for their constant support (and to Angie Morey for sharing her symphony tickets), and to my earliest readers, cheerleaders, sanity-keepers, and, it goes without saying, friends: Jason and Karen Clarke, Rob and Karissa Kloss, Steve Himmer and Sage Brousseau, Kevin Fanning, Vanessa Ramos (LitTeamBoston 4-life), Laura Q. Messersmith, Krista Kitowicz, Rose White, Alyssa and Kristin aka the Sisters Osiecki, and my dear BAWs: Manda Betts, Sandra Lau, and Jenna Lay. None of this without you, still.

Dad, for plopping giant headphones over my tender ears, and Mom, for harmonizing with me in the car — for taking me to all those rehearsals and lessons, attending all those concerts and NYSSMA competitions, and raising me to believe music was not only fun but important — I can never thank you both enough (yes, even for making me practice). To all the VanSkivers and Racculias, thank you for filling my life with so many songs.

This book would not exist if I hadn't been a music nerd in high school, if it hadn't been for the other bassoonists (McKenzie Field and Tanya Maslak, I'm looking at you), all the bands and pits and orchestras, and all the conductors and teachers, especially Mr. D, in whose excellent company I learned to understand music, and to love it more than I thought possible.

And last but not least: thank you, Ellen Ermingard Raskin, for showing a weird little girl who loved to read that other people were full of such strange and beautiful mysteries.